HOUSE HUNTING FINNISH STYLE

MEGAN DAVIES

Copyright © 2014 Megan Davies

All rights reserved.

ISBN:1502719150
ISBN-13:978-1502719157

DEDICATION

To family and friends and of course all Finns everywhere.

MEGAN DAVIES

PROLOGUE

As is sometimes the way with farmers, Mr Karhu's life had the same parameters as his farm. 'Life', 'farm' – the two words were almost interchangeable. In addition to arable land he had pigs and a small herd of dairy cows and some chickens, plus a wife and a son. A little of everything in fact, at least of things that could thrive in the part of Finland where he lived. His day began with milking, ran through working on his fields, and returned via evening milking to an early bedtime.

His wife, Mrs. Karhu, kept the farmhouse like a palace. It was spotless, in spite of her having a little part-time bookkeeping job in the town. She went there daily; her days were regular all year round, whether daylight shone or darkness pressed against the windows. Mr. Karhu's life was governed by daylight hours and the seasons; in winter when the days almost vanished and the land was under snow, he became more taciturn, if that was possible, and a little morose.

Of course, after twenty-odd years of marriage, there is often not very much left to say. Whatever was worth saying has long since been said, in the days when the presence of a spouse was a novelty, and time through the years carves out separate, parallel grooves for man and for wife, with little need for surplus communication. Thus it was that it was quite some time before the Karhus discovered that they both thought the boy was somehow getting worse. In the end it was sheer exasperation that drove them to speak of it to each other. Mrs. Karhu saw him as getting more slovenly and rude, Mr. Karhu as becoming more stubborn. Of course, he had always been stubborn, if by 'stubborn' was meant 'slow', but now there seemed to be a different quality to his slowness. A kind of rebelliousness, a sort of resentment. Or else the boy was in his private world, a world that left the cows unmilked while he stood staring into space. The farmer wondered where and what that world was, but he for one had no time to try and find out. Someone had to do the milking.

She supposed it was his age, said Mrs. Karhu. He was growing up. But what did 'growing up' mean, if it meant that he was three times as irresponsible as ever? Half the time she had to remind him to take his muddy shoes off in the house. She hoped it would pass. He wasn't a bad boy.

And now he was back at school. The long summer holiday was over, the new school year had just begun. That was another thing. The boy should have left school before the summer, but his grades had not been good. He was having to repeat his final year; maybe that was the cause of his constant glumness.

Today was the second day of term, but the afternoon already, the slow-paced hours of a hot, still, sleepy August day. The boy would be home soon; he never went anywhere after school. The farmer kept a lookout for him from the tractor shed. It would take the two of them to go and bring in logs on the tractor. Then the boy could start to chop them – they would need wood for the sauna and the winter heating. All in all, mused Mr. Karhu, the lad was good at farm work, if only he could just snap out of his present attitude. They hadn't had to employ a farmhand now for a couple of years.

When he saw his son go past the window on his way to the house he shouted to him, but the boy did not answer, or even turn his head. Mr. Karhu cursed him briefly and went out after him, towards the house and into it and right to the door of the room where the boy had gone. The room where the outdoor shoes were kept and the ancient hunting rifle hung on its hook on the wall. Beyond the door he noticed that the boy had not yet taken his shoes off. He had lifted the gun down from the wall and was playing with it. Mr. Karhu stepped inside.

"What are you doing?"

The farmer was a practical man, prosaic and down-to-earth; he knew where he stood on matters. He had never expected to finish his life with a question.

CHAPTER 1

London, 1980

Dr. Noel Fisher would never of his own accord have taken in a lodger, least of all one from somewhere dubious, such as overseas. After all, as he pointed out to his colleague Dr. Phillips, he was a university professor, not a lodging-house keeper. Which meant that he had become more intransigent at each blithe suggestion from Phillips that a lodger was just what was needed. Yet now, as he made his way home on the final day of term, Dr. Phillips was harassing him again.

"I just thought you might be glad of the company – someone else around to take your mind off things. You'll be rattling round in that place if you're on your own."

Fisher felt a sudden stab of indignant self-pity. "You don't seem to understand what it's like to be left by one's wife," he said petulantly. "After twenty-three years. The nature of the emotions involved. The – the heartbreak." He allowed his mouth to set in a grim line and began to steer a course towards the car park.

"Of course I do!" Phillips's voice was reassuring. "But she'll be back, we all think she'll be back. She'll see sense, eventually."

"She tells me she has."

"Well, it might not happen overnight."

Fisher felt disinclined to continue the conversation. But Phillips kept alongside, adjusting his step annoyingly to stay in time with him. Whenever Fisher speeded up Phillips did a little hop and skip to keep up level. After twenty yards he resolutely broke the silence again.

"It's just that while you're on your own, old man, it would really be doing us a favour. If you could take in, say the fellow. For a couple of months." Fisher made no reply.

"You're going to have oodles of space. Till Millicent sees sense, I mean. And there isn't anywhere else to put him. Cheryl's desperate. It's her first job. She doesn't dare to tell them she's screwed up."

Fisher stopped suddenly short, so that Phillips was obliged to stop too. "I am going through the equivalent of being in mourning. I do not wish to have strange people in my home. Most of all feckless students."

"The man's around thirty, I understand. An engineering graduate."

"No."

They resumed their journey, one angry and disgruntled, the other forlorn.

"What is it Cheryl's done, anyway?" As he said it, Fisher cursed himself for asking.

Phillips gave the short, soft sigh of one who senses that he is about to get a foot in the door.

"Well, she's double booked. I mean, she's in the accommodation office, as you know. And they've put her in charge of booking the rooms for overseas students. I don't think they should have given her that responsibility by herself at this stage, I…"

"Get to the point."

"Well, that is the point. She's put some male and some female who don't even know each other in the same single room from September through till the end of next May. All names just look foreign to Cheryl, if that's what they are, and these two she just got confused. It wasn't till she noticed the different photos that she realised what she'd done. So now it's getting late and everywhere's full and she has to find somewhere else for one of them. She's frightened they'll give her the sack if they realise how stupid she's been."

"Well, I can't take anyone," said Fisher firmly. "Both for reasons I've given and because I need to start on my book. I want to get preliminary notes made before my sabbatical next year. Besides which, now you're saying it's till May. Just now you said for a couple of months."

"Just till Cheryl manages to sort out something else." The tone was placatory.

They had reached the point just opposite the car park that formed the short cut to Fisher's block of flats. Fisher stopped and waited for the lights to change, to cross the road.

"What about the woman?" asked Phillips, his face brightening hopefully. "Or rather, girl, I think she is. She's from somewhere Pacific, and some sort of aristocrat. A Tongan princess would certainly wipe the smile off Millicent's face."

"No." said Fisher testily, alarmed to suspect the idea did have its charms. "Absolutely not." Not, he added ruefully to himself, that a Tongan princess was likely to end up smitten by a middle-aged, greying professor, at least before the publication of his book.

"Only trying to help," he heard Phillips retort in a huffy tone, as the lights changed and they stepped off the pavement. It annoyed him to notice that Phillips did not detach himself from him at this spot to go his own way, as he usually did.

"Don't you usually go straight up Grosvenor Street from here?"

"Cheryl's picking me up. She's got herself a little second-hand car, just a week ago." Phillips's eyes were busy scanning the hot, shining metal domes of the car roofs. "There she is!" He raised his arms and waved, and Fisher caught sight of Cheryl just as she vanished again from view through an open sun roof.

"She'll want to know if I've had any luck," said Phillips. "What am I to say?"

They were heading straight for the car. It was too late for Fisher to disappear, for Cheryl had seen him. Now she was lolling again in the driver's seat, the window wound down because of the heat. She peered up.

"Hello, Dr. Fisher." She leant across to open the passenger door for her father. "Have you asked him? About you-know-what?"

"He says he can't," said Phillips shortly. "He has to write a book."

Cheryl gave a short gasp, then sighed and slumped back in the seat. She stared straight ahead through the windscreen, past the dangling green dice and the miniature teddy bear that sat on the driver's mirror, her face a picture of desolate and absolute despair. She did not ask about the book. She had short dark hair clipped back from her face, which still had a rounded, scrubbed look despite the make-up that rendered its hue a uniform, muddy beige. A spot on her chin had pushed itself up like a tiny volcano through the silt, and seemed all but set to erupt.

Fisher experienced a sudden, unreasonable pang of guilt, like a rogue attack of indigestion. As if a section of his digestive tract had suddenly solidified into a heavy iron bar. Cheryl turned her face slowly to look at him, her eyes brim-full of disappointment. He noticed that her make-up went no further than her chin; beneath her woebegone, monochrome face her throat was its normal colour. Another pimple was either coming or going on her nose.

"Are you sure you couldn't? Just for a couple of months? A few weeks?" She exhibited nothing of her father's jovial false camaraderie, just a plain, straightforward attitude of utter hopelessness. Fisher sighed. He hated himself for what he was about to say.

"A month then. But only till you find somewhere else. I shall be awfully busy with my book." His spirits plummeted. Really, he thought, sometimes he drove himself to despair. In contrast, a new pulsation of life seemed to pass through Cheryl; it roused her body and parted her lips in a wide, artless smile and chased the tragic expression from her eyes with a joy that welled up and flashed and sparkled. Even her hairgrips seemed to perk up. She still did not ask about the book.

Standing beside the car Fisher straightened up to keep Phillips out of his line of vision as Cheryl tumbled out her thanks. He regretted his weakness to the point of fury with himself. As she drove off Cheryl circled once before she left, and as she passed she gave him a cheery wave.

"The man, mind," Fisher called out after her without even giving it a thought. He was annoyed to notice later his annoyance at having made that spineless stipulation.

CHAPTER 2

Fisher sat on the washing machine in his laundry room and watched Heikki hanging up his wet socks to dry. It had been four months now since the Scandinavian had come to lodge with him, and on this gloomy December afternoon he had asked that Fisher come and find him the minute he got in from the university. He was here in the laundry room, deep in the rituals of his twice-weekly wash. There were ten pairs of socks already on the line, white, boomerang-shaped, all identical, their toes aligned neatly to face the north. They were whiter than white, not a trace of dinginess on even their undersides. The line behind bore a long row of snowy-white identical T-shirts. Heikki stretched and stooped, his pink face gleaming with steam and exertion, in an uninterrupted rite of alternate pegging and abeyance. He wore rubber beach sandals and his glistening upper half was bare.

Under normal circumstances it would have irritated Fisher to sit and wait while Heikki went placidly about his business, but on this cheerless day something in the cosy, reassuring smell of the laundry room and the rhythmic, monotonous action of the sturdy back, now bending, now rising, was strangely relaxing. A soothing, domestic, detergent-scented balm began to creep in, easing the turmoil and loneliness of his soul.

All the same, the procedure seemed never-ending. Fisher allowed his gaze to drift to the window in search of diversion, but nothing was visible in the pitch black behind the glittering lines of rain-drops on the glass. He eyed once more the rows of sturdy, wholesome, male garments strung across the room and wished yet again, now safe in the impossibility of the unchosen past, that he had opted for the

Tongan princess to come and stay. He had thought at the time that such rashness might have stopped Millicent coming back when she otherwise would have. Now it looked as if he might as well have chosen the Polynesian temptress after all.

Mr Heikki Heikkila, fruit of that cursed gesture of good will, had arrived in time for the autumn term. He was not tall and slim, as anticipated, like Bjorn Borg, or even blonde. He was tallish but somewhat bulky, with tow-coloured hair in a crew cut, and a curiously clean and boyish look. Behind his rimless glasses his features were set, so it seemed, to constantly register polite expectation.

He had come with a sports bag the size of a coffee table, no other luggage, and was dressed to Fisher's vague consternation in a vast pair of khaki Bermuda shorts. Below them his bare calves with their sparse down of fair, curly hair were as broad as boat paddles. They bulged obscenely in their hairy nakedness against the midnight-blue satin upholstery of the drawing room sofa. Fisher had served sherry, which his new guest had downed in a single mouthful.

In the tortured failure of small talk which Fisher had gamely tried to maintain, it transpired at least that the newcomer was neither from Stockholm or Gothenburg, the only parts of Sweden that Fisher could refer to with confidence. He had changed track.

"And have you been to London before?" At this question the tiniest spark of interest had enlivened Mr. Heikkila's eyes, but only for a second.

"No. This is first time."

There was something strange about his 'f's and 's's, something fuffing and hissing.

"I think you'll like London. There's plenty to do here. Theatres, concerts. What sort of thing are you interested in?"

It seemed from the silence that followed that his new companion had drifted off to sleep, except that his face still wore the same inscrutable half-smile of politeness. When he spoke, his words had the air of an answer long deliberated over.

"I have heard that here is wery good peer. And bups."

Fisher had stared at him, then fallen back on the only words that came to mind.

"Yes, quite."

It had to be said that conversation that was certainly not the strongest suit of his guest. It had been two weeks, for example, before he had gathered by chance from Cheryl that the lodger was not, after all, from Sweden anyway but from somewhere else.

Heikki when questioned had merely blinked placidly behind his glasses and agreed that he was not from Sweden. "I have never peen there. I am from Finland."

Then, after a silence, "Do you know where is Finland?"

Fisher had given a short laugh. "Of course."

And that being the case, his new guest had volunteered no more information on the matter.

It could not be said that Heikki was a difficult lodger, even given that the time had stretched out long past the one month Fisher had specified. He was unobtrusive and retiring, kept early hours, paid his rent on time, did not smoke, and was ruthlessly spotless in the kitchen.

He had joined a sports and sauna club and began to come back glowing from his sauna bath, which he endured, it was rumoured, until he was red as a lobster and the heat far more dastardly than anyone else could stand. It seemed that he worshipped perspiration, and all that produces it, yet he was also fastidiously clean. More fastidious than Millicent, or even Fisher, who was fairly fastidious himself. Twice a week he would boil himself in his sauna, and twice a week he boiled and ironed all his clothes, the entire contents of the giant sports bag. His favourite colour was pristine white. His clothes stayed white. In his free time, to Fisher's mortification, he cleaned the flat, scaling off layers of dust and grime which Fisher had never even noticed. Such projects took up a major part of his weekend.

No, it could not be said that Heikki was troublesome. But nor, Fisher found, was he nearly as easy to live with as his virtues might seem to indicate. It seemed, on the contrary, remarkably trying to share one's living space with someone who was, or appeared to be, permanently sleepy. For Heikkki seemed to have just woken up from hibernation when even at his most alert, and oddest of all, even in circumstances that ran completely counter to sleeping. He retained an air of sleepiness when jogging or playing squash, an aura of somnolent fogginess when dredging up pedantically accurate facts and figures. Worse than this was his habit if not prodded remorselessly, of remaining mute for hours or, so it sometimes seemed to Fisher, for days.

Had he not, Fisher admonished himself, prayed for someone who would not drive him mad with idle chatter? Yet Heikki drove him all but mad with his lack of it. He found himself wanting to hurry the slow bear, chivvy him up, make him do things quickly. Goad him into sparkling communication. But whatever the nature of Fisher's questioning technique, be it rapier, bludgeon or caress, the Finn would blink his white-lashed eyes and ponder deeply before replying. There were times when Fisher swore to abandon politeness and just give up talking to him at all. They could live in silence till the maddening fellow left in May. For that, it looked like, was the length of time Heikki would be staying after all.

Heikki pegged up the final pair of underpants and wiped his hands on the tiniest of snowy hand towels. "There," he said, with a look of satisfaction towards Fisher, "It is finished." He wiped the basket and filled it with the neatly-folded clean, dry laundry he had taken down. "Shall we go?"

Fisher stretched himself and slid down from the top of the washing machine, tottering slightly as he touched down onto the tiled floor. He was stiff from his prolonged encampment on the hard metal surface and his legs had fallen asleep.

"I'm not as young as I was," passed through his mind. "Any Tongan princess would think I was a fossil." He opened the door wide for Heikki. "She wouldn't be far wrong." The bulky ensemble of Heikki and his basket passed slowly through the doorway and ahead of Fisher along the hallway to the main part of the flat.

"It is old apartment," Heikki had given his thoughtful verdict, "But you have plenty of space here."

"Yes," Fisher had answered. Phillips had been right. It was almost too much, since Millicent had gone.

Just as bad as the smooth, unoccupied side of the bed were the spaces where her clothes and personal possessions had been, and the empty space on the sofa where she had liked to sit. Her carefree presence had filled the room, her perfume, her aura had filled the flat. She wore high-heeled shoes and low-necked dresses, with nowadays ropes of pearls setting off the sophisticated neckline. Heikki's ample backside ahead of Fisher was encased in shapeless blue tracksuit bottoms. His rubber sandals flip-flapped as he made his way, placid and self-contained, towards his own door. For the thousandth time Fisher felt the maddening promptings of conversation, the impulse to puncture the bubble of silence in which they were imprisoned.

"I see you had a parcel this morning." The postman had woken him up with the bloody thing. "Was it Finnish vodka?" Heikki beamed mysteriously, but without turning round. Fisher saw only his faint reflection in a darkened window as they passed. The ghostly double had the air of one who held the key to an immensely satisfying secret.

"It is present", came from Heikki's earthly version. "For you. For the so-called Little Christmas. And to thank you for these accommodations."

In the midst of his genuine surprise Fisher noted that a small spark of pleasure had been ignited. It was a kind thought, even if vodka was not his drink. He could maybe even trade it quietly for a decent bottle of Scotch.

They had come to the room that Heikki occupied. He paused with his hand on the door knob.

"Please, come to wisit, when I have had time to sort my laundry." Heikki hitched the basket a little higher under his arm and disappeared.

It was some time later that Fisher knocked at the door. He had decided on reflection that he might just sample the vodka himself. He had noted at the time the giveaway heaviness and hard, smooth bulk of the parcel; there must be two bottles in there at least. In Heikki's room two chairs had been pulled up to the coffee table, now in the centre of the room, and the table itself had been set with two small glasses and an open bottle of Irish whiskey. Heikki poured drinks. In front of one chair the large, brown-paper-wrapped parcel which had come that morning had been prominently placed, still unopened. Heikki motioned towards it.

"I am sorry. I did not have time to unwrap parcel and wrap it as gift. I hope you don't mind."

"Not at all," said Fisher, generously. That meant he was getting both bottles.

"Please, unwrap."

The outer layer of strong, brown paper was lavishly covered and criss-crossed with sellotape, but at last it surrendered, and Fisher began to strip off the layers of protective newspaper wadding underneath. As he worked they began to loosen and unfurl like petals, as if they understood what was expected of them. He was almost to the treasure. He was reaching into the innermost nest of newspaper sheets, smoothing them down against the table around the parcel's final prize offering, its glass and alcohol double-chambered heart. Heikki beamed proudly and expectantly.

The object inside the promising layers was hideous.

Its sides rose sheer and glassy, in undulating, vertical waves, the loosely corrugated walls defining a central space in the form of an amoeba. At the bottom of the hollow space, when Fisher looked more closely, was a thick glass base. He stared at the startling monstrosity, disconcerted.

"It's…..Oh, thank you!"

"I knew you would like it. I noticed you have wery much glass things and china." Heikki swivelled it admiringly on its newspaper sheets, his eyes moving reverently over its asymmetrical bulges. Whatever it was, if anything, Fisher knew only that he hated it more with very passing second.

"I'm extremely touched. But are you sure you want me to have it?"

"Of course. I ordered it especially for you. My mother has sent it." Heikki raised his eyes reluctantly from its gleaming flanks and sat back on his chair, clearly struggling to find the words of expression. "I know you have interest in peautiful things. And that you don't have here already nothing that is same type. This is wase by wery famous designer."

Fisher gave a smile, and what he hoped would come across as a nod of appreciative admiration. He longed to hustle the thing back into its wrappings, out of view. "It's magnificent. But where, I wonder, should we put it?" His mind ranged over his collection of antique crystal and delicate porcelain. To destroy its harmony with a large, crude invader was unthinkable. "I rather think it should go in my bedroom. There's a spot on the mantelshelf there which would be just perfect". He picked the vase up. It weighed like a rock.

Heikki stood up to let him out of the room. He was nodding with a satisfied air, the air of a good deed well done. "It is for flowers. Some tulips, for example."

In his room Fisher viewed the glass creation, anthem to

Scandinavian aesthetics, with infinite distaste. It would have to go out on display, he supposed, at least until Heikki had left. He forced his gaze away with a shudder, and meticulously smoothed out its newspaper wrappings. They flattened out beneath his hand, a half-page picture of a winter scene, of a snowy house set in snow at the edge of a dark, snowy forest, at a time that seemed to be approaching dusk. Fisher paused. The picture glowed up from the page with a radiance that seemed almost warm, strangely full of soft pinks and off-whites set off against muted blue-blacks and gently darkening greens. It caught Fisher's eye, held him oddly spellbound; there was something magical about it. He had never before seen a snow scene that looked so inviting. It took a minute before he understood what gave it that effect. The house itself was painted an astonishing shade of rich and glorious pink.

A sumptuous pink, somewhat deeper but a trifle more sugary than rose. He wondered at first if it might be a flaw in the printing inks, but it wasn't. The other colours of the photograph were all as they should be. In the gathering dimness the snow had lost its sparkle, but was still softly luminous against the darkness of the forest. And against them both the house glowed like a warm-toned jewel. Fisher stared at its uninhibited pinkness, quite disconcerted. It seemed such a fanciful colour to paint one's house, especially for a race of people as serious as Heikki.

Oh well, there was no accounting for taste. Or maybe that was the point. Maybe it was for the house's outrageous colour that it was in the paper.

At any rate, the whole effect was really rather beautiful. Incredibly beautiful, in fact, like a scene from a fairy tale. It was certainly a fairytale house. It had white fancy woodwork around the windows and from every overhang and every window ledge hung icicles, long and pointed, some twisted sideways by the wind. It was capped with snow, and snow lay smooth and undisturbed around its walls. It was not until Fisher imagined himself in the picture and wading through that snow that he noticed that no-one had dug a path through to the front door. The beckoning house was inaccessible.

Perhaps it was just a film set, not a real house at all. Fisher dropped his gaze to the caption below the photograph. 'Talo, jossa poika tappoi isänsä.' No help there. Not a whisper of a clue. What a madly impossible language Finnish was. No wonder Heikki always sounded on the phone to his mother as if he were engaging in some sort of verbal keep-fit. For the first week Fisher had eavesdropped mesmerised and appalled, held reluctantly captive by the rat-tat of exploding consonants and the rack-stretched moan of unfamiliar vowels. It was a side to Heikki that had taken him by surprise.

Fisher let his eyes roam on down the page, seeking vainly to get the smallest grasp of its subject matter, then began to leaf through the other pages. The complete opacity of the words before him sapped the impact of headlines and suffused the adverts with a poignant dignity and depth. On page two was a photograph of a president Fisher had long assumed to be dead. He checked the date of the paper. The tenth of February, 1978. It was almost three years old.

It was no good. Gift or not, he really could not stand that vase. Fisher woke in the middle of the night and was immediately aware of its presence. Through the window the light of the streetlamp, wanly warm as it entered the room, threw a gleam on its flanks that turned cold and slick on contact. The thing was an alien, vulgar, tasteless aberration. Fisher got out of bed, wrapped the vase back up in the winter wonderland, and thrust it deep in the wardrobe.

CHAPTER 3

The afternoon was warm, so warm that the windows were open as wide as they would go, to admit what there was of a blossom-scented breeze to the room where Heikki was packing. He packed smoothly, methodically, and with effortless concentration, untroubled as always, it seemed, by any thoughts beyond the task that he was performing. He appeared to have completely forgotten Fisher, who had come in for the final rent cheque and now stood watching, leaning against the chest of drawers. It was late May, their incongruous cohabitation was almost over, and Heikki, with his seriousness and his white socks and insatiable passion for saunas would soon be gone. Back up north to the arctic country from which he had come, while in balmy London Fisher could readjust creakily to the full use of all his rooms again. In the autumn when Heikki came back he would be in regular student accommodation. Otherwise young Cheryl's head would roll.

It seemed odd to Fisher that he would soon have his flat back to himself. The prospect was immensely appealing, and at the same time he was apprehensive. More than anything he had wanted to have his flat back; he begrudged the fact that he had somehow got used to Heikki. But though the substitution of the Finn for Millicent was nothing short of a rather bad joke, he provided at least some sort of buffer from the loneliness that Fisher dared not feel.

It was a shame, he told himself yet again, that he hadn't taken the girl, and then more truthfully he pointed out to himself that it was almost definitely just as well. He was fifty-three, and anyway still in love with Millicent. Besides, come the autumn, his precious sabbatical year lay ahead, and with it *the book*. The key to the recognition he had long since considered he deserved. He would get to work on his brilliant treatise on the nature of truth and beauty, elucidate definitively the enigma to which even Keats had only alluded briefly. It would make his name.

But first there was the summer to spend in preparation. He must try to enjoy it and not to mope, start roughing out notes for the book. Besides, in a fortnight's time, he too would be off. Standing there in the sunny room Fisher felt a sudden surge of anxiety, while a chilly cloak seemed to descend around his body. The trip. Whatever had he let himself in for?

Why, oh why, had he ever let himself be persuaded? He dared not think about it. He tried instead to concentrate on the soothing ritual of Heikki packing, following his movements back and forth as he emptied drawers and cupboards to feed the insatiable sports bag on the bed. Soon the room would be his again, without the slightest trace that Heikki had ever been there.

Back in his own room Fisher sank down listlessly on the side of the bed, overcome with indecisiveness. Though what he felt indecisive about he could not say - it was too late now. In two weeks' time he would be there with Heikki, in his far-north homeland of snow and all-pervasive darkness. He would be there for three weeks, if he survived, and not a known soul, bar one he hardly felt he knew at all. Why on earth had he agreed to such an ordeal? Had there really been no choice? Fisher shivered, and allowed his body and spirits to continue to droop.

It was the mould that had started it all.

Or rather, no, the mould had been the final straw. The final straw and, Fisher told himself, the only reason why he had ever submitted to Heikki's entreaties. Indeed, it had been some considerable time before he had taken these seriously. It was not until the gift of the vase that he had understood that his polite but somehow unfathomable lodger regarded him as some sort of benefactor. The vase had been to show him his gratitude. And from that point it became more apparent that the quiet Finn held Fisher in high regard.

"You must come to Finland," he began to say as the months went past. "To my summer cottage." And Fisher would laugh a little, to show he appreciated the joke, and say that he only liked ice in his whisky. Then Heikki would give a little smile too. It was not for a long time, well into spring, that Fisher understood the most disconcerting factor.

That Heikki was serious.

He began to decline politely Heikki's stalwart efforts, steadily intensifying, to lure him to the arctic. Brighton beach on a windy, overcast day was bad enough, and the summer was always too short anyway, without deliberately sacrificing what there was of it. But Heikki was undeterred. He spoke repeatedly of his summer cottage, of fishing, saunas, days drinking Finnish beer. Fisher should even meet his parents. Heikki's face almost glowed. He heard with disbelief that Fisher did not fish. He must fish, how was his name? Through the infinite black vacuum of Fisher's imagination flowed icebergs, walruses, snowstorms, the agony of frozen feet.

"I don't really like cold weather. Or darkness."

"Now is spring. Ice is melting."

"But the dark..."

"When you come it is June. There is no dark. It is light almost all of time."

Fisher set out on a new, more promising line of discouragement. A tiny sigh. A rueful, wistful smile. "No summer holiday anywhere, this year, I'm afraid. I have to get started on my book."

He waited for Heikki to question him further, but to his disappointment, the Finn only waved his arms in benign dismissiveness. "You can read it at cottage." A ghost of a smile curved Fisher's lips.

"I have to write it, not read it. I've taken a year off, from the autumn, to get it done, but I have to start as soon as I can. It's a major work. I'm going to need all the time I can get."

"But you have whole year!" said Heikki. "It is first summer. Summer is so short. You need to take preak. You cannot work *whole* time." He stressed the word 'whole', and his voice was shocked and sincere. Nonetheless, Fisher was irked that Heikki had not asked him anything else about the book. It had come to Fisher more than once that his lodger would be the ideal 'common man' to test his theories on. He had many sterling qualities, but was undeniably of promisingly nonexistent philosophical insight. And totally lacking, it appeared, in aesthetic sensitivities. If he, Fisher, could manage to make his theories inviting and clear to such as Heikki, then his power to influence the rest of 'common man' was virtually assured. Put more plainly, if Heikki could understand his message, then anyone could.

Not that he was belittling Heikki, of course. The man was honest and serious and practical and reliable.

That aside, Fisher had yet another, more immediately pressing reason for desiring Heikki's imminent enrolment as guinea-pig. For if Heikki could only appreciate the importance of the impending project, he would understand why Fisher could not possibly take him up on his offer of a summer holiday. So Fisher braced himself and planned how to set about the daunting task of educating Heikki. It would never do to start off in the oxygen-thin realms of pure theory, that was obvious. No, he must start from something concrete, that Heikki could assimilate into his world of saunas and new technology and spectator passion for rally driving. It wouldn't be easy, that was for sure. But Fisher should start his lesson the next time they perceived some object of beauty together. For example, it came to him, they could start in his very own, elegantly furnished drawing room. He was certain that Heikki gave its aesthetic ambience not the slightest thought, during his lustful and regular pursuit of germs there. When Heikki ran his hairy-backed finger over the top of the chiffonier, he was not admiring the deep, seasoned glow of its antique mahogany. He was checking the surface for particles of dust. Fisher had seen that concentrated look in Heikki's eye many times. He was quite sure the man did not understand the real rarity of the air he was breathing.

A few days later found Fisher leading Heikki into his very first adventure in aesthetics, a guided tour of the treasures of the drawing room. The object in this initial lesson was simple; merely to open Heikki's mind to values that had nothing to do with how new or even how hygienic an item was. They could move on to abstract concepts later, but for now it sufficed to enlarge on the finer points of each piece of furniture, each priceless rug, each lovingly selected piece of crystal and chinaware. Point out how the room depended for its flawless coherence on the background setting, a subtle paint shade and tapestry wallpaper exactly replicating at great expense a late Jacobean design. Fisher ran a fingertip lovingly down the wall, delighting in the rhythmic alternation of texture and smoothness. Below a cloudy-blue velour flower spray was a small, greenish stain. He scratched it. It turned to brown.

"I have seen same in my room," said Heikki. "I think it is mould."

The mould would take two or three weeks to deal with. It sprang from a seam of dampness within the wall, culprit the guttering. It could have been worse, as the man who had to be called in was quick to point out, but it would have to be done. And the wallpaper would all have to come off, of course, and then be replaced. Fisher listened devastated to the sentencing of his tapestry wallpaper, but worse was to come. There would be noxious chemicals, the rooms affected would be unliveable in. It would be simplest if all occupants of the flat could go and stay somewhere else for a few weeks while it was being done. Fisher's disbelief and misery were complete. A few weeks! His summer plans had been ruined in an instant. He groused to himself, muttering darkly, sinking down into his chair.

"Confounded nuisance. And I don't have anywhere else to go." He experienced a mysterious, dragging feeling as he said the words out loud, was aware of Heikki suddenly looming over him, large, prosaic, slightly accusing.

"You have cottage in Finland. I inwite you. It is waiting you."

And now he was supposedly packing his things, so that Heikki could inspect them before he left. He must be quite sure that everything was just what was needed. Since the fateful discovery of the mould and his enforced capitulation to Heikki's summer plans he had found himself tossed between denial, fear, nervousness and excitement. In an appropriate equipment selection there would be some security at least.

"I have an hour to pack," he had said to Heikki.

"You have two weeks!"

"Yes, but I want to know before you leave that everything is correct."

He would take his notebooks, of course. He put them ready on the bed with his winter boots and a set of thick, worsted underwear. He really had no idea what to take. A sudden homesickness flooded through him, even now, before he had even set out. He looked around him at the pleasant room, in which the broad bed with its unfamiliar cargo of arctic necessities floated motionless on the blue Wilton carpet like a raft becalmed on the open sea. All this safe, beloved familiarity he was about to leave.

Heikki when he came in took off and polished and replaced his glasses while he cast his eyes slowly over the tottering piles of jackets and underwear. More slowly still, it seemed, his gaze took in the fur-lined boots and woollen hats, the hitherto unused scarves and sweaters from the relentless knitting needles of Millicent's mother.

"Ye-es." His tone was thoughtful. "Actually you will not need so many things. You have shorts?"

The final pack was as small and neat as only an expert can manage. It stood in the centre of the bed, well clear of the tideline of rejected articles heaped up against the headboard. Heikki nodded with satisfaction at his handiwork, then consulted his watch.

"Hey! But I have to go!" He clicked his heels together and raised his arm in a mock salute. "So. But, see you soon."

"Yes, see you soon. In…" But Fisher could not pronounce or even bring to mind the name of the small town Heikki came from. He followed him out of the front door of the flat and down in the lift.

"It is not long now."

"No, not long at all," responded Fisher bravely. Outside Heikki heaved his sports bags into the taxi.

"So. We see in Finland."

"Yes. Have a good flight."

The taxi left.

A twinge of anxiety robbed the evening air of its mellowness as Fisher stood for a minute in the street. "I should have said I was looking forward to it," it came to him. He hoped that Heikki had not noticed this omission. He doubted that he had. All the same, an uncomfortable feeling accompanied him as he went back inside.

CHAPTER 4

He had dozed off. When he opened his eyes once more the mist was thinning, and the sun was already visible again like a dull silver coin. The grey sea of moisture around them turned to white and began to sink; soon the tops of grey barns were floating in it, as if rising back up out of a flood, and as the sun struggled finally out from behind its veils it began to shine on the clearest, most beautiful landscape that Fisher had ever seen. It was nothing majestic, nothing dramatic. It was rolling countryside, like the fields and forests of a children's picture book, set here and there with a glittering ribbon of river or a farmstead with wooden buildings the colour of red earth. But every detail of it, near and far, was suffused with light of a clarity he had never experienced before. As the day took hold the sky grew bluer, the greens and reds more resonant, till it seemed to Fisher that everything around them sang together in a harmony of colour and form and light. On and on; ahead the road curved then straightened up, wove back and forth then straightened out again, then wove and wove until Fisher's ecstasy began to be undermined by an unpleasant nausea. On the plane he had dined on gin and tonics and hardly slept. He shut his eyes to lessen the queasiness, and when next he opened them the bus had stopped, and there was Heikki.

Fisher hoped, as he settled himself into Heikki's car, that the final stage of his journey would not take long. A lungful of fresh air had settled his stomach, but he needed coffee and some solid food. He had not realised Finland was so big.

Yet before he knew it they were passing again through the pastoral dreamscape. Fields, forests, farmsteads, all bathed in sunlight. It was half an hour before they came to the outskirts of another one-horse town. Heikki bent down and stabbed with his finger as the car speeded smoothly through the streets. "There is my house where I live. In there." They were passing a block of flats. Fisher glanced back at it, then looked at Heikki in consternation.

"And we are going where?"

"We go to my parents'. To my mum and dad. They live near lake where is summer cottage." Fisher relapsed into silence.

The house outside which they drew up was of wood, but of dull green, not the earth red of most of the houses they had passed. It was neat and well-kept up, a single storey, with hanging baskets of flowering plants along the front and clay urns of geraniums beneath the windows. The lower part of every window pane was enhanced by a white lace curtain, and from the small neat lawn in front of the house rose a graceful flagpole, proclaiming patriotic and domestic pride. All the same Fisher could not quite convince himself that a wooden house could really be a very permanent dwelling. He climbed from the car and followed Heikki up the path.

The front door was adorned on each side by a showy brass carriage lamp, which to Fisher's mind hardly fitted the rest of the ambience at all. Beneath the lamp on one side was an oval plaque made from a piece of wood, on which a single word was burnt out in pokerwork. 'Hilppala'.

"It means 'Hilppa's place.' It is house name. From my mother, Hilppa." As Heikki spoke, the front door opened, and Fisher looked down at the tiny woman who stood before them. She was not much bigger than a girl, but her skin was wrinkled and the hand she extended to Fisher was arthritic. From behind her came a smell of baking so heavenly, so overpowering, that Fisher imagined he would swoon. His mouth began to water, his soul to yearn hopelessly once more for coffee, hot, plentiful and strong.

"My mum," said Heikki.

It relieved Fisher later to recall that he had smiled intrepidly, even while inwardly registering two points. Firstly, that Heikki's mother could gabble out more words in a minute than Heikki could plod out in a month, and secondly, that despite his preparatory language studies he hadn't even clearly distinguished, let alone understood, a single one. He gave another rather self-conscious smile as she ushered them in.

"Does your mum speak English?" he whispered furtively to Heikki, when the deluge seemed at last to have slackened.

"No," said Heikki, placidly, at normal volume, and opened a door that led off the hall in which they now stood. The room before them was shrouded in darkness, lit only by the shimmering screen of a black and white TV. From the shadowy box came the unmistakable sound of a tennis ball bounding rhythmically from racquet to racquet, an occasional murmur from a hidden crowd. A new smell, grossly human, that of clothing and slightly perspiring flesh, began to mingle with the baking aroma as a large form, illuminated only down the TV side, turned slowly towards them, and just as slowly began to rise.

"My father," said Heikki. "Urpo." Urpo grunted. He might have been repeating his name. His teeth, Fisher noticed as he stood up, were not in his mouth, but sitting on the arm of his chair, as if they too were riveted by the tennis. "He has new teeth", said Heikki. "He is not quite used." Fisher shook the proffered hand and in the uneven light that flickered on the plump face stared unnerved at the image that would be Heikki's in a matter of thirty years from now. Mr. Heikkila senior was fatter and shorter than his son; he was balding, and surprisingly slovenly in dress, but the face, if one took away the jowls and the drooping moustache, was the same. The same expression, or lack of it, in the pale eyes behind the glasses. His bodily form had the same intangible likeness to some sort of bear. Only his hands were different, they were calloused. At that very moment the unseen crowd gave a roar and Urpo released his handclasp, returning to his seat. It was clear where Heikki had inherited his speaking skills from.

They returned to the hall, where Hilppa was waiting for them expectantly.

"Otatekokarfyanootvyodotetaaarnkoseehenastykunessooerdaaaghn?"

Fisher urged himself not to be discouraged. It was early days yet. Heikki answered briefly then turned to Fisher. "She asks if we like to have coffee. I say we don't need. We have peer. But first I will show you your room."

They drank the beer sitting on a terrace behind the house. It was some kind of lager, not unpleasant, but its coldness made Fisher shiver slightly. He was feeling chilly, in spite of the sun. And with every mouthful of beer the soft mist of sleep caressed his brain a little more compellingly.

"Shall we go to see poat?" suggested Heikki. As he spoke he heaved himself up from his chair, with the help of the arm-rests.

"Good idea!" agreed Fisher heartily, rising too, although the suggestion itself meant nothing to him. His head felt a little muzzy; the lager, it seemed, was deceptively strong. It was probably as well to walk as to sit. They crossed the grass and immediately entered a small wood; just as quickly, they started to make their way downhill. Not straight, but tacking back and forth along a tiny path so ill-defined as to be for the most part almost imaginary. All around them crowded firs and birches and alders, a real, proper forest all of a sudden, but nothing like an English one. Beneath their feet the path was springy with fallen needles. It was overgrown by straggling bushes and perilous with looping tree roots and uneven stones, but Heikki bounded this way and that with the nimbleness of a mountain goat. Fisher had to give all his energy to keeping up.

They popped out suddenly, onto a broad, deserted, dirt road, where Heikki swung left and strode on, with Fisher scuttling behind him. Then he stopped, and Fisher, drawing level at last, let out a quite involuntary gasp of surprise. They had come to the edge.

The edge of everything, so it seemed. For there before them, a few yards off, was a wooden jetty with a boat, and beyond it a stretch of shimmering water so immense that Fisher imagined he must have lost the battle to stay awake and be dreaming. Here and there quite far out its surface was broken by tiny islands, some crowned with trees, others no more than rocky outcrops. The furthest away were mere silhouettes against the faint blue smudge that Fisher realised now must be the far shore. A few boats were cruising in the distance, and high above the water seagulls circled, their cries faintly audible.

"So, here is lake."

As Fisher looked the water rippled for an instant, and burst into a thousand twinkling star-points where it caught the light. For a moment a thin white foaming line marked the base of the nearest islands, then the water subsided once more into stillness, stretching tranquilly beneath a cloudless sky.

"And poat."

Fisher pulled his mind back to his nearby surroundings. The white craft moored to the jetty in front of him was almost completely covered by a canvas tarpaulin, beneath which he could make out the contour of a windscreen, and a bit of roof. It was obviously some sort of motorboat; more than that he couldn't say. He was wary of boats.

To his left lay a tiny beach of pebble and sand; the forest they had come through came right down to the back of it. It petered out not far along into rocks and bulrushes, but near the jetty, set back more towards the trees, was a wooden building, earth red, trimmed in white.

The summer cottage. The summer cottage by the lake. That was why they had come to his parents' house - to come here.

There was something rather odd about the building, he could not put his finger on what.

"And that's the summer cottage?" He pointed. Heikki gave him a blank look, as if he was not sure whether Fisher was joking or not.

"That is poat house." His tone was neutral. He turned his face towards the open lake beyond the jetty and nodded. "Cottage is out there. We wisit tomorrow. With parents."

"Oh." Fisher tried to follow the nod. "Where out there, exactly?"

Heikki gave another nod. "On island. It is why we have poat."

"Ah." Fisher threw the little vessel an apprehensive look and scanned the vast expanse of water once more. "Is it far?"

"Not so far. Do you see gap between islands there?" Heikki pointed.

"No-oo."

Heikki lowered his arm. "One minute. Wait."

He turned around and crossed to the boat house, disappeared and returned in a matter of seconds with a pair of binoculars. He focussed them across the water, looked steadily in one direction for an instant, and handed them to Fisher, who put them obediently to his eyes. He could make out nothing but a wavering, twitching patch of black scarred with fuzzy white spots. "That is island we must go past," encouraged Heikki. He took the binoculars back. "And there," - he squinted through them, then pressed them hard against the bridge of Fisher's nose - "There is island where is cottage." The white spots had disappeared, the black itself seemed to blink and flutter. The metal rim of the binoculars pressed deep into Fisher's flesh. "You see it now?"

"Oh, yes!" cried Fisher enthusiastically, "Yes! Wow!" He pushed the binoculars away and massaged his nose surreptitiously. "Yes, indeed. Wow." Heikki beamed with pleasure.

"How long does it take to get across to it?" The answer would be "quite long" or "not so long".

"It takes twenty-two minutes, if water is calm." Heikki fastened the binoculars back in their waterproof case. "Forty one minutes to row with oars. If water is calm." Fisher prayed silently that the water would be calm.

"And we go tomorrow, eh?" When he had rested properly he was sure the trip would appeal.

"Yes, tomorrow. You must take with you swim suit of course, and sandals for peach. We have wery good sauna there." They left the jetty and made their way along the first short strip of road, to a seemingly unmarked spot where Heikki plunged once again into the forest. He gave a final, vague wave up the road as he did so. "By road one can come by car. But we take now short cut again."

The short cut seemed somehow shorter going back than the way they had come, in spite of being uphill. When they reached the house it occurred to Fisher that there had been no windows in the building he had mistaken for the cottage. That was what was wrong with it.

CHAPTER 5

Heikki's parents would not be coming with them to the island after all. A place had come up unexpectedly for the week after next at the Moose Walk Retirement Home, for which they had put down their names. They would spend their time until then getting ready, and only go to the island for the midsummer weekend. The day after midsummer day, on the Monday, they would be moving.

It was possibly just as well, thought Fisher, as they loaded the boat at the jetty, that they wouldn't be coming. The boat was so full there was scarcely any room left for passengers. He was proud that his own contribution had been modest – just a small canvas holdall with the basic necessities for a beach day. He always took too much, but this was to be a brand new start. Even Heikki had commented on how small his bag was.

The jetty was finally empty and Heikki had climbed up beside him again. "So. Now is only most important thing." He signalled a knowing look to Fisher, then crossed the short stretch of beach to the boathouse. "Come, please." The boathouse was dark inside, and smelt of petrol and lake water. It took a minute before he could make out what Heikki was standing beside - a stack of beer crates almost as tall as himself.

The beer crates were Heikki's crowning masterpiece of packing. When they were stowed on board he stood and surveyed his handiwork with pride.

"And now, we are ready." He turned to help Fisher, who clutched him wildly as he clambered in. "So now at cottage will be only us two. But I think we enjoy." He nodded significantly towards the beer. He had dug out from somewhere a baseball cap which he put on his head, with the peak towards the back. It altered his image as much as was probably ever possible, from bumbling bear to dashing boater.

"What will happen to the house?"

Heikki gave the dashboard a final loving polish and fitted the key in the ignition. "They are selling. That is why they have now much to do."

"We should have stayed to help them, maybe."

Heikki waved his hand dismissively. "They can manage. They need only clean. I rent van to take away furnitures when they have gone." He turned back blissfully towards the controls. Fisher stood up to get a better look, feeling quite the sea-dog. The boat rocked gently, causing him to sway and stagger. "Please. Sit down." Heikki turned the key, and in another minute they were curving away across the water.

The shore from which they had started out was already almost out of sight when the small boat drew level with the first of the islands and started to pass between them. To his surprise Fisher could see now that on every island of any size there was a cottage. A flagpole, a jetty. A tiny slip of a beach.

"Here is one hundred islands," said Heikki, in a tone of pride, and it seemed that he was right. As they went on, new islands constantly appeared from nowhere and flowed towards them, and still the further shore seemed to come no nearer. Fisher sat mesmerised, thinking neither of things that had been nor even things that might be to come. He hardly noticed when Heikki cut the speed of the engine and the small craft turned and began to aim like a homing bird towards the land. "So, we are here."

Fisher came to, and saw the shores of an island drawing rapidly nearer. It was not large, his gaze could encompass it from side to side with only the merest turn of his head, but nor was it the smallest they had passed. He could make out a landing stage, a small beach, bulrushes, red wooden buildings by the water. Behind them rocky slopes and boulders rose up towards the now familiar crown of densely packed trees. It looked deserted there. Heikki lifted an arm for an instant and pointed.

"There is cottage."

Fisher twisted round and looked. High up on the rocks, almost camouflaged against the trees, was a brown wooden chalet. He dropped his gaze to the red wooden huts at the water's edge.

"So what are those?"

"That is sauna. And poathouse."

"And who uses them?"

"Only we. We are owning all."

"But who owns the island?"

"We. We own." Heikki continued to steer the boat straight ahead, with rapturous concentration.

"You own the island?" Fisher looked out speechless at the tiny independent country that was fast approaching.

"Almost. There is one other couple. Name is –" - Heikki rattled off something quite ungraspable. "They have cottage on other side of vood. But everything this side is ours, and all what does not belong to them." His tone was contented but factual, devoid of boastfulness. He pulled the boat in smartly beside the jetty.

The cottage was a modest but sturdy building of unpainted logs, with large square windows and a log veranda. It stood by itself on a flattish piece of high ground some way back from the shore, and was reached apparently by simply climbing up over the rocks from wherever one happened to be. Behind it the thick wood of birch and pine trees formed a screen that cut off the rest of the island, except to one side where there rose up a small, bald, rocky hill.

It felt to Fisher like a dozen trips before the boat was empty and the cottage veranda piled high with all they had brought. But at last it had all been carried up. Fisher, free finally to take in the breathtaking panorama spread before him, became reluctantly aware instead of a growing need to empty his bladder.

"So. We go inside." Heikki took a key which was simply hanging by the door. The cottage consisted of a large room which seemed to be a living room and kitchen, a small hall, and two other rooms. Heikki waved an arm through the doorway of both. "Here is pedroom. And here is another." There appeared to be no more rooms in the building, for the only other door turned out to lead to a cupboard. Heikki disappeared into one of the bedrooms. Fisher followed him.

"Is there a toilet?" The smallest glint slipped into Heikki's eye, as he turned and pointed through the window at a small, red, narrow, wooden hut, like a guard's hut, across the rocks at the fringes of the wood.

"There is toilet. Smallest room." He turned back in towards the bedroom. " And here is your ped."

Fisher was faintly confused, though he tried not to show it. "My bed? So we are here tonight?"

"Of course," said Heikki, turning back towards the window again.

"Oh," said Fisher. He supposed it was all right. He had made up his mind, after all, to immerse himself wholeheartedly in the spirit of adventure. But it irked him the way that Heikki never thought to mention anything in advance, always kept things to himself. Had he known, he would have brought his pyjamas.

"We are here many nights," said Heikki. He looked out happily at the sun-dappled trees, the deserted rocks, his own small kingdom. "Until the midsummer, at least." But Fisher did not hear him. He was already halfway to the smallest room.

Fisher stood up from brushing his teeth at the water's edge and gazed out over the magical lake with its one hundred islands. They had been here three or four days now; he felt already like an old hand. He was wearing his swimming trunks, and wellingtons that were possibly Urpo's. He knew that if he looked down past the white froth of toothpaste the water would be crystal clear, so clear that one could count every small fish that swam in it, every pebble, every slip of weed and grain of gravel if one wanted. Such numerical nature surveys, thought Fisher, he might very well have time and soon insanity enough to embark on.

Further out he could make out Heikki, already rowing the small boat out to check his nets, his passage quickening the sinuous reflections of the lake. The heat-haze that had earlier covered the water had lifted, laying the way clear for another day of glorious high-summer weather. The daily programme had been lazily established. They would sunbathe on the rocks and drink beer and swim, which Fisher did reluctantly as one more occupation to stave off madness. Heikki would gut the fish he had caught and cook it for dinner, and in the evening they would sauna, a rite to which Fisher was now initiated. In broad daylight they would run out from the small wooden sauna house in the bulrushes, naked and red as lobsters, to plunge sweating and gasping into the midnight waters of the lake.

All in all, island life included many pastimes which Fisher had never indulged in before. And in between, or even during, he would gaze out over the vast and infinitely beautiful lake that imprisoned them and wonder just how soon, or even just how, he could escape.

Heikki lay for hours on the rocks like a giant seal, turning gradually from blubber pale to a rather reddish shade of brown. Fisher burnt quickly in the unaccustomed clarity of the air, and took to permanently wearing his only shirt, which he washed out nightly and spread out under a couple of stones to dry. In terms of achievement he rated sauna second only to the loss of his virginity, but all the same, it remained a ritual in which he never felt entirely at ease. Washing his clothes out helped to shorten it. With sinking heart there came to him one possible explanation of why Millicent liked to put the washing in last thing at night.

The only change to routine was provided now and then by the island's only other inhabitants, the neighbours with the unpronounceable name. Fisher had discovered them himself one afternoon, when on a time-killing mission of exploration. Pushing his way through the wood he had stumbled on their territory, bursting unexpectedly into a clearing where a man was mowing a small patch of lawn behind a cabin. He was mowing round the edges; in the centre of the lawn was a woman lying stretched out on a sunbed. Apart from a white scarf draped across her eyes she was naked. Fisher retreated.

He said nothing about his discovery, but the next day the couple paid them a visit. The white scarf must have been of thin gauze, for the man had never turned in Fisher's direction. They drank beer and stayed for what seemed to Fisher a very long time. They spoke no English. Their names, as now introduced by Heikki, were Seppo and Sirkka.

They came twice more during the days that followed, once by paddling round the shoreline at midday and once through the wood at four in the afternoon. Fisher bore their visits bravely. On the visit round the coast they stayed for an hour, and on the trip through the woodlands, four. Behind his amiable mask Fisher tried to secretly fortify his mind with the chapter headings and sub-divisions of his book. There was nothing to write on in the cottage, except the holiday novel he had brought to read. At one stage he slipped away and wrote his synopsis on the inside cover. It was an hour of bliss.

On the only other challenging territory of the island, the hill, was a telescope. This too, Fisher had discovered while prowling about one day. The hill was not really much of a hill, just a barren hump of granite that that rose to form the island's modest high point. The telescope was mounted on its rounded summit and angled out to face the north. Fisher tried in vain to work it. He supposed it must belong to Seppo and Sirkka. Heikki looked at him in sleepy surprise when he mentioned this.

"To them? No, it is ours. You can see house from it. You have not tried?"

"I couldn't work it. I didn't know how."

Heikki's look of surprise became less sleepy. "But it's easy! Come. I show you." He threw down the knife he was cleaning fish with, wiped his hands on a rag and led the way up the rock. There he fiddled around with the telescope and pushed Fisher's face up hard against the viewing lens, just as he had with the binoculars.

"I'm a bit short-sighted," apologised Fisher, as Heikki fixed his hand round Fisher's and adjusted the focus. Fisher was once again amazed at the power in the grip. His knuckles felt as if they were in a vice. The giant fingers guided his, and then suddenly the scene at the other end of the telescope jerked into focus. "Oh, yes!"

Heikki released his grip. The view continued to jerk up and down, but Fisher's control grew greater. He saw water, more water, and then the scene jerked suddenly and included a jetty and a boat house. Fisher recognised them as the ones he had left a few days before. "I can see the jetty." He felt the iron fingers clamp down on his.

"So now if you look up. There is forest, yes?" Fisher admitted that there was. Heikki bent down and squinted through the telescope himself. "And there – there is house." He made way for Fisher to look again. There it was. Hilppala. One could see almost all of it, if one got the angle right, but from the side. One could make out a part of the fence and the windows. A slip of the road they had driven along.

"Well, I never!" said Fisher. It was truly incredible. And after Heikki had gone back down to rescue his gutted fish from the gulls, Fisher continued to look through the telescope alone. He managed to turn it round and still to focus it – on some birds in the water, on a far-off island, a nearer island, the branch of a tree, a woman at the water's edge. It was the key to a whole new world.

The next time he tried to use it, he could not get it to work.

He took to rowing, in the small boat that Heikki kept on the island, in which he went out daily to check the nets. To his own surprise, and even more to Heikki's, who was visibly impressed, it turned out that Fisher could still pull a pretty good oar. He had been pretty keen at Cambridge; now would be just the time to brush up his rowing skills. He rowed about in front of the island and even, eventually, under patient instruction, began to use the outboard motor attached to the boat. Then he would cruise about as far from the island as he dared.

It was difficult to get out of Heikki just how long their stay on this island paradise was going to last. Fisher had no wish to give the slightest hint that he was not enjoying himself, still less that he looked on his surroundings as a luxury Alcatraz. It was without doubt the most exquisitely beautiful place he had ever seen. But he needed something to do. He needed brutal, mental activity.

"When you are here," said Heikki, with an air of luxuriousness, "There is no sense of time. Time - disappears." He had a satisfied look.

"Quite." said Fisher. "And shall we be here for midsummer?" It appeared they would. There was to be a bonfire on the beach with the Unpronounceables.

"Ah." Fisher smiled, an exceptionally radiant smile.

"And my parents, of course. I go to fetch them in afternoon. I hope there will not be not too many drunken drivers on lake." Fisher was amused. He had never thought of drunken boaters before.

"We have sauna together," Heikki continued, "And then midsummer. It is best night of year." The prospect of a sauna with Hilppa and Urpo removed all traces of merriment from Fisher's mind.

On the morning of what turned out to be midsummer's eve, a minor accident occurred with the rowing boat. That very morning, Fisher knocked the boat on the edge of the jetty when coming in to land from his outboard-motor practice. The result was a jagged hole just above the water-line. It was not big, but when Heikki climbed down into the boat to take a look at it, the vessel sank down, and a thick little column water spurted in.

"Climb out of poat," Heikki ordered, but even when the miserable Fisher had scrambled penitently into knee-deep water, with Heikki on board the hole was still below the surface of the lake.

Heikki dragged the boat up out of the water and turned it over on the beach, with Fisher, red and embarrassed, trying to help.

"It is small hole," said Heikki, pacifyingly. "It is easy to mend."

But there would be no time today. Heikki left in the larger boat to pick up his parents, leaving Fisher standing forlornly by the jetty. He did not dare to ask to go for the ride, as he had planned. After a while he climbed the hill and looked out forlornly over the blue silk lake.

It was truly astounding, thought Fisher, with a certain woozy detachment, how much his fellow drinkers could all put away. Even Hilppa, if his impressions were not mistaken, was knocking it back like a navvy. Down it went, bottle after bottle, into that withered, dried-up, frail old frame. He wondered how those dry old fibres could absorb it all. She must be ten years older than him, maybe fifteen. He had given up drinking at that speed before he was thirty. And as for the others, the Unpronounceables and Heikki and Urpo, he could hardly imagine how much beer and rum and vodka they had got through. Far more than he could manage, that was for sure.

Heikki rose stiffly to his feet. "We go to light ponfire," he said. He took a smouldering stick from the barbecue and the small party made their way to the beach, which seemed to tilt rather unsteadily. Seppo threw the contents of a canister at the bonfire. The stick produced nothing but a sulky wisp of smoke, but when Heikki threw in a lighted match the whole stack burst into glorious, upward-shooting flames in a matter of seconds. They stood and looked at it, enraptured. Then Heikki led the way back up towards the place where they had been sitting.

It disgruntled Fisher to notice that, try as he might, he was losing the spirit of the thing. The rocks were hard, it was the longest day of the year, and though for once there was lively conversation, he was excluded. In his mellow state Heikki's translation services were foundering badly. His well-intentioned offerings in English were becoming fewer and increasingly difficult to follow. The words were becoming spaced out, which made it impossible to always know to which thought a certain word belonged. Fisher found himself slipping away, becoming sober.

He was surprised to find, when he stood up to go and relieve himself, that he was still drunk. Rocks which he had always known to be flat and reliable beneath his feet had taken to heaving and reeling unpredictably. While urinating at the edge of the wood he had to hold on to the trunk of a tree to keep his balance. On turning round ready to rejoin the party he realised no-one had even noticed he had gone. Heikki was putting more sausages on the grill.

He found himself floating towards the telescope, but as before, when he tried to make it work, its secret stubbornly evaded him. He tried a few more times, then stood beside it, looking out across the midsummer lake and the islands. On every shore, or so it seemed, a bonfire glowed like a new sun being kindled, and beneath each one a second sun shone up, from somewhere in the mirror-calm water.

"So beautiful," Fisher heard himself exclaim, though no thoughts seemed to stay in his mind for very long. It seemed somehow hard to retain them. Yet his visual faculties seemed to be enhanced.

He was vaguely aware of voices becoming louder, no longer just a far-off murmur punctuated by a mercifully faint shrill laugh. It was Heikki, followed by the Unpronounceables, coming up to him over the rocks. His absence had been noted. Heikki ambled amiably towards the telescope.

"You have been using.....?" His voice was slow, the right word nowhere to be found. He seemed to stare at Fisher with great intensity, then his gaze slid away. He smelt of alcohol.

"Trying to," said Fisher. He thought if he did not confess at once to his lack of success, then Heikki would ask him to point out something. But Heikki was no longer listening. He had turned back round to the Unpronounceables. "You have used telephone?"

"Telescope," volunteered Fisher, diffidently. Heikki adjusted the instrument and the Unpronounceables looked through it. The smoke from Sirkka's cigarette drifted slowly up around the barrel. She was swaying slightly. In the background Urpo and Hilppa appeared at long last, struggling slowly towards them. "We look though telephone," said Heikki, again in English, as if they could suddenly all understand that language. He looked through the telescope himself and then pushed the lens towards Fisher. "You see house?" Fisher noticed that he pressed a lever as he spoke before adjusting the lens. At last he understood why the telescope had never worked for him.

"I saw the house last time," he said, but he bent down and looked again obediently. The house was not quite in focus. Heikki was twiddling something. As the image sharpened Fisher could see the house wall, the roof, the windows, the tree in the yard.

"Oh yes." He drew his head back and Heikki looked again, then let out an exclamation.

"Hey! Hey, but window is open!" He reported in Finnish to the old folk, and then Urpo took hold of the telescope and had a look. "Window is open!" repeated Heikki to Fisher. Hilppa looked. Urpo looked again. There followed an animated discussion.

They started to make their way down the rock, still jabbering among themselves. It was several minutes before Heikki turned to Fisher again. He still was not his usual calm self. "My mother has left open. She is getting little forgetful. That is other reason why new home is good idea." They sat down, but the mood of the party seemed to have changed. The discussion was heated, and Heikki seemed to become a little sulky. "They do not like that window is open," he repeated to Fisher.

"They think it is not safe." He stared glumly at nothing in particular. "They want that I go across lake and shut it. I say that I don't want to go." He waved his beer bottle vaguely in the air. "We have party here."

"I could go," said Fisher, without really knowing why. Then a shock of fear ran through him. Supposing Heikki said yes? But of course he wouldn't. Heikki looked at him. Fisher could see from his eyes that he was unmistakeably unbelievably drunk.

"Ye-es. Hey, of course! You can work motor poat now!" Fisher felt his spine turn to ice, in spite of the slight warmth that still came from the grill. He opened his mouth to say that, after all, it would not be a good idea, but Heikki had turned away and was talking to his parents again. He turned back round. "I told them" – Fisher noticed his voice was horribly slurred – "That you are really a poatman now. I said them you will go. My mother is wery pleased." He turned and spoke again to Hilppa, who replied effusively.

"I told her you are wery good poatman now."

Fisher found himself somehow being steered towards the jetty, hemmed in by Heikki and the Unpronounceables. They were keeping close, almost as if he were under guard, and as Fisher felt the jetty's planks beneath his feet he was overcome by a sudden sense of unreality, like a doomed man going to the scaffold. He couldn't believe he had suggested anything so stupid. He had never even been in the boat out of shouting distance for help from Heikki, never even had to beach it by himself. And if Heikki had not had far too much to drink, he would never have gone along with such utter madness.

He remembered now anyway that the boat had a hole in it. It wasn't lakeworthy. If the lake was choppy in any part, the water would come in. He turned to make this point to Heikki, but Heikki had vanished. A moment later he reappeared, coming down from the cottage with a rather staggering step. When he drew near he slipped on a rock at the edge of the water and almost fell over. The others pulled him upright as he grabbed for the side of the jetty to steady himself. "He's completely drunk," went through Fisher's mind again. "If he was sober he would never allow me go." And he wanted to explain to the others about the hole, and about his totally inadequate boating skills, but felt his tongue locked by language. He felt as hopeless as if he had not had the gift of speech at all. He could only wait for them to realise Heikki's thoroughly untrustworthy condition, but they seemed to consider his behaviour perfectly acceptable. Heikki was holding the key to Hilppala in his hand; he had hung on tightly to it even when he had slipped. Now he waved it at Fisher.

"You go to house. You open door." He demonstrated how this should be done, a turn of the key in an airy lock. "You close window —so. You take one peer to relax. You come back." He waved towards the Unpronounceables. "We are waiting party for you." He nodded, with obvious satisfaction. "Soon you are real captain. Now you are only hero." Fisher sensed that the boat had been unfastened ready for him. On the jetty Seppo stood with the cast-off mooring rope in his hand, as if the little vessel were some kind of large and ungainly but amiable dog on a lead. It bobbed and dipped on the surface of the water, lifted by ripples. Its stern was less than a yard from dry land. Heikki seized the wooden rim and pulled the boat up closer for Fisher.

"It won't float," said Fisher urgently, "It's got that hole." Heikki waved a hand breezily.

"It will float."

There was nothing for it but to prove him wrong. Resolutely Fisher climbed in and tried surreptitiously to depress the prow, but the little craft bobbed resiliently and the hole stayed inches above the water-line. It was no good, he wasn't heavy enough to prove the boat unfit. At least not here, near the safety of the jetty, with the Finns looking on. On the open lake it would hit a rogue wave and sink, he was sure of it. Or a drunken midsummer speedboat driver would crash his pottering little ark to smithereens. Fisher fastened the toggles on his life-jacket fearfully, just as Heikki pushed the boat out.

It was only then that Urpo finally made it to the head of the jetty; it had taken the old pair all this time to clamber down from the rocks. He began to shout at his son, gesticulating, distorting his features and pointing at Fisher. He was clearly agitated. That old bear, thank God, could see the total imbecility of it all. Heikki was taking note; he began to wave Fisher frantically back in towards the shore. With immeasurable relief Fisher plied the oars to bring the boat back in, and Heikki stepped into the shallow water to grab at the stern. Fisher stood up.

"His teeth. He has forgotten to bring his teeth with. If you could look for them, please, while you are there. It has been wery difficult for him to eat." Heikki rammed the boat out once again, bringing Fisher down into sitting position with a thump. Fisher grabbed at the side.

"Teeth," he repeated. His own voice sounded somehow odd. "O.K." There must have been some force in Heikki's shove, for the boat was already some way out. Fisher shipped the oars and wound the wet, coarse starter cord of the outboard motor round his hand. It was bound not to start.

"They are in pox," floated Heikki's voice across the water, "small plastic pox." Fisher pulled the cord. The motor spluttered immediately into life. He hoped there was fuel. The partymakers watched from the jetty as the boat sped away, in a wide, capricious arc of the engine's very own choosing.

"Take two peers" shouted Heikki, waving his arms. "And remember, teeth." He continued to wave until Fisher was no more than the smallest ineptly zigzagging dot, but Fisher had no strength for even the briefest of responses. He was trying to calm himself, to unlock his paralysed brain, and gain some sort of mastery over the self-willed boat.

CHAPTER 6

If there was one thing Fisher had learnt during his time on the lake, it was how to tell an island when he saw one. This was a great help in recognising the far-off, uninterrupted coastline when, through sheer good luck, it finally came into view. But no sooner had Fisher relaxed a little than he realised that he did not have the faintest idea where to head for, or if the beach and the boathouse would be straight ahead, to the left or the right. As he squinted and put his hand up to shelter his eyes, he felt his blood drain suddenly, and a crop of sweat beads burst out on his temples. The entire coastline was one long unbroken string of beaches, boathouses and jetties. Worst of all, he hardly knew what he was looking for. He had only seen Heikki's jetty a couple of times.

But it really was, he marvelled later, as if the wretched boat had a mind of its own. The water itself almost seemed to bring him in towards the shore, albeit side on, and when he dared to turn his head, there on his portside was a beach and a boathouse that certainly looked like Heikki's. With hands that were curiously trembling Fisher fastened the boat and climbed out shakily into the shallow water. He must make sure, before he pulled the motor up, that this was really the place.

The boathouse was not locked. He opened the door and saw the concrete slab where the beer crates had stood. Yes, this was it. And there before him was the dirt road leading up from the beach, which would take him past the front gate of Hilppala.

Fisher set off. It seemed that midsummer revelries had kindly left this part of the mainland behind, for the place seemed deserted. His feet crunched quietly in the peace and stillness of the luminous northern night.

He did not want to go up the road. Despite the instruction to drink two beers, and having to find Urpo's teeth, he was going to need all the time he could get. It might take him hours to find his way back across the water to the island, since he really had no idea how to get there. And even longer if the motor wouldn't start. He would go up the same way he had with Heikki, through the forest. Fisher rounded the corner and made his way to the short cut where it came out onto the road.

The tiny path was just as enchanting as it had been when he had stumbled down and up it in Heikki's wake. It seemed to Fisher that he had become more agile over the course of even a week or so; he was surer-footed, could go along it faster and with much greater confidence. But after a while it got more difficult all the same. He was getting tired, he had been climbing now for half an hour. It had taken less than fifteen minutes with Heikki, more like ten. Fisher stared dubiously upwards through the trees – there was certainly no sign of the house. He suppressed the unpleasant thought that he was lost. He had followed the path, he must just keep going up. But he cursed himself. Why had he not simply taken the road and walked briskly? Now he was lost in a Finnish forest. It might be small, but he might as well be lost in the jungle. Added to which the mosquitoes were practically eating him alive.

He could be anywhere. The unfamiliar wilderness around him seemed suddenly ominous, threatening. This was Scandinavia, after all. Supposing there were bears? Or wolves? Fisher struggled to allay his own alarm. He reminded himself that there were houses at the edge of the forest. Hilppala at least, and probably others. It must be safe here. And he could still see where the lake was, could still see the glitter of water through the trees. But what of the road, the one that ran from the lakeshore up past the house? He tried to picture how the road swung round. Supposing he were now climbing parallel to it, instead of heading towards it? He had no way of knowing. And Heikki would soon be wondering where he was.

There was nothing for it. He would have to go down again, towards the lake, his only reference point, and follow the shoreline back round to the boathouse. Then come up the road, which is what he should have done in the first place. He reminded himself that Heikki was far too inebriated to measure the passing of time.

It would not do to try and clamber down to the lakeshore through the unmarked wilderness of bushes and saplings. He would have to locate a path. It was as he was searching for one that he heard the car.

He stood stock still and strained his ears, trying to shut out the maddening trilling of nearby birdsong that threatened to drown it out. The car sound was quite far off. It came from behind him on his left, grew louder, passed him and faded away again ahead of him. He struck out towards it, away from the lake. He noticed suddenly that there was not just one path, the one he had followed, but dozens of them, weaving in and out of the bushes. There were probably hundreds of paths all in all, in fact it was little wonder he had gone wrong. But now at least he knew in which direction to go. In less than ten minutes he came out suddenly out onto the road.

The road did not look familiar, but at least it was a road, and to his left it went downhill. There could not be so very many roads in the district. This was more than likely the one that went down to the lake. In the uphill direction, to the right, it curved away off round a corner and then appeared to run along past open fields, but across the road, near the corner, exactly opposite to where he now stood, was a house.

Not Hilppala, but civilisation, at least. Fisher heaved a sigh of relief. He made his way across to the gateway and wondered if he could make himself understood if he asked for directions. Only then did he remember it was probably the middle of the night. There certainly seemed to be no-one around. The house itself, almost hidden behind magnificent lilacs, was set at the far side of a yard, and like Hilppala backed onto forest, but its style was more rambling than Hilppala, and the atmosphere of the whole place much less smart. The large, grassy yard was overgrown, and surrounded by a hotchpotch of tumbledown outbuildings. There was no gate between the gateposts. Not all Finns were as house-proud as the Heikkilas, it seemed. Yet one thing about the house caught Fisher's attention, even in his present state. Behind the lilacs the house was pink, like the house in the paper.

But was there anybody round to ask for help at this hour? He eyed the house dubiously. It looked deserted. The residents were almost certainly at their cottage, or celebrating midsummer elsewhere. He would just have to go down the hill - that was really the only sensible option. He had wasted enough time already. Without more ado, Fisher set off at a lolloping trot. He had not gone more than half a mile before he began to recognise the road. He took a left fork and in another minute saw the white fence of Hilppala come into view. Commanding his weary body forwards Fisher crossed the neat front yard with its baskets of flowers, and took out the key. It had been the longest ten-minute walk in history.

He stood like an interloper in the hall. For a moment he could not remember why he had come, had to go back through his memory to rake up the reason. Oh yes, to shut the window. Or rather, 'windows', for Fisher noticed now that the window was double, an inner pane and an outer one, for better insulation. At another time this would have intrigued him, but now he was tired and in a hurry. He shut them both. If he was to 'drink one peer' it would have to be quick, he had already wasted hours. But he certainly needed one.

It would be of immeasurable help, he reflected, if he could only lay hands on the map which Heikki had used to show him where the island was. He was not good with maps, but Heikki had marked both the jetty and the island with a blue ink cross; it would be a godsend for trying to calculate his route. Fisher began to rifle through the kitchen drawers. The map was there, in the second one he tried. The drawers were fastidiously lined with paper; once again, he could guess where Heikki's training had come from. When he picked the map up, what was underneath it immediately caught his eye. The newspaper picture of the winter wonderland – the drawer was lined with the very same paper. Fisher stared in disbelief at the leafless barrenness, the snow, the icicles sprouting like pointed teeth along the eaves of the fairytale house. He could not even start to reconcile its image with what was around him. It had turned out the country was warm, and everything that could grow grew abundantly – the constant daylight didn't give it time to stop. There was nothing to associate this place with winter and snow. It addled his brains to even try.

He pushed the drawer shut, then bent down to take out a bottle of beer from the cupboard beneath the kitchen sink. As he stood up, his eyes fell on a black plastic box behind the tap. Teeth. It was the teeth box he had been asked to find. It was empty. Fisher glanced dismally round the kitchen, then tried the bathroom, as being the simplest place to start looking. The teeth were there, sitting on the small glass shelf above the basin, like the Cheshire cat's grin. He eyed them with revulsion, and went to find something he could pick them up in. In a bedroom he opened the small top drawer of a chest. It was lined of course, but empty except for a pair of socks and a hearing aid. He took the socks. When the pink and white grinning abhorrence had been captured Fisher took his beer and went to the living room. He must make haste. He sat down on the sofa and began to study the map.

"So. You are taking your rest."

Fisher struggled from the depths of sleep and tried to open his eyes. Something slid off his stomach as he moved, and dropped with a rustle onto the floor. He noticed blearily that Heikki was standing over him, silhouetted large and solid against the light. He sat up. He could see that what had fallen to the floor was a map. From outside he could hear the sound of voices. He looked round, at a loss for a moment to remember where he was and what he was doing there. He was on the sofa in the living room of Heikki's parents's house. Heikki stopped leaning over him and sat down on a chair.

"So. You did not come back to island. You are sleeping. I do not plame you. I have headache, and I too am tired." Heikki took off his glasses and began to polish them. "But we have to come today, because tomorrow is day when parents go to new home." He replaced his glasses and blinked experimentally. "I am sorry you did not see island till end. But you had nice trip in poat." He did not seem to be angry about the incident. On the contrary, he seemed in mellow mood, despite the headache. Fisher glanced at his watch. The hands stood at quarter to six.

"You must have got up very early."

"It is evening. It is quarter to six p.m."

Evening! Then he must have slept for... but Fisher could not remember what time he had got to the house. It was hard to hang on to time when night scarcely put in an appearance. "You must have been worried sick, when I didn't come back."

"Nooo. We have looked through telescope. We have seen that poat is at peach, and window is shut. We know you have got here. We decide that you are drinking wery big glass of peer."

From the kitchen came the sounds of Hilppa bustling about. She bustled as she had presumably bustled all her life, as she set the table with bread and gherkins and hard-boiled eggs. One would never have guessed that this was to be her last day in her home.

"I got lost." said Fisher. "When I tried to come up through the forest from the boat house. It took forever."

"Put churney up through forest is so short." exclaimed Heikki.

"Not for me." Fisher followed him to the kitchen. "I came out miles away. Much higher up the road. Near a house on the opposite side, near a corner." He opened the drawer to replace the map, and tapped the newspaper lining with his finger. "It was painted pink. Like this one." Heikki glanced indifferently.

"It is same house."

Fisher lifted the newspaper lining slightly for him to see. "The same house? I hardly think so. They don't look a bit alike apart from the colour."

Heikki shrugged. He helped himself to bread and said indistinctly "Now is summer. That is winter, in photograph. Do you come and eat?" They sat down at the table.

Considering the excesses their tired old bodies had been put through, for Urpo and Hilppa too the meal was really quite a hearty affair. It was not till the table was almost bare that the party, the alcohol, and the exertion began to take their toll of the family members. By the time that Hilppa rose to clear away Urpo had nodded off on his chair, snoring raggedly and sliding gently sideways. Fisher looked round for Heikki, but he wasn't there. If the old man fell to the floor, it would be his duty to pick him up. A kind of revulsion, like that for the false teeth, filled him. Fisher stood up quickly and took some dirty plates to the sink, then stepped out onto the terrace as if to briefly take a breath of air. It was beautiful out. The evening air was fresh and limpid, and Fisher himself felt refreshed. His long sleep had done him good, the simple, plentiful meal had restored his strength. He was off the island, they would not be going back there. He was ready for anything.

When he went back indoors the others were all asleep. It was eight o'clock in the evening.

It was not the most graceful of exits, nor the fastest, through his bedroom window, but Fisher did not want to advertise that he wasn't sleeping. When finally he had made it he brushed the imprint of his shoes from the urn beneath the window and listened, glowing with pain and triumph, but nothing seemed to have happened inside the house. He was free. Outside and free in the luminous evening, while the others were snoring soundly in their beds. Another ten minutes, and the house, the intriguing pink house that Heikki claimed was the one in the picture, was before him.

It was the first time Fisher had really enjoyed himself since he had arrived. He felt alive and wicked and alert, now he no longer had to keep up a smile or pretend that he understood a word of what anyone was saying. The air was fresh on his face, the world undemanding. He stood in the shelter of the forest across the road from the house and pulled out the newspaper page which Hilppa had used to line the drawer. It was certainly hard to believe that the house in the picture and the house across the road were one and the same. The colour of the wooden walls looked similar, it was true, but no more than that. Nor was it just the difficulty of substituting snow for summer. For a start, while the house in the photograph stood proud and complete, of the real house across the country road he could make out no more than a slice, for the rest was obscured by a wooden fence and by stout, thriving lilac trees on either side of the gateway. The house in the picture had no such fence.

But supposing the photo had been taken from between the gateposts? You could do quite deceptive things with distance in a photograph. In the quiet emptiness of the evening he ventured nearer, right up to the fence, so close that he could sense the warmth that radiated from it, and concealed himself behind the thick, rough chunk of wood that formed one gatepost. Before him was the yard. It was so overgrown with uncut grass as to form a kind of miniature prairie, and surrounded by a motley collection of sheds and outhouses. Beyond it, at the far side, stood the house. It was barely visible through the lilacs, which seemed to have been allowed to flourish irrespective of where the windows were placed. From their random foliage projected a large wooden porch around the front door, reached by steps and surmounted by an upper-storey balcony. The windows, or those that were visible, had white crocheted strips like those of Hilppala and were trimmed with broad white bands of decorative woodwork; set against them the pink of the walls glowed deliciously. To the right side of the slumbering house was an orchard, full of bent, twisted apple trees, and to the left, an open patch of yet more prairie grass with a washing line strung across, on which a single garment was hung out to dry. Behind the house stretched a deep, impenetrable band of birches and firs.

It was hard to tell. Probably half the houses in Finland backed onto a forest, and were made of wood. There might even be quite a few that were painted hot rosy pink. Fisher Fisher studied the photograph, comparing it to the building before him.

The lines of the wooden porch and the windows matched, as far as he could tell, and the roof had the same distinguishing feature. It stopped short at one end and became a flat roof, to allow for a second balcony, with a handsome white balustrade. An unexpected thrill of excitement ran through Fisher, like a wave, like an oncoming orgasm. It must be the house! This was the winter jewel, whose picture he held in his hand. After all, Heikki had been perfectly matter-of-fact. Fisher longed to get nearer. He watched the house as boldly as he dared. There was no-one around, nor was there any sign of life at the windows, which nearly all had their blinds and curtains pulled. A sly breath of wind ran its hand across the prairie grass as if stroking it, and wafted yet more lilac scent through the air, but the house remained unresponsive. It must be eleven; Fisher checked his watch. If they were there its occupants must be sleeping, like the Heikkilas down the road, snoring deeply through an imaginary night.

But more likely, they were probably still away. It was still the midsummer weekend, after all. If they had been home there would have been some signs of recent celebration, but everything seemed to be in tranquil order. Fisher was tempted to brave the yard and snoop around, but did not quite dare. At last he turned reluctantly and started walking back down the road.

It was as he was passing the corner of the tottering white wooden fence that he noticed a small path that ran along the left side of the yard, then turned and ran along between the house and the forest. It beckoned him; it would bring him nearer to the house itself. If he was quick, he could spend a few more minutes checking out its secrets.

He went cautiously in spite of his fervour. Every few yards he stood again stock still, but nothing happened, and he reached the end of the fence where the path turned the corner. On this side the 'fence' was nothing more than a simple barrier of wire, giving suddenly an uninterrupted view of the house, for here on the north side, the shady side facing the forest, the lilacs had not taken such a hold. They were smaller and there were fewer of them, revealing the house's own gloriously coloured flank. Beneath the eaves white wooden carving ran the length of the building, its pattern echoing that of the decorative window frames. It was the house! The carved wooden trimmings were identical. But how extraordinary, that it should be here, so close to Heikki's!

Excitement emboldened Fisher to creep on past the back of the house. It wasn't actually very well kept up, he noticed. Not trim and manicured, as it had been in the paper. He cast an anxious eye at the nearest window, but only the whitish curtaining stared blankly back at him. Beyond the house he followed the path past the orchard, after which the path became even smaller, and trailed off into a copse of trees which seemed to border onto a road. Fisher turned back. He had survived his trespass and no-one had challenged him. It was obvious there was no-one at home. He began to relax a little. The grass of the orchard, he noticed on his return trip, was overgrown, and nasturtiums had all but engulfed the wooden steps that led down from the house's narrow terrace. In spite of himself Fisher gave the windows a final apprehensive glance as he passed them. The curtains of some of them, he saw now, were not hung properly but makeshift, pinned up with tacks. At the base of one of the windows, inside, was a decorative bowl, its rim encrusted by a dead amaryllis, reduced to a fragile streak. It was hardly what he would have expected from the well-presented house in the photo. Yet Fisher was still sure this was the place. He tried to picture it in winter, bare of grass and lilacs, steeped in snow and glowing in the darkness.

Back round the corner he noticed for the first time a small wooden gate in the fence It was even slightly open, just as if it were beckoning him in. Of course, at the roadside gateway there was no gate at all, just open access, but this was different. This was more like a real invitation. Fisher found his feet disobeying his strictest instructions to decline. In a few seconds' time, he was nearing the house. He wanted to go right up to it, to touch its walls and see if they were warm. In his agitation he clutched at the small Finnish dictionary in his pocket, which Heikki had lent him. If someone came out he would have to pull it out and pretend to ask them something. But the soul of the house stayed empty, and Fisher stood finally on the overgrown gravel in front of it, and studied it openly. The truth seeped into him gradually. The house was deserted, his intellect told him that. But it was not just deserted, it was abandoned.

CHAPTER 7

The following morning Heikki drove his parents to their new home, the Moose Walk Retirement Home, while Fisher was left to continue to enjoy his return to civilization. The old couple left for the final lap of their life with the air of popping out for a local shopping trip. It seemed odd to Fisher that they showed so little trace of emotion as they left their home; he had hardly been able to tear himself away from his own flat for a three-week holiday.

It was two p.m. when Heikki returned. They would no doubt be off soon, to Heikki's flat in town, which seemed an immensely attractive proposition.

"And this house will be sold now, now that your parents have gone?" Fisher reconfirmed.

"Sold, yes. Tomorrow we must take keys to agent, then he can show if someone will look round. Pecause on Wednesday, after men have peen for furnitures, we are ourselves no more here. We are going fishing."

"Fishing?" Fisher feared at once that his horror had shown itself all too readily in his face.

"Yes, fishing," said Heikki, who seemed to have noticed nothing amiss.

"Where?"

"On a lake. About two hundred kilometres north-east from here."

"How long for?" Fisher could not believe that his host was oblivious to his dismay.

Heikki pulled a face. "Two weeks, maybe, or three.... You have time, I think?"

Fisher had been about to rise, but now he sank back onto his chair again, staring dumbly at Heikki. He did not really see him, however. Instead, in that instant, his world rearranged itself, like the particles in a kaleidoscope undergoing momentary chaos, then dropping into a brand new pattern. First every fragment of the whole disintegrated, as it had when Millicent had finally told him about Peter, but then miraculously, within a second, it reunited itself into a previously quite unpredicted form.

"On Wednesday?" He heard himself confirming dreamily. He must contact England. He must somehow get himself recalled. "Oh... That sounds..."

Heikki smiled, happy and unruffled. "We go with Seppo, he has inwited us. His firm has cottage on an island up in north. Sirkka doesn't come. Daughter is waiting paby."

"Like the island where we were just now?"

"No, this one is wery small, where we are going." Heikki stood up and fetched a map that was new to Fisher. He spread it out. The region it covered looked ominously free of major towns and completely devoid of motorways. Heikki placed his bulky finger on a small dot near the centre of the lower edge. "So. We are here. And we go - " He propelled his finger along the tiniest of black lines and then along an almost imperceptible red line snaking crookedly and rather unprogressively up the page. Fisher began to feel queasy simply following it with his eyes. The finger went on, in a zigzag, looping motion up the map, and came to rest at last on a small blue misshapen blot. "We shall be here. This is lake." Heikki looked at Fisher for his approval.

"It looks wonderful. Is it – near anywhere?"

"No," said Heikki. "It is fully in the nature." His voice had a touch of bliss. They studied together the area round Heikki's finger, while Fisher felt an odd sensation, like that of warm tears, rise up from his stomach to behind his eyeballs. Heikki folded the map up and began to fan himself with it absentmindedly.

"Cottage is quite same than ours on island. But smaller, and it has not gas. Or electricity. But it is wery" – he broke off and fixed his eyes on Fisher's face, searching earnestly for the word. "– cosy. It is wery cosy place." Fisher, with Heikki's eyes still on him, smiled brightly, feeling the tears now burning hotly behind his eyes. He must. He must find some way to escape. He was silent, battling against foreboding and despair.

"Seppo comes in evening on Wednesday. We will go in two cars." Heikki pulled himself back to the present and looked round. "But now, we have verk. Big furnitures we must clean, and put label to what mum and dad want in new home. Rest goes to store. Small things we put now to garage, it is wery good storeplace." He gave what sounded like a sigh of pleasure. "We have quite much verk. But remember, fish are waiting." He rose, and Fisher miserably followed suit.

The estate agent's office, when they called there the following morning, was still deserted, so they drove round to Heikki's first to pick up the items that were going to be needed for the trip. Stepping out of the lift on the fourth floor, Heikki snapped a light on and opened his own front door against a heavy, rustling resistance.

"Here has come newspapers still while I am away. It is not worth to stop them for so short time. But now when we are going for longer time, I must cancel order." He scooped up the pile and took them to the kitchen table to sort out his personal mail from among them. It would not take long. He had only to check there was nothing important, and then put his fishing clothes in a bag. And mosquito coils, they must remember to buy some. He pushed his glasses to the top of his head and squinted at the envelopes, while Fisher stood at the window, looking out at the street below through the slats in the lowered Venetian blind. His mind was on mosquitoes.

"Here is one for you." Heikki stood up and held out the letter to Fisher, then disappeared into his bedroom to pack. Fisher took the envelope in surprise and looked at it. It bore a crest.

"It's from the university," he said to Heikki's back. "I'd forgotten I'd given them my address here." He ripped the letter open, mystified, and took it back to the window to read, adjusting the blind.

'Dear Colleague,' the letter hailed him from thick, stiff, emblem-encrusted paper, before passing on with tactful delicacy to its main thrust. It seemed that the faculty's 'splendid librarian' Patty Doublethwaite was now in hospital after a by-pass operation. It would be a friendly and appropriate gesture if the whole department could get together to send Patty flowers, with its very best wishes for a speedy recovery. The letter meandered through a list of Patty's professional virtues before naming the day by which donations were to arrive. The date had already passed. Amazing how these irritating, useless messages always managed to reach one wherever one was, thought Fisher. Marooned on Mars an invitation to the local infant school bring-and-buy would probably find one.

Who on earth was Patty Doublethwaite, anyway? He frowned, then stood staring unseeingly from the window. Unless she was the colourless crone that sat behind the etymology desk.

He became aware only gradually that Heikki was speaking to him, had been speaking to him for some time, while he had been lost, trying pointlessly to recall the face of Patty Doublethwaite.

"You have pad news?" Heikki was enquiring anxiously. Fisher turned his head as if in a dream. "You are frowning."

"No, no," Fisher hastened to reassure him, "I just….." He looked down and saw that he still had the letter in his hand. A shortish, printed letter on thick, quality paper, with his department heading and the university coat-of-arms at the top. And then it was that the wicked idea of the century, an idea utterly deplorable yet at the same time sinfully attractive, opened a hitherto unused door in Fisher's morally upright, uptight deepest being and stepped right in. Unforeseen, unbidden. One couldn't call it a wicked plan, for it never was planned, but wicked it certainly was. Fisher felt a blush of shame, a glow of burning fire to his cheek as reckless inspiration took relentless possession. He ran the risk, he knew, of despising himself henceforth forever, yet something had hold of him, made him soldier on. He folded the letter ostentatiously with shaking hands, crest uppermost, message well hidden between the folds, and returned it to its envelope. Then he looked down, eyeing it still, avoiding Heikki's gaze. "I have to go back to London. To teach a summer course. Somebody has been taken ill."

Heikki drove the few blocks back to the estate agent's office looking woebegone, while Fisher sat beside him, his mind in tumult.

"I'm so sorry," he repeated, for the tenth time. "There really is nothing I can do. But maybe next year…" Then he bit his tongue. Oh, cursed desire to please, that lured him time and time again into setting traps for himself. But remembering Heikki's stunned expression as he stood holding two sets of waders, Fisher felt again his own lack of gratitude. Still, there was no going back. He had already lied. Cruelty now was the only way to save their friendship, he told himself. There was no return; he had no choice now but to lie his way to freedom and sanity, and make it up to Heikki the rest of his life. "You must go to puy tickets tomorrow while I wait men for furnitures," said Heikki, as the car pulled up outside the agent's. "Yes, that's a good idea," said Fisher humbly. And somewhere not so deep in his guilty conscience his spirits began to sing.

With all his recently acquired experience, it was still a shock to Fisher that no-one in the travel office could manage a word of English. Nor could they at the railway station, and in the end his only achievement was to miss the bus that would have taken him back to Heikki's. It was almost two before he turned the corner, hot and footsore, onto the final stretch of road where Hilppala stood. Heikki was just driving off in the car.

"Probably coming to look for me," thought Fisher, as the car pulled up beside him, and Heikki ran the window down. "You have had lunch?" It was not quite the question Fisher had been expecting. "Oh, yes, thank you." That was clearly the answer that was required.

Heikki was looking a little put out, a little anxious, no doubt because he had not known where Fisher was.

"Men have not come yet for furnitures. I am just on my way to phone. Do you come with me?" Heikki opened the passenger door as he spoke. Fisher climbed in obediently.

"Where will you phone from?" The phone at Hilppala had been disconnected the previous day.

"From kiosk, at top of hill."

They drove off at what seemed like reckless speed along the country road, up the hill past the pink house, round the corner, and further on into the open country, where on the outside of a bend in the road, its back against a broad expanse of pale green grain, stood a brown wooden shack. It had dark wooden steps in the front, and a swinging shop sign. Rusting beer and butter adverts, printed on tin, were screwed immovably into the rough, long planks of its sides. Outside were a litter bin and a picnic table and benches. There was no sign of a telephone kiosk. Heikki stopped the car at the side of the road and leapt out.

"This is kiosk." The inside of the wayside grocery store with its one tiny window was thickly murky after the light outside, but Fisher could see that it was plentifully stocked with unfamiliar foodstuffs, sweets, newspapers and cigarettes. Heikki made a call on a telephone which the shopkeeper took from behind the counter. It seemed from his facial expression and intonation that all was not well, but then, with Finnish, one could never tell. As they left the shop he turned to Fisher. His voice was exasperated.

"They come tomorrow! They have wrong day! They have written down wrong date!" He seemed understandably thrown by their inefficiency. "Now what we can do? Tomorrow we are already gone. Seppo comes at five o'clock this evening. And you have train." He turned to look at Fisher. "You have ticket?" They were already speeding down the hill.

"Actually, no," said Fisher, recalling the failure of his morning mission. He turned to Heikki as the obvious solution dawned. "So I could wait here and meet the men when they come tomorrow. Then go to Helsinki tomorrow evening. I can still get a plane on Friday, I'm sure."

Heikki seemed gratifyingly grateful for Fisher's suggestion. Even Fisher felt the burden of his conscience shift a little, now that Heikki was actually going to benefit from his deception. For if Fisher could be there, Heikki wouldn't have to alter his plans.

So it was that the evening found Fisher sole master of Hilppala.

It felt strangely odd to be on his own, much odder than expected. Heikki had fished a frying pan, a pan slice, a fork and a vicious-looking knife back out from the items stored in the garage. All the food Fisher wanted he would have to buy from the kiosk, a twenty minute walk up the hill.

He had been looking forward to this moment all afternoon, the moment when Heikki and Seppo would be gone, but now that the time had come, he felt at a loose end. He wandered down to the jetty and sat there staring out to where the picturesque islands rose from the shining surface of the lake. And somewhere in their midst was Heikki's island, and the cottage.

How unhappy he had been here. How ungratefully bored and fed up. It hadn't been Heikki's fault, of course. It was simply that their interests, their approaches to life, were so very different. But now at last, he could breathe again, he could relax. He was free. He had freed himself from all those most wearisome of burdens, the social obligations of a guest.

Tomorrow he would be leaving this exquisite world, where

boredom had been refined to an art form, and in forty-eight hours he would be back in dear old London. And suddenly, looking out across the glittering waters, Fisher realised with a shock that the idea did not appeal.

Now, in the silence of freedom, Fisher heard too late the whispering voices of a new world calling, a magical world that invited him to explore it, while he had the chance. But it was no good. He had made his arrangements to go. And after a while Fisher turned, and made his way reluctantly up the beach.

He slept badly, for it was spooky alone in the house, and was awakened finally from fitful dreaming by a purposeful rapping at the door. He sat up with a start and looked at his watch. It was seven fifteen. He could just make out the luminous hands, for the room was in darkness, a phenomenon Fisher had almost forgotten. He glanced apprehensively towards the window, which seemed now to look out onto a blank wall, very close to. It was several seconds before he realised it was not a wall, but the side of a giant vehicle. The removal men! They were here.

Fisher ran to the front door and opened it, thrusting the envelope with Heikki's instructions at the two men that stood there. They scooped up the furniture with a speed and strength he would not have thought possible. The house was stripped, the lorry doors battened into place, Fisher was made to sign his name, and the lorry drove off. It was seven forty five. Seven forty five! And the men had come and gone already. No wonder, thought Fisher, that he was always so tired in the afternoons, when everything always happened so early in the mornings. And his train would not leave until the evening. He wondered how to spend his day, but no great inspiration came, except that it should start with breakfast. He set off accordingly up the hill towards the kiosk, to try and identify anything that looked like rye bread, or milk; Heikki had left him with margarine, and a paper screw of coffee. On the way down he passed the pink house, coming first to what must be its proper main gateway, round the corner from the smaller, gateless one. He stepped up to see what he could see from there, but it wasn't much, for the outhouses got in the way. He regretted still that he had not been able to see inside it. It was as he was stepping back from the entrance that he noticed a wooden board in the grass verge beside him, already half overgrown in nettles. A keep-out notice, no doubt, except that its one-word message was followed by a string of digits. A phone number, possibly. It even looked familiar. Fisher pulled from his pocket the business card that the agent had pressed on him just as a matter of routine. Well, well.

The place was for sale. Before he had finished his second cup of breakfast coffee, Fisher had thought of an irresistible way to pass the day.

To Fisher's surprise, when he reached the office the agent, Mr. Laine, was outside, loading up his car. He was struggling to put the final touches to a bristling cargo of fishing rods, boat oars, wicker baskets, and rubber boots. His face took on a disconcerted expression when Fisher appeared, and he nodded curtly, as if their previous acquaintance had somehow displeased him. At this Fisher's courage all but failed him, but he summoned it back. He could not give up now. His plan was too delightful.

"I remember you speak English," he said, a little more hesitantly than he would have wanted. The agent continued stowing away a canvas holdall full of thermos flasks.

"There is something I can do?"

Fisher steeled himself to give an impression of firmness and decisiveness. "I would like to see round a property - "

The agent made an ineffectual effort to slam the boot shut, and shot a sudden look at Fisher.

" - that you have for sale." Fisher felt his voice thin and formless, like old sacking. It was no good, he had always been timid. The agent continued to stare at him, but now his look was one of simple surprise. "You are wanting to buy? A property?"

Fisher shrugged. "Perhaps. I don't know till I've seen it inside." He had prepared all his answers. The agent's face mutated smoothly through a range of fleeting expressions – from surprise to interest to a faint but predatory gleam of hope. He seemed to have forgotten about his packing.

"You are thinking to move here?" He sounded impressed.

Fisher pulled a face and waggled his head from side to side in a show of non-committal nonchalance. "Maybe. It's a very attractive country."

It was odd, he noticed, how his English had become more stilted since he had come here. As if the Finns would understand him better that way. Yet Laine, he noticed now, spoke English surprisingly well. His speech was quicker and sharper than Heikki's, and he seemed to have more control over problem letters. But perhaps he was just a quicker and sharper type than Heikki. More of a go-getter.

As he watched, the agent's face clouded over. "You are a foreigner. You cannot take a loan here. You can buy, but you cannot take a loan from the Finnish bank."

"Oh, I have the money," said Fisher airily. "I have just sold my house." That at least was more or less true, in its way. He had indeed just let Millicent buy him out of the place in Sussex. All the same, he mustn't raise the poor man's hopes too high. "But of course, at this stage I'm only looking."

"Well, that is fine!" The agent exclaimed. "Then we have no problem." He almost smiled, but before he could do so, his forehead began to wrinkle into a frown. "But aren't you going away? I thought that Mr. Heikkila said that you were leaving to England."

"Oh, I am, I am. But not till tonight. That is why I need to look round today. Then should the place be suitable I shall come back." The agent glanced uncertainly at the loaded car.

"I was actually just off. On a fishing trip. Just a couple of days. I'll be back after that to start selling Mr. Heikkila's house."

"But I must look round before I go," cried Fisher. His chance for a day's entertainment was slipping away. "Otherwise I'll have no idea. And it's very near. At the top of the hill, near Mr. Heikkila's. The pink house there."

"Ah." It was hard to tell if the agent was rubbing his hands or wringing them. "Ah, really. That one?" The agent glanced once more rather woefully towards his car, his features full of indecision. Then his face suddenly brightened. "But of course, you can see round house by yourself. I can give you a lift there. Then when you are in England you can write to me if you want to buy." With a sudden briskness he unlocked his office, went swiftly to a cupboard and selected a large key, checking the label attached.

"I can take you there, you can look round, then put key in through letter box here, before you get train. There is kiosk nearby, they will call you taxi." And with that he ushered Fisher out and locked the door again behind them. In another minute Fisher found himself crammed into the back seat of the ancient car with a plastic box full of wriggling bait on his lap.

CHAPTER 8

He was standing on the threshold of an old-fashioned farmhouse kitchen, a room so large that it spanned the house from front to back, with an open staircase leading up to the upper storey. It was furnished with a large wooden table and benches, a wooden settle, a dresser with plates on the shelves, and still it gave the impression of space. On the opposite side between two doors the room was graced – there was no better way to describe it - by an elegant, old-fashioned, white-tiled ceramic heating stove, so tall it reached up almost to the ceiling.

It took a moment to understand why the whole room was sunk in a greenish half-light, till Fisher realised that the only daylight filtered in through the lilac trees outside the windows at the front. The windows at the back of the kitchen had their curtains carelessly drawn. He made his way across the room to open them. As he did so he noticed behind the staircase a doorway leading to a smaller kitchen, in which he could just make out the mighty iron fortress of an old-fashioned kitchen range. It was not alone there; it shared its quarters with a sink, a boiler, and a none-too-modern electric stove.

Fisher drew back one of the curtains, which tore with a tiny ripping noise in his hands, and stared out at the forest just beyond the fence. So here he was! He was inside the wooden jewel of the photograph. The key to its secrets was literally in his hand. It was his to explore, to poke around in. Then, whenever he afterwards looked at its picture, he would know exactly what was inside.

But only if he didn't waste time. He had until three, when the bus left from the bottom of the hill. Fisher looked at his watch. It was nearly twelve. He must get a move on. With a thrilling sensation of sampling forbidden fruits, he drew back the rest of the curtains in the kitchen, and set to work.

It was a big house, much bigger even than it looked from the outside, and to Fisher's pleasure mostly charmingly old-fashioned. He wandered ecstatically from room to room as he warmed to his adventure. In its furnishings, its decoration, the house was delightfully ethnic; it was quite unlike anything in England. It had wooden floors, woven rag mats, and old-fashioned, delicate china. It was strange that there was so much furniture in the house – perhaps the agent had been telling the truth after all, when he had said that it had not been empty for very long. From the upstairs front balcony he could make out through the distant trees just the tiniest flickering glitter of the lake.

Between the kitchen and the end of the house on the forest side was a pleasant room attractively furnished in the Russian style, with an elegant oval table of white-painted wood, surrounded by a matching set of white and gold, ornate, round-backed chairs. In Fisher's mind it was at once 'the garden room', for from it a door led out to the garden, or rather the scrubland, where the washing line was. Fisher opened it and sank down onto the wooden steps outside, feeling their warmth beneath him, closing his eyes and allowing the dappled orange sunlight to play on his eyelids. Behind him, all around him, the house and yard and garden carried on with their private occupations. As if he didn't exist.

It was heaven sitting here. Even the hurt about Millicent seemed somehow far away. Fisher leaned back against a plant pot on the steps and began to wonder idly what to say to the agent to explain that he did not want to buy the house. He should leave a note when he dropped the key off, it was only courteous. The house was too big. Too small. Too old. But was it old? Compared to his London flat it was virtually new. Was too isolated. Was too close to other dwellings. The agent might get his address out of Heikki, might try to sell him something else. He would have to stall. Behind his back Fisher felt the heavy plant pot shift, then heard a crack as it pressed against the wooden edging to the step.

He opened his eyes and turned to look at the damaged wood. There were certainly some rather fragile bits to the property. He remembered now that a part of the porch steps had broken off underneath the agent's foot. As he stared out across the garden again he could see now that the 'garment' on the washing line was an old rag, pinned up with a single peg, a shapeless bit of grey. But the sunlight had turned it to some sumptuous item of raiment, touched the clothes line, and turned it to a silver thread. Touched the whole of the straggling, untended 'garden' and turned it to a jewel-set field of wispy radiance. Fisher let his eyes rove round once more, then checked his watch, stretched, and rose stiffly to go back into the house.

It was odd, how it had become for him in this short time a summer house, with no connection to the other one, the winter house that had haunted him. This house left the winter jewel as what it was, a newspaper image. The house around him was just as intriguing, but had a character and a personality of its own. It was vibrant, mysterious, enchanting. And spacious. Fisher gave a sigh. It would not be easy to spend all his time in the coming year in his flat, cooped up writing. But he must be strong. One was really nothing in the academic world nowadays unless one had produced at least one book. He must get a move on, or he would be writing it as a pensioner.

He sighed again. He should make a move, it wouldn't do to be in a rush. He put his hand in his inside pocket to check for the key and found again the agent's paper with the details of the house. It was all in Finnish, in the blur of words only figures stood out comprehensibly here and there; the price, the area of the land, the year the house was built. There had been more land, apparently, only that had been sold. He returned the paper to his pocket. He must fix his attention now on deciding what message of discouragement to leave for Mr Laine. He would have to trawl through the house again to look for plausible defects.

By the time he was halfway up the wooden staircase, he had all but forgotten his mission and was again engrossed. On the front upper balcony he paused once more, and searched for the far-off sparkle of the lake. It was then, as he turned back to look at the house, that it came to him, in the form of a crazy idea that simply arrived. He wasn't at all sure where from. But as soon as it had infiltrated his thoughts, he became quite breathless with it. Crazy? But why not? Fisher's depression lifted suddenly for the first time since Millicent had left him. He was thunderstruck with the sudden force of his own inspiration, could hardly contain his excitement.

Why have to tell the agent that he couldn't buy the house? Why not buy it? It would be absolutely just the perfect place to write his book. There would be no distractions. He did not need to be in London. He would not have to face the patronising sympathy of his colleagues. He could think of no logical reason why the sense of distance appalled him so. After all, Heikki had come to London to study; the distance couldn't really be such a very big factor. And it must be perfectly possible to live here, seeing that some people did it all the time. They had shops, roads, food, trains. One only had to crack the language. Only. But he could try again. And meanwhile he could buy this fabulous place and write his book here. The house must be in better condition than it looked, for the agent had said it was fine. It was common knowledge how honest the Finns were. Gloomy, but honest.

The idea gobbled him like a monster eating its prey. He was entirely consumed, he found himself pacing back and forwards doing sums. He would use this place for a year to write his book, and after he would use it as a holiday home. He would try and buy the furniture with it, the oval table and painted Russian chairs.

He did more sums in five minutes than he had done in the whole of his previous life. The results smiled back at him from the margin of the agent's paper. The place was actually going for a song. If he rented his London flat out for part of the year, he would be able to make ends meet quite reasonably. He saw already that it was a chance that he absolutely mustn't miss. He must get back to the agent. And then he remembered that the agent had gone fishing for the weekend.

He should go. He would miss his train. He could write from England.

But what if he went? Supposing the agent came back and sold the house on Monday? Supposing there really had been a string of prospective buyers? He wanted this house. Nothing had ever felt such a masterstroke, so right, as his sudden conversion from trespasser to owner. That had always been his trouble, thought Fisher, he had never trusted his intuition enough. If anything, this had hampered his development as an aesthete.

He should postpone his trip back to London, obviously, and get this purchase in the bag. He must stay here on the spot. Though not at Hilppala, that wouldn't be right. He would go down into town and find a hotel.

On trying to leave, however, there was once again some problem with the door. On arrival the agent had struggled to unlock it, and now, quite simply, it was being impossible to lock. The tongue and the groove would not align. At best the door looked shut, but a stout kick from the outside could no doubt cave it in. As Fisher sat in frustration on the front porch the solution came, just as it had with the purchasing decision, and again so obvious that he did not understand why he had not thought of it before. He could not leave the house unlocked, that would be irresponsible. He would stay here the few days till the agent returned.

Fisher, lying in improvised curtain sheets on an iron bedstead, did not sleep as well in his new home-to-be as he had hoped. He had chosen a bedroom at the back of the house, overlooking the thin strip of grass that ran between the house and the forest, but found himself strangely restless, and conscious of the closeness of the air. If he opened the window, he was plagued by mosquitoes, if he shut it he was once again stifled, for the night was warm.

The mattress beneath him was nothing but lumps; he regretted now that he had not yet gone down to Hilppala to bring his bags up and his sleeping bag. He fell at last into a light doze, and woke up with a suffocating feeling. He must have air, mosquitoes or not. Fisher got off the bed, had the outer window halfway open, before he looked down. Down below, in the middle of the grass strip, was a wolf.

There was no mistaking it. It was large, rough and grey against the soft, bright green of the grass. When it heard the window open it looked up, straight at Fisher, who stared back, petrified. The beast drew back on its haunches, crouched, snarled and bared its teeth. Fisher slammed the window shut, fumbling to get the bolts and latches home, then rammed the inner window into place. From down below, almost drowned out by the pounding of his heart, he heard the wolf let out a single yelp, like a bark. He wondered if wolves could spring as high as an upper storey window, if the animals could break a double layer of glass; he tensed himself ready for its leap. But when it leapt, the wolf leapt not at the window, but away across the scrubland.

Fisher sat down weakly on the bed, and proceeded to wipe the sweat off his forehead. Of course there were wolves here. How stupid of him not to bear that in mind. 'Elks, wolves, bears', Heikki had listed phlegmatically, as if they were everyday phenomena. But a wolf round here! That put a different light on everything, although Fisher warned himself not to be defeatist. It must have come from the forest behind the house; he would have to make sure the back fence was wolf-proof. They must appear, he reassured himself, just at night, for certainly no-one had warned him to watch out for them by day.

But how, Fisher wondered, did the wolves know, in the middle of summer, when it was day and when it was night? This tricky question he resolved to ask the agent.

The following morning, however, he was tempted to try and convince himself that the episode had merely been a dream. The wolf had gone. The strip of grass where it had pounced was not even flattened. It was the start of another glorious, flawless summer day, to be packed with boy-scout resourcefulness and purposeful exploration. He reminded himself that people wouldn't live round here, which they did, if the prospect of being eaten were very real. All the same, he resolved to clean up a gun and keep it handy. He had come across a couple in a shed; they had made his blood run cold until he remembered that Heikki's father had one too. It seemed everyone had one round here.

It was the weekend holiday of a lifetime. Fisher prowled the house, making plans, his future unfolding before him like the unexpected blossoming of a flower. He was infinitely grateful to Heikki for having brought him to this wonderful, unimaginable place.

It would be a new start; a new life in which he would be both bold and practical, in contrast to cautious and impractical, which was how he had heard himself described. Particularly by people who knew him well, and who should have therefore seen his trapped potential, such as Millicent and Phillips. In this dreamlike house in this hauntingly beautiful country he would rise like a phoenix from the ashes of his stagnant career and spoiled marriage, to a life of brilliance, as clear and radiant as the northern light.

The wolf did not reappear.

He discovered, during the course of the next three days, by chance, where to turn the electricity on. He pushed a grimy black switch in a cupboard and to his surprise, the dead grey light bulb in the kitchen behind him changed colour and began to glow dully. Its light was dense and yellow in the lilac-green daylight that swamped it, and no more vital than the colour from a child's cheap paintbox. When Fisher tried the cooker, the hotplates warmed with only the faintest singeing smell of frying dust.

The whereabouts of the water tap eluded him. On an impulse Fisher went down through the orchard to the well, but it was disused, and the wooden boards that formed the cover were nailed down. He was forced to go all the way down to the lake to bring up water.

On Monday morning, with a smug sense of coping, he was able to heat up some water for a shave. There were half a dozen saucepans, trailing spiders' webs, in a cupboard under the sink. Fisher neatened himself up as best as he could, pushed the door to firmly and set off, catching the ten o'clock bus into town to see the agent. But the office was closed.

The agent was not yet back from his trip. Fisher hung round, but the agent did not appear, and five in the afternoon found the office still closed. He was deeply disappointed.

He had called in at a supermarket during the day and stocked up on real food - steak meat, potatoes, vegetables. He had been living the whole weekend on foodstuffs the kiosk sold and he could identify; the novelty of its narrow range of national favourites had already worn very thin. He would have a 'proper' meal tonight, and come back down to the agent's office tomorrow. Mr. Laine was bound to be back by then. With some decent food inside him he should be able to sleep well, at least. And consoling himself with this thought, Fisher got the six o'clock bus up the hill.

That evening he ate in style, with steak and a salad, and potatoes boiled in their skins and then fried. It was capital.

Perhaps the meal was too heavy, for instead of sleeping better, he found it impossible to sleep at all. The night seemed particularly bright, the house full of strange disturbances, anonymous creakings and rustlings. There were so many questions. Would the agent come back early in the morning and wonder where the key was? Would he be able to buy the house at once? If so he could simply fly to England to arrange things, then come back. While in town he had posted a letter to his bank to ask them to transfer a large sum of money here. But was it all, after all, a big mistake?

They were odd, these nagging preoccupations. He had been in a good mood when he ate, for the meal had been to celebrate his new life. A faint smell of meat still lingered in the house, even though he had eaten outside. It was no good. Fisher rose irritably and made his way restlessly to the head of the staircase. The kitchen below was sunk in its half light, a little deeper that it would be during the day. But all Fisher's senses were concentrated suddenly on the unmistakable. There were noises coming from the porch outside. It was certain. Yet no shape passed in front of the window, no shadows deepened the even twilight within the house. Fisher crept down to the hall and stood there, feeling unaccountably scared, his eyes upon the front door. Then, as if he could simply no longer stand the tension, he flung it open. There, rooting among the remains of the meat chop, was the wolf.

Except that it wasn't a wolf. It was, Fisher noticed to his relief, a dog. It was mangy, unkempt and thin, but enormous, with the remnants of a rope around its neck. Not that Fisher took the last of these details in. He slammed the door shut and stood with his back against it, inexplicably shaky. He supposed he should have kicked it, thrown something at it, to make it go away, but it might have attacked him. It looked filthy; it was probably jumping with fleas. They might be the least of its infections.

In default of any more clearly indicated action he returned to his bed, where he lay awake and tense. The dog had presumably finished the meat chop, for now it was scratching at the door. Then it began to whine and bark, though whether at the closed door or for more meat was impossible to say. As its barks rose in volume Fisher began to fear that someone would hear it and come to investigate the house. He must silence the thing at all costs. He would have to get it to leave. He dressed quickly and armed himself with a broom, then steeled himself to open the front door once again and fend it off. He dodged clumsily as the dog made a lunge at him, then to his amazement it ran in through his legs and into the kitchen. For an instant he found himself astride its hairy, bony back, and then it was behind him. He tried half-heartedly to chase it out, but was forced to give up and retreat upstairs, where he flopped down, dismayed and perturbed, on his bed. Surprisingly soon, considering the germ-ridden monster down below, he fell asleep.

From time to time during the next few days, the dog absented itself, but to Fisher's frustration it always returned. Whenever it saw him it went for him, yelping and snarling. He tried to appease it when he dared, but always he feared from the glitter in its eye as it pranced that it planned to make a bid for his throat, to rip out those faltering words of pacifism for once and for all. Those were the moments when his mouth became dry, and something in his stomach began to quiver strangely.

Wherever it went, however, Fisher noticed that it always came back to one of the sheds in the yard. He could see it from the window, always foraging round it, always snuffling around the closed door, trying to get in. At last it would give up, with an outburst of furious barks, and spring towards the house, where it let itself in by lunging against the door.

At a time when he was quite sure that the dog was absent, Fisher went out himself to prowl around the shed. There seemed to be nothing special about it. It was made of greyish, unpainted wooden planks, and was girded round by a lush defence of nettles, spindly alder saplings and weeds. Behind these some of the wooden planks were starting to rot, but the wooden door was still sturdy, and firmly set in its frame. The bolt when Fisher tried it would not budge. A rusty spade was still propped beside the door, and deep in the tangle of plants nearby was a rusty scythe. Fisher braved the nettles to try and look in through the tiny window, but could make out nothing of what was inside. He felt a nettle sting his calf, and then another, lightly, almost affectionately, and moved his leg in irritation. What was the secret of the shed? What attracted the dog? It was probably a rat. Or a dead cat, though Fisher hoped fervently that it wouldn't be. Not here in his dream house. But if he was going to buy the place, he needed to know.

He picked the spade up and struck it hard against the handle of the bolt. In the earthy cleft where the spade had been worms writhed and tiny insects dithered and scurried, caught by surprise. The bolt shot back. With mixed emotions Fisher prodded the door.

The shed was empty.

Empty except for an empty bowl inside by the door, and a chain secured to the wall. There were odours, it was true, but not of rotting flesh. Fisher stepped inside. As soon as his blinking eyes had adjusted to the dim light he looked round, but there was nothing else.

To the free end of the chain an extra length of rope had been fastened, with some kind of collar attached. The bowl was a dog's bowl. It was dirty and dented, and marked round with crudely painted letters. He made them out in the light of the doorway. 'Kosto'.

Fisher put the bowl down as fast as he could. It needed no further deductions to work out who Kosto was. Now he understood. The vile monster was not just a stray dog, come to taunt him. It had belonged here. This was its home.

And suddenly he saw the whole thing differently, understood that in the dog's mind, that primitive organ, it was he himself that was the intruder.

He was struck by an overwhelming wish to get back quickly to safety. It was vital that 'Kosto' should not come home to find him here, in his inner sanctuary, his personal den. With a furtive glance from the window and another from the door, Fisher hastened outside.

By the very next morning the dog had returned and made the shed its own. After that, it seemed to Fisher that it came less often up to the house, but stood in its very own doorway, guarding the yard. It barked and raced out fiercely at whoever came by, which was of course only Fisher, who was prompted to work out a new route via the little wooden side gate to reach the porch.

It seemed best to use this route until the agent got back. He would know what to do about the dog. All the same, Fisher put out food for it when it wasn't there, small offerings to keep it pacified, and filled up the bowl with water. If he didn't, he feared it would come to the house again, bringing vermin, and leaving behind it a tell-tale open door. It could push its way in, but it could not get out if the door were pushed to behind it, nor could Fisher get it to leave by himself. He wondered who had owned it since the owners had left. Perhaps no-one, it was so thin.

CHAPTER 9

It was, in retrospect, Fisher saw clearly, unreasonable to expect the agent to be in his office on the Monday after his trip. He would have all his fishing tackle to unload, would certainly have to clean out his car. But on Tuesday there was still no sign of him, nor on Wednesday, nor Thursday, by which time Fisher was beginning to tire of his daily trip, not to mention grow rather despondent. He wondered whether he shouldn't just put a message through the agent's door, confess where he was, and ask him to come up to the pink wooden house on his return, but something told him it was certainly best that Laine never know he had been staying there. He would rather pretend he was at the hotel in the town.

He was beginning to think that he must have misunderstood, and that the agent had said a week, not a weekend. That would certainly partly explain the amount of luggage that he had. But well, that week was almost up, which meant that the agent must be returning soon. He had promised to spend the summer showing buyers round Hilppala. And the good thing was, Fisher told himself, that by now he himself would have had enough time to go to England and perfectly plausibly come back. As his second weekend in the house rolled around, Fisher posted the key back in through the agent's door. It fell with a muffled clunk, down beside the coconut-matting doormat just inside. He never locked the door of the pink house anyway – it was easier just to push the door to into its hole.

It must have been somewhere in the early hours when Fisher awoke to hear the dog. Its barks rose in a chilling, full-throated crescendo, and then went on and on, so loud that they rasped through Fisher's night sleep. Sharp, urgent, barks, like the sound of faintly muffled gunshots. Fisher lay rigid, ears strained, feeling the perspiration creep out in a cold, wet film between his back and the blue nylon cover of his sleeping bag. Someone was coming. He would be discovered. The barking continued, then gradually, after what seemed an eternity, it grew more sporadic, became interspersed with growls, and finally, to Fisher's unspeakable relief, stopped altogether. He listened, but now there was only an unnerving silence.

What was it now that had roused the dog, in the middle of what passed for night? Perhaps no more than a passing car, or a stray fox stalking the yard, Fisher told himself. All the same, to make sure, he padded out and across the landing to the window. The yard outside was already perfectly light, the brief span of dusky darkness had come and gone, and only the quietness round about gave an indication that this was not yet really day. The white sky was bland and sunless, but pearly and luminous; the lilac trees, the grass, the reddish soil, the white fence, were all their normal hue. There was no sign of a fox. It must have already gone on its way. Fisher grew bolder. He leaned from the window and imagined he could see why the dog had been making such a fuss. The spade had fallen across the door of its shed and had somehow got lodged there through the handle; the dog must have knocked it as it was jumping against the door. Now it couldn't get out. As he watched, he saw it jump against the window, saw the dim, pale flash of its teeth, and seemed to hear a final brief canine shriek.

Fisher withdrew his head. He supposed he should go and release it, if he could figure out how to do so safely. He should go now; the longer he left it there, the madder it would be when it got out finally.

Or, it came to him, he could leave it in there to starve and be done with the problem, since in theory he shouldn't be here to rescue it anyway. Fisher stood on the landing and searched his soul, to see whether he could sanction such cruelty. So ridiculous to be agonising, now the monster was for once locked up. His body gave a start while his brain was still busy. It took a second for his senses to percolate his thoughts. The door was creaking down below. It was opening. Someone was entering the house.

It was hard to move. Nothing moved. There was silence downstairs. Fisher stood rooted to the spot. Could the front door have opened in the wind? He swivelled his eyes back stiffly to the window he had just been looking out of. The topmost leaves of the lilac tree were still. And the door fitted snugly. That was why there was no point in battling with the key. Fisher forced his legs to creep his body back to the bedroom, tried to open noiselessly the little drawer with the gun he had loaded to keep off the wolf. Of course, he wouldn't fire it, but at least it was some form of protection. After all, he was dressed in only pyjamas. He moved to the cover of the wall at the top of the stairs.

When he forced himself to look, there was no-one in the area of kitchen he could see, but the door from the hallway stood open. It seemed to Fisher in his nervous state that the light from the open front doorway threw a long, faint, human shadow across the kitchen floor. He set his foot on the top stair, then down to the next one, slowly, carefully, and crouched down to peer though the banisters. Someone stood in the kitchen, their head and shoulders outlined by the dull, greenish light from the window. They stood with their back towards the banisters, quite still, as if surveying the room. But it wasn't the agent, or a tramp. Fisher raised the gun, to be on the safe side, but his hand shook ridiculously as he tried to point it down at the white cotton shirt. He willed himself to issue a challenge, but no words came. They wouldn't have been understood anyway. A thousand possible actions seemed to jostle impotently in his brain. The intruder did not move.

It was Fisher's knee that betrayed him, unable to tolerate the awkward crouched position any longer. He had to move, he could not last out. The stair board creaked, Fisher sat back with a thump, overbalancing. The gun clattered noisily down the stairs before bouncing and spinning to a halt. It did not go off.

The intruder did not start. Simply turned and looked up, then stepped round out of the shadows, into the light.

She was unutterably beautiful.

CHAPTER 10

She was dressed in jeans, and not as thin as all too many young girls nowadays. Fisher stared at her. It shocked him to notice that even now, in this most bizarre of meetings, his greatest attention was drawn towards her contours. The denim fabric fitted smoothly over her thighs, her neatly-rounded buttocks. She was dressed in a man's shirt, crumpled and too big; the breasts that filled out its billowing folds appeared to be two perfect hemispheres. Round and high, like those of a Hindu goddess, or a figurehead on a wooden ship. Yes, that was exactly what she looked like, a figurehead, an idealised epitome of beauty. Except that she was real. Alive. The old jeans, the ill-fitting shirt, the battered trainers did nothing to diminish the figurehead effect. She had hair like a mermaid's, or maybe too straight for that, but so heavy that not a strand had wafted out of place. It hung down her back in a thick, shifting curtain the colour of sun-bleached corn. But most startling of all, the childlike face that it surrounded was more stunningly exquisite than anything Fisher had ever seen. Lured away from her figurehead charms his eyes travelled upwards, were held transfixed by the flawless symmetry of her features, set off against the golden frame of smooth, dense hair. The being that stood before him was perfect, divine, more fabulously beautiful than anyone he had ever set eyes on before; her expression as she returned his gaze was unfathomable, yet serene. She had the face of an angel, a Madonna, Mona Lisa without a smile; her look was so calm, so deep and pure. So inscrutable. She was…..he realised he had said it already to himself. She was divine.

She was a goddess.

He became aware that he was staring at her rudely, and lowered his eyes in embarrassment, but got no further than the faint, arresting glint of the small gold cross at her throat. Below the cross the fair skin sloped gently towards the curves of her cleavage; he could not look there. That was holy ground now. He raised his eyes again. She was watching him still. It was hard to make out the shade of her eyes, except that it was beautiful. In the murky green lilac-light of the kitchen it seemed that they were the colour of the sea.

Beneath her gaze he remembered he was dressed in nightwear, and felt a little awkward. He should introduce himself, he thought, for the silence was beginning to be tangible. "Fisher." The word sounded somehow clumsy and odd, as if he were making some surprise assault on the air. Or as if he were sneezing weakly. – "I'm Noel Fisher."

He came down the last few stairs and held out his hand, but the goddess ignored it, still holding him in the power of that look. He began to wonder if he was hallucinating, or if somehow the intruder had killed him and this was some dying vision of his life's deepest unfulfilled desires. He faltered and let his hand drop, his initiative drained away. Only his eyes remained fixed on her, as if he were under a spell. As he watched, the goddess bent down and picked up from by the table leg a battered black rucksack that Fisher had not even noticed. She swung its straps over one perfect shoulder, and turned away.

She was leaving. Fisher attempted to take a step, to raise and reach out his hand towards her, but it seemed as if he was rooted to the spot. He watched, helpless, as the shimmering curtain of pale gold hair swayed impassively from side to side and the shapely form retreated. But the goddess did not make for the front door. Instead she crossed the kitchen to the doors on either side of the tall white stove, turned the handle of the door on the left and went in, shutting the door behind her. Fisher heard what might have been the soft thud of her rucksack hitting the floor, then a louder thud, that he could not explain.

He stood for some time in the middle of the kitchen, uncertain what to do, but the goddess did not reappear. Not did there come any further sound from the room. He began to suspect once again that he must be going crazy in this strange daily limbo, and must have simply imagined the whole thing.

Finally rousing himself, he tiptoed to the door through which the goddess had disappeared and tried to listen, but all he could hear was the tell-tale, humiliating thump of his own unruly heart. Putting his hand on the handle he pushed it down, trembling. The door moved, opened slightly under the pressure. The goddess was asleep on the sofa there, the back of which had keeled backwards onto the floor. That must have been the thud. She was sprawled out crosswise on her back, but he knew she could not be dead, for her bosom beneath the man's shirt rose and fell in unhurried rhythm, the tiny gold cross tumbling a little this way and that, as the heavenly body beneath it undulated peacefully. She was fully dressed, her legs splayed and her feet in their trainers sticking out, her hair cascading like a molten gold waterfall down the sofa-side and over the broken sofa-back lying next to it.

Fisher shut the door again, and deeply preoccupied mounted the stairs where, unable to fix his thoughts upon anything sensible or concrete, he returned to his bed. Soon the night hours would be over, and it would be at least be rational, manageable daytime again. They were quite uncanny, these nights that weren't really proper night, they spawned all sorts of odd goings-on.

He was not sure what to do about the goddess. On waking and recalling the events of the night, he had mourned them tragically as a fantastic dream, the creation of his love-starved body and apparently unhinging mind; perhaps the eight days he had spent in solitude here were beginning to tell. He had resolved to be stricter with himself and to work hard on maintaining his sanity, but on going to the upstairs window to take in the air he started. The spade was still across the door of Kosto's shed.

So that much at least was not a dream. Now he stood once more with his hand on the handle of the door where the goddess had been, unsure whether he wanted to know the answer or not. But he had to know.

She was still there. She was still on the sofa, but had moved in her sleep, so that her hair now spread out all around her as if she was floating on the surface of the sea. But her spun-gold tresses were full and luxurious, not lank and wet. He wanted to reach out and run them through his fingers.

Instead, he shut the door and stood irresolute. Who was she? What was she doing here? Why had she come? For the sake of activity he set about the daily tasks, trying to do them softly, as if careful not to disturb a sleeping child.

At midday the door across the kitchen opened and Fisher spun round nervously. There on the threshold stood the golden vision, the goddess, gazing out and turning her head from side to side. Slowly, majestically. Fisher nearly dropped the saucepan he was wiping. He stared at her, his ears began to redden, and every word he had prepared to communicate to her, to explain himself, deserted him. He looked at her soundlessly.

The goddess did not seem to be as disconcerted by the situation as he did. Her gaze, as Fisher trembled within it, was as calm and tranquil and inscrutable as it had been in the small hours of the morning. Fisher put down the tee-shirt that served as a wiping up cloth.

"I'm Noel Fisher." He was immediately painfully aware that that was the one thing he had said already. "Doctor Noel Fisher." His mouth seemed suddenly to be fashioned out of chunks of wood; it gave his voice a strange and unnatural clacking quality.

The goddess continued to regard him silently. There was something aristocratic about her, about her composure. She was certainly young, it came to him. If she were human, she would be not more than fifteen, sixteen at most. Her face was still childlike in its smoothness, though her body had moved already towards the full-flowering dignity of womanhood. Despite her youth and her silence, she seemed completely in control of the situation, which, as she was divine, was of course not surprising. Fisher imagined now that her eyes were ice-blue, not actually sea-coloured at all. They were fringed by long, curved eyelashes that were dark, despite the fairness of her skin and hair. Now, after sleeping, her cheeks bore the faintest flush of rose-petal pink.

"I'm just staying here," Fisher said.

Nothing else came to mind. He noticed with annoyance that he had stuttered slightly, and feared that his words had had the sound of something between an apology and a request. It felt somehow awkward that the goddess did not speak. He wished she would break the silence. But just then without a word she bent down, just as she had in the early morning, picked up her rucksack, slung it over her shoulder, and walked out through the front door. She left the door partway open behind her, and as Fisher ran quickly to the window to watch, she walked across the front yard without turning round. The dog barked, and she maybe answered it, but her voice was inaudible over the racket that it made.

He watched her go with wistfulness tinged with relief. It was no use trying to explain her to himself. There might be, there was, there could be, no explanation. A goddess. He would remember for the rest of his life that he had once seen a real, live goddess here. It did not matter if he had merely been hallucinating. He would look on it forever as yet another magical experience in this fairytale house, set in this fairytale, captivating land. Yet it left him in an unsettled, strangely nostalgic frame of mind.

It was not until Fisher's second restless pilgrimage that afternoon to the goddess's recently-vacated shrine that he noticed the little heap of articles behind the door. A sweater, some pairs of pants, a half-empty bottle of coca-cola, and a pair of pink patterned fabric shoes, the sort a young girl might wear to a party. Fisher stared at them, scarcely daring to accept the conclusion that was winging towards him like an angel. The goddess was coming back.

Or why else should she choose to empty her rucksack here before she left?

But if she was coming back he must catch her this time, catch her and talk to her. Again he was on tenterhooks, could settle to nothing all day. He dared not go to the town to check on the agent in case the goddess came again while he was out.

He was upstairs in the evening when the dog began to bark, and ran at once towards the stairs. He heard the sound of the door scrape over the ground as it was pushed, saw the beautiful figurehead, the goddess, reappear. She looked neither right nor left as she came, let alone up the stairs to the point where Fisher stood, dressed in his final clean set of clothes. Instead she crossed the kitchen to her previous den, went in and closed the door behind her. She seemed quite unflustered by the dog giving vent to its outrage in the yard, for Fisher had had to let it out of the shed. She left behind her a savoury odour of hamburger and chips. No doubt, thought Fisher, the dog had been maddened even further by the smell of meat. While he still stood on the stairs the goddess came back out to the kitchen again and began to open all the cupboards. She looked inside them then shut them again, while the smell of food floated ever more seductively through the open doorway. Her eyes travelled all around, but down low, never upwards to Fisher. Then she crossed the kitchen once more and her graceful arm shot out across the little table where Fisher had taken to arranging his supplies. Her slim fingers coiled around the ketchup bottle, and she disappeared back into her room.

By the end of two days, Fisher had almost grown accustomed to her presence, whether real or imaginary. She came and went, using the room beside the garden room as her own, without ever glancing any more in his direction. She was silent, regal, infinitely charismatic. She made not the least attempt to speak, nor even, so it seemed, did she feel any need to do so. Only the barking of the dog alerted Fisher to her comings and goings across the yard, and only her words to the dog revealed that she did have the power of speech. To Fisher's envy and amazement she had skills that were fittingly deific with the fiend; she was able to trap it in its shed with the spade, or attach it to the chain with the collar and the piece of rope. With the monster secure she would walk through the yard without the slightest tremble. But the words that she cast before it as she passed, whatever language they were in, were always drowned by the infernal volleys of its wrath.

For his own part, Fisher did not dare to address her, especially if she wasn't really real. But the goddess tormented deliciously his every moment, filled his dreams at night. His restless desire for the agent to return became tempered by his newer obsession, entangled with desire to be somehow forever in this dream. It was a fantasy, a dream of exquisite sweetness which all the same exhausted him, a riddle which could have a solution only when - he was not sure when.

She was no good for writing his book. Despite her silence she made it impossible for him to work. When he sat down she would walk across the kitchen, the room where he had to be in order not to miss a glimpse of her. He would raise his eyes from his notes and follow her, for she never looked in his direction, and long after she had disappeared he would come to, and find himself staring and seeing her still, in his imagination.

She obsessed him. Sometimes he even peeked through her keyhole to see if she were still there. He could concentrate on nothing. Even his long trips to town in search of the agent filled him now with anxious impatience. Suppose she had gone when he got back? Taken her things? Fisher would hurry up the hill, despite his worries that his heart was about to start playing up again, only to slow down with a sigh of relief as he saw her smoking tranquilly on the porch. Cigarettes were something that he disapproved of absolutely, especially in the young. But the goddess smoked with such grace and elegance, such beauty and composure. It seemed that the health risks would just float away on a coil of smoke. And after all, she was divine.

CHAPTER 11

At about the same time that Fisher met the goddess, Laine the agent on his fishing trip set eyes on, and fell for hopelessly, a goddess of his own. Her name was Linda. She was seven metres long with a hard-top cabin and horse-power of up to two hundred and fifty.

Not least of all her unbelievable attractions, she was for sale.

But as with Fisher, Laine's new-found love played immediate havoc with his burgeoning plans for his career. Laine had little intention of staying in Alajärvi all his life, in this dull, sleepy backwater which was simply an undistinguished void on the property map. He had only stood it this long because the river was a first class place for indulging his passion for boats. But no-one ever wanted to move here now, and the people that lived here rarely saw any reason to change their house. He would be heartily glad to be out of this place, he had long-since felt, and now saw his chance. He had managed before the summer to tie up a much more profitable business in Kuopio, and would move to that town after the second leg of his fishing holiday. He had not yet managed to sell the Alajärvi business, but until he did, he would only need to pop in whenever he was passing. Besides, he wanted to keep the Linda moored here on the river.

But yes, his time in this property graveyard was almost up. He was returning now, after three weeks on the lakes, just to open his post and to ask for a second loan from his bank, to enable him to purchase the Linda. The Kuopio venture had already put him into negative equity. It was not the best time to ask for more money, but he was in love, and what man can know in advance when that will happen?

HOUSE HUNTING FNNISH STYLE

Besides, the manager was a yachting man himself.

That being the case, it was hard to understand why the manager of Alajärvi's only bank could not find it in himself to be more visionary. He refused point blank to set up a further loan, became unreasonably stubborn on the subject of collateral. Laine sighed impatiently. Of course the collateral would be there. It would be there as soon as the brand new business was up and running. The prospects were bright. But the manager stolidly refused to budge, and Laine, who had called in to see him directly on his way back from the trip, went home to his sauna in a very bad mood. He dreamed that night that a rival buyer had incompetently shipwrecked the Linda.

The following morning he called in briefly at his office, still licking his wounds about the unkind loan refusal. The post was sparse, but included a letter from Heikki Heikkila, enquiring how the sale of his parents' house was progressing. Laine grumbled crossly to himself. He might have sold the place if it hadn't come up exactly when he'd planned to go fishing. He reached for another envelope and noticed a shadow had fallen across his desk. He looked up.

A man dressed in shorts was fiddling with the handle of the outer door. Laine got up to let him in, but it was not till he heard the words 'Good morning' that he realised that the visitor was somehow familiar. The pile of post and even the Linda faded away as he struggled back over time, the sound of English still strange in his ears.

"I'm Fisher, Dr. Noel Fisher. I came here before." Fisher was flustered; he had been unprepared for actually finding the agent here. "I've come about the house."

From the agent's expression it seemed that he found the information unenlightening. "Ah, yes, the house."

"The pink house," said Fisher. "Near Mr. Heikkila's. You left me to look round it, remember?"

And suddenly it all came back. The Englishman that had come with Heikki Heikkila, and who had wanted to look round that house.

"I thought you were in England?"

Fisher became more flustered. It was going to get complicated. He knew he would stammer.

"I – I was. I put the key through your door. But now I'm back."

Laine nodded politely in acknowledgement. His mine was already drifting back towards the wreck of the Linda. He produced a ghost of a smile.

"And what about the property? Are you interested in looking round some others?"

"I would like to buy it."

Laine's attention had already started to wander again, but now he threw Fisher a startled look. The office around him seemed to roll, very slightly. Perhaps it was the heat. He searched for the phrase that at school had convinced him of the madness of the English.

"I beg your pardon?"

Fisher felt his fragile assertiveness crumbling. He supposed that he did not look like a man of property. He had given up wearing his good clothes to town as the weather turned hotter, and had supplemented his only shorts with a pair that looked dismally like Heikki's. These he wore now. He had no choice but to try and fall back on natural dignity.

"I would like to put in an offer. For the place that I looked round. At the top of the hill."

Laine had pulled himself together. "A first rate choice. An excellent decision." He was vaguely grateful, as he spoke, despite his dedication to selling houses, that he was leaving the district. "How much can you offer?" He moved to the shelf as he spoke, and took down a file. His own voice rang a little oddly in his ears, as if something strange was happening to the blood in his head. "The price they are asking is two hundred thousand Finnish marks."

Two hundred thousand! It was a snip, compared with what one would pay in London. Fisher felt himself on a roller coaster of ecstatic emotion. Though of course, he would have to bargain. He had had to buy Millicent out of the London flat. But people always bargained.

"I can offer one seventy five." He could let the London flat out while he was away, that would help.

Laine pulled a face. "I have buyers looking round tomorrow. If they like the property and offer full price..."

Fisher looked at him aghast. Tomorrow! He had only just got here in time. That was probably why the agent was here now. "A hundred and eighty thousand?" It truly was all he had. "But I can pay the deposit now. Ten percent? Fifteen? In cash." It was true. The money he had ordered from England had arrived. He had accidentally drawn out the whole sum, due to language complications, and now it was hidden in his sleeping bag.

Laine looked at him sharply. A hundred and eighty thousand. That would of course be more than acceptable. The seller would no doubt be thrilled to be shot of the place. But ten percent deposit in cash - the seller would never be expecting that. He need not mention it. It would be money over the odds, superfluous, at least until the final transaction. His expression became a little sharper still.

"Twenty percent," pleaded Fisher, beneath the penetrating gaze. "I can pay it whenever you like."

Twenty percent deposit – that meant thirty six thousand marks. And suddenly Laine no longer saw Fisher, though his eyes still appeared to be piercing him through and through. The Linda, made whole again and gleaming white, was emerging from a veil of mist and growing every second less ghostlike. As she glided towards him he could see that there was no-one at the helm.

"You could pay a deposit of twenty percent? And immediately, in cash? I will contact the owner about your offer today."

"You think they'll accept it?"

Laine tried to extinguish the glow in his own eyes, or at least reduce it to a level that could be read as merely professional empathy for his client. "I imagine there is excellent chance. Especially if you can put down a deposit. Can you be here at eight o'clock tomorrow morning? By then I will have the reply. If it's 'yes' then you can pay deposit. I shall cancel the people who should come later, and we can draw up a document of sale."

"Eight o'clock," agreed Fisher, with far more than his usual enthusiasm for such an hour. The two shook hands and Fisher found himself outside in the dusty, near-deserted street again, his heart as light as a feather.

CHAPTER 12

The early morning bus passed the bottom of the hill just after seven o'clock, paused for Fisher at the roadside, and meandered down into town, overtaken by a thin stream of faster traffic. In the opposite direction a single vehicle sped unimpeded up the empty side of the road.

The office was still closed when Fisher got there. He stared anxiously through the window till almost eight, when the agent's car drew up and Laine stepped out. Like the summer streets, the car was dusty; it seemed that Laine had not had time to clean it since his fishing trip. He shook hands and opened the office door, but to Fisher's surprise his face bore a somewhat preoccupied look. Once inside he said at once, "I have not been able to contact owner yet."

Fisher looked at him in mild dismay. "Which means?"

"That we can't set the sale today." Laine sighed irritably and stared out dismally towards the street. "Of course, it is the holiday month, but all the same…"

Fisher tried to conceal how suddenly devastated he was. He had not slept. He had lain awake the whole night, gloating over his plans. The house would be his; the goddess would live there in her own suite of rooms. The agent could explain to her the situation.

And now there would be a delay. "How soon do you think you'll be able to contact them?" He waited anxiously for Laine's reply.

Laine shrugged. "Very soon, I hope. But it's not so easy". He sighed again. He did not see Fisher. Before him the sleekly rounded stern of the Linda was retreating again towards the horizon. He watched her diminishing form brokenheartedly.

Perhaps he should cancel his second trip, stay here and just try and hunt down the owner? But it wouldn't help, not if they were away on holiday. They would not be back before he had lost his chance to buy his dream boat.

"How soon is very soon?" asked Fisher disconsolately. He sank his hand gloomily into a pocket and produced an envelope with a wad of notes. "I brought the deposit. Twenty per cent." He took out the money and rifled through it, then set it on the desk and gazed at the neat block of notes in its paper band. Laine gazed too, and a great, unbearable misery seemed to squeeze at his heart.

"I thought that if I had paid the deposit," said Fisher, "you could perhaps give me the key again, so I can have access. I would like to look round and plan out repairs and alterations. While I'm here in Finland."

Then he need not be afraid that the agent would turn up and catch him there unawares.

Laine did not answer. He was mournfully scanning the spot where the Linda had disappeared. Fisher tried to rouse him.

" About the owner. You really think you can contact him very shortly?"

"She. It is woman. And yes, she is probably just in holidays till the end of the month." There was silence again.

"I don't suppose," ventured Fisher timidly, "that you could sort of rent me the place for a month, while you wait for her? I can pay you whatever is required in terms of rent. And then we can knock it off the sale price later." As he spoke, Fisher absentmindedly ruffled the heap of notes with his thumb. And as he ruffled, Laine came slowly back to life.

The rental agreement was for eight thousand Finnmarks. Four thousand per month, but as Laine pointed out, a two-month contract would be sensible, in case the owner's holiday was protracted. Fisher privately thought the price rather steep, but understood when Laine explained about hidden costs. It would come off the sale price anyway. "We discuss a refund, of course," said Laine, "if the sale does not materialise. But I'm sure it will." Fisher nodded. His eyes were glowing as he watched Laine wind a sheet of paper into the typewriter.

"You do think she will sell it for the price that I said I could offer?"

"I am sure she says yes," said Laine, who suddenly seemed to be rather cheerful himself.

The rental contract was in Finnish, but Fisher could make out the date and the sum, and the start and finish dates of the agreement. By which time, he hoped, the house would in any case be his. The two men signed it in duplicate.

"So," said Laine, "place is to you. For now, and soon, we hope, forever. I will give you the key."

He had found the key only after Fisher's visit the day before. Now he went to take it again from the metal-fronted cupboard. As he did so a shadow passed across his face, a look of annoyance. "At least, I hope the place is to you. This morning, I went to the house myself, to see if I could find there another address or telephone number for the owner. There was a dog there, quite huge, and very dirty, just running round in the yard." Fisher opened his mouth to say that he had meant to mention that, then shut it again. He gave a laugh.

"I shouldn't want a dog there. No, I certainly wouldn't want a dog as part of the agreement. Perhaps if it's still there when the sale goes through, you could have it removed?"

"It is removed already," responded Laine. "Because, I have to tell you a very strange thing. And not pleasant, but I hope that it is all right now. There was a girl there."

"Oh," exclaimed Fisher, lamely. He suspected that the colour had drained from his cheeks.

"It is possible, I think, that you did not completely lock it that day, when I left you to see the house. Because today it was unlocked, and when I got inside, there was this girl!" Laine appeared not to have noticed the sudden pallor beneath Fisher's tan. "A teenager! As if she was living there. Blankets and everything! I don't know what young people are becoming these days. I threw her away, of course. I told her, 'Someone is coming to live here. Out you go!' And I took her from the arm. Then she started shouting, 'My things, my things,' I told her, 'take your things.' She started to say that she is not the only one, there is others there, it is not fair that she must go, and so on. She was screaming. I threw her away with some clothes and her bag and locked the door. I told her, 'Take your terrible dog and go', and then she left. I made quite sure. But if ever there is any more trouble, you must let me know. And if you are there yourself and someone comes, so call police. And most important of all, make sure always to lock the door."

"Of course." Fisher wondered fleetingly how one summoned the police without a car and without a telephone, but mainly he hoped that Laine would not notice that he was trembling.

The estate agent's story of how he had kicked out the goddess had diminishing impact on Fisher's euphoria, as he made his triumphal return to the house that was the winter jewel. He felt quite shaken up by the fact that Laine had gone round there, and even more disturbed by his account of how he had shouted at the goddess, but on reflection he thought it more than likely that the goddess would have come back already. The agent had no idea of the real situation.

If anything, he felt somewhat jealous that the agent had got the goddess to respond, if only to defend herself. In all the days they had now been together, Fisher pondered ruefully, she had never attempted to speak to him. If only he could speak a little Finnish, that was the problem.

The dog was not in the yard when he arrived, which was always a relief. He wondered if it was still with the goddess. She could manage it better than he could, though it didn't like her. It liked no-one, that was certain, except perhaps viewed as a snack.

The nervousness of anticipation that Fisher felt on mounting the porch steps did nothing to dislodge the sense of thrill and the song of joy that soared and vibrated through his being. He struggled long and rather clumsily with the firmly locked, badly fitting door, then stood at last on the newly-opened threshold of the winter jewel, the house that represented nothing less than a new life laid out before him. It was still only morning, and the east-facing rooms were flooded with light, while the luminous green of the kitchen was bright and light-hearted. Oh, to think that this heavenly paradise was really to be his! Fisher placed the rental agreement on the kitchen table and set out to look with a new sense of ecstasy at what was so very soon to be his domain. He went all over it, upstairs and down, until at last he could force the other matter to the back of his mind no longer. It was no good. He left the last rooms of the upper storey unexplored, and went downstairs.

The door to the goddess's room was closed. He hesitated before its blank facade, reluctant to find out what he already dreaded to find true. He listened, thought, stood. There was silence, a deep, peaceful silence from the other side of the door. Behind him, in the kitchen, the grandfather clock ticked reprovingly. He had never before disturbed the goddess in her room. He knocked. Still silence. He wanted to call out her name, her earthly name, but it came to him that he did not even know it. A beam of light shone suddenly on the handle before him, like a favourable omen. He opened the door. Every trace that the goddess had ever existed had disappeared. Fisher stared at the room in simple, life-saving disbelief. Then his heart sank like a stone, and his stomach felt sick.

He had been quite sure that the goddess had simply left till the coast was clear. He had tried to ignore the vague impression he had got that there didn't seem to be any articles of hers around the place. The goddess was in turns rather casual, that is, extremely untidy, and rather private and secretive, collecting things up and bundling them into her room. That was where, Fisher had tried to convince himself, they all were now.

He turned away at last, overcome by profoundest grief. Perhaps the goddess had never existed. Perhaps she had merely been a figment of his desire and fevered imagination.

But the agent had distinctly claimed that he had thrown her out.

In his sorrow, and to ward off thoughts of impending insanity, Fisher vented his anguish and wrath upon the wretched agent. How could the man have been so uncouth, so insensitive, as to act with such brutality towards the goddess? He was a Philistine, chained to the petty, devoid of imagination, like Heikki. Had he shown her respect, perceived that she was a deity? No. He had shouted at her, driven her away. Angry tears began to glitter in Fisher's eyes. It was harrowing to imagine the goddess's distress.

He stumbled dispiritedly towards the table, and slumping down with his head in his hands he allowed the tears to roll down his face. He remained there hour after hour, until at last he raised his head blearily. "There has been too much excitement for one day," he told himself. And too tired to think of anything, using the banister to assist himself, Fisher hauled himself off to bed in his money-padded sleeping bag.

He awoke during the meagre slip of night that currently separated the days from each other. His eyelids still felt hot and tender after the tears he had shed, and his eyes stung and prickled as he opened them. The goddess was standing at the open doorway of his room.

Or so he imagined. He raised himself on one elbow and rubbed his burning eyes with his hand, but the vision stayed put. After what seemed an age she half-turned and shut the door behind her, then came and stood beside the bed, so close that Fisher could almost breathe in the heavenly odour of her body. The arm on which he had propped himself began to ache, but he dared not move. It took all his courage to keep his eyes on her face; at the same time he could not drag them away.

Still holding his gaze with her own the goddess knelt down, quite near to him, and suddenly ran her fingers down his forearm, where the hairs were standing up on end. Then she spoke and her voice, now that Fisher heard it, was sweet and still slightly girlish, without a hint of the detonating consonants and whining vowels that seemed to be the mainstay of the Finnish language. She was so close she needed only to whisper, and it took a moment before he realised that he had understood every word. For the charmingly accented words were not in Finnish, but in his own tongue.

"I love you," said the goddess.

There were times in the weeks that followed when Fisher scarcely dared to breathe, for fear that his cup of happiness would overflow. The great work hovered somewhere in the stratosphere, to be started some time, while Fisher bathed each day in the radiance of heaven, and watched the astounding revelations of maturing summer. By night he made love to the goddess, rediscovering lost arts, cautiously inventing new ones. It was all so incredible. As if God, the creator he had dutifully acknowledged all his life, had from his store of meanly distributed blessings suddenly meted several out by mistake. The bag had fallen open, and they had all tumbled out. Onto him, Noel Fisher, before God had had a chance to retract them. So many blessings, simultaneously, and just one humble recipient.

Somewhere deep down Fisher felt the dim conviction that at some point he would be called on to pay for this, or that God would realise his mistake and suddenly take all his blessings back, but for the present he was too drunk with pleasure to really care. In a surge of happiness he stuck a note through the door of Heikki's flat in town, to let him know the good news. About the house, that is. The good news about the goddess he chose not to mention just yet.

The goddess lost none of her mystery with the change in

circumstances. It appeared that apart from 'I love you' she could say little else, in English at least. And even these words she never said again. As if to say them once should be sufficient for all time. But she had said them. She had found the words in his tongue. And he loved her, with a passion he had never experienced before.

CHAPTER 13

Fisher was restless. Perhaps it was the moonlight. It was almost August; the moon was back in season, though the nights were still very short. He stirred in his narrow bed and wondered where the goddess was, and if she was coming up to see him. It was after midnight. Her company would help to pass the time. He pulled on his trousers and went to the head of the stairs, where looking down he saw the goddess, carrying a bowl of heated water from the stove. She was dressed in a towel, with another round her head, as if she intended to rinse her hair out after washing it. When she sensed his presence she stopped, looked up, and gave him the deep, long, considering look that he could never quite interpret.

She was standing there still when the front door opened with a mighty bang, as if it had just been kicked. Fisher jumped; even the goddess slopped most of the water out of the bowl. But she did not react when the falling liquid scalded her feet. Instead, with one accord, she and Fisher both stood rigid, their eyes on the figure in the doorway.

A young man stood there. He was standing motionless, as if he was sizing up what he saw before him. It seemed to Fisher one of the longest moments he could remember. There was silence, except for the jerky ticking of the clock. The young man began to glance around. He looked at the walls, the windows, up at Fisher, with an indefinable, sphinx-like expression, such as the goddess's had been on her arrival. But hers had been mysterious and beautiful. The present intruder was frankly ugly, not to mention unsavoury. He was poorly shaven, and his short hair stood up untidily. Fisher registered that it looked a long time since he had washed.

Then the young man dropped his gaze to the goddess, and his face and body leapt into life. He lunged in and made a grab for her, the air was suddenly filled with unintelligible exclamations. He was shouting something at the goddess. Fisher gave a start, it was all so unexpected. He expected the goddess to scream but she didn't, and with admirable presence of mind turned hastily to set the bowl of still steaming water on the table.

"Taavi" he seemed to hear her gasp, as the young man grabbed. It might have been a name, or merely the Finnish for 'don't'. Or some other exclamation. She broke free and ran towards her room but he caught her up, and flinging his arms around her held her close. To Fisher's horror she sank her head upon his shoulder, while the towels unwound themselves from her body and tumbled unheeded to the floor. It wasn't the Finnish for 'don't'. Their bodies fell together into the goddess's room and the door shut behind them with a whacking sound, as if that too had been kicked. In the kitchen the water the goddess had spilt spread lazily across the floor.

Fisher stood lost, uncertain what to do. He wondered dimly if he should go down and pick up the towels and close the front door. The night breeze was blowing across the kitchen. But he could not bring himself to descend the stairs, to intrude in a drama where he didn't belong, even though the goddess and the young man were no longer there. He felt sick and shaken, worse than that. Almost bludgeoned to death. The goddess had a lover.

Of course she did. Fisher wondered how he could ever have been so naïve. She must have come here to meet him, a lovers' tryst. She had been waiting for him all this time, in a house that they had assumed would be deserted. She had probably even been getting ready for him tonight. No wonder, though Fisher, she had never tried to tell him more about herself.

And yet, she had told him that she loved him! They had lived in rapturous oblivion. And now someone else had come, this young, ugly, pasty fellow, and taken possession of her. It was so unjust, it was all so difficult to understand. But one thing was obvious. The blessings had played their trick.

By the end of three days, it seemed clear that the goddess's lover had come to stay. She called him Taavi. He called her Katja. Her earthly name. He was clearly surly by nature, and the glances he threw at Fisher were chillingly unpleasant.

"It's my house," Fisher protested to himself. "I'm buying it. I'm the only one that has a right to be here." But it didn't help. His paradise had been invaded. And his goddess prised away.

She never came to him, of course, in the night any more – why should she? How could she? Her real boyfriend had claimed her. And as time went on, it even became unclear to Fisher, why the goddess had ever given him her attentions in the first place.

There was no point in hurting himself. He never went downstairs once he had retired to his own room. He did not want to know of their life together. And it was all too obvious that they found his presence a strain. They were awkward and silent with each other when he was around them.

"My house," he almost sobbed to himself. "My goddess." But he should have known all along that it wasn't to be.

On about the fifth day after his arrival, the young man went out and came back driving a van, an old, battered white thing. Fisher hoped for an optimistic hour or two that he might be leaving, then feared for a morbidly anxious afternoon that he and the goddess might be leaving together, but the van just remained from then on in the yard, where the young man spent much time tinkering with it.

So the days passed, and threatened to turn into weeks, while Fisher, indecisive but powerless, lived on in uneasy cohabitation with the goddess and her mystery boyfriend. And still no word came from the agent to say that the deal could be clinched, and that Fisher could finish buying the house. He had to hang on desperately to the idea that this news would represent a turning point, a point when something decisive must happen, while meanwhile his anguish and burning jealousy only festered and grew more destructive day by day. It seemed to him that he lived in a paradise that was now a nightmare, in which all attempts at action faded away in weakness and inertia, and each sight of his beloved or her hateful companion brought him pain.

Then, on what was actually the tenth day after the young man's arrival, although Fisher had given up counting, something quite extraordinary but unmistakable happened. The goddess and her boyfriend had a lovers' tiff. There was no mistaking it. He emerged from his room to the startling noise of angry, squabbling voices in the kitchen downstairs, just in time to hear the sound of the front door being pulled hard to, as if someone were leaving. Looking out of the window, Fisher saw the goddess crossing the yard. She was marching furiously, paused only to let the dog loose with an angry toss of the rope, then she stalked off through the gateway and down the road without looking back. As she disappeared the young man too crossed the yard from the house. He ignored the dog and made straight for the broken-down van. Its engine roared rapidly and clumsily, an ugly explosion rent the air, and the ramshackle heap of metal and wheels took off in a cloud of exhaust smoke. It went in the opposite direction to the way that the goddess had gone.

It was one in the morning when he heard the dog, then the sound of it being shut in its shed. Not long after he heard front door opening, and then the footsteps whose very sound he had come to live for. It was the goddess. Moreover, he had not heard the sound of the van. She had come on her own. Fisher raised himself up, listening alertly, heard her moving about a little downstairs. He wondered if he should go down and try and speak to her. It distressed him so, that she had been upset. But what could he say? If only they had some common language, if only he could talk to her. Comfort her, tell her he would always be there for her. He loved her. She had said once that she loved him. But what good would it do now? She had chosen. She had chosen, and he had lost. He lay in the dark, his body rigid with longing and misery.

When he was finally dozing, the goddess came and climbed into bed.

She came to him quite often now, when her other lover wasn't around. The young man had taken to driving off in his ramshackle van for hours or even whole days on end, and when he came back he would start bringing all sorts of bits and pieces into the house. Old TVs and radios, broken machinery, clapped-out electrical appliances and knick-knacks that he dumped in the kitchen and around the sheds.

"My kitchen! My house!" and even "My sheds!" protested Fisher to himself in outrage, but it did not help. He had no way to protest to the offender.

He wanted to explain to the goddess, in the hope that she would speak to her boyfriend, and get him to break this escalating obsession. The house was beginning to look like the nest of a giant magpie, and all because of someone who didn't even have the right to be here. Fisher took the goddess by the hand and gave her a tour of the TV valves and dissected lawnmowers laid out all around the house, but her face took on a baffled look and she merely shrugged.

Not that the young man was simply accumulating things; he tinkered with the items he brought back and drove them away again in the van. But he always seemed to be bringing back two things for each one that left. It was enough to give a sensitive person, an aesthete such as himself, a nervous breakdown. Fisher felt he could kill the young man for his electronics habit alone, let alone for what the fellow had done to his love life. He was desecrating the house, degrading it. He must be got rid of, Fisher determined. As soon as possible, and at all costs.

As for the goddess's taste in lovers, Fisher had no idea what to think. She herself was so exceptional in her magnificence, yet her boyfriend seemed more wanting in blessings than the goddess was blessed. His habitual expression fell somewhere between moronic and morose, and nor was he otherwise anything to look at. He was pale and of average height, and overall too scruffy to pass for nondescript. When not plain bad-tempered he seemed by turns awkward, sullen and uncouth, leaving Fisher only able to conclude to his anguish that the rough diamond must be a powerhouse in bed. He wondered sometimes if his rival knew of his own secret life of passion with the goddess, but was sure that he didn't, for the fellow simply stared right through him when they passed. For the first time Fisher was grateful for his own unprepossessing looks. They constituted no doubt the perfect protective camouflage.

He would slip out to watch the goddess as she sat on the porch in the evening sun smoking cigarettes, would go unobtrusively to gaze on her time and time again as the sun sank lower and the shadows lengthened. If the young man had gone out in his van and had not come back, the goddess might mount the stairs and come to him, softly, wordlessly, and Fisher's heart would open up with wonder and rapture. "Katja," he would murmur, for at these times only he dared to call her by her earthly name. "Katja" he would utter stupidly, as his lips descended onto hers. Then the planets would sing in their orbits.

Lying in bed with Fisher Katja would feel for the reassuring, thick, hard square of the sleeping bag with her knee. And sometimes when he had gone downstairs, when he thought she was still asleep, she would check it and clasp her hand around the thick wad of notes that was still there. It seemed to her somehow that it was thinner now than when she had first discovered it, but it hadn't thinned any more since the night she had come back after the agent had thrown her out.

It was nothing short of a miracle that she had found it. She had simply sat on it while going through his things. She had sat down and felt the difference in resistance of that one particular section. She had no idea what the old man was doing here unless, as a miser, which he obviously was, he wanted to live somewhere free, but she was grateful. She was even grateful that he had not been here when the agent turned up and so had not been thrown out. She must stick around him, disgusting as it all was. She was going to need all the money she could get.

CHAPTER 14

Through his rather hazy grip on time, Fisher guessed that August must be well past its mid point. The corn in the fields behind the kiosk had been harvested, the rowans were thick with reddening berries and the birches draped with strands of yellow, and still the agent had not got back in touch.

In the house's orchard the apples, though small, were turning red and rosy-looking. They hung in their hundreds in the autumn sunshine, looking juicy and tempting. On an impulse, Fisher went out one day and picked all those he could reach. He filled buckets and bowls with them; there were far more apples than he knew what to do with. They had apples enough to last them through the winter, that was sure, although he had all but stopped believing in such a thing. It was good to have them harvested anyway. Fisher felt a sudden pride of self-sufficiency. He picked out an apple out and sank his teeth in. The flesh was white and sweet, stained pink to a little way beneath the skin, but the texture was somehow pappy and soft. He bit another one. It was soft too. He was deeply disappointed. Perhaps they would have to be for cider. The second apple had a maggot in it as well. One had to be careful.

The apples were a let-down. So much so, that Fisher left the bowl he had sampled on the table and went for a walk.

On his return the pile of apple cores was the first thing Fisher noticed as he came up the steps of the porch. It was there by the top step, just where the goddess was accustomed to sit. He experienced rapture, astonishment, emotions apple cores had never aroused in him before. Especially abandoned ones. But they must be the goddess's, the pile was neat. And it was just there, just in her favourite spot. She was eating his apples, partaking of something he had provided. And by the dozen, so it seemed, unless that greedy ape of a boyfriend was scoffing them too.

But the young man was not at home. After nightfall Fisher waited hopefully for the goddess to come upstairs, but she tarried on the front porch, so long that Fisher peeked out from an upper window to see what she was up to. He was just in time to hear the unmistakable sounds of mastication, then the moonlight picked out a small white missile as it flew in a rising then a falling arc. A few seconds later the goddess came up the stairs.

The young man came back early in the morning, just after Fisher had got up, but he did not come in. He gestured sullenly for Fisher to help him load the van up with a washing machine, then he wiped his hands on a rag, climbed into the driver's seat, and started the engine. From somewhere the dog shot out and jumped up into the passenger side. Fisher heard it baying as the van left the yard and belched its way noisily down the road.

The goddess was up when he went inside, and running down the stairs, but she did not run to Fisher. She ran across the hallway into the toilet and began to throw up. It seemed that the apples were taking their toll.

"She ate too many," thought Fisher ruefully, "and if some had a maggot…" He felt somehow responsible. His own guts churned in an agony of remorse.

He watched her uncertainly through the open door, not knowing whether to show concern or to pretend that nothing untoward was happening. It was then that he realised that a vehicle was drawing up outside. Not the van, which could not stop without a ritual of geriatric seizures and convulsions, but a healthy engine. Fisher froze in terror. The agent! He threw the goddess's back view a desperate glance. She was still crouching over the toilet bowl, her body wracked in spasms of evacuation. Above the belching interposed with gasps and lamentations came the thud of footsteps mounting the porch, then almost immediately the sound of imperious knocking. As Fisher ran to close the door on the goddess she looked up, her face tinged with green, and let out a long, wailing moan. Behind him the knocking on the front door was repeated, but before he could reach it, it opened by itself in response to the weight of the blows.

It was Heikki.

He stood in the doorway, blinking a little owlishly. It must be quite dark in the house, Fisher realised, after the bright light outside. He felt like laughing, he was so relieved, and even Heikki looked shyly pleased at his warm reception. As Fisher ushered him to the kitchen it seemed that he did pause and listen, but when Fisher shut the door behind them the groans of the goddess disappeared.

Fisher motioned him towards the wooden table. "Sit down, do. Shall I make some coffee?"

Heikki sat down on the wooden bench and began to blink again. He was suntanned to a pinkish brown that the green light rendered an extraordinary shade, and had possibly lost a little weight. He was still rather sleepy. He looked around the kitchen and then at Fisher with a slightly bemused expression. "So. You are here."

Fisher spread his hands in a gesture of resigned acknowledgement.

"But why you are here?" Behind his glasses Heikki was earnest, enquiring. Joy rose up unbidden like a bubble inside Fisher, and burst out in a sudden, involuntary grin.

"I'm buying it. I'm buying this house to work in. Didn't you get my note?" Heikki had. But Fisher had gone to England. How was he here? In the tone of voice there was no accusation, merely puzzlement. Fisher felt humble. For a second, in his pleasure and relief at seeing Heikki, he had forgotten the circumstances in which they had separated.

"Ah, it's a long and complicated story." He hoped that this might suffice, but saw that Heikki was waiting trustingly for an answer. Where could he start? How could he explain?

"Well, they asked me to teach the course, but..." And then it suddenly came to Fisher that even the agent assumed he had gone back to England and then come back here. His tale was watertight, if he could only remember how to tell it himself.

"Well, I went back. But that day I was here alone, before I left, I came and I looked at this house, just for something to do. Then I went back, and the whole time I was in London, I only thought about this place here. I mean Finland. How it's beautiful and clean and peaceful, and the people are so...." The words flowed out of his mouth, as if they were already there, without ever having had to come from his brain. Heikki looked radiant with pleasure. Fisher found himself almost sensing which stepping stone to put his foot on next.

"And then it came to me that that is precisely the environment that I need to write my book. Somewhere far away from the hustle and bustle. If only I could be over here! London is much too busy and noisy, there are far too many distractions. And I don't really need to be there.

And then I recalled that this house was for sale, and everything fell into place. I wrote to the agent, and put in an offer. So here I am. Except that we haven't completed the sale yet, it's more on a sort of rental basis just now."

Heikki's face had lost its glow of national pride and was now a touch lugubrious. "Why you didn't pought Hilppala?"

Fisher felt a slight twinge of guilt. He hazarded, "It was too expensive. This house was cheap. Of course, I know it needs things doing."

Heikki glanced about him rather sharply.

"Agent has told you everything? He has peen quite honest?"

"Oh yes."

"And still you want to puy?"

"Of course. I'm sure I can take it all in my stride." Heikki seemed quite impressed. Fisher looked at him a little anxiously. "He said that the things to be done were just superficial." There was something a little pleading in his voice.

Heikki was looking round him at the kitchen and its ancient fittings, its shabby furnishings, with the closest expression to curiosity that Fisher had ever seen him wear. He was suddenly painfully conscious of the front door that would not even shut, the splintering woodwork, the crumbling plaster in the wall above Heikki's head.

"It's a nice house. I want to save its soul."

Heikki threw Fisher an odd look. "Save its soul?"

"I just – really like this house," insisted Fisher, lamely. Heikki's attitude was to be expected. The man had no imagination, no vision. "The condition isn't too bad, is it?"

Heikki began to look a little more like his usual self. "It needs much repairs." He took off his glasses and moved his eyes around the kitchen with a slowness that filled Fisher with trepidation. "Here needs new door, new windows, new equipments, and quite much work done on walls and ceiling. Rest I have not seen, of course." He threw Fisher a sudden penetrating look, quite unlike his usual sleepy expression. "Floors were clean when you came?" Fisher was rather taken aback. The national obsession with cleanliness was no joke.

"Oh, yes." He had not even noticed. "You could look round the other rooms if you like. Give me your advice." Fisher stood up and led the way out into the hall.

"The scullery. Toilet. Living room. That's a sort of vestibule." Heikki could even take a quick look at the toilet cistern, if he wouldn't mind. It didn't always work, and he was good at that sort of thing. Fisher moved to the toilet door, but before he could even quite reach it, it opened, and suddenly the goddess stood before them.

Her pale face still had the greenish, mermaidish tinge. She had been sitting quiet and exhausted on the floor by the toilet bowl behind the closed door, and now drifted listlessly off to her own room and shut the door. Even on Fisher she left a crumpled, subdued impression.

"She's not feeling well," he excused her.

"Who she is?" Heikki asked.

Fisher had forgotten for the minute that the presence of the goddess needed to be explained. He stood stock still for a second to think. A hundred possible explanations of who or what the goddess might be stacked themselves up quickly into a mountain, and then, asced upon the summit, the mountain toppled. Who was the goddess?

"I don't know," he said. "She just turned up. But she's living here. That's why I can't leave. If I do, she'll become a squatter. She'll get rights. Then I will never be able to get her out when the house is mine." "Not that I'd want to," he added, but quietly, so that Heikki would not hear.

Heikki appeared in any case not to have heard Fisher's explanation. "Why she is living here? She is paying you?"

"No. She's with her boyfriend. He's here too."

"Why they poth are here?"

"I don't know," said Fisher, a little irritably. The conversation seemed to be a quest for pointless facts. Yet Heikki had not even mentioned the goddess's breathtaking beauty, which even her present queasiness could not dispel. He remembered once more how irksome Heikki's unrelentingly mundane approach to simply everything could be.

"You must kick poth out." stated Heikki, matter-of-factly.

"But I love her," screamed Fisher's soul, "She is a goddess." Though he knew that he could not say this aloud. Heikki's mind ran in weights and measures, facts and statistics, not in spirits and divinities and romance and souls.

Heikki glanced towards the goddess's closed bedroom door and nodded sagely. "Kick them poth."

Fisher nodded weakly. "I expect I will. But not while she's ill."

They returned to the kitchen.

"So Hilppala isn't sold yet?" Fisher asked, to change the subject. A cloud of slight displeasure passed over Heikki's countenance. There was still no buyer for the house yet, despite the agent's assurance that there had been widespread interest. Heikki was most disappointed. Fisher wondered vaguely whether to let on that the agent had not even been in town, but decided that that would simply make his friend more disgruntled.

"I expect in the autumn…"

"In autumn, yes. But then I shall be back to my studies in London. And you will be here!"

"Yes, indeed. When is it you go?"

"In few days." Heikki blinked sleepily and his face returned once more to happy placidity. He had been all this time on the lake, it transpired, and had only come home now to prepare for England. The discovery of Fisher's note on his doormat had amazed him. He had come right away to check its truth out, for tomorrow he would be visiting his parents, and the day after that he must fly to England. He doubted his new apartment there would rival the hospitality of Fisher's.

"It was a joy to have you," Fisher said stoutly. "I hope the year goes well."

His words were interrupted by an audible groan from the goddess, who came out and floated across the kitchen like a pale ghost towards the toilet again. Fisher prayed that at least her boyfriend would not turn up until after Heikki had left – if Heikki met him he would take this for a real madhouse. But the sight of the goddess seemed to bring Heikki's thoughts back to the present.

"Why you live here when house is like this?" he asked. "Why don't you live in Hilppala while it is empty? Then you can start repairworks here and mess will not disturb."

"That's very kind." Fisher was touched. He jerked his head

towards the toilet door. "But as I told you, I can't leave them here."

"Put you are kicking them out." asserted Heikki. He rose from the bench. "I must go. We must see again before I leave for England." Fisher rose too, and accompanied him towards the door.

"Don't forget my very best wishes to your parents. I trust they have settled in well in their home?"

It was one of those questions that seemed to make Heikki pause to ponder. It was always impossible to know in advance which questions would have this effect. "Quite well," he said finally. "But Hey!" His face brightened suddenly. "Come with me to visit them tomorrow, why not? It would be nice for them to see you."

Far away, at the borders of his consciousness, Fisher heard the barely perceptible but nevertheless unmistakable sound of the young man's van passing by the on the road outside the house, and disappearing. He had gone to get petrol, or some food from the kiosk before coming back. He would certainly not be long; it was time to get Heikki out of the way.

"We can go by my car," Heikki was saying. "I can come to pick you, say, at eleven a.m."

"That would be lovely," said Fisher. "I'll wait for you just outside the gate."

CHAPTER 15

It seemed to Fisher that Heikki's parents had visibly aged since he had last seen them, as if to be more in keeping with their surroundings. A white-clad assistant ushered them into the couple's small private sitting room, where the lowered Venetian blinds reduced the daylight intake to long, thin, pale stripes that hooked their way across the furniture. As if the previously tough old couple were now fragile specimens that might disintegrate in too much sunlight. Or as if they had had enough of the surrounding beauty and had opted to retreat to this snug cocoon, to spend their final days in unimaginative comfort. As his eyes adjusted Fisher saw a low glass coffee table set between the armchairs and the sofa, laid out with coffee cups and a plate of cinnamon buns. He took his place on the edge of a too-soft chair while Heikki translated.

"They say it is pleasure to see you again. I called to tell them we are coming poth."

Hilppa motioned the assistant to serve Fisher first with refreshments, as guest of honour. There was no escape from the buns. Heikki and Urpo helped themselves and began to chew stoically.

"I'm delighted to be able to see them." Fisher eyed the ball of coiled, sugared dough on his plate with covert wariness. It would, he already knew, behave like cotton wool in his mouth and then like a six course meal in his stomach. Still, it was nice to see the old pair again, and they had made him welcome, although Hilppa was clearly displeased with Urpo over something. She was scolding him, her voice becoming shriller the faster she gabbled. Urpo dipped and munched stolidly.

"She is angry pecause he has taken pun," explained Heikki. "He has sugar disease."

Fisher nodded understandingly.

"He has peen to hospital. They have forbidden him to eat such food."

"That must be hard." For a moment Fisher half wished that he could be diabetic too. That he might avoid such morsels as the one in front of him on medical grounds. At that very instant Hilppa's expression changed, and she gestured encouraging at Fisher.

"She says you can eat," said Heikki. Fisher smiled wanly, and began to nibble decorously. He wondered how much he could leave without it being noticed. He allowed the plate to rest on his knee and took up the rapt, attentive smile of total immersion in the conversation round about. It must be quite a story that Heikki was relating now, for even Urpo had risen from his primeval sloth and was taking an interest. His eyes were wide open. The story must be about some fish caught on the fishing trip. From Hilppa's expression they were probably comparing gutting techniques. It was only when he raised his eyes from sipping his coffee that Fisher noticed that Hilppa and Urpo had fallen silent and were looking at him, just as engrossed as he had pretended to be.

Heikki came to his aid. "They want to know if you know what happened at house. I said 'of course'."

"What happened at what house?" Under Hilppa's scrutiny Fisher pulled off the tiniest portion of bun and set it ostentatiously in his mouth.

"In your house. House what you are puying."

"Why? What did happen?"

"They want to know if you knew that man has peen shot there. Py his son. If you knew that it is famous murder house." There was something almost reproving in Heikki's tone. "I told them of course you know. Agent has told. Put you didn't mind."

The accident that happened then to the coffee and the plate and the bun that Fisher was holding was perfectly genuine.

The car ate up the miles of the homeward trip steadily, as if some mission had been accomplished. It was a new car and went quite smoothly even over roads that were pot-holed or not even surfaced.

"I'm sorry about the coffee," said Fisher. "And the cup."

Heikki shrugged indifferently. "It wasn't expensive one. And service nurse will clean up."

"It's just such an utter shock. I had no idea...." Even now, Fisher noticed, his voice was a little shaky. He felt, too, curiously reluctant to reach the place to which they were heading.

"Put you really didn't know?"

"No, I had no idea."

"Laine didn't say you anything?"

"No, not a word. And then, when you came to visit, nor did you."

"You didn't tell, that Laine did not say you nothing."

Fisher suppressed a feeling of perplexed exasperation.

"It is pecause he wants to sell you house," continued Heikki. "You are not going to puy it if you know that previous owner has peen shot there. And py own poy."

Fisher digested this assertion. Despite the sense it made he hoped that Laine could not be capable of any such deviousness. "Perhaps the agent really doesn't know," he said timidly. "It's the owner that he is trying to contact for me to buy it."

"That is owner's wife. Owner is dead."

"Maybe Laine doesn't know that."

"Of course he knows. It is quite famous murder. It was wery popular case. That is why photo of house is in papers."

Fisher sighed. "I thought it was just because the place is so beautiful." He stared glumly through the windscreen; the unmoving features of his face belying the heaving chaos of his thoughts.

"It is long time ago, said Heikki, in a tone that was partly defensive, partly pacifying. "Four, five years. That perhaps is why I didn't pother to tell you. It is nowadays only ordinary house."

Fisher was silent. It looked as if Laine had deliberately deceived him.

"I cannot know you want to puy it. I think you are in England."

Fisher sighed. "I know."

All the same, Heikki could have told him. The average person would have done so just as soon as anyone mentioned the picture. Or the house. Fisher continued to stare before him, his eyes full of tragedy. How could anybody do such an ugly thing? To violate such an exquisite place? A place where himself had seen only peace and a perfect existence.

"Condition is not so good now," said Heikki, "Now that no-one has peen living there. If you are puying you have wery much work to do, to get it back into shape." Fisher found himself marvelling absently at Heikki's phlegmatism regarding the house's horrifying history. Beside that, the relevance of its current shabbiness faded to nothing.

"I'm not sure any more if I'm going to buy it. I have to think it over." Fisher watched the sunlit landscape of the afternoon go rolling past, the green-gold patchwork of meadows and harvested cornfields, but the slightly darkened windows of Heikki's car glazed them all with a sinister tint he had never really noticed before. For once he could not lose himself in the beauty of the fields and forests all around them.

"Why did he shoot his father?"

Heikki checked the road before making a turn. The route was beginning to look familiar. "It is mystery. Nobody knows."

"But there must have been a reason."

Heikki shrugged. "I don't think he ever said. He just came home from school one day and…PAM!!"

"What happened to him?" Fisher hated himself for asking. Every new piece of information was only torture.

"They put him to young person's prison. He was under age."

"And the rest of the family?"

"There was only mother. Dad is gone."

Fisher longed to ask more, but at the same time knowing made it worse. A shadow had suddenly been thrown across the house that had shone like a beacon in his life. It had been tainted, never to be purified again. His dream was disintegrating in the grip of some hideous disease, and with every question he was encouraging its grim metamorphosis.

To his surprise and reluctance, he noticed that they were almost there. But now he looked at the wooden house with different eyes as Heikki drove his car in, straight across the yard. The place was a grizzly crime scene, not a house of happiness at all. Even its brightness in the crystal-clear light was suddenly threatening; it was ominous, too vibrant, not benign. It worried Fisher now that he had been so taken in by what he had thought of as olde worlde charm. It shook his faith in his judgement. Did he really want to buy the house and live there, walking on floorboards where a gunshot victim had poured away his life-blood? The very thought seemed suddenly morbid. He understood now, why Heikki had asked about the floor.

But what about the goddess? He felt suddenly tired, completely drained. Damn Laine, for saying nothing. No wonder the man had been so keen to oblige. Only weariness kept Fisher's anger in check.

Heikki had already stopped the car. He ducked his head down and peered past Fisher towards the front door, then pointed with his finger towards the window just to its right. The window of the sort-of-vestibule. The white wooden trim glowed sprucely against the rich solid colour of the wall.

"In there. That is where he did it." Heikki straightened up. "Well, let me know. What is going to happen. I like to know." He started the engine. "Maybe we see in England wery soon. Or maybe you will puy still? You could puy somewhere else. Why you don't puy Hilppala? We keep in touch."

With a feeling of something approaching pain Fisher watched as Heikki disappeared in a spray of dust, back down towards the town and his own apartment. He would leave for England the following day. Fisher stopped waving then turned back to face the house. Now Heikki had gone there was no longer any protective barrier between him and what he had himself initiated; the purchase of a crime-tainted property. The place loomed over him now, oddly creepy. As if it knew he had found out, and was waiting to see what he would do next. Fisher forced himself to mount the porch steps, and reluctantly entered the door.

The sort-of-vestibule was just as he remembered it. It was sparsely furnished, just a very small table, a mat, a dresser, and a small corner cupboard. The room itself was pleasant enough, but one he had hardly been in, despite its position, for something about it had always left him slightly uncomfortable. Besides, there was no particular point to it, it was simply there. On one wall there was a tapestry picture of some game birds, and in the wall beside the dresser an empty hook.

This time, despite his preoccupation, Fisher understood as soon as he opened the door what it was about the room that made him feel unsettled. It wasn't the sense that someone had been murdered in here. It was something much slighter that had disturbed him, something so slight he hadn't even analysed it.

The mat was in the wrong place. The room was unaesthetically arranged.

It was quite a small mat, made of woven cotton strips, of the sort that had been everywhere in Hilppala and were also here. In some rooms they had been rolled up, in others, they were laid mid-floor, with the perfect Finnish eye for symmetry. But here the mat was too near the door and one of the walls. Most offensive of all, it was slightly askew. Fisher wondered why he hadn't automatically straightened it himself.

He bent down and lifted it clear, with a strange sensation in his stomach that was not to do with the trifling weight of the mat. The floor underneath it was clean.

So clean, that it was overall paler than the darker floorboards all around. But whereas the darker boards were uniform in colour, the pale patch was faintly piebald, with indistinct patches of a shade so subtle as to give them a kind of beauty. Nothing eye-catching. Just delicate tints, as if the area had all been scrubbed.

CHAPTER 16

It was cold in the evenings now, especially after darkness fell, and the crisp, bright moon that rose that evening looked down curiously on the small, hunched figure far below, huddled desolately on the disused well in the copse of trees past the orchard. He would have to abandon his plan to buy, thought Fisher. It was frightful, it was grotesque, to take on a house where someone had died so very gruesomely. Especially at the hands of his child. And that was only half of it. The atmosphere had suddenly changed here, he could swear it. Instead of mellow warmth he now felt evil leering out at him from every corner. As if the house was unhappy that its fraudulent cover of charm had been blown, and now was resentful and malicious. As for the sort-of-vestibule, the evil was tangible there; Fisher had dropped the mat back into place as if he was covering up a nest of snakes. Through his weariness and his jolted nerves he felt yet another searing burst of anger at the agent. To cancel his offer would serve him right.

Upstairs he looked around him at the small room with its single bed where he had camped now for more than two months. Was this where the boy himself had slept? Or rather not slept, probably, but lay and planned out his unthinkable, unspeakably hideous deed? The though was abhorrent. Only lack of alternative moved Fisher to even sit on the bed. He must pack his things, leave tomorrow, he could contact Laine from London. But one thing was certain, his dream was now nothing but a nightmare.

He was surprised in the morning to find himself waking up, after what he had thought of as a sleepless night. The goddess had not been to visit him. When he rose and went downstairs she was asleep on the wooden settle in the kitchen, breathing quietly, looking divine. He slipped past her and outside. There was a hint of autumn about the morning air. The warmth was a little thinner, the colours a little sharper and brighter than in the full, heavy summer. The sky was somehow a purer blue, the grass a more saturated green, the trees in the yard were tinged with glowing yellows and vibrant golds and reds. The whole scale of colours was more intense, as if the house was consciously trying to present itself at its best. It would not be easy to tear himself away, even though he now knew that the place was cursed.

And what of the goddess? If he left she would be no more than a torturing memory. He supposed that she and her lover would continue to live here after he went, for how could he ever explain to her the gruesome tragedy that had happened? If only he could get her to come with him to England! But he lacked the language to persuade her. He would not only have to tell her of the house's past, but dissipate her loyalty to her boyfriend.

Through the window he could see her head, for she had woken up, and was sitting at the table inside. He was tempted to go in to be with her but turned instead and set off restlessly up the road past the fields of stubble towards the distant forests, where the tumbling golden tresses of the birches reminded him of the goddess's hair and aspen leaves glowed like pale, bright coins against the sombre branches of the firs. When he came back, tired and still distraught, the house was unoccupied, regarding him forlornly through empty windows. He felt a sudden pang of pity for it. It wasn't, after all, the house's fault, what had gone on within its walls. The house itself was innocent, a victim splashed with blood. A bystander. Perhaps it even felt itself the shame of the memory it harboured, the secret stain it bore. That was why it was shabby now, no longer proud.

And suddenly Fisher felt a sense of loyalty towards it. He had come with love; the house had showered him with miracles when he did not accuse it for its past. It had changed his life, when his mind had been open. It had shown him new possibilities, it had even brought him the goddess. Suppose his mission was to bring back happiness to the house, to give it hope for itself? To restore it its warmth after the chill of sadness and abandonment and shame? 'I want to save its soul' – even Heikki had latched onto those words.

The magic, the goddess, the beauty, it was not just a one-way thing. He was here to help the house, to help it recuperate, and forget. Start anew. That was probably why all this had come about.

There was no need to leave it, no need even to be parted from the goddess or try and explain to her what had happened in the house they had come to share. It had healed his soul with beauty, and beauty is truth, and as such the key to all that is good. He would not abandon the house, he would rescue it. He owed it that.

The days and weeks that followed were idyllic. Fisher had once again opened his heart; his reward was to watch the pink house grow each day in peace and loveliness, set in the sumptuous beauty of the autumn. Even the goddess seemed to grow if anything more beautiful, somehow softer, even gentler, and even more shapely, if that were possible. Her form, as she slipped in beside him beneath the sleeping bag, seemed to Fisher since his crisis to be firmer and more substantial to the touch.

The only worry in those halcyon days was the lack of news from the agent, though September the tenth, the day when Fisher's rental contract expired, had come and gone. It made him nervous about being caught out unexpectedly in the house. Not long after, however, a letter from the agent did arrive, forwarded by Phillips from England, in which he said that he had not yet found the owner, but was looking still.

Meanwhile Fisher tried once again to make a desultory start on his book, but it was hard to concentrate, what with the goddess's presence, and the uncertainty, and the breathtaking autumn that so often called him to the window to look.

It did seem that the dog was getting even worse. Even the goddess seemed to have more trouble nowadays keeping the upper hand. She was somehow now less nifty at tying it up or getting out of its way, which could only mean that the dog had got quicker, unless the goddess had got slower. Or maybe she was simply tired of having to try and dodge it. At any rate, only the boyfriend could control it. Perhaps it liked his churlish manner and sullen face.

As soon as Laine got back to him, Fisher promised himself, the dog could go. The dog seemed to sense his plans, and give him a hard time accordingly.

It was odd to Fisher to bring to mind that the goddess and her lover almost certainly knew nothing of the house's past. In its charm and emptiness it must have seemed to them the perfect place for their tryst. Its bloodstained history was a secret that he and the house shared alone, and even he only knew of the event. Its circumstances had been lost already to the past. Or so he thought, until one afternoon when sitting on the porch it came to him that there was indeed one final link in existence. One living being that had probably witnessed not just the shooting, but everything else that went on. And now that being, guardian of that fateful secret, had come snuffling from out from its shed and was drawing near him, snouting in the grass as it came. As he watched it with loathing it looked up, curling its upper lip back from its fangs.

"What do you know about it all?" asked Fisher, and realised he had spoken out loud. A long, thin, string of drooling spittle made its way down from the corner of the brute's mouth and hung suspended.

"Eh?"

With a bark as sharp as an explosion, the dog leapt up suddenly high in the air at Fisher on the porch, its jaws wide open, yellow teeth flashing. Fisher scrambled rapidly to his feet and ran inside, pushing the door shut and leaning against it, scarcely able to even draw breath.

It seemed forever before he dared to move, dared to creep upstairs and look down from the window. The vile animal was digging in the refuse heap in the corner of the yard, its greyish-brown bony haunches sticking up in the air. He did not see it as first, because it almost blended in. As he watched it lifted its head and shoulders, and scoffed what it had dug up with a single toss and snap of its jaws. Then it shook itself, groomed itself briefly but obscenely, and trotted away.

Fisher became afraid to go to sleep. For sleep consisted now all too often, it seemed, of a nightmare about the dog. In his dream the fanged yellow arcs of its teeth were about to close about his nape and throat, engulfing his whole head in that stinking mouth. He would wake to find the saliva that it swam with was his own perspiration.

There was no doubt about it after what had happened to him on the porch; the animal really was getting worse. He wondered if there hadn't been some way he could have prevented it getting this hold on them all. But now it seemed even the goddess was losing her touch.

He remembered once again how she had penned it in its own shed with the spade as soon as she arrived; he remembered being drawn to the window by the sound of its demon howls. He didn't remember it making a fuss when her boyfriend turned up. It must have been out on its midnight ramblings, which was a shame. At that stage it might still have torn the callow young lout into shreds.

Against his will, the night of the young man's arrival began to run itself once more through Fisher's mind. It filled his mouth with a sour taste, but at least it was better than falling asleep and dreaming of the dog. He endured once more the pain of seeing the lovers in their embrace, felt again the hard wooden boards of the stairs as he mounted forlornly to his room. He had not slept. He had come down to close the door and pick up the towels and - wait! The dog was there! It was capering about in the moonlight on its rope. So it had been there, but the young man had somehow managed to keep it from barking.

Even now, it was galling, how that hopeless dolt could make the thing obey him, how he could tie it up or even chastise it without it attacking him. There were days when he even took it out with him in his van. It somehow seemed that only the obnoxious could discipline the vile with impunity. But what was his secret? Whatever it was, it seemed to come naturally to him.

At this point Fisher surrendered involuntarily to sleep, and dreamt not only of being messily devoured, but of the young man rewarding the dog for its gruesome good deed. He tossed it a biscuit or a lump of meat and then ran off, skipping and dancing, the savage beast frisking at his heels. As they ran, as they grew a little more distant, it seemed they grew younger; that the dog grew faster and lost its grizzle, and the young man became so young that he was almost back to a child.

When Fisher awoke he lay for a while, letting the pieces fall into place. And when they had fallen, completely of their own accord, he saw that the pattern they made was complete. As if a curtain had just been drawn back. The dog did not bark when the young man came because it knew him, and the dog obeyed him now as if he were its master, because he was. About the goddess there were only more questions, but Fisher knew now, like a dark void opening before him, who her lover was. He was the murderer. The boy.

CHAPTER 17

The boy was quiet on the bus journey home, but then, he was always quiet. That's what they all said afterwards – that, and that 'you never could tell, could you?'

It was August, the schools had only just gone back. If the boy had plans to murder his father or anyone else, he did not share them, although several people on the bus said later that they had distinctly seen a murderous look upon his face. It turned out they were not all thinking of the right boy.

His own friends said he looked out the window, with a nothing-in-particular expression. At his own stop he had said good-bye and got off the bus. Or maybe he had merely nodded.

The boy stood waiting by the side of the road until the bus had pulled away and disappeared, then he turned and made his way up the hill towards the farm where he lived. His bag was heavy; he had packed up his school books as usual, though he knew he would scarcely be opening them this afternoon. Perhaps he wanted even to keep life normal for as long as possible.

Near the top of the hill he turned in through the gate, and crossed the yard. The dog ran to greet him, but he kept on walking. He could see his father in the shed where the tractor was kept. When the boy reached the porch steps he mounted them slowly, then he went inside and put his bag down on a chair. He must not allow himself to waver, he had rehearsed it all. It was now. Commanding his mind to be empty he crossed the hall to the room on the other side, then he reached up and lifted the gun down from the wall.

CHAPTER 18

Fisher found himself horribly shaken to think that he had been living with a murderer for all these weeks. He could not for the life of him imagine what fragile shred of luck had preserved him up to this point. No wonder the fiend always wore that sour, vicious look.

It sent a chill down Fisher's back to recall that he had tried to think good of the fellow, unnerved him to think that he had misread evil for simple sulkiness. And as for the danger to the goddess – he could hardly contain himself when he thought of that. He must get away, and take the unsuspecting goddess with him, as fast as possible. He hated to abandon the house, to break his promise to it, but what else could he do? The evil still wormed around inside it, like a poisonous maggot.

It was nothing short of bizarre, Fisher mused, to find himself living with the son of the very person the agent was looking for. The murderer would know where his mother was. But it wouldn't do to contact Laine and thus give himself away; he would just have to hope that Laine was doing his own detective work. Meanwhile, to stay here was infinitely dangerous. Suppose that the young man had killed his father because of a hatred of father figures? If he had, Fisher himself might be living precariously on borrowed time. He was tempted to put a chair beneath the handle of his bedroom door at night, but couldn't, because he lived in hopes of visits from the goddess. Instead he took Heikki's kitchen knife and hid it beneath his mattress.

The goddess, he was sure, could know nothing of her lover's past. She would have been simply a child at the time. He wondered what stories the monster had spun to her, what lies he had used to lure her to be with him. And what were his intentions towards her? Did he love her or, unspeakable thought, (and here Fisher's blood invariably ran cold) was he also "planning" something for her? He watched her in agony, trying to work out ways of explaining to her who and what her boyfriend was, ways of convincing her of her predicament. If he could only get her to understand, they could leave at once, he could take her away with him back to England. He couldn't leave without her, and not just because he couldn't bear to leave her. It was vital to get her away from here while she was still alive. He dared not trust to her immortality, and she was precious to him beyond all measure.

Against the background of his own continual fear Fisher followed her as she went about her affairs, and each day as he followed her she seemed to him softer, more womanly and less girlish. As if it were becoming obvious that she was indeed truly intended for him. He had began to buy her little food treats from the supermarket down in the town, for she did not eat very well, he noticed, and nor did her lover. The estate agent's office, when he passed it, was always shut up.

It was in some ways easy enough to keep an eye on the goddess, for she didn't seem to do very much, but then, as a goddess, she was of course not required to. She never went anywhere except to the kiosk, to buy herself snacks or cigarettes, and still spent much of her time on the front porch, smoking and drinking beer. Such a beverage must, thought Fisher, feel like amber nectar flowing down her throat. Her only real activity was to heat up the sauna twice a week in one of the outhouses. She went to sauna alone, for the young man never seemed to go near anything cleansing if he could help it. The door she kept firmly shut, to keep the dog out, as Fisher explained to himself. It was the time that Fisher was most nervous for her, for it was dark there, with only the light from the wood stove, and a lamp in the dressing room. It filled him with fear, and when not with fear, with jealousy, for he could have joined her there in the cosy darkness, he was sure, if it weren't for his rival. For her safety he took to watching her from the darkness of another shed, armed once again with the knife, in case the young man or the dog attacked unexpectedly. Through his window he could see the window of the dressing room, and supervise the private rituals from which he was excluded.

It was seventh heaven to spy on her as she stood in the little room, arms raised, drying her hair, like a mermaid who had just risen up from the sea. She stood naked, which she never did when she was with Fisher, she was much too modest. The dusty panes of glass through which he peered distorted her somewhat, making her pink body dumpier and mischievously playing with her curves, but still it was a sight worth seeing.

It came as a shock when one night, when the young man and his van were not around, the goddess turned back on her way to the sauna and signalled to Fisher as he loitered in the yard, quite unmistakably beckoning him to join her. In the single small light of the dressing room distorting shadows seemed to give her face a challenging, almost amused look, then with a smile she motioned him into the flickering half-light and shadows of the sauna room, where only the woodstove fended off the darkness, and the air was stiff with solid, searing heat.

The goddess climbed up to an upper bench and threw down water onto the stove from a copper scoop. There was a hiss, and Fisher felt as if flames of heat were licking his face and running up inside his nose. He endured it for as long as he could, then ran out into the dressing room, showered and sat down to wait for the goddess to surrender. He would never understand how the Finns could stand it for so long, or even how or why they had invented that particular form of torture in the first place. But the heat was not the only thing in his mind at the moment; there was something else there niggling away, half unconsciously. It was not until the goddess came finally out to shower and dress, that he understood as he watched her, what it was. The distorting glass of the windows had not been distorting her at all. She was the same shape in the flesh. Somehow stouter and thicker than the image of her which he had worshipped daily. He had thought of her as the Mona Lisa, but naked she reminded him more of a Rubens. Why was it he had never seen the Rubens in her before?

There were only two explanations; that he had noticed her figure incorrectly, or that the she had put on weight. But how come? It wasn't the food snacks he had been buying her; he had found out that in her kindness she had been feeding them to the dog. This had grieved him, in spite of her altruism, but also surprised him, for in bed too she seemed to be plumpening up, and he had thought that it was the food. That she was accepting his tokens of love and care, and eating them in his absence.

The sound of the white van was suddenly audible, as it clumsily turned the corner at the bottom of the hill. Fisher had only time to seize his shoes and scuttle off across the yard to the house. There he dwelt much on the mystery of the goddess's changing form.

When she came to him a few nights later he slipped his hands around her buttocks, and then to her stomach, but she pushed him away and sprang up out of the bed. She tossed her hair and stood glaring at him rather resentfully, and he knew that by such movements he had transgressed the rights she had given him, but for once he ignored the expression in her eyes and stared at her figure, as she stood a few feet distant from him. He remembered the feel of her stomach when they had first made love, how it had yielded so softly to his touch that he felt it must be almost touching her backbone, but now it felt different. It felt solid, and refused to give, as if it were protecting something. It looked solid too, with curves that were heavy and self-assured. But it wasn't the food, she hardly ate. The goddess turned and left the room and went downstairs. He could hear from the sound of her feet that she was indignant, but the vision of her as she stood by the bed remained before his eyes, as he struggled to accept his own conclusions. This was not a situation that Fisher had personally met with before, but now he was sure that his senses were not deceiving him. The obvious, which he had never even dreamt of, had happened. The goddess was pregnant.

Fisher's first reaction was one of horror. How could it have not crossed his mind that he might get her pregnant? What was he to do? He felt stupid, not to have given it a thought. He remembered the mornings he had come upon her looking pale and dishevelled, and how he had merely retreated back upstairs, reluctant to acknowledge that there were times when even the goddess was not at her best. He could never have imagined her doing anything so grossly terrestrial as having a baby. Especially when she could not be more than fifteen or sixteen years old.

It was only his second reaction to acknowledge that the baby might not be his. He had, after all, only been her lover for a couple of months. He had no idea how pregnant she was, or how soon babies began to show; he and Millicent had never been blessed with offspring. She was certainly filling out. It would take nine months. When she gave birth, that might point to who the likely father was, but then again, not necessarily. Perhaps, as she was a goddess, there wasn't any earthly father anyway. Fisher had no idea, but one thing he knew; that, assuming there was, he wanted with all his heart for the child the goddess was carrying to be his. Because one, he loved her, and two, he had always wanted children, and not least three, because the all-too-likely alternative did not bear thinking about. That the father of the child was that odious young psychopath, the murderer.

The goddess, of course, could have no idea that the probable father of her baby was a dangerous criminal, nor, in her innocence and purity, would she ever suspect such a thing. If she were told she might not believe it. Or she might break down. Or, more rewardingly, once the truth had sunk in, she might fling herself on Fisher and beg him in the faltering English of his fantasies to rescue her, to save her from the monster and to take care of her and the unborn child that she carried.

And as he lay on his narrow bed and juggled endlessly with dates and likelihoods and possibilities, Fisher saw nonetheless that it did not really matter, for practical purposes, whose the baby was. His duty as concerned the goddess was in every scenario identical and perfectly clear, and her pregnancy only made it still more urgent to push on and execute his plan. He must rescue her, whether he could explain to her what he was doing or not. They must run away together, fly to England, start a new life with the baby. She could learn English, he would bring up the child as his own. The only problem that remained was, as before, how to bring it about.

He watched the goddess anxiously as she sat on the porch with a cigarette. Unruffled, lost in her own thoughts, as the white smoke wafted up in rings. As he observed her Fisher felt his whole being soothed and lulled, despite himself. In her contemplative state there was something statuesque about her. She had abandoned her denim jeans today and was wearing simply a bed sheet around the lower part of her body, for it seemed that the jeans no longer fitted and she had no skirts. The soft folds came down to her ankles, as if she was dressed in the style of the ancient Greeks. Around her shoulders she wore a jacket of the young man's, for the days themselves now scarcely carried any real warmth. Her face as she sucked and puffed was calm, almost noble, apart from the rounded softness it too had taken on. She looked at the same time both more womanly and more divine, thought Fisher. He suspected that she had seen him, and was tempted to blow her a kiss, but she looked so tranquil, so deeply engrossed, that he could not bear to disturb her. So he did not indicate that he knew she had noticed him, but retreated quietly indoors, his eyes brim-full of adoration. Then, from behind the living-room curtains, he watched her secretly as she sat there, Goddess on Olympus, musing dreamily against the wooden railings of the porch.

Katja pulled the jacket closer round her shoulders, rolled another cigarette and sat back against the wooden balustrade to reflect.

It was ok. Things were going ok. They could be worse. She would just have to keep a cool head and think.

She had already worked out where she would dump the baby when it was born. She did not actually turn her head towards the old well at the far end of the orchard, but in her mind's eye she reviewed again her preparations. And another good thing, she told herself, she knew where to put her hands on a lot of money. That always helped. And in case it vanished, she had kept back what she had taken when she first found it and hidden it safely.

But so far, the wad of money hadn't vanished, nor even got very much smaller since that memorable day when the agent had turned up and thrown her out. It seemed that since that time the disgusting old miser had hardly spent anything on himself. As she rolled with him under the sleeping bag she would check up on the smooth, stiff patch that the notes made, caressing them and feeling them safe inside their blue, quilted square. It helped her to take her mind off what was going on, to make it worthwhile. Of course, the whole thing was revolting, but she had no choice. It was simply a question of survival. And later, when all this was over, she could look back, not that she intended to do that, and know that it had all been for the best. After all, in its own weird way, the miser's presence here had also been a stroke of luck.

In her mind she saw herself standing once more at the gateway of the yard, as she had done those few months earlier, on her arrival. How relieved she had been to get here, and then how uncertain, as she stood there in the summer night, that this could really be the place where her aunt had lived. The yard was a wilderness, the house had bits hanging loose. Could it really have gone downhill in so short a time? Her aunt had been forbiddingly house-proud. For a fleeting instant, Katja had felt almost sorry for the woman.

She still held it had been a brainwave to come here, to have remembered the place would be empty. And best of all, no-one would ever come to look for her here. It would be a sanctuary till she got this baby mess sorted out. She had tossed her hair back and set about getting in, skirting round and approaching the house from the orchard, to be on the safe side. And then suddenly, in a frenzy of outraged barking, there was Kosto in the middle of the yard. She supposed it was Kosto. The beast was crazy enough, but it looked so thin. Wild and unkempt, as it always looked, but more so. And poised for attack. She would have to take a chance, do what they always did to fend it off.

Bending down, she had picked up a windfall apple from the orchard grass, and thrown it with all her might across the yard into one of the sheds. The dog had leapt high in the air, done a spin there, landed, and run in after the flying green object, so that Katja, running behind it, had only had to push the door shut, and ram the spade through the handle.

It was certainly Kosto. The thing's brain had always been its weak point. Its barks were much less audible from inside the stout walls of the shed. But what was it doing here? She had waited, but no-one had come out to see what the noise was. In the silence after the animal had given up barking, she had mounted the porch steps to the door. She had expected to find it locked but instead, as she prodded, it began to swing open. The familiar hall stood before her, deserted. She had stood with a sense of relief and triumph in the doorway of the kitchen. She had arrived. She could stay here to hide, to think, to sort things out till it was over; she must just first find somewhere to go and kip. She had turned round. At the top of the stairs stood a sleep-rumpled, gawping, middle-aged man in pyjamas.

And here he was now, nearly three months on, still gawping at her, but now from behind the curtains, those infernal strips of crochet that her aunt was always making. God, how he drove her mad, always staring. And even when he wasn't touching her, she could feel him undressing her with his eyes. But then, she was used to men doing that. The thought of his touch made her long to wash, to purify herself.

She had tried at first to pretend quite simply that he didn't exist.

She was tired, she couldn't be bothered with questions or answers. And anyway, it seemed that the man was quite incapable of talking. He always looked trapped, as if there was something he wanted to say, but he couldn't. It wasn't until she had been through his bags and found his passport that she had finally understood what was wrong with him. The ugly old git was a foreigner. English. Which meant, she supposed, that he didn't speak anything but that. She had been putting far too much effort into ignoring him.

She knew a bit of English herself, in fact. But that was something that she never intended to let on. She ignored him still; she had gone through his things because they were there. But the money, that hadn't been there in the beginning, she was sure of that. She had seen him through the crack in the door one afternoon, just counting it out, note after note, groaning and examining the unfamiliar slips of paper. There were more wads done up in paper bands on the bed. It came to her then that the goggling fool might be nothing short of a gift from heaven, if she stuck around and watched out for some sort of chance. She needed whatever it cost for an abortion.

It was next day that the agent had come and turned her out. She had come back, hoping to find the coast clear, and discovered in total surprise how the land really lay. A rental agreement made out to the miser lay on the table. He was not just an oddball wanderer, he was here officially. Why, she could not start to imagine. But the next thing would be, he would throw her out. Or get the agent to do it again. She would be homeless, and separated too from the money she had seen, if the miser hadn't given it all for the rent. She had checked the sum. He had had more money than that; he must still have a good stash somewhere. She must hang on to him, look for it, and hang on to a safe place to stay. She had fought down a sense of revulsion, as she had grasped just exactly what it would take, not to get thrown out. But she had to be strong. And as she had lain with him that first night, on his lumpy, makeshift bed, feigning passion and gritting her teeth, she had been aware of an oddly heavy square of quilt upon her midriff, and understood everything she needed to know. But she couldn't just take the money and run. She had no place to go. She didn't know where to get abortions. She had to stay put until she had worked out a plan.

And here she still was. She stretched against the hard wooden railings a little stiffly, for she had been sitting now for quite some time. It seemed fresh air was the only thing that made you less queasy when you were pregnant. The whole thing was ghastly. She didn't have the faintest idea whose the baby was or when it would come. Only, she supposed, that at some point it almost certainly would. She never had found out where they did abortions. Katja lit another cigarette, and wished she had brought out a can of lager. She didn't want to go inside for one. Even now she could feel his eyes gazing mournfully at her from the kitchen. She sighed.

She wondered if the miser had noticed that she was putting on weight. She didn't suppose that he had, he was doting, but completely stupid. Would he realise that she must be pregnant? She doubted it. A baby couldn't make you that fat, after all. Katja looked down. She was still quite slim, despite the sheet, really. Those jeans had always been on the tight side.

Taavi. That had been the biggest shock. She had never expected him to turn up. It appeared he had run off from wherever they had put him, and come here to hide, just as she had. She had tried to ignore him, as she had tried to ignore the miser, but all the same, she knew that she must be terribly careful. There was no more teasing the idiot, that was for sure. Not now they had all seen what he could do when provoked. If she needed to stay here, if she valued her life, he was someone she had to assess and to manage and placate. He had always hated her, she knew, just as she loathed him. She was never quite sure from minute to minute who had the upper hand. But just let him try and kill her. She would show him.

By mutual consent, they avoided each other as much as possible. But they got on each other's taut nerves, all the same.

Her cousin, the miser, a baby. What a situation! Katja wrinkled her nose in disgust, picked up her cigarettes and lighter, rose heavily to her feet and went inside.

By the time that Fisher saw the goddess walk through the room, the wrinkle had been absorbed back into her young, elastic skin, and her face had assumed the look of deep composure that was its passive state. Expressions took effort, she couldn't be bothered. She juggled with her problems inside. She was too young, her skin too firm, for life to have fixed the corners of her mouth in a downturn. As the goddess crossed the room, the look on her face was distant and serene.

CHAPTER 19

Fisher sat down at the table, aware that his stomach was churning uncomfortably. The letter was all in Finnish, beneath the estate agent's stamp, and dated the first of October. Attached to the page with a paperclip was a half sheet of English, hand printed.

Mr Fisher.
Here is the situation of the house you are interested to buy. I am sorry about the delay. It now seems that the owner is dead – you remember, that I had difficulties to find her. As my English is not good, I have written the situation to you in Finnish, I hope that Mr. Heikkila can translate it to you. Then let me know what you want to do. The house is now her son's, It would be his decision, if he wants to sell. I have tried to search him, but I cannot find him also. He is maybe abroad. I am sorry to disappoint you. Please return to me the key.
Best regards.
Markus Laine.

So that was that. The trail had disintegrated. Come to nothing, because the owner was dead. Fisher felt dumbfounded and disappointed and relieved. Yet a few blessed seconds still had to pass, before he understood the total import of the letter. That he himself actually knew where the son was, that the house would belong to. There was only one son: that dreadful, taciturn, patricidal lout with the dirty fingernails, who was right here under his roof. All this would be his! The house, the orchard, the sheds, the whole estate. Not only had he himself not got the house, it would have submit once again to that monster's tyranny. Fisher glanced about him in an agony of sheer disbelief.

There was something about the wording of the letter that puzzled him. What did Laine mean, tell him what he wanted to do? Did he mean that he would carry on searching, to ask the young man if he wanted to sell it? Well, the young man would never sell it if he knew who was buying it, that was certain. It was plain to Fisher that the fellow hated the sight of him. If Fisher wanted it, his only chance was to be an unknown buyer, from abroad.

There was also something else. If this was his house now, and he knew that his mother was dead, why had the young man not thrown him out? Perhaps he had killed his mother himself, and was playing the innocent. It didn't bear thinking about, yet Fisher found himself doing just that. Perhaps his own turn was coming next. Deeply troubled, Fisher put the letter down and went upstairs rather nervously. However he looked at things, it was high time to leave. But it must be with the goddess.

Things had lately become more urgent in any case. Time was moving on. The leaves of full, ripe September had fluttered away, and already the trees round the house lifted thin, crooked, naked branches to sky. But while the once-lush world around her was reduced to bare sticks and stems, the goddess by contrast was becoming plumper and more imposingly majestic every day. If he didn't come up with something soon, Fisher's senses told him, the goddess would be too enormous to board a plane.

As Fisher pondered these things in his heart the day drew on, and beneath him the goddess and the young man returned to the house, from their various and separate wanderings.

Katja came first, from her trip to the kiosk for food. She had only just noticed the letter to Fisher left lying on the kitchen table when she heard the sound of her cousin crossing the porch. Tucking the letter into her clothing she ignored him and retreated to her room, going in and closing the door behind her. Once in private she read the letter through. Then through again and again and again.

After this she sat on the broken-backed sofa while answers to the questions she had been asking herself rained down on her like falling stars from the sky.

He was trying to buy the house; that was why the ghastly old miser kept hanging on here. But did he actually know who Taavi was? Did either of them know who the other one was, or what they were doing here? She doubted it, since they couldn't share a word in common. So the miser wouldn't think of just asking Taavi where his mother was, and anyway he couldn't if he wanted to.

And all the while her aunt was dead! That answered that one. It crossed Katja's mind that her cousin had probably killed her – why stop with a job half done? Once again her heart gave a thrill, intermingled with a spiteful little tweak of satisfaction. It didn't protect you from anything, being house-proud. But that meant – oh horror of horrors, – that the house, this whole place, would indeed belong to her cousin! And here Katja's heart seemed to shrivel with bitterness a thousand times stronger than her fleeting pleasure of a moment before.

The blow was devastating. Unimaginable. It almost stunned her.

But she wouldn't be beaten. Facts were facts, it was what you did with them that mattered. It wasn't so much the information that was important, it was having it, especially having more of it than other people. It gave her the chance to do what she liked to do best in the world. The chance to scheme.

With any luck she could use those facts. To better her position, and maybe even to simply have some fun. It upset her that her cousin owned the house she was in, and eased the pain to think that he didn't know it, since nobody knew where he was to tell him, except for her. It amused her to think that the miser had no idea who his housemate was. But she still had to think on these things, to formulate a plan.

She copied down the agent's details, in case they should come in handy, checked the kitchen was empty, then going to the table bent down and placed the letter on the floor. Carefully but casually, as if it had fallen. Where Fisher would find it, because he would be looking, but the young man would not.

Fisher, on picking it up and rereading it, felt once more desperately disappointed. He was in love with the house. He wanted it. He wanted it to be rid of its evil.

He tried to reason himself into being philosophical. It was, he told himself, no more than a minor setback, a temporary delay. Laine might soon get news of the young man, and write to him; the young man might want to sell. What would someone of his sort want with a house like this? Fisher raised his head and stared absent-mindedly at the young man himself, who was currently stirring a saucepan of something meaty on the stove. Feeling the eyes on his back, the young man turned, and bored the penetrating gaze of one pale-lashed eye right into Fisher, with a sullen, unmistakeably vengeful look. There was a sty on his other eye that made it look smaller, reduced it a hooded, disfigured glint. He rarely looked at Fisher so directly, but today he did, as if he could read his thoughts. It was ten to one, Fisher deduced from that look, that the fellow had murdered his mother.

CHAPTER 20

The murderer's electronics business was going rather well. It was something he had learnt how to do "inside". He had set up a workshop in one of the sheds and went door-to-door in places where he was unknown, begging items to mend and then selling them on where he could. He was a genius with bits of wire, and careful to be honest. He dreamt of a new van. The one he had was always playing up.

Katja, watching him from the porch while he tinkered with the engine, registered absently that he wasn't bad looking these days. Till you got to know him. She was still on fire about the house. It was a sore that compelled her to pick at it constantly. It was all wrong that the half-baked cretin could murder his father, run off from jail, and then simply get back on his feet. It maddened her that she needed his goodwill, had to toe the line, keep his secrets, in order to be able to hide out here herself. He wasn't pregnant, nor did anyone even bug him. He had changed during his time inside, no-one recognised him. And now this. Some people had the most incredible luck. Except that Taavi's luck was something he didn't know of yet.

It was, all the same, a mistake to ask him, as she did in the grip of intolerable heartburn, how he felt about 'living here now', with respect to 'what had gone on in there'. She had nodded towards the sort-of-vestibule as she spoke, and succumbed to an ill-tempered belch.

She had expected a curt reply, but not quite what happened next. The young man turned white, then seized her by the neck and began to shake her. Katja put her hands on his wrists and let out a piercing scream.

"Don't! Don't! The baby.." The young man's voice when he spoke was merely a whisper. "You can get out, baby or not."

A door opened up above and he quickly released her.

Fisher understood at once that he had interrupted a quarrel and withdrew, embarrassed, but the sudden shrill scream and the look on the young man's face had frightened him. How could the goddess ever defend herself if the murderer turned violent once again?

Even Katja understood that this time she had overstepped the line. She had gone too far with baiting him, and now he was going to make life hell.

He would kick her out for the slightest reason, just as he had said. She would have to apologise to him in order to survive. She would have to grovel, and beg him to allow her to stay, to wash his clothes for him and make his food. She would have to accept humiliation until she could hit on revenge. If push came to shove, she could hardly rely on the love-sick ghost for protection. He seemed to keep out the way himself when her cousin was around.

The young man made new rules. They were her last chance. The stranger drove him wild, but Katja was beginning to make his blood seethe. He hated the sight of her more each day, hated the very sense of her presence in the house.

Even his new decree that she must make herself useful and do the cooking turned out only to make things worse, for as a cook she was reluctant and inexperienced. Beyond the realms of sausage she was ill-equipped to cope with the catering. It was always sausage with Katja as housekeeper. Sausage soup, roasted sausage, sausage chopped into cubes or slices, sausage with potatoes. Sausage with ketchup. Potatoes with ketchup. Potatoes. Sometimes the young man got meat from somewhere, and then he cooked and ate it himself. Perfected the art of braising carrots and onions.

The electricity one night just ceased without a pop or a flicker, and thereafter no longer jumped to attention when the switch was thrown, or rose to the hotplates of the cooker when summoned; they had to cook on the old-fashioned kitchen range.

It was on a sausage night that Katja after the meal collected up what was left unused of the firewood and started to carry it towards the door. The young man cleared his plate and dumped it in the sink. "You haven't washed up."

"I'm off to the sauna." Her arms were full of wood. "You can wash up yourself."

"It's your job. And by the way, you are taking the wood. Which we need for heating the water up."

"I got the meal. There's plenty of hot water left. Check it yourself if you don't believe me." The young man turned and lifted the lid of the large aluminium saucepan that was still on the range. It was almost full of steaming water. He pulled it back onto the hottest part of the surface. She could bloody well wash up before she went. And leave the firewood. As he put the lid back down he heard the door close, softly and sweetly now, because he had filed down its edges. He ran and opened it, in time to see Katja leave the porch and go loping clumsily across the withered grass of the yard. It was cold out. Winter would not be long. Behind him he heard a hiss as the water boiled and bubbled over onto the range. By the time he had stopped and lifted the lid off and run out after her she had locked herself into the sauna shed, where the light from the fire as she fed it with fresh wood flickered softly over the unpainted walls. The door was firm and its lock well-oiled now and quick to turn. The young man could only bang ineffectually on its stout wooden surface.

"I'll kick you out, you lazy slut. You see if I don't. You and it." He rapped on the window and glared in, pressing his face against the pane. Katja attempted quickly to cover her nakedness, but the towel was no longer big enough to cover the vastness of her body.

"It's not your house. Your mother doesn't know you're here."

If he had killed his mother, now surely he would say so. Her own boldness scared her. What would she do, if he did say that? He would certainly kill her too.

"It is my house. It's my family's house. I have the right to be here. You don't."

Katja pulled a face at him through the window, as bad as she dared, then the thought came to take the key from the lock. So he couldn't get in with any fancy tricks.

"Your mother wouldn't want you back here!" She shouted through the keyhole, when she could feel the night air blowing through it. "You mur – She was going to shout 'murderer', but thought better of it, and stopped before he could recognise the word.

All the same, the young man was visibly stung by the probable truth of what she had said.

"Well she certainly wouldn't want you," he shouted, bending to the keyhole himself. "I'll find her and tell her you're here and she'll kick you out. She'll be disgusted. You just wait."

"You've no idea where she is. You'll never find her."

"I will. I haven't had time to look yet. But I will."

"I don't think so," shouted Katja. "You'll never find her!"

"How do you know?"

She was back on dangerous ground. She must change track. And somehow escape. She couldn't stay here all night. She lowered her voice. "And anyway, she's trying to sell this house. That's why she wouldn't want you here."

"How do you know?" the young man repeated. She didn't know whether he'd heard the bit about selling the house. He raised his voice, its tone became angrier.

"You know where she is. You know where, don't you? Well, I'm not going to let you out until you tell. I want to know."

"I've no idea where she is. And I've got the key."

"You tell me! You tell me where she is, this minute! You're a lying, deceitful, rotten, stinking piece of..."

"I don't know where she is!" bawled Katja, as loudly as she could. The shouting was beginning to give her a headache. The baby gave a kick, with a violence she felt compelled to pass on. A viciousness she had to discharge. She stabbed the key back into the lock, spun it round and flung the door open suddenly. The young man jumped back in surprise.

"I just happen to know she's been trying to sell this house. To be shot of it. So it looks like she wasn't expecting you. Or planning to have you back."

"How do you know? Who told you?"

"I just heard. I don't remember who from."

"So you don't know it's true."

"I bet it is. How could she know you were going to turn up? You're supposed to be still in jail. And if someone else bought it, you'd have to pack up and go."

"I'm going to find her." In the light from the sauna she could see his eyes begin to glitter and spark. "I'm going to tell her what's going on here. And she'll kick you out, whatever she does about me. You just wait!" and the young man turned from her abruptly and strode back across the yard. Katja's anger rose again as the parasite behind her navel gave another kick.

"You'll never find her!" she shouted after him, through the darkness. He turned round on the porch.

"I hate you! I hate you, you fucking bitch!"

"Your mother is dead!" shouted Katja after him, at the top of her lungs.

But the young man did not hear her, because he had just slammed the door.

It was only from the fact that she was still alive that Katja knew her cousin had not heard the final line. She was very lucky, and she had been very unwise. It had been a decidedly close shave.

She could not bring herself to apologise, but she did her best to act contritely. When the young man began to grill her again on the subject the next day, she answered only that it was something that her mother had said was being considered, she didn't know any more than that. But the young man was dissatisfied. A nagging feeling obsessed him, and a memory of an unsettling incident which he had suppressed. Well, she wouldn't get away with it. He would check out the broken 'for sale' notice he had come across in the shed. It must have a number on it, or a name, some indication of where it had come from. The young man rose and went to his workshop where he mended things, and where he had cleared the rubbish from the front room into the back, to set up his workbench.

The second room looked strangely neat and bare, although he had put all sorts of stuff there. And then he remembered. He had one day pulled out anything wooden and chopped it up for firewood. It created more space and saved a couple of trips to the forest.

The advertising board had gone. He had probably already fed it into the range.

As she looked from her window, the young man's expression as he crossed the yard struck terror into Katja's heart. He was going to kill her! She knew it for sure. With regard to what happened next, Fisher was, as he was for most things that happened in his life, completely unprepared. Drawn out of his room by some sort of feeble intuition, he saw the goddess already lumbering up the stairs towards him, hauling herself up step by step with the aid of the wooden banister. She was puffing and gasping for breath, and with her free hand she held up the hem of the sheet that she wore, to prevent herself stumbling. She was half way up when the young man came slamming in through the door, his face full of thunder, but he only glowered at the back of the goddess as if to warn her that her time was almost at hand. Not yet, but soon. Then he strode off into another room.

There was murder in that look! Fisher grabbed the goddess and tried to pull her into his own room, which was easy, for she did not resist. On the contrary, she seemed quite anxious to get there. Behind the closed door, shaking with his fear and his boldness, Fisher held her hands in his and stared imploringly into the ice-blue eyes while the words he had withheld for so long came tumbling out.

"England," he said. "England. We must run away!" Taking both her hands in one hand he began to fumble for his passport from among his belongings. "Run away. You, me." He had found it. Releasing her he marked out a triangle in the air with his forefinger, tracing it out between the passport, his own breast and hers.

"You, me, England. I love you."

To his exultation the goddess seemed to understand him at once, for bursting into tears and breaking down into a stream of unintelligible protestations, she gave her obvious consent with a series of vigorous nods of her head.

When she got to the village it seemed to Katja she had lived there only in a previous life. It was afternoon, and apart from memories, the place seemed deserted. As she passed the houses of people she had known she viewed each one with equal revulsion, but no-one from the past came out to meet her, and after a while her own home came into view.

She did not have long. She must go about her business quickly. She knew where her passport was. And at this very moment, to go to England would be like getting to the Promised Land. She would be free from her troubles, and from Taavi, and out of the trap she was in. Of course, she would be lumbered with the miser, but he came with money.

It was too bad she couldn't simply rid herself of the baby. That was the cause of all the trouble. But it couldn't be long now; she was awfully big. It was bound be born dead or die at birth. An escape to England would be just the thing to tide her over.

It was better than that. London was a place she had always wanted to go.

Fisher noticed as soon as he awoke next morning that the goddess had come back and pushed the passport under his door. He felt immediately buzzing with excitement, as he took the passport back to bed to savour its contents.

It was not just that this was the document on which all depended. It would tell him all those things about her which he longed to know. Her age, her full name. Where she came from. He opened the passport at the photograph page. Her image stared up from it, a chubby little girl, rather disconcerting him. The features were hers, in a way, but they were rounded, babyish. They were rounded now too, because she had put on weight, but in a different way. He looked at her date of birth, her full name; it was wonderful to have all that information before him. She was sixteen. He rifled through the visa stamp pages but they were empty save a single stamp on one page. Perhaps a school trip. He returned to her photograph. She looked so young. He looked at the issue and expiry dates.

The passport was out of date.

The expired passport was like a portcullis coming down in front of Fisher, trapping them both. He had not the faintest idea how to get her a new one, in this foreign country. He would have to write to Heikki, confide in him, ask him for advice. It would all take time, and the goddess would not be able to travel, very soon. It was beginning to look as if they would be stuck here until the little one was born.

CHAPTER 21

On a winter's day, when the stillness of the air was palpable, and the cold bit Fisher's hands and stung his cheeks when he went out, he noticed that a little snow had fallen in the night. So scantily there was scarcely more than a white thread along the branches of the trees, a light dust on and between the black, curled corpses of the leaves on the ground, but all the same, it lent a new, invigorated aspect to the world. It reminded Fisher that the winter was really on its way. He was sorry that the snow had come while he was asleep, and that he had missed that most symbolic moment. But that afternoon as he sat by the window more snow began to fall, first the odd flake, then more and more. It began to come down silently, abundantly; when Fisher looked up to the grey, cloudy sky it was full of dark flakes springing from nothing and growing larger, turning white on their downward passage as they passed him. Snowflakes flew to the window pane just in front of him and clung there, dark against the white blur behind them, while the in the yard the bare ground had almost disappeared. And though agitation still burned in Fisher's breast, there was at least a part of him that as he watched became calm and stilled.

The young man too looked out at the gathering snow, but its beauty slid off his black depression like water off a duck's back. This was his twenty third winter, and he set out merely to take it in his stride. He scraped the ice and snow from the windscreen of the van, broke the ice on the water in the dog's bowl, chopped wood and hunted out the snow shovel. He ignored the stranger whom he could not account for and devoted himself to making life miserable for Katja. It was the only way he could make her presence bearable to himself. And in between, as he stared at the soundless, pristine beauty of the snow and the dark, heavy, snow-loaded promise of the winter skies, he gave himself over to anger and despair. He berated himself for his cowardice - time was getting short, it had as good as run out. It was winter already. He had been here for months, almost half a year, and he had not yet carried out his vow. He had come here and mended TVs, fought with Katja and ignored the stranger, and now he chopped up wood for the fire, but all that only ran counter to the real reason why he had come here.

He had come here to die.

It was because there were others here, because he was not alone, that he could not find peace to get it done. He had escaped from one place where he was always watched to another place where privacy was denied him. It had been a total mystery what they were doing here, in a place where there should be no-one but him. Why Katja was here he now understood, the stupid cow, but the weirdo? Who was he? And what was he doing there? Always standing gawping from somewhere, like some ancient fool in a trance. He believed his cousin when she said she had no idea who he was. That he had simply been there when she got there, goggling at her from the top of the stairs.

They flustered him, they threw him off his stride, though he wasn't sure why. There should be nothing about their presence that should stop him from carrying out his plan. Dead was dead. But it disturbed him that they were here. They were intruders, in his home, in his head. They had no right to be here.

It had been summer when he had escaped. All about him as he had taken his first breath of freedom the world had been growing, pulsating, unfolding. Unfrozen at last it was bursting into blossom in the sun. The lake had sparkled as he walked beside it; above it birds wheeled and soared in a sky so huge that their forms were often no more than pinpricks in its brightness. As if life was reaffirming itself through everything round him. But inside the young man himself was nothing but a hard, black kernel of anger, the only thing living in an otherwise dead grey soul.

They were calling to him, his accusing demons, as real and tangible to him once again as if they were true flesh and blood. As if they were living beasts, with hide and hair and weight. Upbraiding him, demanding that he do his duty, reminding him that they shouldn't have to wait any longer. Making clear that he was betraying the truth with his weakness.

He bargained with them. He wanted to see his own home. Make his peace with what had gone on here, touch its walls one more time. He would leave his body here while his soul, released, flew off into the infinite darkness. He was not prepared, as he walked to his own Gethsemane, to walk into Katja. He had leapt upon her when they had met, to throw her out. She had sunk her teeth in the soft flesh where his neck met his shoulder. Like a vampire. She had had her teeth in his flesh ever since.

So now when the young man stared from the ice-patterned windows at the white layer deepening round about, he did not look on the whirling snowflakes with the same mix of boyish delight and awe as Fisher, or even the same bored indifference as the jaded, bad-tempered mother-to-be. He noticed only that in contrast to the joyful abundance of the summer, the world around him now sang in perfect harmony with his mood. In the monochrome yard beyond the window the trees were stark beneath a sky the colour and weight of lead, while around them the snowflakes hurtled listlessly down on their flight towards the dreary, dispirited earth.

Now, if ever, was the right time to add the final note to the sombre chord. As the winter wrapped him round the young man's inner promptings began to grow louder and more insistent, and at the same time he grew more fearful every day.

The truth was, his own plans scared him more, now that so much time had elapsed. Perhaps it was the thought of the pain, or else, despite himself, the irreversibility of it all. Yet he still saw, as clearly as he had on that first day, the day of his endarkenment, that none of it, none of the tedious process of being alive, had even the slightest jot of common sense behind it. The whole thing was nothing more than an endless succession of ultimately pointless routines and rituals designed to stop one glimpsing or worse still falling through to the infinite nothingness underneath. There was no point behind any of it in the end, and now that the he had seen that, the young man's very existence had become to him a source of shame. A mark of weakness. It fell to him, it was clear, to efface that existence, to pull the hands of the world from its eyes by his own example.

As for those he had come across who claimed they had 'seen the light', the young man did not know if he envied or pitied them, for he had seen the dark, and knew which one was the great and ultimate, underlying truth. Knew towards which state his own path irreversibly lay.

Yet whatever the reason, he had still not carried out the necessary deed. His father was dead, and he himself was still around. And meanwhile, day and night rotated, time rolled on, and around him the rest of the world was still complacent in its blindness. Would continue so, until he had been the first to make a stand.

To run from his plans until he could get rid of Katja and the mournful ghost the young man busied himself and did odd jobs round the house, for that was his nature. To fend off a daily inner fear of what he must do, he grew more industrious, sought to displace his conscience with activity. He put the house in order, not because he was planning to live there, or even because he was planning to die there, but because it needed to be done, for the neglect that it had suffered was beginning to affect its condition. He collected TVs and vacuum cleaners and mended them; each unfinished job postponed his departure, for it wasn't fair, he told himself, to let his customers down.

Quickly, quietly, remorselessly, the snow had taken possession of the land. The nights were now no longer impenetrably black, but the contours of the land were always visible, and on clear nights the snowy fields glowed in the moonlight and sparkled in the light of the stars.

Katja did not smoke on the porch these days, but in the kitchen, staring out of the window. She was heavy, quiet and withdrawn, and had ceased to pay any attention to her dress. She seemed somehow terse and rather unhappy; indeed, if she had not been a goddess, Fisher might almost have thought her expression a little sulky. In the yard the snow lay spread out between the buildings, wall to wall and door to door; at first rumpled, like a sheet on an unmade bed, and then gradually smoother and smoother, re-forming after every snowfall. It hid its depths treacherously and the rough places were indeed made plain; in places its white mass drifted to over a metre deep. Fisher, returning from a short winter walk at dusk, while the young man was out in his van, stopped short on the road, just opposite the house. The weather was clear, the sky a luminous but darkening blue above the ragged, snow-capped fringes of the forest.

Though the moon had already risen high enough to turn to silver, and in the house the lamp in the kitchen was already lit, the night had not yet leached all the colours from the earth. In the biting cold Fisher stood stock still, lost totally in exaltation. There before him, in the bluing snow, framed by the forest and the last strands of pale daylight in the sky, was the winter jewel, the fairytale house of the magazine.

CHAPTER 22

In the homely yellow lamp-light of the kitchen, on a freezing January night, the goddess gave a little scream. The young man was out. Fisher, who had given up hoping that she would rouse herself to show him any attention, turned round on the stairs and came back down again, disconcerted, but the goddess ignored him. She was gripping the edge of the table with both hands, and had lowered herself to the bench with a little gasp; behind her, her shadow sank in a spreading mountain across the wall. When she did look at Fisher, it was somehow as if she looked straight through him, except for a shade of what seemed almost like resentment. As he hovered, the goddess let out a long, moaning howl, put her hands on the enormous basin belly that threatened to suck in the rest of her, and then a hand on her back. Anxiously Fisher rushed across to her, but she waved him away, with a look he was almost obliged to interpret as fury. He slunk back up to his room, and left the door there open a crack.

It was indigestion. It was probably no more than that. And anyway, the young man would be back soon. The goddess was quite quiet, really, apart from periodic groans and shrieks, accompanied by exclamations he could not interpret. In between it would all go silent again. When Fisher peeped down surreptitiously she was standing by the window, looking out, as if waiting for the young man to come home. She was holding the small of her back.

It must be indigestion. Let it be that. Not in heaven's name the baby, which Fisher had long since come to imagine would never happen. He supposed he should check by timing her cries and making sure they were subsiding, getting fewer and further apart. He took off his wristwatch and laid it on the bed. Where, oh where was the blasted murderer, when for once he was wanted? The goddess gave a moan, then screamed and shouted at the top of her lungs. Fisher shot out and flung himself down the stairs. When he stood before her she stared at him gasping, mouth ajar, panting. Her forehead was wet.

Fisher stared back. He must do something. Fetch a neighbour, get her to hospital. Run out and look for the murderer. She was having a baby, here in the house, with nobody here except him.

"Don't worry," he heard himself say to her, feeling the panic surge through his own frame like in a cold, foaming wave. "Don't worry, I'll get help." He left her and leapt up the stairs, pulled on more clothes with fumbling fingers. It seemed that a cold draught wrapped around him even as he put on the extra layers. When he came downstairs the front door was open.

The kitchen was deserted. When he looked out, the goddess was ploughing her way across the yard to the sauna, stumbling and lumbering through the knee-high drifts of snow. Fisher hesitated. Should he put on his boots, or just run straight out after her in his socks along the deep, pitted tracks she had left? Where was she going? And where was the dog? Then in spite of himself he felt the freezing snow beneath the balls of his feet like a shock, like a pain, as he plunged and scrambled in the goddess's footsteps to catch her up.

He was too late; his moment's hesitation had cost him dear. By the time he had almost got to her the goddess had reached the sauna, pushed her way in through the door and shut it behind her. He heard the short, sharp clack of the bolt being driven home, against the longer drawn-out sound of a piteous groan. Locked out, he stood at a loss what to do, until the pain from his stockinged feet in their cradles of white, trampled snow became unbearable, upon which he returned disconsolately to the house.

His feet burned and stabbed. They were numb and clumsy, as Fisher hobbled round the kitchen. He did not know how to rid himself of the pain. And all the while, his mind was busy with the problem of the goddess. What should he do? Fetch a neighbour, get help? But the neighbours were scattered. And anyway, how could he explain? He should try to help her himself, but she had shut him out. In any case, he knew nothing of babies and how to deliver them. Truth to tell, he knew nothing about babies. At that moment of anguish, mental and physical, he heard the sound of the young man coming home.

The goddess's lover, Fisher told himself, would see the light on in the sauna when he parked the van. The goddess would hear his arrival with relief, and avail him of her plight. It would not do for him to interfere. He could not in any case have been of any use. He had not even understood the words that the goddess had shouted in her pain. Fisher dragged himself wincing to his room and zipped himself quickly into his sleeping bag, but pull it as high as he might his ears still heard the distant shrieks and groanings of the goddess. They went on hour after hour, muffled and half imaginary, till he felt he could no longer stand it, but was too tired to do anything but lie. Then came the distant coughing sound of the young man's van and the sound of its engine starting up then fading rapidly away. There were no more noises from the goddess, Fisher noticed anxiously, whatever that meant. He should get up. He should go and see what had happened. But the pain in his feet when he put them down to the floor was still unbearable. Before he could bring himself to make a second attempt, he fell asleep.

It had not snowed in the night. The sky was a clear, bright cloudless blue when Fisher awoke, and sunlight sparkled on the smooth cones of snow that capped the trees. From the strength of the light he could guess that it was already quite far into the morning. It was a moment before he recollected the events of the night before. The goddess's baby! How could he possibly have slept at such a time? The goddess's baby had come. His baby? The young man's? He must work out the number of months. Fisher listened. There was an eerie silence that filled him with an inexplicable dread. The house had an empty feeling. When he opened the door and went out onto the landing he could sense that the kitchen below him was deserted; what daylight there was these days poured in freely through the windows, now that it no longer had to pass through lilac leaves. The room lay quiet and self-possessed, as if, like the rest of the house, it had a life of its own quite apart from that of those who inhabited it. There was no sign that anything had happened there. And no-one about. No goddess, no tiny new baby, no young man. Fisher went gingerly down the stairs, and summoned the courage to open the goddess's door. The room was empty. Looking out from the window he noticed that the young man's van was still gone. When Fisher had carefully eased on his boots, he went out. The yard too was empty, but now the snow there no longer looked like a bed-sheet; its white expanse was heavily criss-crossed by the marks of feet. In a trail of miniature chasms and waves countless paths ploughed haphazardly across the once-smooth wastes, the sunlight glinting on their tiny peaks and troughs. If it had snowed at all in the night there had been but a sprinkling. Not enough to cover whatever the small, pink, ragged flowers were that had sprung up and were now blooming everywhere.

Like little pink daisies in the snow they were scattered in the tracks that led between the front door and the sauna, and in the tracks that led across to the space where the young man parked his van. Fisher could see from where he stood that the snow round the sauna door was thick with them. He had left his glasses upstairs; he bent down and peered short-sightedly at one of the flowers. It had a deep red, slightly fringed centre, around which radiated soft pink petals, their edges so delicate they all but faded imperceptibly away. He reached down and touched one gently. It wasn't a flower. More like a bloodspot on the snow. He stood up. With an unpleasant faintness he made his way along the flower-strewn tracks across to the sauna. It was empty.

The dressing room had just been left in disorder. There were clothes and other items strewn around, and a bowl of frozen pink ice with a half-submerged frozen piece of sponge. There were brown-stained cloths, an empty bottle. From the sauna room itself, where the door stood half ajar, came a faint but disagreeable, unidentifiable smell. Fisher pushed the door open nervously. The windowless room with its wooden benches was in total darkness, for the only light came from the dressing-room window and the doorway now occupied by Fisher. It was some time before he could make out the brown stains on the benches, but as soon as he did, he feared they were blood. He waved a hand across them, to see if they were shadows, but they weren't. They were pool-shaped with tiny outgoing channels, as if blood had run along the grooves in the bench; there were streaks down the bench side, as if blood had overflowed from somewhere and started to run down onto the floor.

Was it blood? Was it still wet? Squeamishly Fisher moved to touch it. As he did so his foot touched on something that blocked its way softly and spongily, the something from which the strange and slightly unpleasant smell was emanating. He bent down, and realised then that he had not till that moment ever really understood what squeamishness meant. His foot was nudging into a small heap of something that looked like offal, as far as he could make out. A strange, messy lump of something fleshy, to do with the body, surrounded by a dark pool of what was all too obviously blood. Fisher stared down, unable to draw his gaze away from the dimly-lit, mysterious heap, and felt his own guts rise to his throat. He forced himself to try and imagine what it could be; he felt somehow a gruesome duty to know the worst. He should never have let the murderer stay loose. But the heap was not a baby, not even a dead one. It had no bits that could have been arms or legs. It was too flat and limp to be a head. Was it part of the goddess? Had that feckless brute finally killed her too? Fisher stared again at the vile mess that was a body part. It was lank, flat and bloody, slapped carelessly down in a mess of congealed gore. He crouched down. Its faint smell wafted up to him. If it were not half-frozen, it was clear that it would reek to high heaven.

With a start Fisher realised that the young man's van had come back into the yard and pulled up just outside the shed that did for a winter garage. Quickly he ran outside and pulled the door to behind him, just a second before the van door opened and the young man climbed out. Behind him he could see the dog untethered on the front seat, leaping up and down. Its barks grazed his ears like volleys of gunfire.

"What have you done with my goddess? Where is Katja?" shouted Fisher, at the top of his lungs, but his words were drowned by the non-stop fire of noise from the dog. The young man ignored the questions and made his way towards the house. He had not heard. And of course he would not understand. Although, thought Fisher wrathfully, he could probably guess.

He would show him. Now was the time. Fisher started to plough his way across the yard towards the wooden house, staggering and stumbling though the soft white freezing trenches. He missed his footing and sank to his knees in the snow, was obliged to perform laborious antics to right himself again. He would show that murderer. He must know what had happened to the goddess and her baby, must find out what the young man had done. He must make him understand, that he was being called to account.

Halfway across the yard Fisher gave up the uneven struggle and stood panting. Of course, he should go back first to the sauna. Take in all the evidence. Weigh up what might have happened. Then, when he had forced the young man to understand him, he would have more idea of whether the fellow was lying. Fisher retraced his steps more carefully in the deep, scuffed holes he had already made, feeling his feet like ice and his trousers clinging wetly to his legs, and pushed the door of the sauna open again. There once more were the dressing room, the frozen bowl, the tumbled clothes and sheets. More resolutely this time, he opened the inner door. A thin strip of dull light from the dressing room fell across the floor and crept up the bench. Beside it in the gloom lay the small, fetid mass of he-wasn't-sure-what, in its own little lake of blood. Again that faint, sickening smell, only kept in check by the cold.

It only took a second. The dog nearly knocked him down. For once, he did not hear it coming. It bounded in silently, without a bark, just no more than a panting noise as it got up close. Fisher heard it wheezing as it passed him, felt its waving, muscular tail smite his legs again and again. It sniffed the heap. Fisher took a timid step forward to restrain it, but even he was not prepared for what happened next. In a single movement the dog bobbed and lifted its head, as it tossed the lump of flesh down its throat. He could only look on paralysed with horror, as the dog shook its head side to side while the slivers of tinted ice melted and dripped down from its jaws. Before it had even licked them clean, Fisher had rushed outside and was sick.

CHAPTER 23

What preoccupied and fortified Katja as the taxi dropped her off at the pink house were not the joys and challenges of motherhood, but the vision that had come to her in her two-week stay at the hospital. A prospect of revenge and advancement rolled irresistibly, fool-proofly into one. Lying musing in the endless hours while the nurses tended her baby she had hit upon a wonderful plan, a stroke of genius compared with simply running off. They should not go to England. She should hide her passport when it came. She must fix things so that Taavi sold the house to the miser, and then, as the lady by the miser's side, it would all be hers. She would make well sure then that Taavi noticed who was really taking over his childhood home. She would walk around with a notebook, taking measurements, and make out she was going to modernise completely. The thought was delightful.

The baby was crying. It brought her back to where she was, which was out in the snow at the roadside with a babe-in-arms and a towering mountain of equipment. With a peevish sigh Katja tucked the screaming baby under one arm, took a couple of carrier bags in her free hand, and crossed the road.

The sauna was silent and closed up as she passed it, its traumas already buried deep under endless layers of soothing, peacefully falling snow. The land's white crust as she plodded through it revealed no trace of the little pink daisies that had sprung up in her wake as the young man had propelled her across the yard.

She hated him. She hated him for the way he had treated her the night that the wretched baby was born. Like a pig. Like one of his father's farm pigs. She would give her own life, if only to get him for that. And when she had screamed at him that she was dying, he had shoved her in the back of the van, where the TVs went, and put the baby on the front seat. He had dumped them both at the hospital and gone away.

Fisher since the disappearance of the goddess on that night had been going almost mad with worry and despair. Where was she? Was she safe? Was she even alive? Supposing, heaven forbid, that her immortality had failed her? It didn't bear thinking about. And what about the baby? The baby that Fisher now realised, sadly, could not be his; nine months would take it back to April, before he had even come here. He longed to ask the young man where the goddess was, and where was his baby, but the young man kept himself to himself. Most incredibly, he went about his life as normal. It was as if the goddess had never existed. It was classic psychology, the mark of the abnormal mind. If all was fine with the goddess, and the young man a father, then where was his joy? Or his grief, if something terrible had happened? Or if, as Fisher could not stop himself from suspecting, the young man had turned his hand again to evil, then where was his repentance, and his guilt? How could the young man just live like this, from day to day?

It was while he was staring mournfully from the window one morning that the goddess came trudging across the snow with a baby under her arm.

It was hard for Katja as she walked in, to know which was worse – her cousin's expression or the miser's, the maudlin longing in his tear-filled eyes, red-rimmed and drooping, like a bloodhound's. Her cousin's face expressed simply horror. As if, she noted bitterly, he expected her to have died. Certainly not to have come back here. She would have to convince him that as soon as she could, she would go off to join the baby's father abroad. Otherwise he might throw her out, or worse still do her in.

She got the impression he had practically had his fill, which meant that as grace time in the house now she had just until the brand new passport arrived. Or at most until Taavi found out she had received it. But how long did that give her? From now, six weeks at the most, in all likelihood. Six weeks of clinging to the miser like a limpet. Six weeks to make it all happen.

The best thing was, the plan could not fail. It could not fail, because she was the only one who held all the cards. Who knew everything about everyone. Her hand was superb. And when it was over, and Taavi vanquished, she could ditch the baby, take the money, and make herself scarce. With her passport she could even go abroad.

That Taavi would be keen to sell the house, she did not doubt. It was simply a matter of the agent getting in touch, and letting her cousin know that it was his now. The only snag was, the agent was probably not even looking for him any more. And if he was, he would probably never come here. It was up to her, to get the ball rolling there. She must think of something.

CHAPTER 24

On one of his rather rare visits to his previous office Markus Laine turned the hand-written letter with its single paragraph over and over in his hands. He looked at the envelope. The letter spoke the truth, it seemed, for the envelope was postmarked Alajärvi and addressed to his office here; it had taken a while for him to come here and find it.

It was just an extraordinary coincidence, except that it hadn't quite all coincided enough. All that effort to try and find the owner of that house, and the great mess the fall-through of the sale had put him in, and now the son was writing to him, out of the blue. And out of wherever they had put him. Laine read the letter once again. It was short and to the point, in printed letters that were almost childish.

I am out of prison now, and back at my home in spite of what happened here. I have heard from someone you were looking for me. Get in touch. I am waiting for what you have to say.
Taavi Karhu

Yes, it was extraordinary. Laine wondered who could have told him. Not that it mattered. The little letter was a godsend. If he went to work quickly he might still catch the Englishman, before he had had a chance to buy somewhere else. No-one ever bought in the winter anyway. And no doubt the boy would be more than grateful to have that reminder of his own grizzly doings off his hands.

All the same, Laine hesitated, stood uncertainly with the letter in his hand. He needed the money. It might just tide him over, save his skin. But he had to remember that the writer was a psychopath who had already struck. Did he really want to get involved – was it wise? They had all seen now what the lad could do.

His own father, too! And at seventeen.

Laine set the letter aside.

It comforted Katja at first to think that her letter to the agent had probably already done its work, and that any day now his answer might be waiting there for her cousin in the mail box. The knowledge of what she had set in motion consoled her in her exhausted nights, kept awake by the whining baby. It sustained her through the grotesque, covert courtship of the miser to which she set herself anew. Yet there was still no word from Mr. Laine. On the morning when Katja opened the mail box to find that her passport had arrived, she said nothing. But she wouldn't be able to hang out long, pretending that she hadn't had it.

When the smart little document was safely secreted away she returned to the kitchen to unpack the boxes that had just arrived, and to ponder on why the agent hadn't responded to the letter. She had ordered a consignment of formula milk to be delivered to the house, to scare her cousin, and because it would never do to be seen buying baby stuff in the town.

It seemed that the baby had cried itself to sleep. The young man sat watching her from across the kitchen as she opened the first of the cardboard cartons and started unpacking. There seemed to be an awful lot of milk. She wondered if she had made a mistake in the order.

"How much fucking food are you going to give it?" The young man's voice was almost scornful. "I don't eat that much myself."

Katja kept taking out the packets and wondering what to do with them.

"I ordered it in bulk, to save having to go down into town for it all the time."

"You wouldn't have to do that anyway," said the young man, although he was not usually given to extending conversations. "Because you're not staying. It's time to go. I said you could stay here until the baby came and now it's come so now you can bugger off. I don't know what you're still doing here."

Katja was taken aback at the unexpectedness and the length of this outburst, but quickly recovered. She flipped her head defiantly. "You do know. I can't leave until I get my passport. As soon as it comes then I'll go. And you can stay here with your precious secret about who you are and where you are. And what you are."

The young man made an angry noise. All was quiet apart from the sound of Katja slapping formula packets wrathfully into haphazard piles. Then the young man said:

"Shouldn't you breastfeed it, anyway? Isn't that what tits are for?"

Katja snorted with irritation. "You breastfeed it, if you're so keen." She lapsed into silence, as Fisher appeared and hovered uncertainly at the door. He felt awkward at intruding. They made such an intimate little family scene.

On a balmy day in the autumn, when he was just off to see the Linda, an unfortunate thing had happened to Markus Laine. He himself had supposed that his ardent passion for her would last till the end of time, but the house of love is built on sands, and on that very day Laine saw and fell hopelessly, hook, line and sinker, for a new amour called Gabriella, who had just moved into Linda's boatyard. It was a change of loves that cost him dear, for the Gabriella was a bigger and more expensive boat, so much so that the total sale price of the Linda covered not much more than her enviably-contoured successor's huge deposit.

It was not long after getting the murderer's letter, that Laine checked his post and found himself holding the final demand for a payment on the Gabriella. A demand for money that he did not have. He dreamed that night that the wooden cradle where his sweetheart was berthed for the winter was empty, with weeds growing up around the wooden posts, while the canvas shroud that had protected her flapped and billowed mournfully in the wind.

It was the very next day when Laine's car pulled in through the gates to the pink house and drew up outside the porch. He had set out early to make this call, and it was early still when he arrived. There was no-one about, but the blinds were open, and an old van was drawn up on the far side of the yard.

Laine turned off the engine and went to get out, but before he could do so a great dog sprang from nowhere and hurled itself against the car, barking vigorously and flashing its teeth at the windows. Laine kept the doors tight shut and wondered nervously what to do. He recognized the dog as the same one he had sent packing earlier with the girl. He was faintly puzzled as to why it was back, but he didn't want to cross its tracks again, that was for sure. He was just about to drive off when the front door opened and a figure appeared, brought out by the noise of the dog's attack. A young man, dirty and dishevelled. For a moment Laine was at a loss; it dawned on him only gradually that of course, the boy would no longer be just a boy. Unlikely as it seemed, this could be him. Inside Katja glanced from the window, saw the car and faded inconspicuously away to her room. Upstairs Fisher was still asleep, worn out by worrying into the small hours.

Laine wound down the window a fraction. "Mr. Karhu?" It seemed that the young man's lips muttered something non-committal, but at least not 'no'. It was hard to hear over the barking of the dog.

"Could you tie the dog up? Then we can talk." The young man called the dog and kept his hand on the piece of rope it had round its neck, watching Laine with suspicion. Laine opened the door very carefully and put his feet out.

"You know who I am?" he asked, when the young man's wary, hostile expression remained unchanged.

"Nope."

"I'm the estate agent. Markus Laine. You asked me to come."

The young man opened his mouth a fraction, as if to speak, then closed it slowly. His expression became a little more wary still. The coldness of the snow outside the car door began to come up through the thin soles of Laine's office shoes. He made a little gesture.

"Do you mind if I come in? Then we can talk."

With apparent reluctance, the young man led the way inside. He kept his hand on the dog's rope and pulled it in with him, then pushed the animal into a side room and closed the door. Laine sat down nervously at the kitchen table without being asked. Despite the cold, he noticed that the palms of his hands were damp with sweat. He wondered what it must be like, to shoot your father. He must be very careful. It was just as well he was only the bringer of good news. He wiped his hands surreptitiously on his trousers, gave a cough and lifted his briefcase onto the wooden bench beside him.

"Well?" said the young man curtly. He stood in the open space between the table and the door behind which the dog was growling.

His hands were by his sides, but poised, it seemed to Laine, for possible action.

"I've come about the house."

"Meaning?"

His voice was almost insolent, but Laine was once more painfully aware that the young man would snuff him out like a candle, should he aggravate him.

"About selling it. I'm the agent your mother put in charge of that."

The young man was already staring straight at him, but now the whole expression of his face changed. "Why is she selling it?" He looked visibly shaken. Shocked. Angry. Laine fancied the already pasty face had turned a little paler. There was something else. He had said 'is'. An unwelcome suspicion began to form in the agent's mind.

"Perhaps you had better sit down."

The young man scowled, but after a minute he came and lowered himself onto the bench opposite Laine. "What do you mean, selling?"

The agent clutched at the straw, the changed phraseology that allowed him to procrastinate.

"You didn't know she had decided to put the house up for sale?"

"No. We weren't in touch."

He had fought with all his might against the vision of the wooden board. Fought and more or less won. In her room, Katja pressed her ear more firmly to the keyhole. If only the wretched baby would stay asleep until the agent had finished telling what he had to tell. She turned and glared warningly at the cardboard box that served as its cradle, then turned her attention back again to the conversation in the other room. The conversation that was to kick-start her prospects as lady of the manor. "Well, she did," the agent was saying. "Soon after she moved away."

"I don't know when that was." Her cousin's voice was sulky and complaining. "She didn't tell me herself. I only heard."

"It was quite soon after you'd left."

The young man was silent, then he raised his face to the agent with sudden eagerness. It transformed his features completely. "But you know where she is?"

Laine experienced a sudden sinking sensation, quite unrelated to any fear of being summarily murdered where he sat.

"Well, yes and no." The face in front of him looked childishly young and full of hope. Not like the face of a criminal at all. Laine found himself wishing he could give any message other than the one he had no choice but to give. "I am afraid she's died. I am afraid that your mother is dead."

And from the expression on the young man's face, it appeared that he had in many ways just died too. But even Laine was taken aback at what happened next. The young man burst into tears. His face crumpled, tears welled up and flowed down his cheeks, he turned suddenly from pale to red and slowly to pale again.

"No, no. You're teasing me. It can't be true." His breath came suddenly in gasps as he fought to get the words out. "She's not dead. She isn't dead!" At which Katja knew that the reckless words she had shrieked from the doorway of the sauna that day had been carried away by the wind. Now she feared that her cousin's noisy, disbelieving anguish would wake the baby. If that happened, she would be revealed, and all before the agent could get to the point. That the house would be Taavi's.

Laine, not himself a father, was astounded to find himself overcome with pity for the young man, amazed to find himself handing a handkerchief to the sobbing psychopath.

"I'm so sorry. There was a buyer for the house. I asked the police to try and find her, and they gave me the name of the hospital where she died. She had pneumonia."

"No, no," cried the young man, but as if to himself, and he began to rock back and forth, with his arms clasped around his body. His words became a plaintive, whining chant. "No, no, no, nooo."

"I'm so sorry," said Laine again. And he was. "Can I get you something to drink?" He stood up and looked around, but could see no obvious means of carrying out his offer, and sat back down again. After a minute he said quite gently, "But I'm afraid your mother is dead. There's nothing we can do."

The young man's sobs were subsiding a little now. "Why didn't they tell me? Why didn't they let me know? They knew where I was, they must have."

The agent shrugged. "I'm afraid I can't answer that."

"But they told you. Why did they tell you?"

"I told you. I asked them to find her for me, because - " Amid the flowing current, the drowning waves of their intercourse that threatened to wash him off his feet, the agent felt his toes touch the shore. Gently, without yet getting a proper grip, but making contact at least. And now, perhaps, he might be able to cheer the fellow up, to shine a little light in the midst of his dark despair of total loss. And secure for himself the money to pay up on the Gabriella.

"There is someone who wants to buy the house here."

"I don't want it sold," wailed the young man. "It's my home." And he began to sob inconsolably again.

"Yes, yes, of course." Laine waited for a pause in the sobbing, but the young man continued, "And anyway, you just said my mother is dead! So she isn't asking you to sell the house any more." He began to sniff, in amongst his sobs.

"My point exactly," Laine exclaimed, and waited again for the sniffs in turn to abate a little. Then he waited further for the young man to ask him what he meant by that comment, but the young man did not ask. It seemed to the agent that he himself would have to push the conversation forward.

"The fact is, that now that she has passed away" - Laine spoke the words clearly and deliberately – "the house is yours. Yours to do what you like with." Once more, he waited for the young man's reaction, but there was none. Laine wondered whether he had tactlessly appeared to know too much. He said contritely, "That is, I believe your mother was a widow at the time of her death?"

The young man's face, which had gone back to ashen after the angry redness of his tears, turned almost a shade of green. 'Like a chameleon,' came irrelevantly to Laine's mind. He said quickly, "And you are, as I understand it, her only child, is that right?"

"I had a sister," said the young man. "She died when I was eight."

"So," said Laine, "That means that the house is going to be yours. I'm sorry about the sister, I had no idea. But just think," - he leant forward persuasively. "YOU could sell the house. I'm willing to take on trust that you'll inherit it." He could hardly afford to hang around for probate – the payment on the Gabriella was already due. He didn't suppose there was anybody else that she could leave it to. The young man said nothing. He looked suddenly very tired. Instead of being overjoyed, he hardly seemed interested. Another tear began to trickle down his cheek.

In her bedroom Katja became aware that her legs were aching, as she crouched against the door. The silence was no guide to anything. At any moment now the baby might wake, they were taking so long.

It was quite a miracle how the brat had slept through the row that Taavi had made. The big ninny. Katja tried in vain to remember the last time she herself had cried. His reaction disgusted her.

In the agent's mind too, the poignancy of the case had receded slightly. Or rather, thoughts of the Gabriella were intruding more urgently. He must get a move on, pull the snivelling fellow back to the practical issues of the here and now.

"And think of it. There is somebody wanting to buy this place, for a really good price. You could sell it and get yourself a super little pad." He started to say "With no memories", but changed it to "With no loans" instead. "At your age! What could be better than that?"

The young man looked up quickly, his face alive again.

"Yes, I mean it," insisted Laine, his heart expanding with a responsive glow. "You might even have enough left over for a car…or a motor bike. When you think that most people have to wait until they're well over thirty…"

"But I live here," cried the young man. "I'm not going to sell." He stopped the agent short with a look of horrified astonishment. "This is my home. I'm going to live here! Even though" – his voice cracked – "even though my mother isn't here." He glared at Laine in outrage through a fresh blur of tears. Laine stared at the streaked, swollen face and saw for an instant the deserted wooden cradle of the Gabriella. He brushed the vision quickly aside and glanced round the room. The walls, the furnishings were shabby, the paint flaking off.

"This place is falling to bits," he said. "It was empty all the time you were in - were away. It really would make excellent business-sense to sell it, especially now you've got the chance. It's almost as if you fail to realise what a golden opportunity this is!" His words rang clearly and convincingly, if with a tiny touch of desperation. On their persuasiveness alone the fate of the Gabriella rested.

"Why didn't you sell it before if it's been empty all this time?" asked the young man sulkily. The agent shrugged. "There were no buyers. This place is old. It's in bad shape. It's hard to sell. The young man leapt angrily to his feet.

"It's a fine house," he shouted. "And it is – not – for – sale." From its prison room the dog gave a bark, as if it had just been roused. Laine waved his hands placatingly.

"You want me to take it off the market then?" he asked. As much to provoke the fool into sense as anything else.

"Yes. I do."

Laine was silent, but only for a second. He said petulantly, "I shall have to charge you fees, if I take it off the market. Since it's your house now. For advertising and things. Because I have been trying to find a buyer for it for a very long time. Anyone sensible, anyone smart, would sell it like a shot, I can tell you."

With any luck the sight of a bill would be enough to bring the young man to his senses. He didn't look as if he had any money to spare. But the young man waved his hand towards the window.

"I run my own repair and maintenance business. I can pay." He seemed to have regained a little composure, though his face was still puffy and tear-stained.

"Then I'll just have to take the house off my books. Tell the buyer you're not interested. But I'll leave you my card and phone number, just in case..." The agent laid his card on the table, as the young man made no move to take it.

"I don't have a phone."

"….And then if I don't hear, I'll send you my expenses bill."

But no expenses bill would help him keep the Gabriella. Laine made his way slowly towards the door then turned round as a thought occurred. "Do you want to meet up with the buyer? Is that what you want?"

"No." The answer was immediate. "I want to be left in peace."

On the threshold Laine held his hand out, rather coldly, but the young man only nodded curtly. As the agent went despondently to his car the dog began jumping up and down at the window, snapping and flashing its frothily gleaming fangs. He could hear its barks even through the double layer of glass. Behind its hellish noise he could have sworn he heard the sound of a baby starting to cry.

The agent waited for word from the young man that he had changed his mind, but none came. Katja, who knew her cousin better, had already given up all hope on that score. The blow was hard, she couldn't believe what an idiot he was, but at the same time her disbelief did not cocoon her in foolish self-deception. She would not after all be flaunting herself in front of Taavi as the mistress of what had formerly been his house. When the agent had gone, it had been some time before she noticed that the baby was crying, so deeply was she sunk in her own disappointment. Eventually she roused herself, as if from a dream, and went to the kitchen to fill its bottle with milk. There she found the young man lying face down on the wooden settle, and a single, crumpled shred of the agent's card on the floor in front of the burning stove. The tableau confirmed the dreary understanding she already come to: one game was over. In the other game, her passport was the only card left to play.

From the window of her room as she sat with the baby, who refused the bottle of scalding milk, Katja saw Fisher come back across the yard from a walk, heard him come in and wearily mount the stairs.

It seemed an age before the hungry baby fell asleep, and not till evening did the young man leave the kitchen settle to feed and tie up the dog.

This was it. It had to be now. Katja took the passport and climbed the stairs resolutely. As soon as she had fixed her expression she knocked on the door to Fisher's room and went straight in, before the young man could come back in and sense that she was not downstairs. Fisher was lying on the bed, but when the goddess entered he leapt up and went towards her. She came to him and held up the slim, new document for him to see, her face wreathed in smiles.

"Englanti. England." She had practised the word with different intonations of joy.

CHAPTER 25

The young man knew that everything had changed. He felt it somehow as he walked across the yard, where even the dog's bark seemed less frenzied, knew instinctively as soon as he entered the door that things were different. In the kitchen there was nothing of Katja's clutter, no discarded half-eaten bits of this and that. No signs of cooking or heating milk on the range. And the door of the room that Katja had commandeered stood ajar, instead of being closed. She had gone! The young man went and looked in. All her things were gone, there was nothing there. All her clothes and the motley assortment of make-up and ashtrays and paraphernalia for the baby had disappeared. The broken sofa stood like a red velvet knoll in the middle of the room, the smaller hump of its broken back beside it.

The young man walked all round the downstairs of the house, but there was no sign of her. It was just as if she had never existed.

So where had she gone? He hadn't believed that stuff about the baby's father, she had always been a terrible liar. But it didn't really matter. She had gone. He fed the dog, and started to prepare a meal for himself. How sweet it felt. As if an unpleasant smell had left the house. He was halfway there. The other half was to rid himself of the goggling ghost that haunted the place. It was odd, there were none of his shoes lying round.

With a strange premonition, the young man stopped in his task and went to listen at the bottom of the stairs. There was silence everywhere, a silence that was graceful, open and wide, a silence that let him breathe, did not suffocate him. He went up the stairs. The landing was clear and quiet, resting peacefully in the late afternoon. A patch of thin winter daylight paved the way to the open door of the room where the ghost lurked when he wasn't haunting. The young man went cautiously towards it. The room was empty once more, except for the iron bedstead and the old chest of drawers that had always been there. One thing was obvious. The man and his stuff were also gone.

Downstairs the young man raised a forkful of cold food absentmindedly to his mouth, still lost in wonder, then lowered it again, They had both gone. But together? Surely not? The thought was ridiculous, impossible. Yet gone they both had. All their things had gone. The young man was suddenly overcome with a great flood of mirthful rapture, quite unlike his usual self. They had gone. He was alone now, he could be in his own peace.

It was several minutes before he remembered. He was free now to face his demons. The thought of this sobered him up.

Tomorrow. He must do it tomorrow. Or even tonight. But nothing was ready. He had no gun, no pills, the lake was frozen, he was not quite sure how to hang himself. He needed time to think it out. And then there was the dog to see to. They would have to wait a short while still, before he answered their call. But he wouldn't be long.

Nothing is ever perfect. In the bathroom the young man experienced a flicker of annoyance when he noticed a bucket there, with a dirty nappy soaking. That was typical Katja. Slovenly to the last. He supposed that she hadn't had time to wash it, or she couldn't be bothered. He only had to empty the bucket and throw out the stinking piece of towelling, but it irritated him none the less. Still, he shouldn't let it get to him. He returned to the landing corridor, now full of shadows, for dusk had fallen but the moon had not yet slipped round far enough to cast its light through the windows. He stood listening. Now in the dark the house was eerie.

He was suddenly scared. Fear surged through his body. He was not used to having the house around him empty, not used to being alone in it in the night. But it wasn't the night itself that was making him nervous, just the steady, dispassionate reminder of the silent house that there was no longer really anything left between him and death. The promise he had made to his accusers, concerning that which he longed to do, longed to have done. The final jump into everlasting, infinite darkness that would exonerate him, write him out with the only worthy exit-line from his part in the farce of life. The time had come for him to fulfil his vow.

Tonight. It had to be tonight after all. The dark, still, empty landing was challenging him. He could leap off from the balcony, free his soul.

He must feed the dog before he went, put out plenty of food for it before he died. He moved to the window and looked out. It would be Kosto who found him first, if he jumped. He should maybe tie him up, to save him distress. From behind the house the moon threw the first of its beams across the yard; soon the greater part of all that space from outhouse to outhouse would be swamped with moonlight. As he watched, lost in thought, a hare sprinted right across that first ray of light. The dog saw it too, and set up a sudden flurry of furious barking down near the porch. Awakened from the trance into which he had slipped the young man turned to go down the stairs. He must not be deterred, he must make preparations.

His hand was on the stair rail when he heard the sound. So faint, so unexpected, as if he was imagining it. But he stopped still and listened, his ears alert. There was silence, then it came again, a small noise from behind the door at the end of the corridor, from the tiny, unused boxroom that overlooked the orchard. The noise sent unpleasant feelings down his spine. More than anything he wanted just to ignore it, to pretend it wasn't there; his hand, still clutching the banister, began to ache from gripping. He took his hand away and listened still. It was no good. Imaginary or not, the noise disturbed him, worried his nerves. He turned back and stole along the landing, apprehensively, but with quiet steps, and opened the box-room door.

The pram that Katja had been given by the welfare was blocking the doorway completely from the inside. It was loaded down with nappies and the cartons of formula milk that she had ordered, with baby clothes and nappy buckets and all the rest of the stuff she had got from the hospital. The young man prodded it dubiously and tried to move it, and an avalanche of nappies and rattles and feeding bottles came tumbling down. The bottles were plastic; they ricocheted off the bare wooden floor. Down below, the dog set up a fresh commotion, but the young man hardly heard it. Badly startled by the noise of barking and then by the bouncing of bottles round the room, the baby redoubled its cries.

CHAPTER 26

Fisher had to hand it to the goddess. For a woman, a divinity, she was pretty much on time. When the taxi turned the corner at half past three, and he saw that beloved face framed in its glory of golden hair, he was more than relieved. All the same, they had no time to lose.

It had been quite a day. The young man had not left home before ten in the morning, which had all but put paid to Fisher's plans to go down early into town and try and get tickets sorted. The young man had sat at the table, going over road maps, and marking off distant points with a biro. It seemed he always went to places a long way away. He had made himself a flask of tea to take, and sandwiches, which was a good sign. It meant he wouldn't be back before the night. And best of all, he would probably take the dog. But his dallying prevented Fisher getting into action. He had to book their plane flight, hotel, train. At this rate he wouldn't have time to come back here. He would simply have to send up a taxi for the goddess.

At last the young man was gone. Fisher rounded up the last of his belongings. It was half past ten – he was going to be pushed for time. He brought the goddess to look at his bags.

"Taxi. Three o'clock," he instructed firmly. He showed her his watch. "Three o'clock. Taxi." He took her to her room, where the baby was starting to bleat and hiccough. "Pack." The goddess looked confused. Fisher made gestures of throwing things together. "Pack. Three o'clock. Taxi. England." Again he tapped his watch. The goddess nodded. Fisher went to kiss her, but by chance at that very second she moved away. There was lots to do, after all.

He had missed the bus. He would have to walk down into town.

On the road he turned to look back at the winter jewel.

The train was not at four o'clock after all. That was its summer time. Now in the winter it was twenty to four. Fisher had sent the taxi up a little early for the goddess, the baby and the luggage, and now waited anxiously at the station.

He had spent almost all his time in the travel office. There had been a clerk this time who spoke English, and the final result of her efforts had been, to Fisher's rapture, to book the last two seats on the late night Heathrow flight from Helsinki this very evening. The young man would never catch them up.

And now the taxi came pulling into the forecourt, just a scant ten minutes before the train was due to depart. Fisher's fears melted into adoration as the taxi driver opened the passenger door and the goddess stepped out. She was looking stunning, if still a little squidgy from the pregnancy. Her arms were full of unidentifiable possessions. The taxi driver took out their bags and cases from the boot and lined them up at the curbside, then lifted out the goddess's rucksack from the back seat and placed it on top. Fisher could not even put his finger for a minute on what was wrong, what the anxious misgiving was that was welling up inside him. The taxi driver got in, closed the door and started revving the engine.

"Stop! Stop!" shouted Fisher, and banged on the bonnet. Surprised, the driver stopped the movement of the taxi. Fisher bent down frantically and looked in through the window. "The baby! Where's the baby?" His voice was an almost womanish scream. He turned to the goddess, but none of the things she was nursing in her arms turned into a tiny being.

"Where's the baby? What have - ?" But even as he uttered these words the goddess bent down and spoke to the driver, as if she were giving instructions. The driver put his foot back down on the accelerator, reversed with impressive speed and shot away in a shower of slush. "Katja", cried Fisher in a tone of panic. "Where is the baby?"

The goddess was already searching for a trolley. When Fisher placed himself in front of her and shouted directly into her face, it seemed that she at last both heard and understood him. She looked up, her eyes wide open in astonishment. "At home." He had shouted at her so emotionally it seemed somehow natural that she should suddenly be able to speak his language. There was something about her voice that sounded as if she was surprised that he should ask. Fisher stared at her, at a loss. The train was due, and the baby was still at the house. It was a disaster he could not start to explain. He glanced at the station clock in agitation, as if that would help. It was twenty five to four. He felt sick.

"The train is coming!"

The goddess looked at him again.

"The train," he repeated.

The goddess obediently began to push the loaded trolley towards the platform. For a young girl she was certainly strong. Fisher ran beside her. "The baby!" he screamed, over the booming of the station loudspeaker. The goddess stopped pushing for a moment. "At home." The train swept into the station. The goddess ran forward to open the door and started to heave things in. Fisher tried to prevent her. After all, she had not long since given birth. Besides, they could not get on the train without the baby. He seized the handle of the bag, his hands next to hers, and tried to wrest it from her. The guard arrived, to see what the delay was, and began to speed them up by loading their luggage.

"No, no," cried Fisher, trying to stop him. "Take it all out, please! We haven't got the baby." But the guard carried on as if he had not understood a word. Implacable, purposeful, item after item. The goddess was already dragging the big case towards the luggage compartment when Fisher climbed into the train to call her back, but his voice was drowned by the slamming of the door and the shriek of a whistle. With initial hesitation, then increasing speed and self-assurance, the train began to move. Fisher wondered if he should pull the emergency cord, but wasn't sure he could identify it. Instead he gave up, just for a moment, and stared blankly out at the station rolling past.

The goddess came and stood beside him in the tiny space at the end of the corridor. She steadied herself against the luggage rack, and sighed as if she considered it all a job well done. She was still a little breathless, but her face had resumed its normal tranquillity.

"Where's the baby?" Fisher repeated desperately, in exhausted disbelief. He was suddenly aware of the train conductor, holding his ticket punch at the ready and waiting stoically. It was obvious to the train conductor from the gentleman's speech that he was foreign, and obvious from his manner that he was confused. When their tickets had been punched Fisher found himself ushered to their seats. He sank down aghast, glanced out helplessly at the passing landscape, then back at the goddess. "The baby - "

The goddess waved a nonchalant hand in the air. "Baby is fine."

It was her first English sentence to him since the words 'I love you'. He leant forward.

"Why did you leave the baby?" He could see from her face that the question was beyond her linguistic powers, but now he could not stop. "What have you done with your baby? Who's looking after him?" Him? It occurred to Fisher with a wrench that he did not even know what sex his own-child-to-be was. He leant still further forward in his agitation. "Baby. Alone."

The goddess gave a small, limp, dismissive movement with her hand. "No. No alone. Taavi."

Taavi? Fisher stared at her, suddenly electrified. He clasped his forearms and moved them wildly to and fro in a rocking movement. "Taavi?" The goddess nodded comfortably, and mimicked his action.

Fisher was silent, lost in his own tangled, still distinctly horrified thoughts. How could she just abandon her baby like that? How could she bear to be without it? And worst of all, to leave it to the mercies of a murderer. He reminded himself that the goddess could not even start to suspect the terrible truth, but this thought did nothing to console him.

Perhaps the young man had come home and caught her just leaving, and forced her to surrender the baby. He looked at her. But the goddess did not look as if she had been forced to do anything. On the contrary, she looked quite composed. She saw him looking at her and actually smiled the shadow of a smile. Fisher forced a faint smile back. If her lover had come home and threatened her, she was taking it very calmly.

It was odd that the fellow should have come back so soon, after all his preparations. And on this day of all days. He must have smelt a rat. But how come he had let her go? Fisher pulled back his sleeve and showed the goddess his watch again.

"Taavi home what time?" It seemed he must still talk like Tarzan, before the goddess understood him. It felt most unnatural, in view of his education, and the number of words he had mastered in his life. "What time Taavi home?"

"Soon," said the goddess. Soon. So not yet. He had not come back. But if he had, the goddess would certainly not even be here. She had had to leave while he was out, to escape with Fisher. But she had left the baby to stay with its father.

It startled Fisher, how much she must love him, to come with him and make that unthinkable sacrifice. Because, of course, the baby was the young man's offspring, however unworthy he was. In her selfless compassion, it seemed that the goddess had felt that she could not deprive him of his first-born, only child. Fisher felt humbled. He only prayed the baby would not come to grief at the murderer's hands.

He hoped too that she had not just left the baby at home. She must have taken it somewhere to have it looked after till the young man returned. He found himself looking at her feet to see if she had been walking through snow, but he couldn't tell. She had stepped in a slushy puddle alighting from the taxi. All the same, she could never have left the baby alone, it was much too small.

He regretted that he was not after all about to become an instant father. He had taken to the idea, though he had not quite got used to it. He stared forlornly at the goddess, who appeared to have fallen asleep, and as he absorbed the beauty of her countenance new, beautiful thoughts began to form themselves of their own accord, as the rhythmic motion of the train began to soothe him. Thoughts so obvious he did not know why he hadn't dared to make more of them earlier. The goddess and he could very soon have a baby all of their own.

And so he began to calm down, as the train headed further and further south towards Helsinki. The goddess was sleeping, catching up, no doubt, on well-deserved rest, now that there was no little baby to attend to and to keep her awake. It would, after all, be easier without the baby to start with, that he had to admit. There would be no broken nights, there need be no explanations. He would not be mistaken for its grandfather. It would give people time to get used to the sight of his peerlessly beautiful young wife. For they should marry soon, as soon as his divorce from Millicent was final.

Katja too, was beginning to relax behind the carefully maintained façade of sleep. It had been a nasty moment. She hadn't realised that Fisher would be upset about the wretched baby. She had assumed that he too had not included it in their plans, but had simply expected her to sort things out somehow. And then he had got in such a state.

It was unbelievable. She couldn't see why he was bothered about the little pest. It was nothing to do with him. But anyhow, he seemed placated at the thought of leaving it for Taavi. She had recognised this as a stroke of genius herself; that murdering psychopath could do what he liked with it, no-one would miss it. The episode would soon be over. If only they could just get well away, off to England, before he came home.

She opened her eyes a crack and noticed that Fisher appeared to have fallen asleep himself. There were papers protruding from his jacket pocket - their train tickets and the air travel reservations. She read them through then leaned back in her seat with contentment. The sleeping form of Fisher was hardly appealing, she registered ruefully. But it wasn't forever, or even long. And anyway, it was all in a very good cause.

CHAPTER 27

Finland, 1977

The boy had gone alone to the beach on that midsummer Sunday, the hottest day of the hottest summer for a decade. He went to the beach because he couldn't think of any other way to pass the time, or anyone to pass it with, and then found that just about everyone in the neighbourhood had had just the same idea.

What else made sense, after all, on a sweltering weekend, than to make for the only chance of coolness, the one possibility of a breeze, at the riverside? So the locals flocked like lemmings to the long, smooth curve of the river where beyond the pines the bank opened out into broad expanses of pebbles and sand - yes, sand; the only proper beach, the locals said, along the whole of the river till it reached the sea.

The whole day the beach path was thronged with people. They parked their cars as near as they could to the head of the path and set off with all they could manage, which for many looked to be a fair part of everything they owned; they came equipped with beach balls and radios and blankets, though the weather was hot enough to melt flesh to blubber, and towed behind them beer crates and children and panting, uncooperative dogs. They bore cool-boxes, airbeds and canvas windbreaks on their shoulders, though there wasn't the faintest puff of wind, and brought for good measure towels, chairs, insect repellent, picnic sets, spades and buckets, racquets, sunhats, skin creams, sunglasses, swimsuits, snorkels, water-wings, cameras, plasters, newspapers, magazines and hampers with stocks of food and drink almost biblical in their glut. They walked slowly of necessity, but at the same time as fast as they could, grimly saving the last of their heat-drained strength to fight for a pitch on the beach. It was a day out. The weather was officially idyllic. They were set to enjoy it.

By half-past ten the day was a scorcher, fulfilling the promise of the early morning river-mist. By midday the trail of cars stretched back for two kilometres from the path head – hot, glittering sealed boxes like the links of a great metal necklace laid out along the sides of the road. Between the cars the narrow gap was crammed with traipsing families and wobbling cyclists. On reaching the riverside they staked out their territory with towels and airbeds, stripped to swimsuits, rubbed their flesh with oil, sheltered beer and babies from the sun as best they could, and lay down to fry.

It surprised the boy to find the way to the beach so jam-packed that afternoon. Among the crowd he felt conspicuous for being alone. He threaded his way through the midst of the slow cavalcade and turned along the forest path. Now and then he tried to walk close to people, so that passers-by would think he was with a group, at other times he walked alone, but quickly, purposefully, as if hastening to some important rendezvous further on.

And all the while he felt uncomfortably how he had felt now for as long as he could remember. As if a wide gulf lay in front of the island on which he found himself the only occupant, and on the far side stood every other person that he knew. And almost certainly, every other person that he didn't know. Even the strangers among whom he walked were no doubt already seeing him now for what he was. An oddball. Peculiar. Someone left behind when everyone else had found themselves in full possession of all one had to know to hold one's head up. An unfair, inbuilt understanding of how to be confidently and indisputably cool.

In fact the people around him as he walked paid the teenager no attention. They were weighed down with pleasureware and held back by dawdling families, while the boy, who carried nothing and came alone, was burdened obscurely, on even this heavenly summer's day, by the weight of his soul. The problem of cool. Or even, he didn't ask that much. Just to know that he was well enough in the know.

There was general agreement among his elders that the outlook for the boy was not very promising. He was having to stay on and redo the final year of school, for his work there had not been going too well of late. The boy himself took a more optimistic view of the future. It was, after all, the only point of hope. Across the bleak, uncharted wasteland of his day-to-day existence where he drifted directionless and forlorn, it beamed at him with a vague but infinitely bright and cheering radiance.

When the future happened he would no longer feel the gulf that separated him from the others. Would no longer fear that they could look in his brain and see all too plainly that anything he didn't seem hopelessly inept at, he was faking. That there was some sort of defect in his understanding. He would make the connection, be in his element with it all. He saw it now, some years further on – fast cars, faster women, a job with unbelievable money, his finger on the pulse of – whatever life was about. He would be respected, even idolised.

The boy naturally did not phrase things to himself in quite these ways, for he was not much given to metaphors and similes; he merely understood that over the lonely struggles of his life, at least the unformed future threw a ray of hope. But before the future there was still yet another school year, and before that, the long hot summer to while away. And first and foremost, the afternoon before him.

If he had been asked the cause of what happened not many hours after this, the boy would have said it was the heat. It oppressed him, put him in a worse mood than usual, made his head ache. It was Sunday, he wasn't needed to help out on the farm. He was free to amuse himself. But the heat drove him mad, made him crabby and lethargic. It prised its way inside his head, expanded and hammered and exploded. Not that anyone did ask about that day, except why he had left his sandals on the beach. He was taciturn by nature, so no-one ever asked him very much. Apart from some weeks later, when they asked him what made him shoot his father. And to that, he never answered anything at all.

Down at the riverside the bank and the nearer reaches of the river were already packed, while beyond the furthest bathers the wide band of water stretched greenish and shimmering to the tree-covered rocky outcrops of the opposite shore. Over those on the beach the calls of the swimmers and paddlers floated high up and faint, as if the sound came from very far off. There was no wind after all, even here. Between the searing hot ground and the cloudless blue hemisphere of sky the air was dense and solid, as hot as an oven.

All day the sun-seekers toasted themselves, from white to pink, to red to bronze to peeling, while between them women suncreamed their children and wrestled them into bathing costumes. A crackling medley rose from a vast array of portable radios, and between the towels dented bottle tops began to glitter like hot coins in the sand. The children played, fought, screamed, wandered off, were caught, fed, dressed again and carried off home. For every family that left, another one bore down ready to take up their pitch.

The boy stood on the concrete slab beneath the shower outlet at the back of the beach and felt the water run cold around the soles of his feet. They were sore and burning, for he had walked barefoot, and the narrow strips left between the crumpled towels were red hot. The water from the nearby shower left little trickles of clear, wet skin across his sandy calves and splashed his clothing, but he did not move. Above the range of the spraying water the sun's heat bit into his shoulders. His headache was setting in.

He stared out idly across the beach at the kissing lovers, the families that fussed eternally, the rows of sunbathers who never seemed to move at all. And how forever, in a lazy, sluggish arc, a beach ball sailed backwards and forwards, light and gaudy among the distant voices of the bathers, and beyond it another, and another.

It was then that it happened, though the boy could never say why. Because he wasn't just then, as far as he knew, thinking anything about anything at all. Perhaps it was just the heat, as he himself was always sure. But later, all the cool air, all the coldness in the world could not cancel out what in that random instant he understood, as he watched the people before him on the beach. That there wasn't any point.

They were all just killing time. They had come here on an aimless Sunday, determined to spend it in a way they had simply been reared to think of as enjoyment. All this coming and going and fussing and stripping and dressing, the age-old ritual of spending a day at the riverside, it was all only passing the time. There was no real point to it, nor any pleasure, But no-one around him, it was clear, had ever given the matter the slightest thought, or ever would. They passed their time that way because it was their custom, and supposed they were happy.

But it wasn't just Sunday. Beneath the glittering sun, the air was full of the nothingness of their lives. Tomorrow would be Monday; they would mark off the days to the following weekend. Year in, year out, they would carry out their lives unthinkingly to the patterns they had accepted without question. Routine, the monotony broken by rituals, ticking box after box on the pages of life set out for them. Without ever thinking, what it was all for.

And what was it for? There was no real sense, in the end. No real use behind it all, it seemed to the boy, that one could really latch onto. As soon as you were dead, you were dead; it was all gone then. And soon no-one remembered you. And soon after that, no-one even knew you had existed. So what were you doing in life, except filling it, keeping busy, making sure there was never time to think of the pointlessness underlying it? That in the end, it would all be for nothing. The whole of life was only a longer version of an aimless Sunday on the beach. Take away that busyness, that blind activity, and nothing would be left but empty time and a boredom as deep as the universe.

It was an insight that came in an instant, which was odd for the boy, who had always been considered rather slow. Rather given to pondering. But now the truth came, the one great universal truth, with a horror that gripped him, that made him feel sick, crept up upon him with a paralysing certainty from behind. Made him feel that he had been poisoned, electrocuted and stabbed all simultaneously. As if it was not so much that he had grasped the truth, but that the truth had suddenly unasked invaded his soul. As if he had suddenly seen, not the light, but the dark.

The boy was taken back, aghast. Up to now he had drifted, forlorn, lost, ashamed, but always hopeful. Yet now, in a revelation that had come in an instant and could never be repealed, he had understood it all. He looked out on the ranks of sunbathers and the bustling families, those self-approving humans he had felt inferior to, with a sudden curious detachment and pity. They were stupid, living under false ideas of purpose and enjoyment. They had been indoctrinated, all their lives. But the boy knew that such illusions would never, ever cradle him again.

Still the devil who had poured this poison into his soul, the heat devil, one might say, had not quite finished with him yet, and dragged him a little further up the visionary hill. There was no point in any of it, which meant, of course, that the boy saw his one true friend, the future, shrivel and then flare up and crumble to a cinder in the heat.

The nearby showerhead had long since ceased to sprinkle, but the boy stood immobile on the empty concrete slab, his face fixed fast in fear and horror. He seemed to be staring at a nearby picnic group, as if he had seen a snake slide in and out.

"Killing time." went through his mind, then, "No, not killing time. Time is emptiness, and how can you kill that?" It was some minutes still before the devil that had stabbed his head with truth and his soul with despair at last sent action to his heels, and jerking to life he fled across the hot sand, pebbles and bottle tops of the beach, to the path that led towards the road.

It seemed to the boy that when he had stood there and seen to the bottom of their lives, and his life, and the lives of those before and to come, and even to the edges of the universe, that some folk had noticed him, but not seen what he saw. They had glared at him for standing there and taking up shower space, then stared at him on seeing his panic-stricken features. They did not know that the devil had drawn back the curtain for him on the whole great fiasco of their existence, so they went on their way, still sandy, resenting him, unaware that they could have broken the spell.

For in his pain and fear at the awful truth that he had just understood, the boy had cried out inside for someone to notice his agony and save him, but nobody did. "Help me," he heard himself crying, "I am falling where I do not want to fall!" But not out loud.

When he started to run, he couldn't say whether anybody noticed at all.

He had run quite far before he realised he had forgotten to put his sandals on. Now he noticed that the hot ground was searing the soles of his feet, and the twigs and stones over which he was running were cutting them. He left the path and hobbled like a cripple along its verge, the long, slow, painful journey to his home. It took an hour to get there, his feet on fire.

In the night he had perhaps a touch of fever, for he half slept and saw before him rows of scantily- costumed bodies, oiled, roasting like sausages in the sun. And lying in bed, his sore feet bandaged, the boy wept, for his heart too was full of pain and grief, and a strange, new, bitter despair.

In the small hours, when the burning in his feet was numbed by painkillers, he crept on hands and knees to the balcony and pulled himself up to kneel on the wooden chair there. Below him the lilac tree beside the porch was blooming, its mauve flowers plump and heavy now it was June. In the night air they dipped and nodded enticingly, floating their perfume up towards him, and between the leaves the boy could see the ground spread out below their branches, firm and inviting beneath its covering of soft, sparse grass. He bent and put one foot on the balcony rail, then squealed, and had to stop himself from screaming with the pain. What had happened to the painkillers? He replaced his leg as it had been before, in kneeling position, then tried again. Again a million fires tore through his flesh. He whinnied and the tears sprang to his eyes.

He could not put paid to his grief and anguish tonight. His feet were too painful. Back in bed, after the slow and arduous return, it was a long time before he fell asleep.

It seemed the boy's feet would be laying him up for several days, if not for a week or more. The doctor asked how come the lad could be seventeen and still forget to wear his shoes home. Mrs. Karhu gave a sigh, which was echoed by Mr. Karhu.

"We don't know what got into him. He can be that daft, especially that day."

"Daft as a brush."

"He wouldn't say what had happened. But we got the sandals back."

The doctor asked if the lad was maybe a little slow.

"Not in that way. More like the boy's got no ambition," grumbled the farmer. "Doesn't seem to know what he wants to do." The doctor grunted understandingly.

But the boy did know. He knew exactly what he wanted to do. Or perhaps 'want' is not the right word. All the same he was coming to see where his duty lay, now that he understood the truth.

From that weekend on, the weather formed a regular routine; roasting hot during the week, a little showery at weekends. Which meant that that June Sunday, so fine and sunny, was for many the high spot of the summer. They marked it in their minds and their journals as a perfect day, an idyll of bliss in which they had basked on golden sands in an azure-vaulted paradise. In well-meant retrospect they stripped the day of grit, mosquitoes, heatstroke, sand-covered food, flies, dog turds, blisters, hangovers, arguments, sunburn and intermittent boredom, fixed and framed the image of blue sky, glittering water and familial harmony in their memories.

They did not know that the strange boy who had stood at the shower point, staring as if he was possessed, looked that way because he was seeing into their souls.

When the boy looked inwards, he found his heart so sore that he was left in agony, for the truth hurt, but he could not avoid it. It had stabbed him through and now the wound was leaking inside him. When he looked outwards, he found himself full of disdain for those around him, but himself he despised most of all. For how could he himself go on living? To see through the whole great con trick that was life, and then to live on as if he believed in this farce, would be unforgivable dishonesty. And besides, there was nothing left now, that he could deceive himself might be ultimately worthwhile to do.

He must spread the word, for it seemed that for some strange reason it was he alone who had been enlightened. Who saw that the whole thing was a very bad joke. He had been the subject, he suspected, of too many jokes in his life, and had not found it pleasant. He refused to be the subject of this one, the direst joke of all.

But he wasn't an orator, had neither the courage nor the skill to preach in words. He could only act. He must extinguish himself. His own extinction was the only message he could give; his death by example the only flag of honour he could fly.

Meanwhile he lay in bed with bandaged feet, and fumed impatiently to be well enough to wipe out the debt of shame that his very existence had become. He was surly and taciturn, angry and despondent. When his feet began to heal, he began to make new plans. Made countless plans and variations throughout what was left of the long, pointless summer.

It was not that he did not want to go. On the contrary, he desired devoutly to have proved himself. Yet it seemed more difficult as the days went on, the violence he must enforce on himself, in order to pass into lightness. It was all very well to see himself floating weightlessly down through the lilacs, as he had done that first night in his fever, or cruising on dark wings towards the welcoming lighted runways of death, but now the act itself began to daunt him. And nor would his parents ever understand.

Still, death was waiting for him. It began to send messengers each day to urge him to hurry. Their presence was physical, weighed on him, he felt them near him, could sometimes almost feel their bodies pressing against him. They resembled the monsters and beasts of his childhood, and he felt them now to be as real as they had been long ago in the dark, murky forests of his storybooks. He who all too often had felt himself too alone would wake to sense their dark, heavy presence around him – death had sent them to collect him, to accuse him, challenge him to get on with the job. In the night he would hear them speaking to him, would wake in the morning to feel them near, could sense their breathing as they waited for him to fulfil his duty.

He wanted to obey them, but found he was frightened, tried to push them out, or steal away from them in fear. He longed devoutly to be gone, yet feared to go. For beyond the pain, beyond that act of duty lay the great unknown, the infinite blackness from which there was no return.

Worst of all, he must bear his suffering alone. For what would happen if he asked for help? They would pity him, as he pitied them. They would draw him back with honeyed words, step by step, from the abyss of darkness, till he was safely far enough to be wrapped around with the gentle threads of their lies, the soft, binding spiders' webs of the great delusion. They would try to persuade him of the rightness of life, until he was helpless again, compliant, a traitor to the great and terrible truth that he had seen. The boy grew quieter than ever, and more withdrawn. He hoped he might die in an accident, and began to expose himself to danger, but the burden of his life remained intact.

It would have to be done.

A gun was the answer. The farm gun hung on the wall. It was used in the hunting season, but the boy had found that he didn't like to shoot things. Didn't like to watch small helpless creatures die.

On the second day back at school he had to acknowledge that time was overtaking him. His accusers were becoming daily more pressing. Ashamed, he chastised himself for his inexcusable weakness. Why, the summer was over and he was still alive! When he got off the school bus and found that his knees were weak and his stomach behaving strangely, the boy knew that this was the day. That he could no longer back out of what he had to do.

He walked up the hill, amazed that his body should carry him forward despite its shaking, noticed that he was crossing the yard and still he had not stopped. The boy willed his feet to keep on going, forbade them to falter. He stared straight ahead, sensed the dog running round him, heard his father call and knew that he must deafen his ears to the sound of his name. His feet took him up the porch steps and inside, where he put his schoolbag down and crossed the hall to the room where the gun was kept, just as Mr. Karhu left the tractor shed and came towards the house.

The boy was clumsy getting the rifle down off the wall, for his hands were slippery and trembling. He was clumsy checking that it was loaded. It gave the farmer time to come up the steps, time to reach him just as he tried to tuck the barrel of the gun beneath his chin. There was just time to struggle and try and wrest it from the stupid boy. Whatever was he doing? The farmer managed to pull the rifle round just a second before it went off.

It caught him in the neck. The worst was the bleeding. The boy could not stop it. He knelt by the tumbled body, dumbstruck, till something inside him told him to run. Told him to wriggle his way out through the half closed door and then to run, run, run, run, run. He had given up running, but was still struck dumb, when they apprehended him in the rye field.

He was underage. Five years in detention seemed the least he should get for murdering his father. The case was clear; he never claimed he hadn't done it.

But then again, he never claimed he had.

CHAPTER 28

The young man stared down at the baby with disbelief. It flapped its arms and reinforced its howls, its features contorted with rage. Now that he was in the room, the noise seemed to almost take the skin off his ears. The din unnerved him, but he stood transfixed, almost hypnotised by the cavernous salmon pink gulf of its mouth, the small, scarlet, angrily curled tongue. Here in the only room in the house which he had not checked was the baby, Katja's baby, small, red and jerking with fury. It was a raging demon, like its mother.

But Katja was gone, the young man was sure of it. The change had hit him as soon as he had come in. It wasn't just that her things were gone. It was the change in the atmosphere. The whole house was breathing with a sense of its freedom, was filled with lightness and airiness and peace. The blissful sense of the very lack of her presence. All the same he had checked just everywhere, bar this one tiny unused attic room.

Yet now here in front of him was the baby, and all too evidently no trick of the imagination. On a sudden impulse the young man left the room and ran round the house again, but still there was no sign of Katja. Or the foreigner. He returned to the upstairs room and stood there looking at the baby, at a loss. It was sopping wet; pale urine had soaked its clothes right up to its chest. The young man was practical by nature. He hunted out a nappy and some dry clothes from the muddle in the room and dressed it again, bending its rubbery limbs back and forth in timid determination. His ventures confirmed his previous vague impression that it was a girl. It continued to yell, but its arms and legs remained intact and returned to waving, as soon as he had forced its garments over each one in turn. When he had finished, it continued screaming. He had a nasty feeling that it wanted to be fed.

He took it down to the kitchen with a box of formula and set about following the instructions to the letter. He was quite sure that Katja had always made the milk too hot. The day when he had told her finally she had to go had not been the only time when she had actually let it boil. The young man tried the milk out nervously on the back of his hand, not quite sure what he was testing for. The white blob maintained its surface tension for a second, then broke and ran across his skin. It was lukewarm. He held the bottle dubiously suspended in the raging mouth. The teat was small compared to the void around it; he rattled it around. After a few more dismal wails, the baby gave a choking cough, and surrendered in surprise. Gripping the sudden intruding object with its gums it began to suck noisily.

It surprised the young man no end, how well he could deal with the baby, with no more training than observing the resentful battles of its mother. He had changed its nappy and warmed its milk, and now it was drinking. He knew it was drinking because the milk in the bottle was getting less, and no milk was coming out anywhere else. Though it seemed that something odd had happened to the nappy; it was no longer wound between the baby's legs but somehow bunched around its waist inside its clothing. Still at least the creature was no longer deafening him with its howls. On the contrary, it seemed to have forgotten its dissatisfactions; the room was silent except for the sound of greedy rhythmic sucking. It was hard to see what people made all the fuss about; you only had to follow the instructions, it appeared.

When the baby had finished it began to whimper again. The young man picked it up. It belched rudely and spewed a little milk on him, and he put it back down again quickly in distaste, with a muttered curse. By the time he had cleaned himself up at the kitchen sink, it had fallen asleep.

He felt a faint but undeniable glow of triumph. Was this really what Katja made such a song and dance about? The young man sat on the bench amid the debris of nappy changing and looked at the baby as it slept in its cardboard box. It lay on its back, its arms flung up over its head, and with what could almost be taken for a smile of satisfaction on its face. The only clothing he had managed to find nearly swamped it, yet its head still seemed much too big for the rest of it. It had somehow relaxed its legs out at the knees in a way quite impossible to imagine, as if its limbs were really made of rubber. As he watched it a small white bubble of milky saliva blew out from its lips, swelled and burst. The baby stirred and carried on sleeping.

But what was it doing here, all alone? Where had Katja gone? And why had she left it here? Especially when she had taken all her things. He could guess from that, that she wasn't planning to return. But to leave the baby! That was weird. And to pack it away like that, just stow it away with all its gear. That was the oddest thing of all. As if it was simply some possession she would not be needing for a while. Or as if the baby would simply exist where it was stored, and would never need feeding, or to have its nappy changed, or its clothes.

As for the oddball, where did he fit into this? It seemed strange that they had disappeared exactly together. On the same day, at least. The young man sat and pondered on these things for so long that he sank into a kind of trance, until the baby woke and had to be changed and fed again. After this the young man stretched out on his customary bench and fell into a deep but restless sleep.

The sight of the baby's box on the floor beside him when he woke next morning gave the young man a shock not much less than the one he had had the day before. It was a minute before he could recall the events of the evening and night, could understand why the baby in its sleeping box was here in the kitchen, and the door to the room his cousin had taken over stood open. Katja had gone. The creeping ghost had gone. The house was his again, he had actually been on his way to kill himself.

And then, he had found the baby.

And now, in the morning light and after too little sleep, his worries flew quickly back to his mind and lodged there, becoming louder and more insistent than the baby's cries, fresher and more real than his child-rearing triumphs of the night. He pondered them while he fixed the baby's bottle. It couldn't stay here. It wasn't his baby, after all. It was Katja's; she had no right just to run off and leave her wretched little bastard here. It was yet another hitch to his plans, so near to being realised. He could hardly kill himself and leave a baby around. But nor could he stay alive and keep it, it would give him away. He would have to hide its existence, as he hid his own.

He couldn't look after a baby, anyway. He didn't know how. Even if he wasn't on the run, he wouldn't know, unless it was a pig or some such. Human babies he knew nothing about. And how would he get all the stuff babies need? Or manage his repair rounds? Besides, he didn't want a baby. Even if there were no neighbours to hear it.

No neighbours. And no-one knew of the baby, apart from him. As he burped it and set it down to sleep the answer came to him, in a small, unpleasant, but irrefutably rational voice. He would have to despatch it. Put it down before he did away with himself. It would hardly be a problem, it was only small.

He fed the baby again when it woke. There was no point in having it screaming till he got round to killing it. And changed its nappy, just for practice; he had still not mastered the skill. The pins were tricky, it was hard to get them through the layers of towelling and yet not pierce the soft, pink, rounded flesh underneath. There were still several nappies clean. Enough to last the baby its lifetime, since that was to be very short.

A pillow or a cushion - that would smother its cries, at the same time as it as it cut off the baby's air. Goodness knows, he had wanted to smother the creature enough times in its little life already. All the same, it was good that it wouldn't understand what he was doing. He would have to bury it, which wouldn't be easy, for the ground was still half-frozen, and out in the forest, not in the yard, or Kosto would dig it up. But glancing from the attic window that afternoon, he hit upon a better idea. He could put it down the well. He had only to wait a few more days, until he was sure that Katja was not coming back.

As soon as that was certain, he could rid himself of this latest complication.

It seemed that the young man could manage the baby a great deal better than Katja had, with a bit of practice. It was all in the booklets she'd been given, after all. The baby itself seemed noticeably less ill-tempered, now its mother had disappeared. There were times when it seemed to be almost complacent, as it slept embedded deep in woollens that were several sizes too big. And it seemed to be getting rounder than when Katja had fed it.

Of course, the baby meant he couldn't go out on his rounds. But anyway, it wouldn't be for long. Very shortly, if there was still no sign its mother, he could dispense with it, and then with himself, so he wouldn't in any case be needing to do his repair jobs any more. They had only been while he was waiting and biding his time.

They were getting more insistent, anyway, his accusers. This new delay, when he had almost made it, had not received their approval, quite the opposite. They reminded him constantly that it had been four years now, nearly five, since that terrible episode and the death of his father, and ten months now that he had been on the run, free to carry out his pledge. Yet he was still here. In the less-than-adequate snatches of sleep that his duties allowed him, his accusers had developed a penchant for regular visits. He came on groups of them in his deepest slumbers, struck against their heavy presence on the fragile edges of his dreams. They began to demand increasingly, sometimes whispering, sometimes clamouring, a proper explanation as to why he was still here, still alive. They told him that the baby was no excuse, nagged him peevishly both sleeping and awake. Their pull was getting stronger.

It would have to go. And soon. After all, it had been a week now, almost, since Katja had gone, maybe more. She was not coming back. However you looked at it, it was high time for the little brat to go. The young man stopped pacing the room, which he had not even noticed he was doing, and came and looked at it again. It was sleeping peacefully; it might not be so easy to deal with as he had first thought. Its roundness gave it a certain protection, its innocent slumbers a harmlessness that rendered a violent assault, well, overkill. In fact, his intentions seemed rather mean. After all, it wasn't really the baby's fault, who its mother was. But smothering it was still the best plan. He steeled his heart.

Tomorrow. He would do the baby tomorrow.

He slept badly that night, and when he got up, he started to fix the baby's milk, then stopped. That was silly. It was pointless to waste time feeding it before it went. The young man wiped his hands with a briskness that belied the discomfort that he felt, and went and looked purposefully at the baby in its sleeping box.

It was lying on its back, bleating crossly and waving its arms and legs in the air, a protest which seemed mild in view of what was about to happen to it. It had kicked off its blanket and had no pillow. It had seemed from Katja's pamphlets that young babies should not have a pillow, and so he had taken it away. It could have suffocated. To die accidentally was completely different to dying as a prearranged necessity. He had already been the cause of death of his father, perhaps his mother. A further mishap would simply have increased his feeling of incompetence. Of course, he had done his father a favour, simply helped him to where he had wanted to be himself, but he knew that his father would not have seen it in this way. And when he saw in dreams his father's body, spiralling lopsidedly to the ground, it was hard to remember to see it always this way himself. He was sorry for the accident, truly sorry. He always had been.

The young man fetched a cushion and placed it gingerly over the baby's face. The baby began to make a strange, whickering noise and waved its arms and legs more vigorously. The young man pressed with his hand a little harder. The squirming of the warm, soft form beneath his grip repulsed him; it was most unpleasant. He watched the short legs pumping and jerking; the round little flannel stubs that were its feet began to pummel him on the forearm, as gently as if they were no more than stroking. The baby showed no sign yet of collapsing limply. He took the cushion away to check how it was getting on, upon which its squawks immediately became more audible. Its face was red. Around the edges of the groin line a yellow-brown, seeping substance had turned the pale-blue flannel of its romper to greenish; there was a long, brown streak below it in the box. The young man paused indecisively then set the cushion aside. Perhaps it was best not to do this before it was clean. It would be dreadfully messy to dispose of if it had soiled itself.

He fetched it clean clothes and a bowl of water, but the stone cold water did not seem to get the mess off very well. He put some water on to warm and when it warmed he took a little off to wash the baby, and put the rest back on to heat up for a shave. The baby began to scream its head off; how he wanted now to block its cries this very minute! When he had washed it properly he began to warm it a bottle. The morning was getting on. He would feed it to keep it quiet while he washed and dressed, and then he would continue.

Of course, he could always slit its throat. That might be easier than smothering it. The young man tapped the baby gently on the nose with a razor blade, to see what happened. The glancing blow left a small, hairline cut from which a little bright red blood welled out and began to trickle. The baby screamed and started; it had just been on the point of nodding off. It began to cry. The young man had not yet finished shaving; by the time he had, the baby had exhausted itself and snivelled its way back to sleep. It seemed to sleep an awful lot, he reflected, much more than it had seemed to sleep when Katja had it. He began to clear away its things, so that they shouldn't be around if anyone did turn up. He rounded them up and pushed them into the cupboard under the sink.

He supposed that it was all right now to go ahead, that there wasn't the slightest chance of Katja turning up. He stood lost in thought, the cushion again in his hands, trying to work out once again what had been in her mind when she had left, and packed the baby away. Why did she do that? And what did she think – or plan - would happen? Had she intended him to find it before it died? If anyone found the baby, of course it would be him, but she had hidden it in a part of the house he never went to. The young man pulled his mind back to what he was doing, and placed the cushion resolutely over the sleeping baby once more, although he did not press down yet. He needed it to be quiet so he could think. There were only two possibilities – no, four. That he would find the baby or he wouldn't. And that if he found it, by that time, it would be still alive, or not.

He could only try to guess, if there was any point to that, what Katja had been thinking. If she had wanted the baby kept safe, but could not take it with her, she would have left it somewhere obvious, not hidden it where she knew it might not survive. But if she hated it that much, which she did, why had she simply not done away with it herself? Instead she had left it where it might be found, or might not.

If he found it dead, she must be expecting him to dispose of it. For how could he explain it? There was no proof that Katja had been here and left it. But if he found it while it was still alive, then what was she expecting him to do? The answer, he saw, was the same. To get rid of it. Because of course, it would have been obvious to Katja that he couldn't keep it here. And how could he get rid of it? He would have no option, but to do – what he was just about to do. And suddenly the young man understood why Katja had not killed the baby before she went, unless she had simply not had the time. Either way, this was a smarter plan, from her point of view. She had left the baby with someone else who would have to kill it, and take the consequences. It would save her the bother, and save her from getting her own hands dirtied. She didn't have to murder her baby. She knew that the person she hated most in the world would do it for her.

And what was he going to do? He was going to do just what she had planned. He was going to kill the wretched baby, thus saving her from getting any blame. And if she were ever caught, she would make up some story to make him a twisted lunatic who had ruined her life. The young man stood looking at the baby with new perception, saw all around it as it slept the gossamer web set to snare him. A second later he felt inside himself a fiery, powerful surging; an urgent, healthy, irresistible need to postpone his going until he had somehow managed to settle the score with Katja.

Before him as he stood he saw revenge soar up on golden wings, felt its driving force, its power and heat. Its glorious imperative banished his accusers for the first time temporarily to the shade; he hoped they would understand that all of a sudden, he still had earthly business to be done. He beseeched them to be tolerant and patient, and let him live freely, until he had avenged himself against that evil fiend.

He was not going to kill her baby. He was not going to sign and seal her plan. She was bound to turn up again some day, and if she didn't, when this, his time of hiding, was over he would go and find her. And then he would hand her baby back to her, and let the whole world know what she had done. It would be his revenge. He was going to keep the baby alive.

When they next met, her millstone would be waiting for her.

He had to think how he was to carry out this task. It would not be easy, in fact it was well nigh impossible, but it would be worth it. At the same time it was something of a relief that he would not after all be called on to despatch it. He had never really enjoyed killing anything, even flies. And the baby was nowhere near that small and squashable. The feel of it kicking and wriggling as he pressed the cushion had made him rather squeamish. But now in any case it was to be spared. It would have to be a prisoner here, with him.

When the young man pulled his eyes away from the all-illuminating fire of his vision and glanced once more at the sleeping baby, the glow of revenge enhanced its forms and rendered it almost beautiful. Made him feel a bond that had not been there previously. He stared at it almost fondly as it lay in its box, allowing his eyes to follow the rounded curves of its head, its tiny, curled hands. A sudden deliciously warm and malicious joy welled up inside him. It should have a name, to give it real identity for Katja.

He picked up the baby's feeding bottle and held it upside down above the round, cosy head. A single drop of milk, and then another, welled out, fell, and splashed upon the baby's forehead, running down and disappearing into a small, expanding wet patch on the sheet. Taavi leant forward and whispered gently. "I christen this baby 'Fuck You'."

The newly-baptised infant stirred and whimpered fretfully at the dripping cold milk and at being disturbed. The young man set the bottle down and quickly wiped the remnants of the trickling fluid from its face and ears. He hadn't long got it off to sleep.

CHAPTER 29

If there was one thing that the young man was determined to be, it was a better mother than Katja. Katja, who was slapdash and clumsy and lazy, who slept when her child cried, disturbed it when it when it was sleeping, made its milk too hot, had no idea how to treat it or even hold it. The young man was determined to care for his new charge expertly. It was only, after all, for a few months until he had lasted his prison sentence out. As soon as he had lain low for long enough, he would find out where Katja was and make sure she got the baby back. All he needed to do was to keep it in good shape till then.

Which was, of course, a daunting challenge. But the young man found himself fuelled by a sudden firm sense of purpose. A task was before him that was not just a lame excuse to postpone his own departure. He pushed his accusing demons firmly away, bade them stay away, and hoped they would do so, until he had seen his cousin unhappily reunited with her child.

He was logical and methodical by nature. He went once more to the room where he had found her, to check what else might be there, now it seemed that the baby was in for a longer stay. The room was piled and littered higgledy piggledy, and the young man too had simply dug out what he needed and scattered the rest. There were blankets and a plastic baby bath and stuff from the social at the hospital, the boxes of formula, jars of creams and tins of powder. He had no idea what half the items were, but it seemed that babies needed several times more equipment than an adult ten times their size. He needed to find more clothes; the baby had soiled everything it had got. He would have to start washing them, disgusting as they smelt. Up to now he had simply thrown them into the stove. And learn to pin nappies, so they stayed together and did what they were supposed to. The young man picked up the bath. It would come in handy. As he did so a wad of papers began to slither from somewhere and waft towards the floor. When he picked them up he could see they were still more leaflets about how to care for one's firstborn. They looked unused; it seemed Katja had not consulted them, either about the baby's short past or its uncertain future. Downstairs it had just begun to cry, when the health service logo on one of the papers caught the young man's eye. He was holding the baby's case-notes from the hospital. It seemed that Katja had given her own name as Matilda, and had refused to name the baby's father at all. The young man threw the papers into the bathtub with the clothes. He would read it all later. The baby was crying more insistently. He realised with a shock that he was already getting used to it.

His own skills impressed him far more than his new charge itself. He had read up some leaflets and practised how to fold and pin up nappies till late in the night, and studied how to hold the creature in the bath so it didn't keep slipping from his grasp when he soaped it. It would ruin everything if it accidentally drowned. He had read, too, that up until the warmer weather he must pack it up in dozens of layers, which he did till it resembled a rather undersized, badly-misshapen woolly seal. Its clothes, like its body, bore usually several thumbprints of engine oil, but were otherwise clean.

It was hard to imagine, all the same, what mothers got so passionately emotional about, over something that was partly boring, partly comical. Beneath the wrappings, the creature's puny top half was out of proportion compared to its bulging, towelling-padded rump; it was only the clothing that evened the disproportion out. Even stripped to a romper it seemed that babies would not or could not do anything more than flail and jerk their arms and legs. And now when he wrapped it up as the booklets instructed, it could hardly move, but only flap its limbs weakly, like a stranded turtle.

It somehow irritated him, in its helpless flapping and struggling. He kept it on its back so its arms and legs could wave more freely, but still it sometimes grumbled and cried.

Worse still, it amazed the young man how demandingly the baby insisted that he move his timetable to fit in exactly with its own. After two weeks he understood that he was being run by a small, round tyrant. He learned to sleep when the baby slept, wake when it woke, programme his day around its feeding and naps. But he couldn't sit around the house all day. He packed the baby into its sleeping box and took it out to the workshop with him, while he worked as best as he could on repairs that were not too noisy. He wrapped it in dozens of blankets in addition to its clothing, for it was still not quite April. It would never do, in the light of his plans, for it to be even ill. In its warm cocoon the baby slept like a dream. There was always an answer, it seemed, its new guardian thought with satisfaction.

But the baby was changing, the young man noticed. After its initial increased contentment it was growing dissatisfied again, although he was doing his best. It seemed restless in its box, and no longer went straight back to sleep when he had fed or changed it or wrapped it up. It lay and kicked the covers off and brandished its legs about and cried. It distracted him, and made it difficult for him to work. But he couldn't just leave it up at the house while he was busy, where someone might come and find it, or Kosto might get it.

He wondered if the baby was ill, but it ate and slept well. He began to suspect it was bored. It certainly had a very boring life. He tried bouncing it about in its box and waving things at it, but he couldn't do that all the time. He made a contraption that dangled things over the baby automatically to save him the bother, but so that it would think that he was entertaining it - door handles, wing mirrors, rolls of different coloured insulating tape. It seemed to help. He could see the baby following them with its eyes.

And all the time his impression grew more certain, that the baby was getting bigger. The legs of its romper were one day mysteriously too short. At first he thought that the garment had shrunk in the wash, but then he understood that it was the baby's legs that were growing. They were getting longer and stronger; it was that which gave it the strength to kick its covers off all the time.

Of course, it was obvious that babies had to grow, they couldn't stay babies all their lives, but all the same, the change was somehow unexpected. He had somehow imagined that it would stay as it was until he had got it back to Katja. He had to cut the feet off its romper suits so it could straighten out its legs in them. Then its bare feet stuck out and he had to put socks on, but then the socks became too small. He put his own socks on it. They covered its legs to the thighs.

The baby continued growing; became too big for the sleeping box the welfare had provided. He made it another bed, from a box that had contained a refrigerator, cut down to size. Made it a cot from a packing crate for use in the house, rubbing the rough wood down to rid it of splinters. But the socks were a problem, It would be a month yet before the weather was warm enough to go without them.

The baby cried less now in the workshop, he was certain. It lay for hours, watching the things he had rigged up over its head. When the wind blew in from the cracks around the door and windows the objects turned slowly. The rolls of insulating tape and the wing mirrors caught the light as they moved. Their stately passage seemed to excite the baby; it gurgled and waved at them. It had even begun to wriggle its body. The young man stopped work on the record player he was mending and watched it absently. It puzzled him, and he envied it, for it didn't seem to have any demons. On the contrary, despite the tediousness of its limited, uncomfortable and, worst of all, involuntary existence it seemed to exude an unmistakable enjoyment. Pinned down by piss-sodden nappies and bulging romper-suits, unable even to turn in its box, it greeted the world with placid smiles, as if it sufficed day in, day out, to wave and stare and go through its range of meaningless noises. To simply revel in its own existence. It slept with a satisfied look on its lips. If it even understood that it had just embarked on a lifetime of pointlessness, it didn't seem to care.

But whether the baby in its contentment was deeply wise or intensely stupid was naturally more difficult to tell. Now, as usual, its eyes were on the objects above it; it was holding its arms in the air towards the slowly circulating cardboard rolls of tape. "Hoi," called the young man, to catch its attention, but the baby took no notice, just continued to chortle at the rotating objects above its head. "Hoi! Fuck You!" The baby did not respond to its name. He felt suddenly slightly sorry for it, about the name. After all, if you didn't take into account where it came from, it was really quite a cute little thing.

The first of May. May Day festival. The first day of spring. This morning, in accordance with some underlying law of nature, the first buds had suddenly appeared on the shining tree twigs that only yesterday had still been smooth and bare. Watery sunlight, weak but gathering in brightness, braved the still icy air and glittered half-heartedly on the grass. The young man had celebrated heavily, though not with any particular relish, for it wasn't the most fun to celebrate alone.

He was woken finally late in the morning by the anguished, accusing howls of the starving, soaking baby. He came to groggily, pulled from the deepest depths of sleep, and realised that the piercing noise in his dream was the baby, and that he had slept through its screams. He managed it clumsily, spewing yellow vomit into a metal bucket beside it, then returned to his bed. His stomach was sour, his head was heavy with lumps of hot lead that hammered and bruised the inside of his skull. The baby whimpered awhile, then drifted off to sleep, and the young man too sank into a doze, in which he carried the pain from his head like a heavy, precious burden that must not be dropped. Its fire went through his hands as he walked. He carried it carefully, the burden which was at the same time a scarcely endurable pain and a baby, almost floating over the grass, looking out to see if he could see his accusers, for he didn't seem to have seen them for quite a while. He knew they would be over there if he looked. There they were, quite near. Dark, cold, solid. They sat with their backs to him, like rough-hewn monuments that would turn, might turn, would draw him to them with their power, their admonitions. He felt their pull. But he was tired. He kept on walking, and fell into a deeper sleep.

It was the baby that woke him again in the afternoon, with more demands to be fed and changed. The young man drank the last of the beer and some tea, and felt better, but not a lot. When he had dealt with the baby he sat on the wooden settle in the kitchen and stared at it limply. His head still hurt each time he moved. His hangover made him moody and morose. He checked on the monsters, his demons; his dream of the morning had brought them closer to him. They were still there, still loomed so close that he could almost touch and smell them, almost feel their rough, hairy hides, but they did not beckon, did not accuse. Perhaps they had really accepted his plan of revenge. Or maybe he was just too tired to care what they thought. He felt ill, he wanted to spare himself from having to think about all that. His head was still swimming, he did not feel quite grounded in himself. He stared gloomily at the baby as it lay on its back and wondered absently, up to the limits set by his own aching head, what was going on in its brain, if anything at all.

Through his own pain it struck him once again as curious how the baby seemed to be tapped into some source of optimism and curiosity. Even setbacks seemed not to bother it. It just kept plugging away. In fact, so long as it was clean and fed, it responded to everything with enthusiasm. As if its natural inclination, the natural predisposition of a baby, was to live, not die.

These thoughts about babies and their essence seemed so profound, if a little detached from reality, that the young man imagined he could think them forever, but it seemed not so, because he gradually fell asleep again.

He dreamt that his accusers stood around him, large and daunting, and now for the first time one of them revealed its face. Up to now he had always been able to sense their presence, their mood, their cold commanding, but their faces had never been towards him. Now one of them turned to look at him, making him feel small before it. He was surprised to find himself speaking, as if it had addressed him, with a braveness of which he was conscious.

"But babies," he was saying. "If you take babies. They don't try to kill themselves. They're made of joy. That's their essence. They're here because they are born, then they try to explore things. That's the way they're made. They don't look for reasons."

The listening accuser did not speak. Not with its voice and mouth. But its answer came from it, flowing in and through the young man's limbs and body, making his muscles weak.

"Why am I saying this?" he heard himself responding, "Well you see, I just wanted to point out, that that's how we are. At least when we're born. You're not there then. Babies have curiosity and joy. And wonder. That's their essence then. It comes from inside. They're not born wondering what they're doing here."

When he woke up, the young man could not remember the accuser's face. He remembered only pointing out to it his singular observations on babies. But it crossed his mind, like a tiny ray of grey doubt in the infinite darkness of his certainty, that maybe he too had simply an inbuilt right to live. That he need not feel so much anger at himself for not agreeing, or worse still, not even daring, to obey the commands of his accusers without delay.

In any case, he couldn't go anyway until he had effected his revenge.

The dream was with him from that day forward, he never forgot it, though he did, in the weeks that followed, begin to wonder if he hadn't exaggerated to his accusers the baby's miraculous qualities.

The main thing in life that seemed to interest it, whenever it wasn't wanting milk, was the dangling roll of insulating tape over its head. He pitied the baby its obsession. It was kind of sad, although the baby did not seem to think it so. It almost treated the insulating tape as a friend. It waved at it and jiggled up and down and cawed at it, and in the slight breeze created by its own jerking body, or wafting secretly from elsewhere, the tape on its cardboard hoop turned slowly and ostentatiously in the air.

It occurred to the young man one day that the baby was trying to catch the tape, to hold it. He noticed how its round eyes followed it, while the podgy, powerless little baby-hands made feeble pawing, grabbing movements in the air. He watched it, feeling its feeble impotence in the face of its self-appointed task. He had half a mind to walk across and take down the tape roll, put it into the reaching hands. But lethargy overcame him, and he could not be bothered. Besides, as usual, the baby did not seem unhappy, just engrossed in its hopeless efforts to bring its hands in contact with the ring. It raised its eyes to it whenever he put it in its box, and waved its hands at it, hour after hour. Happy, inaccurate, untiring, quite undaunted by its lack of success. He was beginning to come to the reluctant conclusion that it must be stupid after all.

On the other hand he was grateful for the opportunity to concentrate on practical matters. He had other aspects of the baby to worry about. It was still getting bigger. This was of course theoretically to be expected but all the same, as before, he hadn't expected it. He was going to have to find it new vests and rompers. It needed once again a bigger box to sleep in. And something other than newspapers for putting it down on. The newsprint made it grubby, made its skin and clothes an inky, dirty shade.

It was one afternoon when the baby managed to grasp the tape ring. To achieve the impossible, after all those hours of hopeless struggle. Hundreds and hundreds of them. When the young man noticed the baby could do it, he imagined it was just by chance. He was quite surprised it had even managed it that way. But soon the baby had it under control, and could do it again and again.

He would have to start to take the baby on his rounds with him in the van, the young man decided. There was just no other way that he could continue to support himself. He had to buy food and cigarettes, to pay off the van, and now it seemed he would have to start buying things for the baby as well. He had not really thought about that, when faced with the treasure trove in the upstairs boxroom. But now the bounty provided by the welfare was all running out, and the baby was nearly out of clothes. The young man began to pore over adverts in the leaflets. Talc, oils, teething rings, dummies – the lists of puzzling necessities seemed endless, so he ignored them, but clothes it seemed that the expanding baby could not do without.

And petrol, he was always needing petrol for the van. It was an old van, and gobbled it up, but he could not take the risk of only making short trips. He had to drive further off, ply for business in places where no-one would know him for the pale boy who had shot his very own father.

But customers he had in plenty, for it had turned out that he was a wizard with his hands, and his false name as a good repairs man was starting to spread. And so on a fresh May morning the young man put a large box in the back of the van, put some milk in a thermos and the baby in the box and set off.

The pig farm was one of his nearer customers. Just ten kilometres or so, it was true, but all the same, it was far enough for him to be unknown there. A generator there had packed up yet again. When the young man reached the farm and parked the van up in the yard he listened for the baby, but there was no sound. He turned and looked back over the seat, and noticed it had gone to sleep. So far so good.

CHAPTER 30

The pig farmer's daughter was waiting for him in the yard by the time that the young man had pulled up and turned off the engine. Her name was Lotta. She had dull brown hair that hung in drooping rat's tails to her shoulders, and a skinny frame that looked to be composed entirely of angles. She must have known he was coming and been looking out for him from the house, for she couldn't have just been walking round outside. She had no jacket on, and spring had not yet filtered the chill out of the air. She stood before him as he climbed from the van, hugging her arms to her chest to keep warm, and eyeing him expectantly. The young man greeted her curtly. He was not sure whether he was flattered or irritated by her attention.

"I've come to show you where the generator is," she said.

"I know where it is. In the same place as last time, I imagine." The young man walked across the yard to the small wooden generator house, but the door was locked. He had to stand aside while Lotta stepped up with the key. She pressed it into the lock and turned it with hands as thin and fleshless as a bird's claws. He went inside.

She watched him from the doorway as he worked. He could feel her presence all the time, though she did not speak, and her lean, flat-chested form hardly blocked the light. From time to time she raised a hand to hook a strand of hair back behind her ear. She disturbed him, standing there. He wished she would go away.

The silence was broken eventually by the sound of footsteps the other side of the yard. A woman was disappearing into the pigsty with a metal pail. Her manner spoke of hard work and gritty endurance. She did not look in their direction. The young man turned back towards the generator.

"I've fixed it for now. But it needs a new part. I'll have to bring it." He wiped his hands on a rag, threw it into his workbox, and closed the lid. As if from a signal, he heard the first bleating whimper from the van. The baby was warming up to cry. As he crossed the yard Lotta followed him like a faithful dog. Close, obedient, as if she adored him, although he hadn't asked her to follow. She did not ask at once what the noise was, but paused and stared blankly at the dirt-spattered vehicle as the cries gathered strength.

"What've you got in there? It sounds like a baby."

The young man flung open the back doors of the van. He must try to ignore her. But Lotta leant in, craning her neck, her eyes darting backwards and forwards into the darkness. He climbed in past her and picked the baby up from its box.

"It is a baby!" she gasped. Her voice held a note of rapture. She followed the sight of the bundle wide-eyed, her mouth slightly open.

"It needs changing," the young man said shortly. He pushed a space clear on the padded plastic seat that ran along one side of the van, and set the baby down on it. Lotta scrambled up behind him, and thrust her head in beside his elbow, as she bent down to get a closer look.

"Is it yours?"

The young man took no notice, and began to strip off the baby's stinking wraps.

"EEyuk!" In the van's dim half-light Lotta's eyes opened just as wide as they would go. Her nose, her whole face, wrinkled up, and her upper lip curled involuntarily in distaste. The young man picked up a can of water to wash the baby down. Lotta followed his actions aghast and mesmerized, as he doused a cloth and began to wipe off the muck.

"It's a girl," she pronounced, to no-one in particular, and continued to stare at the half naked baby thoughtfully. The young man hoicked it up by the ankles with one hand and deftly pushed the folded nappy into place beneath it. He was already something of an expert.

"I didn't know you had a baby," said Lotta. She sounded impressed. "Are you married?"

"Mind your own business."

"How old are you?"

"Don't ask personal questions," said the young man. "How old are you?"

Lotta drew herself up and pushed her chest out. "Fifteen." The young man threw her an absent-minded look. Fifteen. Well, he supposed she must be. It was hard to imagine she was not much younger than Katja. She was strait-laced and serious, thin and scrawny where Katja, if obnoxious, was luscious and womanly.

The baby let out a whining cry.

"I think it's hungry," said Lotta.

"Since when were you such an expert?" The young man held the baby in place with one hand while he reached for the thermos flask, then found he could not fill its bottle without letting go. "You can hold it if you want," he said. He showed Lotta how to hold the baby, how to feed it. She sat on the torn plastic seat and clumsily held the bottle to its mouth, scared stiff and puffed up with pride. When it had finished he showed her how to burp it, a skill she sought to master with selfless diligence.

"What's its name?"

The young man was already tidying up his things. He glanced at the baby. "It's called Fuck You."

Lotta threw him an incredulous look, but her lip was already curled again in horror.

"I don't think that's funny," she said. "You should know quite well, it's wrong to use words like that. It's offensive. And you certainly shouldn't joke about babies by swearing." She threw the baby an angry, pacifying look. "You shouldn't swear at all, it's rude. Especially when people are being polite. What's it really called?"

"That's it. That's the name it's christened."

"But you can't call a baby that. That's disgusting. And anyway, it's not a proper name. It isn't legal. What does your wife say?"

She looked at the young man's hand. "Why aren't you wearing a ring?"

"My wife?" the young man said. "She's left me. She's gone. That's why I bring the baby round with me."

Lotta looked up sharply, her pale face distorted for a second with compassion. Then it hardened. "I'm not surprised, if you call the baby names. She's so sweet."

The young man had already opened his mouth to reply when Lotta froze at the sound of footsteps approaching. Clumping footsteps, as of rubber boots, but a tread too light for a man. She tried to struggle up, the sleeping baby in her arms.

"I should go."

The young man took the baby and laid it in its box; its form was already down below the rim when the pig farmer's wife appeared at the back of the van. Lotta leapt down hastily as her mother gripped the door edge with a bony hand and stuck her head in. Her face, like her hand, was plain and work-worn, and her lank hair drawn severely back from her brow. It was easy to see how Lotta would become, if she stayed on the farm. The farmer's wife blinked for a second, accustoming her eyes to the gloom.

"Come out," she said. "The man's got better things to do than to have you pestering him."

Lotta moved to obey. As she climbed down from the van she turned back. The young man guessed she had something to say about the baby, but on noticing that it had disappeared from view it was clear that she thought it best to hold her tongue.

"Did you get it fixed?" her mother asked him.

"For now. It needs a new part. I'll bring it next week." When he drove out, Lotta looked round, but it seemed that she did not dare to wave. No wonder, when her mother could be taken for the grim reaper's wife.

"You haven't got it very well dressed," said Lotta, critically. "Look, its feet are sticking right out. And this stuff is not very clean." She had taken the baby from its box while the young man was fitting the spare part for the generator, and was playing with it in the back of the van. He threw them both an unrepentant glance.

"I'm a mechanic, not a fucking housewife."

Her criticism partly annoyed him, and partly he brushed it aside. That was typical of women and girls, to fuss over babies. The whole time he was working she was cooing over it, wanting to feed and change it, at which she was hopelessly inexpert. She treated it as if it were a doll.

The next time he went there she had bought it presents. A little dress, because it was a girl. A rattle. A soft, blue, furry dog.

It was suddenly almost summer, the end of May. The spring had crept on past before anyone noticed. In May the earth had finally opened and relaxed, and now green leaves were sprouting everywhere, and a gentle balm began to pervade the air. On the pigman's farm thin grass blades began to push up through the bare muddy soil, and the pig farm began to lose its barren look. It almost thrived, and even the pigs began to look fat and sleek. Amid its scenes of pastoral plenty the gaunt grim reaper's wife looked oddly out of place, as if ungrateful for the ease and bounty that was round her. Even the generator was working for now.

Then the tractor developed a fault.

Lotta heard the news of the ailing tractor with joy and hope in her heart; in deepest secret she allowed her eyes to glow. That meant the mechanic would be called, he would bring the baby. It would be the perfect start to the summer holidays.

The baby's howls were audible the minute the noisy roars of the engine faded away.

"I don't know why you don't fix that van," said Lotta, who had crossed the yard to snatch up the object of her affection. "No wonder the poor thing screams."

The air was warm now; it was really summer. She no longer had to hug her arms to her chest while she waited for the van doors to open.

"It's fractious," said the young man, as she pounced upon the small, red, squalling form. "It keeps struggling. It's hell in the van now. I have to tie it down." He looked at the baby distastefully. "It used to be ok."

"It wants to sit up," said Lotta, who seemed to consider herself now precociously knowledgeable in these matters. She glanced back from the darkness of the van to the sunlit brilliance of the yard. "We could take it outside. It's quite warm. We could get it a mat and the cushions from the swing."

They arranged the baby on a small patch of thick grass underneath a tree. The baby crooned and waved its arms at the insects that beset it, and gurgled and flapped at the bright-yellow faces of surrounding dandelions.

"See?" said Lotta "It's better now. It wants to sit."

She straightened herself with the sudden self-assertiveness of one who has just been proved right, lifting her nose to the sky and stretching her arms out. The sort of movement one only makes on a carefree, warm summer's day. The young man watched idly, his mind full of tractor gears and levers. There was only so much interest, after all, that one could feel in a baby. Lotta raised her arms again and circled them about, as if revelling in their freedom after holding that heavy, precious load. She was looking less somewhat less peaky, it struck the young man, as if the warmth of the summer had somehow filled her out, at least from skinny to very slim. On the backward movement of her armswings her blouse pulled back against her body and sculpted out two small bulges on her chest. So she wasn't quite flat. And when she bent down her arched back betrayed the outline of a bra beneath her blouse. But fifteen! It was quite bizarre, how completely unlike Katja she was, in every way. Where Katja had sprung up into a gorgeous, poisonous flower, it seemed clear that Lotta was destined never to blossom, was doomed to stay scrawny and dour and reserved all her life. Even now, the summer had not teased much effervescence out of her. And where Katja was full of manipulative tricks, Lotta's vice was a straight-spoken sharpness, except towards the baby. She was on again about the creature now.

"You should put it on a mat and cushions at home, so it can see what's going on."

"That's not very easy." he heard himself object. "I have to work. There's always things to mend. And then there's the dog. I don't want the dog to get it."

And he really didn't. Supposing the dog were to savage the baby, after all his hard work?

"I could come and look after her for you," said Lotta, her face coming suddenly alive. "I don't have school now. I have to help out here, but not all the time."

"I live miles away. I don't live anywhere near here." The young man regretted this rejection in an instant, though he wasn't sure why.

"I could come on my bike," suggested Lotta, undeterred. She sounded enthusiastic. "I needn't say where I'm going. They like me to use my bike. It's healthy. I could mind the baby and feed her and so on while you get on with your work. I won't disturb you."

The young man hesitated. It had of course been his unwritten rule that no-one should know who he was, or where he came from, or even what his real name was. But if she did that, if she really came and minded the baby, and didn't simply irritate him with interruptions and her childlike devotion, he could get stuff done and finished and back to its owners so it didn't clutter up the workshop quite so much. He looked at Lotta. The wind was blowing her hair across her face like seaweed tresses moving in the sea. He didn't know why she didn't tie it back. The baby keeled over among its cushions and let out a yell. Lotta bent down and righted it.

"You're so sweet," she cooed to it. "Up you come." Then she straightened up. "Well? What do you say?" She searched his face a little anxiously. "I could come on Saturday."

The young man stared at her at a loss, aware of strange, mixed feelings both urging him onwards and filling him with apprehension. The risk involved in inviting someone to his house was enormous, but it wasn't just that. It was just as much that the person who he might invite was a girl. A girl to visit. There was something challenging, scaring, attractive about the idea. Though of course, it was the baby she was coming to mind.

"There's a map in the van," he said. "I'll show you where I live."

CHAPTER 31

He awaited Lotta's visit on the Saturday with something like nerves. He didn't know why. Apart from a sharpish tongue and a critical streak she was just a child, after all. It was natural for young girls to want to mother babies, to treat them like living dolls.

All week the young man had put the baby out on a mat, as directed, where it struggled and writhed determinedly while he worked. It was sometimes a nuisance, and he had to be careful of the dog. But he knew that Lotta would have a go at him if he hadn't tried.

She came. He was of course expecting her - well, half expecting her, but all the same, he started when he first heard the sound of a bicycle bell outside. He went out to meet her. He had shut the dog away in an upstairs room so it wouldn't bark and scare her out of her wits. If it did that when she arrived she would never come in. He led her up the wooden steps of the porch to the front door, and into the kitchen.

"It's still asleep," he said. "It's in the other room. It'll wake in a minute."

He stood silent. He had run out of things to say. Lotta too, after greeting him, had become quite quiet. She stood before him in his house, his sanctuary, a strange and alien creature that he could not reconcile with his own familiar surroundings.

A girl. A representative, however immature and scrawny, of that dangerous, largely unobtainable yet desperately sought-after species. Girls, those beings he had only dreamed of, that he longed to master and impress; girls, who had tortured him through their absence and sheer impossibility. And now one was here, albeit not a first-class specimen, and he did not know what to do. He offered her coffee. She refused. Beer. She looked doubtful. She drank sourmilk. The baby began to wake.

The young man did not work that day. He assisted Lotta as she mothered the baby, fussing over it under the orchard trees. He relaxed a little as she lost her shyness. When it fell asleep he made her sandwiches and showed her round the house, but not too near the room where Kosto was imprisoned. He had tried to tidy up a little before she came, at least downstairs. He showed her round his workshop and the sheds, and told her of his wife who had run off with someone else.

The baby woke. Lotta took it out once more to the orchard in its stroller, but only briefly. "I must be getting back soon," she said, when he went out to join her. "I can't be gone too long."

She was standing quite close to him. Her hair was less lank today, or perhaps it was only tousled by the bike ride. He wondered what would happen if he reached out and touched her, put his hand through the air to catch back the strands that everlastingly seemed to be blowing across her face.

A beetle landed suddenly on her collar bone, out of nowhere, and folded its shiny black wings against the pale skin. He brushed it off before Lotta had even raised her hand. She jumped away, turning her face towards him a little startled, suddenly wary. He saw it in her eyes.

"It was a beetle."

He was twenty two. He must seem very old to her.

"When shall I come again?"

"During the week. You could come on Thursday." In his mind he saw still the alarmed, defensive look in her eyes. "Then you could mind the baby for me while I do some work."

"I could do some tidying up, while I'm here," said Lotta. "You're not very tidy."

"Suit yourself".

They made their way towards her bicycle. Lotta bent down to croon farewells at the baby. When she stood up she flashed a sudden smile, at no-one and nothing in particular, but which seemed to the young man to probably include him in its range. A bright, warm, totally unexpected smile. It transformed her face, and banished for a second the caution in her eyes. The young man felt slightly perturbed.

He watched her as she cycled off, bouncing in and out of the rutted tracks that led through the entrance. When she had disappeared up the road he let the dog out. Of course it was great, if she was willing to take the baby off his hands. But in addition, it was vital he should think of a plan.

He wasn't a murderer. Deep down, he did not even believe that he was bad. He had never done anything bad, except caused that terrible accident which was never intended. He had felt himself lonely and a misfit, until that summer day when the abyss of truth had opened before him and his soul had been overwhelmed with anger and despair. He had seen the truth for what it was, a black void that rendered all things futile, and found himself faced alone with challenging that heinous lie, the devil's greatest joke. The illusion of a meaning to existence. But he hadn't been bad. He had only tried to do what he knew to be right.

Yet set against the background of all his despair, his useless life, his anguish at the awful duty set before him, was always one small fact that niggled far beyond its minimal status in the greater, cosmic order of things. Belonging as it did to the temporal, and pitiably pointless earthly realm.

He was a virgin.

CHAPTER 32

The van was playing up. It was leaking from somewhere, and making a knocking sound when he turned off the engine. It put the young man in a very bad mood, and to make matters worse, his plans and hopes concerning Lotta were getting nowhere. She had been now three or four times, and each time an iron weight seemed to weigh him down, when he tried to think of how distract her focus from the baby. Her conquest seemed with every visit more impossible, despite his resolutions.

She was coming today. He had meant to meet her at the gate, but when she arrived he was flat on his back beneath the van. He crawled out to greet her and stood before her, tongue-tied and oily, as she parked her bicycle, while across the yard the dog strained greedily towards her. Panting and slobbering it pranced and danced at the end of its rope, and let out the odd snarling yelp. The weather was hot; the young man had simply tethered it, instead of shutting it out of the way in an upstairs room. Lotta eyed it uncertainly and retreated, to which it responded with a deafening onslaught that made its intentions clear. Within the house the baby woke and gave a scream. Lotta paused in an agony of indecision, and stood rooted to the spot while her glance shifted nervously back and forth between the young man and the dog.

"The baby's crying. Are you going to help me get inside? I don't like that dog."

The young man mounted the porch steps with her and pushed the front door open irritably.

"I'll shut it up." Just as soon as she had gathered up the baby he returned to the yard and dragged the dog to its outhouse, where he jammed the door closed, then, since Lotta and the baby had disappeared, he crawled back once more underneath the van. There in the oily blackness armed with tools of wrath he could vent his anger and frustration, about the van, about his miserable failure at conquest, and everything else. For it seemed to the young man he had had to be patient, and to keep himself going on the vague hopes of better times ahead, all his life.

He had been there for a half hour when he heard the front door open, and Lotta came out and crossed the yard towards him. When he turned his head he could see her long, knobbly feet in their sandals, beside the van. "Is it sleeping again?"

"For the moment."

He wanted her to go away and leave him in peace. "I'll be out in a minute. I'm almost done." The feet remained. "Do you want a drink? There's stuff in the kitchen." He inched on his back from under the van till his head was out and gazed up questioningly. "Is everything all right?" It might as well not be. The day was a write-off anyway.

"There's something I want to discuss with you," said Lotta. From his angle on the ground her face was partly obscured by the contours of her body. The young man retreated a little back under the van, and turned his attention again to the low, black, rusty ceiling just above him. . He didn't see it was her job to lecture him on anything.

There was a moment's pause.

"I don't think you should call the baby Fuck You", said Lotta. "I think it's really terrible to call a baby something like that. It's an insult to her." The young man started searching for a spanner. "It isn't even a proper name," he heard her continue. "You can't have a swearword as a name. I've told you that before."

"I think it's good enough," he said, although lately in secret even he had been having his doubts. "I had my reasons."

"It's dreadful. It's an insult. A disgusting insult."

"What should it be called?" The young man moved his head out a fraction and raised his eyes.

"Something beautiful!" Lotta exclaimed. There was something exhorting and despairing in her voice. "Something beautiful. Like, for example," - she waved her arms in the air and looked around at the sun-filled yard - 'Summer Rose'. Or 'Summer Breeze'."

"It was born in fucking January," said the young man. "And those aren't proper names, either."

"Well, something sensible, then. And simple. Like Veera. Or Eeva."

There was silence again. The young man gazed up. He wasn't in the mood for discussing the baby's name. Lotta took a small step nearer, was standing practically over him. The summer breeze of which she had spoken played roguishly with the skirt of her cotton dress. He could see her knees, beyond them, the front of her panties, up, up, through the gently curved valley between the nippled mounds on her chest to the shadowed underside of her chin. Her skirt floated down to return to its prim work of concealment. She had no bra, he noticed, today, and also that her breasts were smallish, but round. Lotta sighed suddenly, and folded both arms firmly across her midriff. The breeze gave a single, billowing, mischievous tweak to her skirt.

"Well, anyway, you simply can't keep calling it that dreadful name. I don't want to say it, even. What do other people say, when you tell them what you call it? What would your wife say? I'm sure she didn't approve."

"I don't really talk to anyone except for you," said the young man, "and my wife isn't here." He wished she would unfold her arms, allow the breeze to do its darnedest.

"Do you think she'll come back?"

"I really can't say."

"Well, I'm sure she'd be shocked to find out what you call that baby."

"Serve her right. I told you I had my reasons."

Lotta looked disapproving. He could tell her expression even upside down from the ground. "You can't go calling her a name like that just to get your own back on someone else! That's appalling! Just think how that poor mite will suffer. And it's not her fault." She glared at him angrily. "Don't you love her?"

The young man did not answer. He had opened his mouth to say that the baby was simply a burden and an inconvenience, but some strange, sudden sense of honesty made him hold his tongue. Such an answer seemed grossly disrespectful to it.

The breeze stirred again. Lotta lifted both hands and tucked the flying strands of hair behind her ears. He wondered what the neat little hillocks of her breasts would taste like, how it would feel to take them in his mouth. The panties were bikini bottoms, he was sure. She seemed to have forgotten that he hadn't answered her question.

"You have to change her name. There must be some way to get you to do it." He could feel her eyes fixed on him, feared she would read the fact that it was not her face on which his own eyes were focussed. He twisted his head.

"Ow!" The sharp metal edge of the toolbox he had pulled in with him hit his cheekbone.

"Are you all right?" Lotta crouched down.

"I just knocked my head. I'm coming out now." The young man wriggled gingerly out from under the van. It still wasn't right. He hoped he wouldn't have to take it to a garage.

Lotta followed him across the yard and up the steps. "Just think how that dear little baby would love it if it found out its real name was Summer Rose."

"In my books, Summer Rose is just as awful as the name it's got." Did she really have to choose today to drive him crazy?

"So you think her name is awful too!" Lotta exulted. "And you know you can't call her that when she goes to school."

"It's not your business," the young man retorted brusquely. "And not your baby, even, though you act as if it is. Just keep your nose out."

"I was only trying to help," exclaimed Lotta. To his disconcertion her eyes filled up unexpectedly with tears. This final weapon exasperated him even more.

"I need to go and wash." He made his way upstairs to the bathroom and made sure she heard him locking the door.

When he came down Lotta was still weeping hot, silent tears of humiliation.

He was suddenly slightly ashamed of his sharpness with her. She was a nice kid. It wasn't her fault the van was playing up, or that her mind ran solely on babies. He said sullenly, "I'm sorry I was rude to you."

Lotta avoided looking at him. "We need some more milk," she said coldly, and gave a noise between a sniff and a sob. "For the baby when it wakes. For this baby without a proper name."

"I'll fetch some."

The young man mounted the stairs again in a crestfallen mood. He hadn't ever crossed swords with Lotta before. He fetched a box of formula and took it down, pausing halfway to look down into the kitchen. Lotta was staring into space at nothing in particular, a woebegone expression on her face. She looked up as he set the milk down on the table.

"Are we still friends?" Her voice was a little uncertain, still a little thick.

"Of course."

"I didn't mean to be a nuisance."

"You're not a nuisance." he conceded, sulkily.

Lotta began to wipe her eyes and her streaming nose with the back of her hand. "I haven't got a hanky."

"I'll get you one." The young man began to rummage in a kitchen drawer for a piece of sheeting or a drying-up cloth. He dug through the drawer for as long as he dared in order to win himself some valuable thinking and preparation time, then he came back with a cleanish duster. Lotta took it humbly and finished drying her face.

He looked at her. Her eyes were still full of tragedy, still damp and red round the edges. But if he was merely gentle with her, and simply cheered her up, he would never get anywhere. He had to make use of the situation, the sacrifices she might run to for the baby in her current mood. He said, "I've thought of something you could do. About the name."

When the baby woke, it had earned the new name of Summer Rose and, after a modest interval, a second name, Veera. 'Summer Rose' would not have been the young man's first choice of name or even his last, but it didn't matter. He could always change it. What Lotta had given she could certainly never ask for back.

CHAPTER 33

The baby had a tooth. It had wept and grizzled and screamed in the night and chewed at its hands in what could be taken for utter grief, till the young man feared that the worst had happened and the great and terrible knowledge of the utter futility of its existence had replaced the baby's inborn essence of happiness and joy. The discovery of the small, sharp cutting edge in its reddened gum brought the young man back from the depths of despair, but still the baby seemed discontented and fractious.

"It needs food," said Lotta. "It's hungry now it's getting some teeth. You should boil it some potato, that's what they give them."

While the young man watched she boiled and mashed a single potato, salted it well, and put a generous spoonful into the baby's mouth. The baby cried angrily and spat it out. "It was probably too hot," said Lotta. "I'll blow on it." She took a second blob of potato onto the spoon, blew vigorously on it for what seemed eternity, and fed it to the baby, who this time spat it halfway across the room. When the baby had forcibly ejected several offerings she sat back and looked at it rather hopelessly.

"I don't think it likes potato." She looked doubtfully at the messy remains in its dish. "Perhaps if we tried it with some jars of baby food from the shop. At least if it's in jars you know it's proper."

She came with jars, teethers, soothing ointments, a teddy-bear bib. But the experiment with the jars was no more successful. This time the baby did not cry when presented with its dinner, but it seemed to have no idea how to swallow it. Or even where its mouth was. At the slightest distraction it turned its head, and allowed the spoon with its precious cargo to come into messy collision with its face. They had to bath it.

In the evening, when Lotta had gone, the young man tried once more, but still the food went everywhere except in the baby's mouth. He consulted the know-it-all leaflets again for guidance on feeding babies, and finally there after hours of searching he noticed the answer. The babies there were strapped into high chairs.

Their will to co-operate was irrelevant, their docility possibly only apparent. They were under control.

It was clear that the baby needed a high chair. The young man pondered for a while, about where to buy one from, and then the answer came to him. He would make one. Moreover, he would make it the most beautiful, elegant high chair in the world. It would be a work of art, not just simply an instrument of constriction. The baby deserved that.

It was late already. Experience had taught him to sleep when the baby slept, but now he ignored that rule. His mind was excitedly full of the image of a beautiful, handmade, painted baby's chair. Crossing his yard without a thought for the demons who usually waited for him there at the midnight hour, the young man went to his workshop and began to saw.

It seemed odd to the young man in the time that followed, that he whose life had been, he now reflected, dismally empty, should suddenly have become, without his planning it, rather full. Out of emptiness had come substance; in the midst of black despair, inextinguishable points of bright light had materialised. From nothing, nothing in the world bar his seething anger and his pact with death, he had found himself with a child to bring up, a business to run, a friend – for Lotta was a friend, and now that long-awaited dream, a sex-life. But it wasn't these things, these points of bright light that lifted his soul from darkness. They were by themselves no more able to do that than the stars overhead could lift up a heavy, blackened wreck from the depth and swell of the ocean. Without support, the dark lamps of the accusers, the darkness of his own soul would have eclipsed them. No, it was something else that allowed them to shine, a small smudge that was lighter than black in the infinite blackness of his soul. The puzzling question mark of the baby, whose innermost essence seemed to be to live, not to die.

Whose life unfolded daily before him, propelled by a seemingly endless fount of curiosity and underlying joy.

As to striving being a part of the baby's essence, it seemed the vibrations of this were becoming amplified. The baby was more and more active and restless, and had taken to rocking about and shifting around. It was well-nigh impossible to change, and its nappy was horrible. It demanded to be fed, and then was messy and resistant; the pantomime took hours.

Lotta dictated little delicacies it should have. It was all a battle, now the baby was no longer something that lived in a box. But the young man was like a bulldog now, with his teeth sunk in. He would not let go. He battled to get the mushes and mashes into its mouth, set it out on an improvised mat near the spot where he was working, where it spent its time struggling and kicking. By the hour, like a half-wit, though the young man hung onto his impression that the baby was not at all stupid, underneath. One day while he was watching absent-mindedly the baby sat up. Lotta acted as if she had taught it to do that herself. Soon sitting up had become the baby's trick, yet it kept on struggling, until it seemed that from sitting it was trying to get down again. Lotta said it was going to start to crawl. The young man waited in scepticism and anticipation. He made renewed promises to his demons, for he feared he was ignoring them dangerously, but the baby fascinated him. And its needs protected him from his duty at the present.

It was certainly becoming plump and strong. Lotta, who seemed to see infant development as her vocation, had reformed her opinions on nutrition and proclaimed that babies should not have salt, and also that Summer Rose should be having home-cooked food.

"Even I don't have that," the young man pointed out. But Lotta was insistent. She boiled a potato again, and a single carrot, and put them through a sieve. Without salt. The baby ate them.

"See?" said Lotta. "You can give her home food. Anything you can put through a sieve: meat, veg, apples, bananas, peas. You can try her with anything, so long as you sieve it. And don't put salt."

The young man was not a gourmet cook. But now and then, to keep Lotta off his back, and help the baby grow, he did his best.

CHAPTER 34

The baby did not like the new food that the young man had prepared. He had mashed a pickled herring finely with a fork and stirred it to a suitable paste with a spoonful of two of tinned pea soup, but not far into the plateful the baby began to grumble and push the spoon fretfully away. The young man gave the rest to the dog and fed the baby on a slice of rye bread dipped in sourmilk, which it seemed to enjoy. It liked things to chew on too, now it had a tooth. He gave it a chunk, and then another chunk, of apple, rather sour, the first from the orchard trees.

In the middle of the evening the baby was violently sick, throwing up on its nightclothes and the bedding of the cot. The young man cleaned it up and put it back down to sleep in the spare cot in the kitchen, which he used for its daytime naps.

From the sounds that the dog was making it seemed that it too must have a stomach ache. The evening was warm; he could hear its grousing through the upstairs window that was open onto the yard. It growled and snarled, then it set to and began to bark. The young man paused and listened. Why was it barking? Had some creature run the risk of bolting across the yard? Then he heard the door. He had shaved it and oiled it and straightened the warp, but it still made a very slight scraping squeak as it opened. He went to the head of the stair and stood there quietly, every muscle tensed, just as Fisher had stood there once before, on the night when the goddess had arrived. Lotta never came in the evening. Not this late, when it was already sunset.

It was only a second later when he saw her face, her hair like a glowing halo as she stood at the kitchen door.

"Out!" He screamed, so loudly that the baby woke with a start and let out a single, piercing scream in response. The owner of the golden hair looked up, then turned and fled as the young man rushed down the stairs and began to chase her. He chased her out across the yard, and the dog joined in and leapt around them, snarling and snapping as they ran. But it didn't bite.

He had to give up halfway down the road. He had bare feet, and the stony ground was cutting them to shreds. Besides, she had had a head start; he had come down from the top of the stairs. But there wasn't the slightest doubt who it was who had stood at the kitchen door, for the sun had been casting its last rays through the windows. It was Katja. The apocalypse had arrived.

She had come back. But why? To the young man's surprise he found himself trembling and shaking, long after the breathlessness of his short, sharp run had worn off. He had to calm himself with a drink.

She had come back. That cruel, manipulating, murderess-by-proxy had returned. And wherever she had got to in her absence, whatever she had been doing, and whatever she was up to now, there could only be one reason why she would ever come back here.

She had come for the baby.

The baby. Ever since it had first begun to exert its hold on him, to fill him with curiosity and questions despite himself, the young man had begun to leave undisturbed in the background the memory of the source from whence it came. So successfully, that it seemed now that the baby had arrived from somewhere all by itself. It had arrived and put itself in his care, and now it belonged to him. It was growing beautifully, it had made him observe that its essence was to live, and not to die. It was hard to recall its original role as an instrument purely of revenge, and the young man hardly ever did so. He had cared for it, and as time went on, the spectre of Katja had faded completely away. That she would never return had been so obvious, he had long since ceased to even bother to think of her at all.

Yet now she was back. She had come to destroy what he had nurtured, to break it, contaminate it, like the vile fiend that was all that she was. Worst of all, she would snatch back the baby she had abandoned, and claim it for her own. She must have changed her mind. God knows why she thought it might still be alive. And what would she do to it when she had stolen it? How would she bring it up? What would any child be like after being with Katja for fifteen or sixteen years? Except that she might kill it. Or neglect it so that it would die, after he himself had gone to such great lengths to preserve it. He had sheltered it, and been rewarded with the one thing he had least expected; a hint of light in the darkness. And now she had come here to take his miracle away.

The young man felt near to tears in his wretchedness, staring out anxiously into the autumn evening. He would defend the baby. He would make sure that Katja never got it back. He was not sure whether she had noticed the cot in the kitchen, she had only stood there for a second, but she might have. If she came back again, he would be prepared. He pushed the cot with its sleeping baby to the living room, to the corner behind the door where it would be least visible, and shut the door. He didn't like to try and take it upstairs, in case it woke. Then he stood for a while at a loss, and wondered what else to do.

It was then that he remembered the gun, the one that Fisher had found in the outhouse and put in the kitchen drawer, to keep off wolves and squatters. The young man had seen it there, but never touched it. He had developed an absolute distaste for firearms. He took another drink and went to the drawer and opened it. The gun was still there. He checked it out. Fisher had loaded it wrongly. He reloaded it. Any nonsense, he would threaten her. He would fire cartridges over her head. She knew what had happened once before. She would believe him.

He sat down at the kitchen table, keeping guard. But nothing happened. He began to half believe after all that he had imagined it, although it startled him to understand how near the surface his underlying fears were.

For why would she come back? She had wanted more than anything else in the world to be rid of the baby. She had left it for dead. Or for him to kill. Either way, it wouldn't still be alive. She would know that.

He was being stupid. His nerves were playing tricks.

The kitchen bench was hard and uncomfortable. The young man went out to feed the dog, but kept it out on its rope instead of shutting it up. At least then he would get a warning of anybody crossing the yard. The door from the kitchen to the hall he kept open, so he could see who was coming in. Then he rested his head on his arms at the kitchen table, the gun beside him, while his mind went through eddies of drifting and alertness, drifting here, there, but his ears listened always for the opening of the front door, or a signal from the dog.

When the world around was quite dark and quiet he heard a sound, and sat up, reaching for the gun. Then came a silence, as if someone might be waiting to make sure the coast was clear. The young man knew what the sound had been. It was the pantry window being opened at the back of the house. She was coming in that way, to avoid confronting the dog. He did not hear her footsteps, they were so soft. When she came in stealthily, through the doorway that led from the back of the house to the hall, she did not look towards the kitchen, where the young man stood waiting hidden behind the half-open door. She stood for a second in the deep dusk, just long enough for him to make out her form, then she moved the few steps across the hall to the living room. The young man turned cold, put his arm round the door, raised the gun and pointed it upwards towards the angle of the ceiling. He felt his whole body squeeze and contract as he pulled the trigger. The gun made a dead sound. Katja might not even have heard it, for at just that moment she opened the living room door, which clicked faintly. Or perhaps she was not quite sure. At any rate, she paused on the threshold for a second, head alerted, then she stepped inside. It was as if she knew just where to go.

CHAPTER 35

It had taken Katja almost no time to realise that London was the reason she had been born. It was like a nectar-hearted flower, unfolding itself for her to sup on, dance over, petal after petal; a whole field of flowers for her to flit across, a carefree, sun-kissed butterfly. She was pampered, indulged, the city's delights were hers to sample, and all the more heady in contrast to what she had been through. She was free. Far from that dreary, collapsing house and her aggravating cousin, released from the heavy, unbearable tedium of her pregnancy. Free from the baby – even her body was her own. It grew light and beautiful again, clad in the clinging designer-label clothes that Fisher purchased for her almost daily. Of course, she was lumbered with the miser himself, which was no small drawback, but the swiftest passing glance at her wardrobe reassured her of the value she was getting for her endurance. And as well as clothes she had freedom, time, money, her marvellous figure. She was in London, the centre of the world.

Since Fisher's own flat was let out for the academic year they rented another, more exclusive apartment, near Marble Arch, so that the goddess could be near Oxford Street. In London it was already spring when they came; and beds of yellow daffodils brought regal splendour to the bright-green, snowless stretches of nearby Hyde Park. Fisher was still rather traumatized that they had not brought the baby, but acknowledged to himself in retrospect that this was for the best.

The presence of the goddess helped enormously to temper his nostalgia for the exquisite land he had left, and to also ward off questions as to why he had not, after all, settled down there to write his book. For certainly no-one could deny the fabulousness of the booty he had brought back unexpectedly from his expedition. More precious than any diamond, the goddess shone and scintillated. Fisher told friends and acquaintances and colleagues, with perfect honesty, that she was the reason he had cut short his previous plans. He had longed to bring her to London. He showed her off at dinner parties, theatres, receptions, a little coyly, for she wasn't even a third his age, but well, as he pointed out, Cupid had always been well-known as a scant respecter of convention.

Of course it was clear that mere conversation between them was not yet possible. "I am sure they can communicate on the bare essentials, at least," quipped Phillips, so incessantly that people started to avoid him. Despite her magnificence and the countless spiritual virtues which Fisher extolled, it seemed that the young girl's English was minimal at best.

"The chemistry is the main thing," said Fisher. "The language can come later. I am going to enrol her on a language course, as soon as she has got her bearings here." And he did.

At which point Katja's bearings changed completely. So completely, that after two months Fisher hardly saw her at all.

The students on her language course were a crowd of young people like herself. Like herself, but of a sort she had never met before, far more exciting in every way. They went to clubs and discos and pizzerias, got noisily rolling drunk in pubs. In one night she could date two men who did not even remotely add up to the miser's age. And as for English, it seemed that twenty words was the maximum anyone might need.

At first she would return in the early hours to the flat, but receiving the repeated impression that Fisher did not like this, she took to staying out and having breakfast instead in a café frequented by fine art students and out-of-work actors. After meeting André she went 'home' only when she needed a change of clothes. And each time she went there it seemed to her that the miser looked somehow even older and greyer than before. More wrinkled and droopy and even less - alive, if that was possible. Yes, Katja could perceive, in her own new abundance of life, that there was something lifeless about him. He was like something that has had the stuffing knocked out.

Yet she was learning English, she learnt it all over the place. She no longer went to the course.

From André she progressed to Dieter, who being older, though not as old as Fisher, was, like Fisher, sufficiently wealthy to buy for her all the clothes she could ever need or desire. This saved her from having to go back to Marble Arch at all, and after a few drinks she could hardly remember what the miser had to do with her life in the first place.

Phillips, coming to pick the couple up to attend a reception one evening, was disconcerted to hear the sound of heartbroken sobs as he approached.
A short time after, Fisher returned to his previous flat.

But Katja did go back. She went back after Dieter had beaten her up for the second time, and found that Fisher had disappeared. When she knocked, a domestic in uniform answered the door, and spoke to her rudely. She returned to Dieter, who locked her up, and soon after that she escaped to find that life had clouded over, and that London was a cold, uncharitable place.
In the end, it was chance that rescued her from the hand-to-mouth, night-to-night existence she had taken up. She was scooped up in a dawn raid on the flat of someone called Spiker, and found herself after a night in the cells on the plane to Helsinki. She arrived there broke, begged a ride from the airport, and set out to find a place to stay for the night.

She had less to drink in the bar than her drinking companion. In the morning she rose before he woke, and combed her hair in his bathroom mirror. Then she took out the last few notes from his wallet, drank the milk from his fridge, shut the front door quietly behind her and caught the train up north.
It wasn't love that was driving her home, to the tiny village she had started out from. She simply had nowhere else to go. But even so, her host had not had quite enough cash left to get her there. She would have to stop off, go back to that godawful house and pick up the money she had stashed away there. The nest-egg pilfered from the miser that the taxi driver, in his haste, had given her no time to pick up in those final moments. She hoped to goodness it would still be there. And if it was, come to think of it, she need scarcely go back home to her parents after all. She smiled wanly. The miser still had a

little bit to offer, if he had but known.

London, she reflected petulantly, had been fabulous, after getting the miser off her back, until the point when Dieter had begun to show his real colours. After that, it had all just been downhill. So much for the so-called golden city, she mused peevishly, in the bilious aftermath of too much beer. She had wound up broke and living on the streets. So all that business, going away with the miser, where had it got her? And what had she even been doing in that ramshackle, murder-sodden house after all? For several minutes Katja could scarcely recall. Her head felt thick and she was tired, as if she was hundreds of hours short on sleep. Then it came back. The baby. She'd had a baby. And an unpleasant feeling turned her stomach. The baby. How odd. She had almost forgotten about that.

There is nothing flesh and blood, nothing solid, about curiosity. It is easy to kill, to extinguish, just a question of attitude. It was best, decided Katja, now she remembered about the baby, to keep herself totally uncurious concerning its fate. She simply made her mind up to that. There was no need ever to know what had happened to the brat she had left in a boxroom at that crazy house. No need even to know what had become of her cousin in the months that she had been away. Just provided – pray God – that the house was just as it had been. She could sneak in, get the money, sneak off and be on her way. If only it was still there!

It was only when she was past the gateway that Katja noticed that the white van was in its usual place. That was a bad sign; it meant that Taavi was at home. But she could see no sign of life at any of the windows. If he had been drinking, if he was sleeping it off…She had gone but a few steps further when the dog came hurling out of the shadows barking and howling. It made her start, but if Taavi was drunk, as she hoped, it would make no difference. She carried on walking and mounted the porch steps, took a look into the empty kitchen.

He startled her. He really startled her, when he shouted at her as she came in through the door. She had run off quickly. But what had really unnerved her, she recalled as she slowed to a halt, was what else in retrospect she thought she seen. And maybe even heard. From the kitchen, lit from the back by the setting sun, came long, striped shadows thrown obliquely across the floor of the hall, hard to identify, like the bars of a prison window or a child's cot. She had hardly had time to flash her eyes in that direction before her cousin had shouted and she had bolted, but just then too she fancied she heard a different noise. A scream. She had fled before she had really taken anything in. Not that it mattered. The shadows were more than likely just the prison bars that that pervert deserved to be behind. In her still rather fragile state she had seen a vision, thought she had heard a sound. Katja forced herself to concentrate on how to return. She would have to wait till Taavi was in bed.

CHAPTER 36

She had got in this time through the pantry window, and now she was standing in the hall. From the kitchen the last of the daylight had long disappeared, but glancing in through the half-open door it seemed that there was nothing there that could have thrown those unfamiliar shadows across the hall. She must have imagined them – her nerves must really have been playing her up. But it didn't matter now. Katja crossed the hall and quietly opened the door to the living room, pausing for a moment on the threshold. In the moonlight that shone with unexpected brightness through the windows at the far end she could see that the L-shaped room looked pretty much as it always had – the table and chairs and the sofa, and the tall, tiled stove in the crook of the L. She roused herself. She must get this over fast, and leave. As soon as she was back out again in the forest, she would be safe, and more important, she would have cash. The hard times would be over. Katja rounded the door and made for the corner behind it, where the tall wooden corner cupboard stood.

Her way was blocked by a cot.

She stood stock still, not quite knowing what to do. The cot again. This time the moonlight reproduced its bars in long, crooked shadows up the wall across the old-fashioned wallpaper. Katja was aware of a sudden, strange sensation, like something cold creeping across her shoulder blades. She had never before felt so oddly fearful.

She didn't feel guilt about anything, so why should she now be seeing a cot? She took a step towards it, saw her own shadow rise a little higher on the wall. She could hear the muffled thumping of her own heart inside her rib-cage, then came a single tiny noise from inside the cot, a sort of snuffle.

She took another step forwards, so she could see inside it. There were blankets there. And beneath the blankets a curved, rounded form, just like an enormous, well-established, slumbering baby. She stood and stared, wondering if the cot and its contents were real, or just a fantasy in front of the cupboard. Mocking her, confirming her to be mad. But it looked real. Even in the moonlight, the bars looked of real wood. Katja stroked the rail of the cot, felt it solid beneath her fingers. Leant over and stretched her hand out to touch the baby.

The side of the cot prevented her falling on it as she went down.

When the young man wiped his hand across his face he realised that what was flowing down from it was perspiration. He looked down at Katja. He could see her face, half white in the moonlight, half in shadow, her hair spread out around her head like a nest of coiling, silvery-coloured snakes. Her lips were open in surprise and she was staring upwards, but not at anything in particular. The odd thing was that apart from her expression, she didn't really look as if anything was wrong. The frying pan had landed on top of her when the hefty blow had knocked it out of his hand, but she didn't seem to care, or even to have noticed. It had slid down and was propped against her ribs on its side, a stubborn morsel of cold, greasy bacon still clinging to its iron features, like a wart. The young man noticed he was beginning to tremble, tremble like a leaf. In the cot the baby was stirring. It had just begun to sense the disturbance. Any minute Katja might jump up and try to take it, the very second it began to cry. He must get it out, take it to somewhere safe.

It was hard to get at the baby with Katja in the way. The young man moved the frying pan and tried to step over her, felt her body curiously heavy and resistant against his feet. She made no attempt to move. Didn't ask what he was doing, or what the noise was. When he picked the baby up there seemed to be no strength left in his arms; all the way up the stairs he was frightened he would drop it. He made it some milk, which wouldn't seem to turn out right, and then it took ages to get it off to sleep. As if it knew that he was nervous.

When the baby had finally settled down, the young man steeled himself to go downstairs and creep back into the living room. Katja had still not moved. When he went and stood behind her, she did not tilt her head back to look at him. Did not even stir. Beneath her head, he noticed this time, was a very dark shadow, like a halo, behind the snakes. He walked round and knelt down beside her, found his eyes drawn gruesomely towards her face. She was looking upwards, her features still, like a mask.

"Get up," he hissed.

There was no reaction.

"Get up," the young man repeated, more loudly and firmly.

She did not move. The young man sat back on his heels and folded his arms. Then he rose and got a sheet of paper and tore off a small piece and put it on the moonlit skin between her nose and her mouth. It stayed there.

He knelt beside her and stared at her motionless form indecisively. He was beginning to force himself, in spite of his shock, to understand why she was lying there, why she had been lying there now for a couple of hours, with never a sound or a movement. Why there seemed to be no air going in or out of her nostrils.

He had killed her. She was dead. He had actually killed her. With one blow from the frying pan. It was somehow ironic. In the kitchen that pan had been her one true friend. He had grabbed it from the range when he saw her go round the door to the cot, and the gun didn't work. Now it seemed one warning blow from an iron pan was enough to – do whatever it had done.

But what had it done? The young man was curious, puzzled, in spite of himself. Was it really possible with a pan to do very much harm? It must have just stunned her, but enough to make her stop breathing for a while. He didn't believe that she was simply fooling. He forced himself to look at her face again, but it seemed that its startled expression was its only imperfection. The halo behind her head seemed possibly a little larger, a little darker. He bent down and laid his head against the ground, and looked at her profile.

He could imagine that the top of her head at the back, where the pan had hit her, was a trifle misshapen, somehow dented, like a ball no longer properly inflated. But he couldn't really tell, her hair was so thick. And then, of course, the back of her head was mainly in shadow.

The young man put out a finger and tested the halo. It was wet. When he took his finger away and held it up, he could see in the moonlight the round dark stain where he had touched the wetness.

He felt slightly sick. Shocked, aghast. It didn't seem proper yet, to let 'relief' in at the head of the queue.

"Get up!" He heard himself urging her again. "Katja, get up!" She did not listen. And then, in a lower voice, but still quite clear, "Get up, or I will BURY YOU."

She did not get up.

The young man picked up the frying pan and took it into the kitchen. He did not care to look at the bottom of it, simply stuck it in the sink and turned the tap on. He picked the useless gun up and threw it back in the kitchen drawer, then he fetched a bottle of vodka and sat down at the table to work out what to do. He didn't feel the slightest bit tired.

He noticed at some point that it was getting light. He would have to hurry now, she had had her chance. He must get things sorted before the outside world came to life, and the baby woke.

For the want of any better idea he rolled her up in the mat she was lying on, pushing the giant roll over and over. She was growing cold; that, if anything, suggested that she really was dead. The mat was a good, thick rag mat, there was hardly a stain on the floor. The young man tied it round with string and did the whole great bundle up in a sheet and tied the ends; in the early dawn he carried it out to the workshop. He would have to think of somewhere to dispose of it the following night.

Even a dry well has its uses, especially one that hasn't been used for many years. It surprised the young man just how easily the first few planks of the cover came away, as if they had been removed only recently, yet the lichen and moss on them was undisturbed. One by one they simply lifted off, and soon left a hole quite big enough to put something small down, the size of a cat. The young man was encouraged, but the rest of the planks did not come free without the aid of a chisel and pliers. He had to work at them with infinite patience and care, so he could put them back without a sign that they had ever been touched.

It was tedious, laborious work, but at last it was done, and the gaping well was before him, dark and hollow and very, very deep. When she slipped away on her final, downward journey, Katja still made not the slightest sound of protest.

It was hard to believe that no-one had seen him. But it seemed that no-one had, for the rest of the week passed quietly till Lotta came, just a few days after Katja's swift visit and departure. She seemed to notice nothing, though she did say that the young man seemed a bit on edge. She accepted the change of mat in the living room without demur, washed and fed the baby, took it out to the orchard, brought it back in and set it on the floor.

"Look!" Her voice was enthusiastic. "She's trying to crawl. But she can only do it backwards." The baby grunted and gyrated clumsily on the spot, then keeled over. Lotta replaced it on all fours and coaxed it encouragingly.

"I'll move the mat back to give her more room."

The young man felt his whole body stiffen, had to force a smile as he followed unseeingly the baby's antics. But when he slid his glance across the floor to the spot where the cot had stood, he could see that it was perfectly clean.

The autumn weather was warm and bountiful. Around the pink house the trees seemed overnight to trade in their dull, tired latesummer greens for glowing attire of russet and crimson and gold. The white hydrangea bush brought forth magnificent blossom and the redcurrant bushes began to look like leafy stacks of translucent rubies. The very perfection of the weather, its complacency, would have been enough in recent times to burn the young man up in anger and frustration. Yet now when he sat on the steps in the sunlight and searched for his anger, he no longer found it. It wasn't there. Instead, amid the darkness, the infinite blackness that he recognised for the truth, he found his eyes drawn constantly towards that small grey light. As if he must watch it, as if it were a riddle he must solve.

But as for his accusers, the young man realised with a jolt, he had nothing left to do any bargaining with. With Katja gone, he had literally thrown his excuses for postponement down the well. There was no need now for revenge. He was once again free to turn his mind to darker matters, fulfil his obligations. As soon as he had lain low for a while longer, he could find another home for the baby. It wouldn't be long now. Then he could go. Permit his demons to win. And yet – he was thankful the time was still not yet. He still had the riddle to answer.

All the same, the baby was tiring alone, and the young man was not maternal. Its gathering speed at crawling surprised him, impressed him, and wore him out. He made it a playpen, but still it was trouble when he tried to do his work. He was always glad when Lotta showed up to play with it and mind it.

Of course, to her he dared not mention his ultimate plan. She knew nothing about his past, or the baby's origins, or even that he was on the run. It disconcerted him profoundly when she started to talk of nurseries and schools, and other matters unbelievably remote. He had no idea how to explain to her that his future was limited, and found himself troubled at the thought of destroying her innocent, animated dreams and plans.

Yet oddly, the young man noticed, if he did not summon such reflections to mind, his accusing demons were apt to keep these days strangely in the background. That just when they had every right to do so, they no longer elbowed their way into his consciousness just as soon as he woke. It was almost as if he was on holiday from them. And to his surprise, as is the way with holidays generally, he found himself wanting to make the most of it while it lasted. At any rate, right now the thought of being picked up for another murder did not appeal.

For the first few weeks, while the moss on the well-top was still settling down, the young man anticipated the arrival of police cars constantly. But no-one came. The autumn continued to swell and mature, then turned and the weather grew colder. All around the leaves began to wither and drop, but as the branches grew barer, in the young man's heart a strange new spring began to unfold.

He was far from sure, after Katja's fate, that he deserved the taste of honey that now seemed to permeate his life. It sometimes unnerved him, how easily he had snuffed out Katja's life to allow the baby to thrive. Be that as it may, as time went on, his fears receded, imperceptibly, gradually, but steadily, like the sea receding after high tide. And as they receded they left behind one fact as firm as a rock rising up through the sand. A fact that no water eddying round it could wash away, a fact that grew warm and inviting, as if that rock were in the sun.

The baby was his. His to keep, if he wanted, for Katja would never be back to get her any more. His to watch in fascination, the essence that was struggle and joy, that had challenged, at least for the present, the power of his demons. There was also another factor, which the young man perhaps would still not have pointed out to himself; he loved the baby.

CHAPTER 37

Krista gasped. The room was full of flowers. It looked like a flower shop! There were flowers everywhere – on the window ledge, on her make-up table, on every surface, even on her pillow. She turned to Julius, who had come in behind her, ducking his tall frame through the low-beamed doorway.

"Are these from you?" She saw at once from the glow on his face that she had guessed correctly.

"It is your birthday." As he beamed at her, almost shyly, her heart was touched.

"They're really beautiful. And just so many. There must be hundreds!" Krista lifted her nose and breathed their perfume, then began to go from flower to flower, bending over each one separately and stroking its petals. "They're exquisite. Thank you."

Julius watched her, an enigmatic smile on his face. It was only when she came at last to the bouquet of flowers upon her pillow, that she noticed hidden among its deep red blooms the tiny velvet-covered box. With trembling fingers Krista

Lotta turned the page. But she did not carry on reading. She had read the story ten times this evening already. Instead she dropped the magazine down beside the bed, drew her knees up under the covers, and acknowledged to herself that she had seen the light. That at last she understood what was so confusing about her passage into Womanhood. For she had been a Woman now for two months almost, and found herself somehow disappointed.

Of course, there was no doubt that the strange events of that afternoon, which had ushered in her new role as the young man's mistress, had all been worth it. Had she not rescued Summer Rose from that cursed name, and adorned her with a name as fresh and beautiful as she deserved? Yet all the same, Lotta felt that Womanhood was not quite all she had expected.

To be honest, before the young man's scandalous suggestion, she had rarely given the matter very much thought. Her hopes for a passionate lover or a marriage offer were set far off, on the other side, she supposed, of some magical change in her body. A metamorphosis from small and thin to statuesque and lusciously curvacious. Yet despite these hopes, to Lotta, so accustomed to her thinness, the mere idea of curves seemed somehow boldly naughty. Not the least in keeping with the virtuous attitudes to which she had been raised. This being so, she resolved her ambivalence by putting all thoughts on the matter on hold and consigning Womanhood to the distant future.

Which made it, of course, much more disconcerting to find she had suddenly arrived there. Had passed the significant milestone one afternoon, without any preparation or proper warning. And there, beyond that milestone, lay her confusion. For shouldn't she be feeling different now, as a regular practiser of the ultimate union? Fulfilled, self-confident, and grown up? Yet by and large, since a certain degree of troublesome soreness had vanished, she had felt just the same as before. She even looked the same in the mirror. It was almost as if, she thought dismally, she had played her trump card in life and nothing had happened. And now there was nothing left to play.

She had tried the Bible, tried to plumb its depths for enlightenment, but it offered her no help in her present dilemma. Besides, she had no doubt sinned away her day of grace. So Lotta turned instead to the only other source she dared to for advice, to her latest discovery, the glossy pages of women's magazines. She had always held them in her ignorance to be superficial, full of trash and tattle, yet now she found them to be just the opposite. From cover to cover they were steeped in enviable knowledge. For the first time in her life their passions spoke to her: she devoured them eagerly in her fervid quest for understanding of the human heart, the deep and subtle soul of woman and man. For weeks she had trawled their pages in the long, secluded hours of the night, in quest of an answer to the question she could never quite put into words, and now she had found it. There, among the fragrant flower bouquets of Krista's humble bedroom it was clear how the young man fell sadly short of

Julius.

He did not adore her. That was his failing. Or if he did adore her, he didn't show it. She shared his bed, she tended his child and tidied his house, he called on her for all these things, but her herself he scarcely noticed. He took her for granted. And finally now, after all her research, she realised what she was she was missing. Why she felt discontent, unfulfilled as a woman. She wanted romance, romantic passion. Women needed that. She wanted him to shower her with attention.

Once more surveying her reflection in the mirror, Lotta sighed and came forlornly to the point of view that it wasn't all the young man's fault that he wasn't more passionate. A pale, unprepossessing creature with watchful eyes stared back at her. Lank, stringy hair, a thin form, breasts developing, but not much yet. She should maybe eat more. At least she should somehow make herself look more alluring. Get some flattering clothes from somewhere, put on make-up. Perfume. She must make him notice her. She should buy a provocative dress, tight and short, the next time she could slip into town without her mother.

The young man had a birthday coming up in a few weeks' time. She would doll herself up to surprise him, wake him up to the glamour that was there inside her.

He didn't know she knew it was his birthday. She would make him a cake. She would bring it round, looking just fantastic. Like a fashion model. He would suddenly see her in a way he had never seen her up to now. He would fall in love with her, he would woo her with passion and romance. He would not be able to help himself.

That way, she would start at last to feel how a woman should.

CHAPTER 38

Far away from the pink house, on the lake that laps at the shores of Kuopio, there sailed a vessel as proud and as effortlessly graceful as a swan. She had smooth white flanks eleven metres long, snow-white sails and a prow so elegant that no other ship's prow on the water could compare. Along her side, or presumably both her sides, ran a single, exquisitely executed turquoise line which emphasised her streamlining; her woodwork, as far as Laine could ascertain, was a shade that had to be mahogany. She was matchless, peerless; these were the very last words he formed to himself before his admiration became so diffused that it rendered him speechless and almost unable to move. With a weak hand he pulled out his binoculars and raised them. He was right, that woodwork was flawless mahogany. The boat deck with its fresh white paint and lacquered floors was spotless, the brasswork winked and glinted with dazzling brilliance.

Her name was Gloria.

Gloria. 'Gloria in excelsis' Laine felt the muscles of his mouth mime, then his mouth remained slightly open as he watched her sweeping silently ahead of him across the lake. She was not using engine-power. Her sails swelled out and bore her smoothly, inexorably across the water, like a siren ghost ship, luring him to follow.

He willed himself back into action, swung the Gabriella round, and set off with her throttle full open in pursuit of the Gloria, and when he had caught her up he cruised beside her, as closely in parallel with her as he dared. From a distance of a dozen metres he checked her out through his binoculars and also with the naked eye. She was beautiful. She was from heaven, a white-winged aquatic angel gliding beside him. He dropped behind her again, to avoid suspicion, but he had to follow her, to see where she came from.

In his heart, though without yet knowing it, he had already tossed aside the Gabriella, now chugging loyally beneath him. He had to have the Gloria. In his mind it seemed to him that he had never before known anything so instinctively, so absolutely clearly, and he realised too that every sacrifice that would have to be made was unfortunately absolutely necessary. He was already hers, had thought of nothing from the moment he had seen her but that she should be his.

And soon she was, for a sum slightly more outrageous than the highest sum that even Laine himself had extravagantly imagined. But he had no choice; he had to have her. And as he sailed her across the lakes through the long, hot summer and the glorious autumn, he understood why. For cruising on a lake in his fleet-running vessel, that shining apparition with the snow-white sails and celestially sparkling brasswork, he was just what on land as a struggling real-estate agent it didn't seem ever possible to be. He was God.

But only in the day, and on the water. On dry land, and especially at night, his troubles began to crowd in and pester him. The business in Kuopio had still not taken off as he would have wanted, and now his expenses included installments on the Gloria, for the sale price of the Gabriella had not been much more than a token offering. He had had to borrow money, shuffle things around to try and rob Peter to pay Paul, but he couldn't carry on ad infinitum. Throughout the autumn he made the most of life and pushed his money worries to the background, but as the weather grew colder Laine began to feel an uncomfortably bleak side to life.

Heikki, on the other hand, was having an excellent autumn. Compared with Laine's his career was blooming robustly. He had passed his exams in England before the summer, and had now come back to start in a brand new job with solid prospects in Alajärvi's district planning office. He took his work seriously, for his post was responsible, but on the whole he relished his duties. As well as reporting to the planning committee, the job involved coming up with ideas of his own. Unpretentiousness notwithstanding, he was now ambitious, and had every intention of working hard and earning a senior position. He had changed his mind about selling Hilppala and had moved there himself, having rented his flat out in the town, but his plan was in a few years to have somewhere new built, to his own requirements.

The only time when his clear skies clouded over was when anything turned his thoughts to his dear friend Fisher, and the current mysterious troubles that person was enduring. The poor man had recently been through a nervous breakdown, of which Heikki had never quite worked out the real cause. He only knew that after his mad plan to buy the house Fisher had suddenly appeared some months later back in England with the girl who had been in the toilet on the morning that Heikki had himself called to visit him.

He wasn't even sure whether Fisher had bought the house or decided not to, or whether in some other way the whole plan had fallen through. He had only heard of the sudden, sad turn of events through Dr Phillips. At the hospital, when Heikki visited with flowers and grapes, Fisher had only sobbed that his life was in ruins, his dreams in ashes, and that truth and beauty were only to be found in the fairytale house which he had so very nearly lived in. He had babbled of homesick goddesses and babies and not being able to continue with his book, now that he was cut off from said truth and beauty. The girl was not there. Heikki had got no sense out of Fisher as to if she was still about.

It distressed Heikki mightily to see his friend in such extremis. On subsequent visits Fisher had been slightly better, under medication, and had spoken of the pink house, and how he had only really discovered the nature of absolute harmony and purity there, in the magical summer nights under northern skies. How he had strolled in the luminous midsummer small hours across the orchard, well away from the stray dog that still held its reign of terror in the yard, and how, sitting on the old well that he had come to think of to himself as the well of truth and wisdom, he had truly understood Keats's claim that truth is beauty, beauty truth. How in that dream world the taunting enigma had simply dissolved. How the house would have been the necessary inspiration for his still uncompleted book. For what could the beauty there around him be, but the utter, utter truth? And vice versa. And Fisher's voice would break down once more while the tears returned to his eyes, and Heikki had nodded each time sympathetically and wondered if his medication could be adjusted.

It was strange to think how that ramshackle house and its overgrown, neglected surroundings could have that effect on anyone. Quite bizarre. Heikki rarely went past the place itself nowadays, but almost always when he drove past the bottom of the hill he thought of Fisher. On one occasion, going into town, a grimy white van shot out of the turning just ahead of him, swerved, stalled, and blocked the road in front of him. He was forced to use the longer, pink house route to reach his office. Driving past the house he slowed and tried to glimpse it through the gateposts, to see what it looked like now that Fisher wasn't there. It was scarcely visible, for it seemed to be covered more thickly than ever with lilac leaves. Heikki saw once more in his mind its outdated, unergonomic kitchen steeped in greenish light, empty now, with Fisher pining for it night and day.

CHAPTER 39

Lotta leant her bicycle against the lilacs and dismounted carefully. It had not been easy to cycle up the hill in a short tight pencil skirt and heels, and each time the bike had wobbled she had feared for the cake in the wicker basket on her handlebars. She could sense it slide around in its tin and was worried that the cream would come off. She had made it as a plain cake in domestic science and spread it with the cream in her bedroom, before finally picking out his name in raisins on the white foamy peaks. His proper name, Taavi, not the name he used with other people. After all, she was hardly 'other people'.

It disappointed her to notice that the van was gone from the yard, for it meant he was out. For the first time ever, she hadn't told him she was coming. She had meant to surprise him, and to do so in several ways, of which, perhaps, the birthday cake was least important. For today he would notice, if he never had before, that she had it in her to be glamorous. That far from being someone he could take for granted, she could look like a siren if she chose to. Or as near to a siren as anyone could ever respectably get. She had added Glamour Weekly to her reading matter, and now on the strength of its advice on just this subject she had spent her savings on stiletto heels, on make-up and elongated earrings.

Perhaps it was just as well that he who was to be seduced was not at home yet. It would give her time to re-enhance her appearance, comb the hair that had somehow tangled itself with her earrings on the ride. But first she must check that the cake had survived, take it indoors, set it out on a plate. Add the blue wax birthday candles that would form its final decoration.

It was as just as she was reaching into the basket that the dog arrived. It came tearing round the side of the building, howling horribly, its yellow fangs dripping and drooling as it bounded towards her. Lotta had never been there with it on the loose, for the young man always tied it up before she came. Not that she reflected now on this point one way or the other. She gave a single scream that rivalled in volume the din that the dog was making, stood paralyzed for what seemed to her to be forever, then turned and ran for dear life to the gate. The dog got one shoe by the heel, Lotta stumbled out of the other, heard the seam of her tight skirt rip and allowed her legs, restored to freedom, to bear her through the gate and down the hill just as fast as they could manage.

Heikki passed her at the bottom of the road, on his way to visit a construction site. He noticed her standing at the bus stop there, though the morning bus had gone by an hour ago. As he stopped to enlighten her he noticed she was crying, and clutching her arms to her chest, and as she sat beside him in the car as he took her into town he noticed that her skirt was ripped and she was shoeless. She was shivering. His instinctive concern for her distress was diluted somewhat with disapproval of her make-up and her style of dress; it was certainly these that had got her into trouble, whatever sort of trouble she had been in. Though one scarcely needed to guess at the matter. That skirt was scarcely more than a pelmet round her thighs, and as for her earrings and mascara, one could only wonder that her parents did not make greater efforts to control her. But he got nothing sensible out of her, and thought it best to leave her to the local police. They would know best what to do, and he himself was already running late.

At the station they gave her hot chocolate to make her talk. They made her tell everything. How she'd taken a birthday cake to a friend and been chased by the dog and left her bicycle behind. And her shoes. They gave her a lift home in a police car, and promised they would send a van up later for the bicycle and get it back to her. "All's well that ends well," said the sergeant, as he handed her over to her parents.

The yard of the pink house was deserted when a constable in a van drove in to pick up Lotta's bicycle a few hours later. After parking he paused a while before alighting, looking thoughtfully round him.

Before him was a farmyard, with the house a bit run down, but somewhere inside his head a bell was ringing. Wasn't it this place there had been that that murder, that had set tongues wagging? He must check it up when he got back to the station. He had always imagined somehow that the house involved had just stood empty after that, but this one, he could see as he walked across the yard, was occupied. A shirt overhung the balcony rail and an upstairs window was open. And after all, the girl had said her friend lived here. When he banged on the front door it opened slightly, though no-one came to answer his knock. There was clearly nobody home. The bicycle was still by the wall of the house, propped up where the girl had left it. He knew it was hers, for it still had the cake tin in the wicker basket on the handlebars, and on lifting the tin he could feel that the cake was still inside. He should leave it for its rightful consumer, as requested; on his own initiative he took it in and put it in the kitchen. The girl had told him it had real cream on, and the day was hot. It seemed, when the constable removed the lid, that the cake had travelled pretty well. Some cream from its sides had adhered to the tin, but the celebrant's name, picked out in raisins, had survived undamaged. "Taavi." murmured the constable to himself, replaced the lid, glanced round appalled at the state of the kitchen, and set off to return the bike to Lotta. He even retrieved her stiletto heels, one slightly bitten, as he went.

It was only later at the station, reading up on that bygone tragedy, its scenes, its players, that he looked up suddenly, with his eyes unnaturally round.

When Taavi came home in the early evening he noticed a number of vehicles round about, ones he couldn't account for. They made him feel inexplicably nervous, and he was relieved on entering the yard to notice that it was empty. It was not until he had parked the van and was lifting the baby out that he saw them all waiting for him, sitting on the edge of the well.

CHAPTER 40

It was one evening, browsing through the tabloid paper which was what he bought now for reasons of economy, that Laine read that the fellow at the pink house, the infamous teenage killer, had been rearrested. They had found out at long last where he was, and come and got him and put him away to finish his sentence. That would, Laine acknowledged, make the world a far safer place, but on the whole his interest in the matter was limited. That whole episode, which had ended in dice-with-death face-to-face contact with the fellow, all seemed distant now, in place and time. He had a new life now, and new preoccupations, and anyway he was nowadays less and less in Alajärvi. He had had to deal with his disappointments over the failed sale, and the trouble it had caused him. The raised hopes that had come to nothing. There had not as yet been any letter from the crazy Englishman, demanding a refund of his 'rent', for which Laine thanked his lucky stars. If only he could sell the Alajärvi business, that would help. He would make a little money, and he wouldn't have to pay a cleaner. Laine turned the page and scanned the sports news dully, then he put the paper down and went to bed, to awaken as usual at the darkest hour in the grip of a terrible despair.

It was as he was nodding off again, towards the dawn, that it suddenly came into his head, for no reason, that he still had the keys and the papers to that dreadful house. He should return them. They had been down there in his Alajärvi office all these months. Not that it mattered now very urgently. The killer would not be using his house now, and therefore wouldn't be needing his door keys to it, for quite some time. Years probably, assuming justice was done.

Laine was almost asleep when, quite unbidden, like the sun

coming out from behind a cloud, the rays of a brilliant solution pierced the dense, dismal gloom of all his troubles. It propelled him from his bed at a laudable hour of the morning, and round to his office, where he threw off the cover from his typewriter, and with trembling fingers began to smite the keys.

Phillips raised his eyes from the letter. "Well, well, well. And will you buy it?"

"Buy it?" said Fisher, "Of course I will. I think it's spiffing of him. Why, what would you do?" His face was glowing. Phillips looked at him. It was truly amazing just how animated Fisher had become, in the hour or so that that must have elapsed since the letter had been delivered. The Fisher that had rushed to greet him with it was so totally different from the apathetic, pitiful creature that in recent months his colleague had become. The man had simply never been the same since the heartless decampment of the golden-haired beauty he had brought back to be some sort of Viking child-bride. Fisher, the most retiring, conservative of men. In retrospect the whole escapade had been quite ludicrously out of character, some sort of middle-aged crisis, and yet the girl's departure had destroyed him utterly. They had all become horrified at his condition. And even now Fisher was still on sick leave, quite unable to take up his teaching duties for the autumn term. He was finding it difficult to eat or sleep, they had not been able to interest him in working on his book.

Yet this morning here he was – up and dressed, if somewhat haphazardly, with an animated manner and eyes bright with something other than the wash of tears. And all because of a letter from which he had learnt that the wooden house he had almost bought on his Finnish trip was once more on the market. The change, thought Phillips, was miraculous – but also disturbing and alarming. For now it was clear that his colleague's mental health was far from the stable affair he had always imagined it to be in their thirty-year acquaintance. Heartwarming though it was to see Fisher happy, it was probably best to try and temper such unpredictable extremities of mood-swing. This state in Fisher, if allowed to progress unchecked, might turn to mania and get him into trouble, or herald an even deeper plunge in his condition. He should at least, Phillips decided, try to keep him in touch with reality.

"It does say that the agent has had to raise the price. You did notice that bit? And a cash sale. Isn't that a little unusual for a property?"

Fisher waved his hands in the air. "Not over there. The agent has always said he likes to have cash. They prefer it. And as you've read, the seller is a young man with a family. It's only natural he needs cash, right away."

As he spoke, Fisher began to dig recklessly through piles of unopened post and papers on his table. "I must have the phone directory somewhere under here. I must phone a travel agent or the airport, book a flight."

"Can't you just write to him?" Phillips stalled. His fears were grounded. Fisher was becoming manic.

"There's no time. As you read yourself, I have to act quickly. There are other buyers waiting. I think it was jolly civil of him to remember me, let alone to give me priority. He couldn't find the young man when I was over there, and that was the only reason that I couldn't buy it then. Now he's decent enough to give me another chance. But I have to act fast. Ah, got it." Fisher pulled the directory's Yellow Pages out from the bottom of the heap, ignoring the resultant avalanche of papers around his shins. "Airport, airport."

"I'll do it for you," said Phillips. The man was all fingers and thumbs. Besides, the easiest way to resolve the matter was simply to ascertain that there were no suitable flights. With procrastination, Fisher's mood of urgency might abate. "When do you need to go?"

"Today. This evening. The first flight possible."

There were seats on the evening flight. There was no way out, for Fisher, hovering anxiously, had heard every word concerning their availability. The only thing he could do now, Phillips understood, was to make sure Fisher in his agitation did not mistakenly board a plane for somewhere outlandish.

"Let me take you to the airport." he offered, resignedly. And Fisher washed, shaved, and packed his bag in the space of an hour, called his bank, and set off a changed man with Phillips to pick up his money and fly to clinch the sale.

Laine too, driving home from his meeting with Fisher, felt as if he was floating on a cloud. He had to park the car up every ten kilometres and pull again from the glove compartment the thick wads of banknotes that would yank him out of the nest of debts that just kept breeding and multiplying. So great was the beauty of those pieces of paper that their glow filled every corner, every nook and cranny of his vision, reducing to insignificance that far-off day when theoretically the young man might be released from prison, and take it into his head to come straight home to his house. How to get out of that mess, if that day ever happened, Laine couldn't imagine. But of course, it was only theoretical. In the name of justice that wicked wretch should never be released. And for justice, Finland was the tops.

No, the risk was well worth taking. More than that, it was clear to Laine, he would have been a fool not to take it. It must have been meant to be, or why else would circumstances have evolved so completely and unexpectedly perfectly as they had? It was right all round. The country was saved from a psychopath, the English professor would get the house that he yearned for, and he himself would be able to pay off all his debts. It would clean his slate, enable him to be a better citizen. And best of all secure for him forever the Gloria, the heavenly vessel that could turn him into a god.

CHAPTER 41

From his first day onwards, Heikki's workdays had been passed in serene enjoyment, until now this week an assignment had arrived which put him in a dreadful quandary.

For the third morning running he spread out on his office desk the final proposal for the road-improvement scheme that the council were planning on commencing, and pulled a face as he studied it. It was his brief to assess all the data and pronounce upon the route's feasibility. If acceptable the chosen route would be properly surfaced, widened slightly and improved with lay-bys. Heikki stared increasingly glumly at the maps and papers in front of him. He could not forget that it was he who had first suggested such a scheme would enhance the area. Encourage more people to at least pass through it.

And now that initiative had caused him the stickiest problem of his career. In theory it was all quite simple. He would make his findings and report on them, then the planning committee would decide in the light of his expertise just how to proceed. Yet Heikki knew already just what he required the final outcome to be, and recognised too that such partiality was not professional. It was just that Fisher was his friend. He had never remotely envisaged when he made his suggestions, Heikki mused perplexedly, that the council would then set their sights on the modest road that skirted the pink house, the place that Fisher was so oddly obsessed with.

The ideas they had for it would ruin Fisher. He was only just getting over the extraordinary breakdown he had had. Heikki cursed himself once again for inciting the council to be forward-looking.

The house itself had been in the papers again only recently, for it seemed that the son, the convicted criminal, had got out from wherever they had put him and had wound up back there. Just as well, thought Heikki, that he hadn't turned up while Fisher had been there. He was found by police with a rabid dog, so the papers said, which a marksman had put down, and, more inexplicably, a baby, which no-one had reported missing. The child had seemed well cared-for. They had put it in a home. Since the murderer's re-arrest, the place had once more stood empty.

Except that Fisher was coming back there, or that was his plan. He was ranting on about the pink house and seeing the orchard and hearing the birches as they whispered in the breeze that wafted through them high above the well of truth and wisdom. He was talking of redemption through trying again to write his book. Apparently he had signed a purchase contract.

He would not be thrilled to come back and find his idyll under bulldozers, even though it was only a small part of the orchard under threat. It was just the bit at the end with the birches and the useless, mouldering well he was always on about. That section had been earmarked for a lay-by, and maybe even a wayside hamburger kiosk. There was no preventing the planners, Heikki knew, if the planning department had once decided that was what it wanted. He had learnt that lesson in the very short time he had worked there. They would have it all cleared and the well dug up to put in the proper road foundations and the lay-by area. The distress would worsen Fisher's condition. He might become permanently mad.

With a troubled heart, Heikki knew he must do just everything in his power to make sure the project was abandoned. He must try to discourage the planning committee when presenting his findings, try to make it clear that some other choice would be preferable - without of course saying anything that wasn't true. He felt uncomfortable. Like some sort of a traitor, whichever way he acted, to either his work integrity or to Fisher. He knew he should weigh up only such factors as traffic flows, drainage, cost and manpower hours, but against these he had to weigh up the value of Fisher as his truest of friends. It was vital for Fisher's health that the copse and the well at the pink house should remain there, intact and just as they had always been.

Of course, Heikki argued to himself, whatever happened wouldn't happen overnight. There was first the surveying, the research, the writing of reports. Perhaps the threat was not so very imminent. He would have to make sure the orchard was surveyed, if that had to happen, at a time when Fisher was safely home in London. For even the faintest suggestion of possible hazard might topple his health. Aside from that, Heikki realised, he would have to resort to the only honest weapon in his armoury: procrastination. It was, after all, the standard procedure of the planning office, as he had so far noticed with disapproval. For Fisher's sake he would have to learn to procrastinate, and having learnt, he would have to procrastinate with all his might. To thwart every tiniest step of progress while appearing to be moving the project along with commendable speed. If he hung his reports and assessments out long enough, the council's interest might well just disintegrate, over time. The whole thing might be shelved or abandoned. At the other extreme, if he acted promptly, he could maybe get the pink house orchard surveyed now, before the snows came. Fisher would not be here yet; he could get it out of the way. But glancing at the window he noticed, inexorable omen, the very first snowflake drifting languidly past.

CHAPTER 42

From his vantage point among the lilac blossoms Laine could push them aside and look in through the window, allowing sunbeams to prance through the sea-green light of the kitchen. Though the room was empty, it was clearly in use. A china teacup and saucer stood upon the table, and that incredible item so beloved by the English, a teapot with a woolly cover. Alongside were a plate and egg cup, a battered eggshell, and a jar of what Laine guessed might be 'marmalade'. The tell-tale signs of an English breakfast, no less. Laine hesitated, then reversed out carefully from among the lilac branches. In the yard he listened; from the open window of the living room came the busy, erratically syncopated clack of typewriter keys. He needed no more proof, but somehow still he had to be certain. And soon he was, for peeking in through a window on the forest side, he saw Fisher sitting at the table. The Englishman was typing briskly, with now and then a pause when he folded his arms and stared up into space.

Laine crept away bent double, then straightened up and returned to his car. He realised now he had half assumed that having bought the place, not even Fisher would actually want to live there. The man had bought it on a whim, the sort of unbalanced thing people did who had far more money than they knew what to do with; it would simply serve as some sort of trophy, a gruesome bauble. He had not really thought very much, Laine now noticed, about Fisher moving in and making the place his home. Not that it mattered too much, he supposed, now that he himself was no longer living in the area.

Fisher of course had not been able to move back over at the drop of a hat. After finishing his sick leave he had gone back to the university, but at Easter he had flown out to clean up and make plans for getting the place into shape. It had shocked him on arrival to notice that nothing, with the single exception of the things for the baby, had disappeared. It seemed that the young man, or whoever it was that had last been living there, had simply left. There was even months-old food there, all but eaten by mice, and the dog's bowl was still in the shed. But of the young man, or the dog, or the baby, there was no sign, and never had been yet. He had found it eerily pleasant to walk the yard or sit on the porch in the sunshine, without the slightest fear of attack.

And now he was here again, for the summer, to revel in his ownership. He had had repairs done while he was away, and redecoration in keeping with the house's original ambience, and now the winter jewel, all spruced up, was in spanking shape. He had had the kind-of-vestibule converted to a library, and though he hadn't used it yet, he considered that it looked very tasteful. The whole had been loyally supervised by Heikki, who had even done a sizeable portion of the work. There was now little left to be done except the installment of discreet central heating for winter visits, an improvement which Heikki, for some unknown reason, had suggested postponing.

Yes, Heikki had been indispensable, thought Fisher, with deepest gratitude. Their relationship had developed, and had reached the level of what Fisher now admitted to himself was somehow friendship. After all, it was good to have all types of friends, not just fellow academics.

Moreover, there had started to be exciting signals. For Heikki had taken to asking him what exactly the pink house and the orchard and the well really meant to him, their true significance. He would ask him earnestly, and listen intently as Fisher enlightened him. The pleasure that the question aroused in Fisher was intense, despite Heikki's patent inability to absorb the answer, for there was only one thing that even asking it could reasonably indicate. That Heikki was waking up to philosophy. He was feeling at last that not-yet-comprehended urge to reach up, to be no longer shackled to the merely prosaic. In short, he was trying to elevate his mental outlook. The thought of this filled Fisher with a generous joy. Yet what could have brought that change about, when one thought about it, except their contact? His personal influence on Heikki. If he himself had helped to cause this subtle development, Fisher reflected, if he had awoken Heikki's soul, he was well content.

CHAPTER 43

A drowsy late-summer afternoon, when the rest of the world seemed content to doze in the heat. In the sun-filled living room of the pink house there was a pause, then Fisher pounded the typewriter keys with a final burst of effort. After that he flung himself backwards on his chair and let out a long, groaning sigh of exhausted rapture. It was finished. Here in this sacred place, this annexe of heaven, the mighty work had just been successfully led to its conclusion. It had taken him longer than expected, for his soul had been weighed down with diverse cares, but now at last he had triumphed. He felt simultaneously drained and exhilarated.

Triumphant but utterly too weak to rise, Fisher cast his eyes out over the orchard, that cherished view that had so inspired and consoled him since his return. Beyond the windows the ancient trees were full of apples that glowed like small red globes amid the branches. They were not yet ripe but they were well on the way; the weather all summer had been perfect, and even now, as it drew to its close, the orchard air was bright with sunlight, and golden rays overflowed into the house.

It had truly just been the summer of a lifetime, despite the work, mused Fisher with satisfaction. It was no surprise that here at last, in this peaceful place, his deepest thoughts had come to fruition. He read this achievement as a blessing from the house, a sign that all the evil that had managed to seep in had finally been expelled.

As for the house itself, it was simply wonderful the way it had responded to his love. His love, and the vigorous attentions of Heikki, of course. It looked strong and happy, and warm and lived-in, and Fisher fell more in love with it every day.

He would have Heikki over, now the book was finished. They could drink champagne.

Fisher stretched, rose at last, and stepped out onto the veranda. It felt strangely heady, but of course quite delightful, to have suddenly no more writing before him, no more racking his brains. As if some tremendous burden had been lifted miraculously from him. He was free now, completely free to enjoy himself in the final weeks before it was time to leave. It was hard to believe. For the first time ever, it seemed to Fisher, his cup of joy was full. Or almost. The house was his, he had written his book. Even the trauma of his break-up with Milllicent was starting to fade into the past. Indeed, there was only one thing now to cause him sadness, a single potent drop of gall most bitter in that joy-cup. The goddess had not come back.

In the midst of his happiness and his prospects of greatness he had yearned for her daily. He realised now, how sure he had been that if he were here, she would reappear. Yet she hadn't come. Her image haunted him with a bitter-sweetness only amplified by his surroundings. It was odd how the house itself did not seem to miss her as he did. He longed to know where she was, what had happened to her. But still something told him, in the midst of his anguish, that if and when she ever came back to her own land, she would make for here. After all, this place was dear to her heart, too. Yet another reason, Fisher would tell himself, for his being here. And always when he took his ease and rested on the sacred well, he felt that she was very, very close.

The rain was grand, though it came as a total surprise. They ran for the house, Heikki covering his half-full glass with his hand, so the hissing raindrops would not dilute its costly contents. Fisher ran with his own glass and the bottle.

"What a cloudburst. And it's been so wonderful all the morning."

"It doesn't last long." At the French window Heikki gazed complacently as rain spears stabbed the puddles on the veranda. Fisher watched as the leafy boughs of the apple trees and beyond them the high noble heads of the birches dipped and writhed beneath the sudden onslaught.

It was all very green. Though of course no longer that vibrant green of early summer. The hues were somehow closer together, more murky and matt. Even the fresher green of the birches was muted in the driving rain.

There was something in amongst those green cascades. Something disconcerting.

It was hard to be sure; hard to focus precisely on the long strings of tossing leaves. It was only as the rain eased off and the birch trees straightened up that Fisher's most appalled suspicions were confirmed.

"There's a strand of yellow. There, in that tree."

Heikki followed the indicating finger placidly. "Now is autumn."

Fisher stared at him in unconcealed dismay. "But it's still only August."

"August is autumn."

Fisher eyed the tell-tale streak of yellow dismally, then anxiously scanned the other birches. He would never get used to just how unbearably short these idyllic summers were. They seemed to be over almost as soon as they had begun.

"Soon is winter." Heikki continued, in a happy tone that sounded to Fisher almost approving. It was almost as if he had read his thoughts.

Fisher felt suddenly inconsolable. "But I want it to be summer for ages yet! It's so perfect. It's so absolutely – sublime." He waved his arms towards the view beyond the window. Heikki had poured himself more champagne, perhaps to toast the approach of winter, but now he paused with his refilled glass partway to his lips. His face had taken on that slightly frowning, preoccupied expression that meant he was building up to conversation. Fisher waited.

"Why they are so important to you, those trees, and the well? What is special about them?"

This again. Once more Fisher felt his body overcome with a warming rush of pleasure, not to do with alcohol. Once more he explained with infinite patience how through this house and its surroundings he had come to know the ultimate, indivisible essence of truth and beauty. How the well had become for him through its inspiration a symbol of truth and wisdom.

He stopped to check the impact of his words on Heikki, who was standing motionless and appeared to be gazing down the orchard at the mouldering object of their discussion. Only his hand moved ever so slightly, swirling the champagne thoughtfully round in his glass. He asked no more questions. Fisher, restored to lightness of spirit, refilled his own glass, and then finally Heikki seemed to come back to the present. His body twitched and he lifted his drink up and drained it, blinking his eyes.

"Rain has stopped. I should go. I am with bicycle."

Riding back to the office Heikki found himself somewhat pensive despite the champagne. There was no doubt his return to the house had caused a miraculous change in Fisher. But he couldn't keep the road enhancement project stalled forever. He had so far kept his bosses happy with a constant stream of calculations and statistics, but it couldn't last. They were getting impatient, very soon they would start demanding more specific data. He would have to at least get the survey done, just as soon as Fisher was safely back out of the way.

Fisher, going out to fetch in the abandoned garden chairs felt the comfort of the re-emerged sun intermingle with the warming glow of champagne. "Autumn my foot." He turned and glared up challengingly at the single length of pale yellow high above him. It was probably just an anomaly of nature.

He had really enjoyed his afternoon with Heikki. The fellow was worth his weight in gold, even if his rather limited perspectives could be somewhat tiring. It was only a difference in culture after all, and he meant well even at his most pedantic. And now of course, anyway, he was starting to see the light.

But now the peerless summer was all but over, as the tell-tale strand in the birch trees had heartlessly warned him. It was almost time to head back to England for the autumn term. Though this time, Fisher consoled himself, he would not be there with the abject aimlessness of the previous autumn. They would hail him now as a brilliant thinker, the turner of the key to some of life's deepest, most challenging issues. His book would guarantee his reputation. New, momentous changes in his life were before him.

They might make him Head of Faculty. This house would be his holiday home.

It was all to the good that he didn't have to pack things up here when he went back to England, and could simply come and carry on living here in his next vacation. It was so much easier, if he could leave things how it suited him. And of course, he wanted it to be ready for the goddess when she came. This might be at any time, for he doubted that she understood about university terms, and that he mightn't be here part of the time. She would see his things and know it was him, that he was still here, that they could start again. He hoped she would want to. Before he flew back for the autumn term he would make a bed up for her, in case she arrived while he was gone and was feeling tired.

CHAPTER 44

Lotta sat down stiffly on the plastic chair in front of the perspex screen. She was wearing lipstick and a navy blue polyester suit, as if she considered formal dress appropriate for prison visiting. From her walk the young man guessed that she was wearing high heels just a little too big.

"It's nice to see you." he said. He wondered what she thought of him, now that she knew him to be a monster. Her expression seemed to him to be apprehensive, but then it often was. He longed to blurt out the same things he had written in his letter, that he didn't do it, he could explain. But something held him back, most likely the presence of the guard just behind him. It made his heart sink, seeing the wariness back in Lotta's face. Still, at least she had come. When he got out he must explain to her properly, before he faced again the dark task that was before him.

"Thank you for coming." he said, to change the topic he had broached to no-one but himself.

There was silence. To Lotta's surprise the offender opposite her looked a little wretched and more than a little awkward. The cuffs of his prison shirt were frayed. She had made up her mind to be frosty, but she heard herself saying, "I'm sorry I didn't write earlier. It took just ages to find out where you were. And even longer to find out what they'd done with Summer Rose."

The young man felt suddenly as if he was choking. He roused himself with transparent eagerness. "You've found out where she is?" It seemed as he spoke that he had to negotiate his voice around some sort of very peculiar lump in his throat. He noticed he had called the baby 'her'. Not 'it'.

"She's in a children's home. Not so very far from where you live."

"Have you seen her?" The lump was getting more troublesome. It was hard to swallow.

"All the time. I said I was a relative. They think I'm her mother." Lotta's voice held a disbelieving tone. "They keep reminding me that 'at some stage' she's going back to you."

So she wasn't lost to him forever! He might even see her again. A sudden burst of warmth and brightness seemed to flare up somewhere in the young man's chest. He stared at Lotta. "I'm getting her back?"

"Of course. Don't you want her back?"

"Of course. More than anything."

"Then you can just carry on like before."

The young man had never for an instant ever envisaged that he would simply carry on as before. But at the moment the complexities of his future were not the matter uppermost in his mind. "How is she?"

"Oh, she's great. Do you want to see a picture?"

Lotta fished in her bag, but the guard made a sudden, prohibiting move forward. "It's only a photo," Lotta cried out in sudden alarm, unnerved. She had to cradle the photo in her hand while the young man studied it. He was not allowed to touch it. A little girl stared up at him, nothing like the baby they had taken from him all those months before. A changeling. So where was his baby, the baby whose unfolding had defiantly challenged his demons? This wasn't it. The childish face looked back at him, a little serious.

"Five minutes," said the guard.

"She's changed," said the young man anxiously. "Are you sure it's her?"

"Of course it's her. I've been going all the time. You just wait till you see what she can do. This was taken in…" - Lotta turned the photo over. The back was marked with the date and a single name, which the young man tried to make out upside down. Lotta frowned. "They don't even call her 'Summer Rose', they just call her 'Veera'".

The young man was on the verge of admitting that her first name had somehow failed to figure in the details he had given to police, but Lotta continued, "I was hopping mad about that." So he said instead, "Oh well, what's in a name?" Resolutely, he motioned for her to show him the photograph again, and scanned the face still more intently, searching for signs that the infant human before him had really evolved from his baby. He could see now that the eyes were the same, the shape of the face. But he realised too that he was looking for other signs, and didn't find them. The face was adequately pretty in the way that most children's faces are, but expressive rather than symmetrical, and framed by soft, curly, mousy, flyaway hair. The expression suggested that the little girl was keen to please; the eyes met the camera with childish openness.

"Time," said the guard.

"Yes," the young man concluded to himself with relief, as Lotta returned the photograph to her bag, that child was going to look nothing like her mother.

It was only a few weeks later, still in September, when the young man left his prison as a free man, took the train to Alajärvi and soon crossed his own yard to his own front door.

It at first intrigued him, then disconcerted him, and finally amused him, to find that his house had changed in numerous mysterious and inexplicable ways during his absence. He had the distinct impression as he walked from the gate that things had been tidied up and mended, repainted even. The pink walls of the house looked brighter and fresher than he remembered them, or maybe it was nothing more than the heart-lifting sunshine and the long-awaited pleasure of being free. The yard was quiet – he had expected Kosto to run out to greet him, but the door to Kosto's shed was shut, and his bowl had disappeared.

Inside it was even eerier. The place was clean and tidy and everywhere had had a facelift. But not too tidy – there were somebody else's possessions left here and there. When the young man looked in some of the cupboards they were full of clothes - men's clothes, so he knew it wasn't Katja, and anyway, he knew where she was keeping quiet. It was only the uncanny atmosphere that somehow put her into his mind. He paused and listened, but the house retained that empty feeling. When he went upstairs, there was a bed made up, as if the place was welcoming him home.

Perhaps that was it. Perhaps it was supernatural intervention, or something that Lotta had arranged to surprise him. After all, he had been away for a year. The odds were in favour of the supernatural, for around the house there were brand-new ashtrays, including by the made-up bed, and an unopened packet of filter cigarettes beside each one. Lotta disapproved of the young man's smoking, although it seemed she had taken his criminal record in her stride. In the upstairs cupboards and drawers there were more clothes, though the young man could find nothing that had previously belonged to himself. He tried some clothes on. They were his size, but absolutely not his taste. They were dreadful. He supposed he could wear them till he could kit himself out with something else. He shouldn't be ungrateful to his mystery benefactor. More welcome was the great, if eccentric, array of tinned goods he found in the kitchen, together with a rack of rather old bottles of wine. The young man made himself something to eat in a stainless steel saucepan, washed and dried himself with lavender-scented soap and a towel that seemed to sop up the moisture in an instant, and went to bed in the bed that was neatly made up ready.

He half expected to hear the sounds of someone else coming home, but nobody came.

He arose next morning and made his way to the children's home, following Lotta's directions. He went on foot; a year without being driven had reduced the van to a paralysed monument of rusted scrap.

He could not believe himself how much he was looking forward to seeing Veera, how excited he was. When they pointed her out and she turned round at the sound of her name the whole of his body seemed suddenly somehow to ignite. She began to walk, yes, walk towards him. But in his arms she writhed and struggled till she managed to free herself and squirm from his grip. When he went to go after her the matron restrained him.

"You can see her again in a minute. We must have a chat first."

They had been expecting him. A table in a side room had been set with refreshments, and the cooks in the adjoining kitchen alerted to listen out for screams or the sound of the matron's alarm. The matron poured coffee and looked at the young man just as disapprovingly as she dared. The young man himself bit his nails and focussed dismally on a cross-stitch sampler on the wall. He was smitten and dismayed at Veera's reaction. He had set so much store on seeing her, he realised now. Only gradually he realised that the matron was speaking.

He would have to get to know her again, the matron was saying.

Regain her trust, before they could let him have her back. It had been a while, quite long enough for that age child to forget completely who he was. He must demonstrate his parenting skills. Only then could they all let bygones be bygones.

The matron studied the effect of her words on the young man. It was hard to tell; there appeared to be none. His expression did not change from a rather absent air of despondency. She carried on. It was natural as the father that he might be disappointed that he couldn't just take her at once, but she hoped for his part he would also understand. It wasn't as if they wanted to make things difficult; after all, they had let the mother visit freely, without ever questioning her legal custody rights. She hadn't said that was who she was, but of course they knew. Or why else would she come?

She paused. She expected the young man to respond, but he didn't. Behind her measured words the matron was far from happy at the thought of returning the child to some lout given to shooting his family members. But the law was the law. The child was his.

She set out the deal. The young man must come every day, or as often as he could, and if he was patient, he would receive the most precious, precious chance that anyone could give him: the chance of a brand new start.

The young man was not at all sure that he wanted a brand new start. He had spent the whole year gearing himself once again toward the opposite, a brand new finish. Another attempt to foil the world with its sham and hypocrisy. But once more it seemed that yet again it wasn't the time to go, for here he was, back fused inexplicably with the riddle. The baby - now a baby no longer!- who seemed to be made up of joy. He must stay with her still, until the riddle no longer intrigued him. Till he knew the answer.

Besides, he wanted to see her, needed to win her back to being his own. He had been just devastated that she didn't know him. The demons had set on him instantly. Without knowing the reason for his misery, the matron had brushed the matter briskly aside. "Don't worry that she doesn't seem to know you," she had said, as Veera had wriggled from his clumsy caresses, "She'll soon get used to you again. Just be persistent." She hoped he wouldn't be.

He began to visit her daily, as instructed, with Lotta, and together they would play with her, or dress her up and take her to a park. They wrapped her up well, for winter was all but just around the corner, but the days, though shortening, seemed full of sunshine to the young man. He could see now, clearly, that this was the child which had been the baby, and on wet days Veera's smile of recognition dissolved the dreariness.

Lotta had been right; the children's home was not that far from the pink house. The distance was perfectly walkable, but he had to be careful. The shortest route led along the river, then it skirted up and round the beach, and then back along the river bank to a point not far from the home.

"It's shorter still if you cut across the beach," said Lotta, but the young man made excuses and went round the long way when he got to that point. As it was, the first day when he had gone by the river the water had sparkled and glinted, as if it was lusting after him; he had had to run, and the next few days had taken a longer route.

It was on the day when the matron had suggested that Veera should come soon to spend a couple of hours at her father's house, that the young man realised he come home via the beach. He had walked across it, his mind on other matters, and caught the demons absent from their place of sacrifice. They had not been there. Or if they had been there, he hadn't given them a thought.

He was getting used now to his house and its metamorphosis. He could still not explain it, especially since Lotta said she had never been there since his sudden departure, but at last he was beginning to know where everything was. Except Kosto, that was the biggest mystery. He had still seen neither hide nor hair of that dog.

It was only a few days later as he braved the river route that the young man noticed a new arrival, a splendid vessel moored to the jetty that ran out from the bank at the point where the water was deepest. There before him was a large white sailboat with white sails neatly furled, the last word in classical modern elegance. In its fineness it made the smaller vessels round about it look quite shabby. Despite his bad relations with the river, the young man drew nearer. There was no-one about or even on board, although a smart, broad gangplank bridged the water between the jetty and the boat. Ready waiting on the jetty was a large stack of what looked like cardboard boxes of supplies. The young man crossed the gangplank and went down the narrow wooden steps that led to the cabin. It was very well furnished, and so was the galley, with an up-to-date version of everything one could need. The windows had curtains of blue and white gingham, each held back neatly in place with a polished brass ring. There was a table that folded into the wall when it wasn't needed, but now it was up and its surface covered with maps. The young man studied them, but it wasn't easy to make them out. He had to turn to the front of several of them for enlightenment. Then he realised how long he had been on board, and made his way quickly back over the gangplank. It wouldn't do for anyone to find him. There was still no-one round. He picked up the top box from the sturdy tower of supplies and made for home quickly. Whoever owned a boat like that could afford to be generous.

The box was full of tinned fruit and jars of a fairly good quality of pickled herring, and pushed down between them was a brand new logbook, which was obviously intended for the boat. It was labelled 'Gloria', but was empty except for a printed sticker on the inside cover, that of Markus Laine, Agent in Real Estate. Above the sticker was printed 'owner' in small, neat letters.

The young man paused in selecting a tin of fruit and raised his head thoughtfully. He had met Laine; that man had come to the house here to try to persuade him to sell it. He had left his agent's card. He had come here in an old battered car and his suit had been shiny at the knees and elbows; he wondered where Laine had got the money to buy himself a boat that wouldn't embarrass a billionaire. The tin of peaches as he opened it fired juice at him. It was as he getting a clean shirt from a drawer full of clothes not his own, that the young man suddenly knew.

CHAPTER 45

It had been Laine's vague intention to make himself scarce well before the young man came out of prison, if he ever did. The killer's unexpected early release for good behaviour threw him into a panic, the more so since he only read of it by chance, in a newspaper he was spreading out to clean his shoes on. He flicked aside a small knob of polish and stared aghast at the brief little column, then shifted his eyes to the paper's date. Ten days ago. The fellow was out already, had been out for almost a couple of weeks.

It was worse than a shock. It was no less than a hideous nightmare, but one coming true. Laine had all but convinced himself that the young man would be inside forever. He had not even started to scan the news apprehensively, alert for an impending reappearance.

He had to get away, put his dimly-formed escape plan into action. There was no other option. And he had to leave now, before the winter; more importantly, before the young man found him. There was absolutely no time to lose; the fellow would certainly have found out already about his house. Laine experienced a sudden pang of guilt about Fisher, and wondered if the young man might have harmed him. Killed him even. After all, it was in his genes. He might have just crept up while Fisher was pouring tea from his woolly teapot. But somehow Laine didn't think that was what would happen, and he hadn't read of any such thing in the news. It was far more likely, he concluded, while his skin turned to gooseflesh, that they would join forces somehow in a fearsome alliance transcending language and set out hotfoot on the trail of revenge. They would bring to their partnership the young man's brutishness and Fisher's eye for detail. The idea made Laine feel oddly faint.

He must pull himself together. He must just drop everything, load the Gloria and disappear.

To somewhere warm, where the living was easy, and not too many questions were ever asked.

The cleaner Laine had hired to give his Alajärvi office the occasional dusting and to shuffle the adverts in the window gave a start at the sudden and urgent opening of the street door. She came and cleaned as she pleased; she had never yet been disturbed by a client. And anyway, it was hardly even time for the office to be open yet. But she guessed at once that the newcomer hadn't come to buy a house.

"Where's the agent? Where is he?"

She didn't like his manner. It was somehow threatening. And there was something odd about his clothes. They were quite respectable, but all the same, they didn't look quite right.

"Mr Laine isn't here."

But the young man insisted he had to see Laine. His voice grew more threatening each time he repeated his demands.

The cleaner's family had all done time. She wasn't susceptible to intimidation.

"I've told you, he isn't here. I'm the cleaner. He was here just yesterday, getting ready to go off on his boat. He's had some bad news, he's taking some time off." The cleaner put the vacuum cleaner back on and raised her voice to make it audible above the roar. "If he's not gone yet he'll be off by this evening. He's got some leave due. Have to make the most of it, a boat like that."

When she lifted her eyes to seek confirmation for this final assertion, she noticed that the young man had already gone.

The boat was still at the jetty, the young man checked it. The supplies had all been taken aboard but the vessel was deserted, its gangplank still straddling the gap between the deck and the land. Laine himself was obviously still at large. The young man could not search any further, it was nearly time for him to go and visit Veera. The matron was unmercifully strict.

Right up to the very last corner before he reached home – his home, somebody else's home – the young man failed to notice the cold wind, and the stiff uphill climb. He was incensed; his whole body burned with fury. He would burn that boat, he would hack up Laine into little pieces, he would find Laine's house and take all he had and then he would burn that too. But if he did it that way, he would still not know who it was who was living in his house. He would burn the boat, then before he killed Laine he would make him tell, and make him sign a paper cancelling the sale. He – the young man slowed down. He was almost home, but ahead of him there seemed to be a number of vehicles round the farm. There were several pulled up along the roadside, and as he watched, a black van came from round the corner, drove towards him, then turned aside into his very own yard.

What were they here for? The young man stopped dead. He didn't even need to ask that question. Then he started walking backwards, trembling, towards the safety of the forest. There hadn't been this many cars there since the day they had come to pick him up to carry on doing his sentence for killing his father. Or maybe all these cars and vans were simply something to do with his unknown house-mate. But he knew that wasn't so. He knew instinctively what they had come for. Who they had come for, and why.

In the shelter of the forest he made his way to the self-same spot where Katja had waited on her final return, a spot where it was possible to be invisible and still peek out at the whole of the pink wooden house and its grounds unobserved. The scene there confirmed his worse suspicions and made his blood run cold, even though he had already pictured what he now saw before him. There were men crawling everywhere, the copse and the orchard were teeming with them. It would only be a matter of minutes, he could tell, before they would all converge on the well, like flies upon a heap of succulent dung.

Heikki was feeling distinctly relieved, at least for the moment. He had managed successfully to put off the survey of the pink house orchard till Fisher had got back to England, and today he had finally managed to get it done. In the morning, to make quite sure that the coast was clear, though he knew of course that it was, he had telephoned Fisher on a pretext to check that he really was in London.

After that he had given the go-ahead for a squad of surveyors and assistants, armed with clipboards and equipment, to go in and survey the site with unstinting thoroughness. Except for the well. They need not check that out in detail at the moment, Heikki had told them - it could wait till later. It was not in use. There was no point in wasting valuable time and resources.

That had been this morning. "So far so good," murmured Heikki, when he heard that the survey had been completed. That was one headache over. But of course, the biggest hurdle had not yet been overcome. It was not enough to keep the surveyors out of sight of Fisher. Success depended, at the end of the day, on ensuring that the road past the pink house was not selected for improvement. The repercussions on Fisher's sanity, if progressive planners tarmacked over his hallowed grove, would be irreversible.

He would have to try to make them favour a different route. To present them with hitherto unconsidered options and plausible reasons why something else might be better. It would not be easy. He had known this area all his life, and knew there was nothing actually to indicate or rule out one route or another. In the end it would all depend on the whims of the planning committee, who would probably simply put it to a vote. They were due to meet next week, when Heikki would have to present and comment on his findings.

Despite his phlegmatic nature Heikki felt nervous at the very thought of that meeting. So much hung on it, the life and health of one of his dearest of friends. And he would have nothing at his disposal but personal eloquence.

He had a week to work out how he was going to phrase things, to be persuasive while not, of course, telling any lies. He was not sure how much of an orator he could ever be. Sighing, Heikki pulled himself together and set off to take a first look at the survey results.

It was cold in the early evening, when Laine walked unobtrusively towards the jetty. He had loaded everything the previous evening, and now carried nothing. He wanted to look as if he was simply going for an evening stroll to potter on his boat. He had no wish to attract more attention than the Gloria usually attracted. He hadn't really wanted to bring her down here to Alajärvi now, it was much too close for comfort to the scene of his villainous fraud, but the boat-yard where he usually kept her wasn't nearly so advantageous for his getaway.

The day had been sunny, but now with the evening a mist was coming. Laine was grateful. It might be thicker out on the water; with any luck he really would be able just to vanish. So engrossed was he in his thoughts, so absorbed, that he was almost at the boat before he noticed there was somebody on it, standing at the top end of the gangplank.

Laine's natural impulse was to run, but then he noticed that the person on his boat had a pushchair. It would have looked very suspicious to run, especially when it seemed after all that it wasn't the person Laine had thought for a dreadful moment that it must be. He started to go on board.

"What are you doing?"

"Where are you going?" asked the person with the pushchair.

Laine felt his heart drop. It was him. He recognised the voice. He could see now that it was him.

He must be careful. The young man had found out, just as he had feared. That was obvious. Make a break for it and the fellow would be after him. He tried to answer casually.

"Just away for a few days. Round about."

"Like where?"

Laine shrugged nonchalantly. "Stockholm, maybe. The archipelago." His mouth felt dry. The young man jerked his head towards the cabin.

"You've got lots of stuff in there. And maps. That sort of gear would all be wasted on Stockholm."

Laine wondered vaguely if he should kill the young man, or if that would only make things worse in the long run. He licked his lips. The young man spoke again.

"What's the furthest you could go in this sort of boat? South America?"

"Not at this time of year."

"Where then?"

Laine suddenly realised that his body felt weak. His nerve had gone, his ingenuity. And the young man had been through his map collection, that was for sure. He had been in the cabin. "Spain," he whispered. "Morocco."

"Good," said the young man. He rolled the pushchair back and forth by its handles, reflectively, then suddenly looked Laine straight in the face. "You sold my house." he said, quietly, but pronouncing each word distinctly. "You owe me, big time."

"I'll pay it back," Laine heard himself promise in a whisper, then tried to make a half-hearted lunge at the young man, as if to push him out of the way. But the young man reached into the plastic folds of the pushchair hood and pulled out a gun.

"You can do me a favour. And her." He jerked his head at the child that was sitting in the pushchair. "And her." Laine followed the movement of the young man's head towards the cabin, where he could make out a smallish, darkish-haired person, looking out of the window.

The young man waved the gun at Laine. "Get in."

When they were all on board and Laine shut up in the galley the young man went back and pulled up the gangplank quickly. He didn't want Lotta jumping ship. She hadn't really wanted to come till he said he was leaving with the baby; she might still change her mind. He had given her reasons for his new, drastic plan in the form of selected half-truths, hastily sieved. She knew something of Laine, and his treacherous house-sale, and nothing, of course, of the furtive activity round the well. But he needed her to come, and not just to help with the baby. He had still not had a chance to explain to her, though he longed to do so, that he hadn't meant to kill his father, it had all been a terrible mistake.

Now it looked as if at some point he was going to have some more explaining to do, about Veera's mother, when the contents of that well came to light. He hoped Lotta would understand and forgive him. She was a true friend, after all, of a sort he had never ever had in his life before. He glanced towards her. She was sitting holding Veera very tightly on her lap and staring out of the window. From time to time she raised a hand and nibbled absent-mindedly at a nail. The young man felt suddenly overwhelmed by emotion, by a great and sentimental affection for her, and a curious feeling of gratitude for all sorts of things. To steady his feelings, bring them to order, he went to the galley and turned the gun once more on Laine, and motioned him into action. The gun wasn't loaded; he had still not overcome his horror of the things, but he didn't take Laine for much of a gun man either.

"Let's go," he said.

The mist had thinned again. Leaving the jetty and setting out across the silvery water that would not darken till the last of the brightness had left the air, the Gloria turned and headed into the sunset, towards the sea.

ABOUT THE AUTHOR

Megan Davies was born and raised in Palmers Green in north London. After reading philosophy at Nottingham University she travelled and worked at a multitude of jobs in a multitude of places, including England, Nigeria, Italy, Finland, the island of Iona and the Shetland Isles. In 1989 she moved with her husband and two sons to Helsinki, Finland, where she qualified as a homeopathic practitioner. She now works as a homeopath and as an interpreter in Finnish and English. *House Hunting Finnish Style* is her first novel.

Made in the USA
Charleston, SC
26 November 2014